SAFE HOUSE

SAFE HOUSE

A NOVEL

SHANNON SYMONDS

BONNEVILLE
BOOKS

AN IMPRINT OF CEDAR FORT, INC.
SPRINGVILLE, UTAH

ISBN 13: 978-1-4621-2036-9

Published by Bonneville Books, an imprint of Cedar Fort, Inc., 2373 W. 700 S., Springville, UT 84663
Distributed by Cedar Fort, Inc., www.cedarfort.com

Names: Symonds, Shannon, 1961- author.
Title: Safe house / Shannon Symonds.
Description: Springville, Utah : Bonneville Books, an imprint of Cedar Fort, Inc., [2017]
Identifiers: LCCN 2017013397 (print) | LCCN 2017023676 (ebook) | ISBN 9781462127931 (e-book) | ISBN 9781462120369 (softcover : acid-free paper)
Subjects: LCSH: Abused women--Fiction. | Family violence--Fiction. | GSAFD: Christian fiction. | Love stories.
Classification: LCC PS3619.Y57 (ebook) | LCC PS3619.Y57 S24 2017 (print) | DDC 813/.6--dc23
LC record available at https://lccn.loc.gov/2017013397

Cover design by M. Shaun McMurdie
Cover design © 2017 by Cedar Fort, Inc.
Edited and typeset by Hali Bird and Erica Myers

Printed in the United States of America

10 9 8 7 6 5 4 3 2 1

Printed on acid-free paper

Special thanks to my beloved sister, Stacy Farmer, for staying on earth long enough to see *Safe House* published. You checked every comma and had faith in my dream. You are my forever sister, and I will never think about this book without thinking about you.

What if home is the most dangerous place?

CHAPTER 1

SEPTEMBER

AMBER LAY IN HER BED, MONITORING THE VOICES. THEY WERE raging, familiar background music in the night. She couldn't hear what they were saying, but she knew her stepfather, Berk, and her mother, Emily, were in their bedroom; and her mother was in trouble. The voices rose and fell; one voice was angry, growing louder, then lower, a menacing rumble. The other voice was soft, soothing, trying to make peace. The peacemaker was losing.

Alert, Amber sat up. Even though she couldn't see Berk, she knew what was happening; he was large, drunk, spitting mad, spewing alcohol-soaked breath into her mother's face. Pushing back the covers, she quietly got out of bed. The voices grew intense. Her mother couldn't stop him when he got like this.

Fear and anger mixed into a poison that ate her heart. No matter how many times this happened, she was still scared, still angry with Berk and furious at herself for being a coward. Gently, she opened her door and slipped out into the hall. Standing between her younger brother's and sister's bedroom doors, she decided to look in on Bjorn first.

Amber opened Bjorn's door and saw him in the shadows, standing in his crib. He let go with one little hand and reached though the bars for her, falling on his side, out of control. Whining in frustration, he tried to roll onto his stomach to see her. Quickly, she crossed to the crib and picked him up, shushing him, frantically rocking and holding him close.

Silently, Amber went to Bjorn's open door and listened to the argument, making sure her parents were still in their room. Carrying Bjorn, she hastily crossed the hall and opened Greta's door. The hinges squeaked loudly. Amber held her breath, afraid to look down the hall. The argument stopped. He had heard her. Sliding the door the rest of the way open, she ran into the room.

Streetlight shone through the bedroom window, silhouetting Greta's small, seven-year-old body. With her back to the window, she stood, quiet and shaking. When she saw Amber, she ran to her big sister like a child to its mother. "Shush," Amber said as she pulled Greta toward the door. Amber froze. Her parents were coming.

"Berk," her mother whispered urgently, "Berk, please . . . don't wake the children."

"Shut it! My house! That little brat should hear this!" he roared. "Greta!"

Bjorn started to cry. Amber looked down the hall and saw Berk lumbering toward them. Instinctively, she pushed Greta into the bedroom closet, depositing Bjorn in her skinny arms. There wasn't time to shut the closet door before her mother backed in the room, her hands on Berk's chest, trying to drive him back, begging him to stop.

"This is my house! Get out of my way!" Berk growled and shoved her mother. What happened next happened all at once, and it felt like time stood still. Amber watched her mother's forehead hit the doorjamb, sounding like a melon smashing on the wood. Falling hard, her mother's body lay still, arms limp at her side. Amber gasped loudly. Dark liquid ran down the white doorjamb in the gray light.

Berk's drunken body swung around to see his wife's motionless form. Staggering backward, he fell against Greta's pink bed. Greta's large eyes reflected moonlight from inside the dark closet. Before Berk could get up, Amber snatched Bjorn, took Greta by the hand, and yanked her out of the closet. Carrying Bjorn and dragging Greta, she ran for the stairs.

Amber didn't let the sound of Berk coming slow her down. Glancing over her shoulder, she saw she had a small lead. Berk growled, "Come back here you . . ." He swore and swayed from one side of the hallway to the other.

Pulling Greta with her free hand, Amber held Bjorn like a football as she took the stairs so fast Greta slipped. Bjorn's screaming covered up the foul names Berk shouted at her.

On the ground floor, she pulled Greta to her feet and ran into the kitchen. Berk yelled as he made his way down the stairs. Letting go of Greta, she frantically dug through her mother's purse for her cell phone. While dialing 911, she ran for the door to the garage, Greta on her heels clutching the back of Amber's nightgown. Pulling Greta into the garage, she locked the door behind them and turned on the light.

"What's your emergency?" she heard the operator say.

"Berk's hitting my mom again, my stepdad, my mom!" Amber screamed into the phone as she looked for a place to hide. Berk was on the other side of the door pounding and yelling.

"Miss, miss, are you all right?" the operator asked.

What a stupid question, Amber thought. Frustrated, she dropped the phone to free her hand. The phone shattered on the cement. She tried the car door; it was locked. Desperately, she tried the other car. Both cars were locked. The keys were in the kitchen with him. Bjorn wiggled, crying in breathless jagged screams. Greta stood halted, looking at the door to the kitchen, sure it would splinter as it threatened to give way to his violence. Amber adjusted Bjorn on her hip.

Suddenly, Berk stopped pounding on the door, and the only noise was Bjorn's cries. The silence frightened her more. Her mind raced. *He must be going for keys*, she thought, *or the garage door remote*. Taking Greta by the hand, she pulled her along the back of the garage, past Berk's refrigerator full of beer, and headed for the other door, the one that led to the backyard.

Amber had her hand on the doorknob and was turning it when it twisted hard in her grasp. Terrified, she jerked back, and Berk threw the door open. As she turned to run, he grabbed a fistful of her hair. Bjorn screamed, slipping helplessly from her grasp, clawing at her nightgown, his chubby body falling hard onto the cement floor. Berk yanked her around, leaned down, and pulled her face close to his, blowing fetid breath into her eyes while Bjorn shrieked in terror at her feet. Berk began slowly lifting her by her hair. Struggling, she rose to her tiptoes, feeling her scalp pulling free from her skull. Clawing at his hands, she tried to get him to let go, her mind spinning. Knowing no matter what she did would be like pouring oil on an inferno, she kicked him with her bare feet.

Sirens sounding in the distance broke through his rage. He dropped her, pulling his rough hands away with strands of long dark hair hanging between his fingers. Wild-eyed, he backed out the door into the dark. Stumbling, he turned and ran erratically into the woods behind the house.

CHAPTER 2

FINDING GRACE

IN THE SHADOWY NIGHT, A COOL OCEAN BREEZE BLEW white curtains in the open bedroom window of a weathered Victorian house. The house was silent except for the ticking of a cuckoo clock and the rhythmic sounds of the ocean washing in and out that came through the window.

It was one thirty in the morning when Grace's cell phone began ringing, shattering the silence at the James home. Eyes closed, Grace rolled toward the edge of her creaky old bed and reached for her cell phone. Her eyes opened when she realized she was falling in the darkness off the side of the bed. Reaching for anything, she took a hold of the charge cord, which pulled the cell from the table as she hit the hardwood floor. Rolling onto her back, she raised it to her ear. Answering, she said, "This is Grace," in her most professional tone. Sitting up against her nightstand, she knocked her water bottle onto the floor where it began to leak.

"Crap!" Jumping up, she took her robe from the end of the bed and wiped the floor.

The voice on the phone said, "Grace? It's Gladys. I have a call for you."

"Oh . . . hi, Gladys," she replied cheerfully and crawled back into bed. "Put them through."

"Hello, Grace?" said a well-known, gravely, female voice. It made Grace smile. *Necanicum,* she thought, *where everyone knows everyone and thing. Life on the edge of nowhere in Oregon.* Grace knew all the police dispatchers. This sexy voice belonged to sixty-year-old, chain-smoking Roxanne, a dispatcher from the Necanicum Police Department.

"Hey, Roxanne. Morning." Grace laughed her easy laugh. "Well, sort of morning."

Roxanne continued, "I have officers out at 1239 Skyline Drive requesting a response from DSAT."

Grace supervised the DSAT team, which stood for the Domestic Sexual Assault Team. It was her eight-year-old baby. The project paired domestic and sexual assault advocates with law enforcement to provide care for victims of violent crimes. The team responded to the scene of domestic or sexual assaults, or met with victims at the local hospital.

"Let the officers know I'll be there in ten minutes. That's the new housing development at the top of the hill, Ocean View, right?" Grace wondered out loud.

"I think so," Roxanne answered.

"I'll call you if I get lost."

"Oh, don't I know it," Roxanne laughed and hung up.

Grace said a prayer. It was her ritual, like a baseball player's lucky socks.

When she ended her prayer, she phoned her mother, Mable, who lived in a small apartment attached to the back of the house. "Mom, gotta go," she whispered.

"Ugh," her mother groaned. "I'm coming."

"It's only a domestic," she whispered. "I should be back early. If I'm not, will you drive Mary to the dentist?"

"Sure," her mother mumbled.

Grace dressed and padded downstairs, wordlessly passing her mother, who was coming up the stairs. Mable went into Grace's room and crawled into Grace's bed to sleep.

Grace turned on the light in the bathroom and caught a look at herself. She shook her head. "Ouch," she said aloud, "It's a good thing you're beautiful." Sarcasm was dripping from every word.

Grace was in her thirties. Her hair was a long mess of unmanageable streaky blonde ringlets that complemented her naturally tan skin. Her eyes were an unusual shade of sky blue. People told her she looked young for her age, but she didn't believe them for a minute. *Tired*, she thought. She just looked tired. Perpetual dark circles under her eyes betrayed sleepless nights. Anyone that knew her said her face was an open book. Her mother said she was too thin, too curly, way too smart for her own good, and "holy cow" clumsy.

Grace tried to run a pick through the tangled ringlets and then caught them up in a hair tie. Realizing her attempts to tame her curls were a waste of time, she shrugged, turned off the light, and went to the living room.

Checking the time, she noted it was only five minutes since the call. Grace had this routine down, but she was already late. Soundlessly, she went to the front door and slipped her shoes on. Just as she was opening the door, she heard their old, blind dog coming down the stairs to go out.

"No, Lady, it's too early. Go back to bed," she whispered.

The sound of the old cocker spaniel's nails on the hardwood floor was exaggerated in the quiet night. Slipping out the door, Grace pushed the dog back inside with her toe. The dog scratched on the door, begging to get out, as Grace went down the front porch steps and headed for the car in the crisp autumn air.

When she started her old, red Jeep, the stereo blared. Jumping, she punched the power button. Her long-legged, seventeen-year-old brother, Nephi, had driven it last. Smiling, she adjusted the seat so she could reach the pedals. Grace turned the heat to full blast, but it didn't keep the cool night air from seeping in through the Jeep's vinyl top. Goose bumps rose on her muscular arms as she drove off.

CHAPTER 3

GRACE OFFERED

GRACE DROVE UP THE WINDING ROAD, HIGH AMONG LARGE new homes. The houses sat along the edge of the lush Oregon forest on the Pacific Coast Range Mountains. The house was easy to spot. An ambulance and two police cars, lights silently rotating, marked the last house at the top of the steep road. Light spilled from every window and the open front door. Ancient pines in a dark old-growth forest swayed in the wind behind the house. On the front porch, a woman holding a bloody rag to her face was arguing with a medic.

The house next door was also well-lit. An older man stood on the porch watching the excitement. A woman in a robe and curlers was crossing the lawn, apparently back to the house next door, with a crying child in her arms and a small girl in tow.

Grace parked across the street. One of the officers, an old favorite and member of her church named Ironpot, came over to meet Grace.

"Hey, Grace," he said with a tired voice.

"Hi, Earl—I mean, Officer Ironpot, sir."

Ironpot gave a short laugh and opened his field notebook.

"Do you know Emily Anderson?" Ironpot asked as he looked through his notes.

"I know her from Parent Teacher Organization meetings, but not as a client."

"Her seventeen-year-old daughter, Amber, called 911 and reported that her stepfather, Berk Anderson, was hitting her mom again, emphasis on the again. The dispatcher heard a loud scream in the background and then heard a man yelling at the caller, Amber, before the line went dead. When we arrived, we found the victim, Emily, with a serious head injury." Ironpot recited the facts to Grace as if he were in court. Grace knew he was already preparing what he would say to a judge in his head.

"Where is he, Earl?" she asked, referring to the batterer.

Earl, knowing exactly what she meant, turned and looked at the dark forest. "He's gone. We're waiting for the county to bring their K-9 unit before we chase him in the woods at night." Earl scanned the black tree-covered mountainside. Grace's eyes followed his.

"Guns?" Grace asked.

"Of course, it's Necanicum."

"He could be anywhere," Grace said, looking at the wooded hillside and then the expensive home, feeling like taking cover. "What does he do for a living?"

"Drives a log truck. He knows the hills, and he comes from money." Grace knew Earl was thinking that meant lawyers and a tough trial. Earl went on, "His family owns the logging company he works for, among other things in the county. According to the victim, his folks bought the house. We can't get her to go in the ambulance. The driver says her excuse is insurance or she doesn't want to pay for the hospital, but I think she needs stitches. We're hoping you can talk her into going to the hospital."

"I can try, but you know it's not really about the insurance or money." Grace smiled at Earl. "Tell me about the children."

"There are three. There's the seventeen-year-old daughter, Amber, a seven-year-old daughter, Greta, and a nine-month-old son, Bjorn. Emily's neighbor, Martha, seems to know the kids and will take care of them if we can get the victim to go to the hospital."

A thin teenage girl Grace assumed was Amber left the house and began crossing the lawn to the neighbors, carrying a bottle in one hand and a diaper bag in the other. The girl didn't even look in her mother's direction, Grace noticed. Face down, as if she was ashamed, she walked with sloped shoulders, deliberate steps, and an air of frustration.

Next door, in a pool of light on the porch, the small seven-year-old girl, Greta, stood without expression next to Martha, the neighbor. Greta's scrawny arms hung limp at her side. She was very thin and had dark circles under her eyes and a vacant look. It seemed a stiff breeze would blow her away, and she would let it carry her without a fight. Words like "failure to thrive" and "trying to be invisible" ran through Grace's mind. Martha held the fat, screaming nine-month-old, his back arched, legs kicking, while she watched the children's mother argue with the ambulance driver.

Grace noticed the victim never looked over at her children. The seventeen-year-old girl took the baby, completely comfortable with the squirming child and the role of mother. Putting the baby on her hip, she stuck the bottle in his mouth and walked inside the neighbor's home.

"Well," Grace said resolutely, "wish me luck."

"Luck."

Making her way to the house, she walked between patrol cars and crossed the lawn. The ambulance driver had a clipboard and was trying to explain to Emily, the victim, that she needed to sign a waiver stating she was refusing services. Ignoring the ambulance driver and looking at Officer Hart, Emily was speaking and gesturing rapidly, demanding they leave her alone.

The officer she was spitting mad at was young and good-looking. Grace didn't know how anyone could yell at Hart. His name was absolutely appropriate. Seeing Grace, he half-smiled, showing dimples, looking grateful for the interruption.

Flashing her own half-grin, her color rose. Looking down, she hoped he hadn't noticed.

"Emily!" Smiling, he turned to the irritated victim to begin introductions. "Emily, this is Grace from the Domestic Sexual Assault Team. Grace is here to help you."

"I don't need any . . . oh, Grace . . . hi." Suddenly, her fiery temper fizzled. "I don't want anyone to see me like this." *She must remember me from school*, Grace thought.

Grace flashed her best "I love you" grin. While shifting her notebook to her left hand, she held out her right hand and said, "This is what I do, Emily. I am here to help you. I'm here just for you. I see everyone at their worst, so don't worry. I won't tell anyone, and you're not going to say anything I haven't heard before."

"Well, I told them I didn't need any help." She looked accusingly at Hart, who kept jotting notes and ignoring her protests.

Interrupting, Grace said, "I brought forms to apply for funds for your medical treatment. So if it's the cost that's holding you back, I've got you covered."

"Oh, I . . . we . . . well . . . crappy insurance, you know?"

Knowing it was an excuse, Grace agreed, "I absolutely do. Who needs a big medical bill? The only catch to the money is you agree to work with the prosecutor if this ever gets to court."

"That's just it. I don't want it to go to court. Berk didn't mean it!"

I bet he never does, Grace thought. "Let's see your head?" Grace said softly, gesturing toward the bloody rag. When Emily raised the soaked towel, her eye drooped as the wound opened. Grace couldn't figure out why Emily hadn't passed out. Concerned, she wondered about a concussion.

Grace's face reflected the worry she felt. "Have you looked at that, Emily?"

"No."

"Let's go in and you have a look at it in a mirror, okay?" Hart's head snapped up and he caught her eye. Winking, she gave him a look that said "trust me and back off."

The medical team looked suspiciously at Grace, but didn't move to stop her. Hart followed her close enough she could smell his aftershave. They stepped into the entryway, where a large mirror was part of an antique coatrack. Facing the mirror, Grace motioned for Emily to remove the blood-soaked rag. Everyone heard a sharp intake of breath as Emily caught a look at her injury. Stepping up,

Grace took a hold of Emily's arm as her knees began to buckle. Hart took her other arm, and Grace felt his arm around both women as Emily's dead weight fell against his tall frame. The wind was totally out of Emily's sails now.

"I guess I better go to the hospital," Emily said sheepishly.

"I guess." Grace smiled at Hart. Emily actually gave an uncomfortable laugh.

"Look," Grace said, "the hospital is only a few blocks from here. If you don't want to pay for the ambulance, and you're sure you'll be all right, I can drive you back down the hill."

"Thanks," Emily said. Grace gave the medic a look and a nod that said "please follow us."

I'm in, Grace thought.

"Okay, let me get my purse and house keys. I need to ask my neighbor Martha if the kids can stay with her."

"I'll do that," Grace offered.

"Thanks." Emily smiled gratefully.

Going back out the open door, Grace winked at Hart again. "We're going to the hospital now."

Stepping closer to her, Hart leaned in, rolling his eyes, and said softly, "Thanks, Grace."

CHAPTER 4

UNRAVELED

GRACE THREW AN OLD BLANKET OVER THE SEAT OF HER CAR to protect it from blood. Out of necessity, she kept strange things in her car: spray for head lice (because you never knew who you'd be transporting or what kind of home you'd end up going to), extra clothes, hygiene kits, a spare car seat, and more. Her car was more like a giant purse than a car. *Blood is better than lice any day,* Grace thought. And cracked vinyl seats could be hosed off.

Soon, Emily was comfortable in Grace's car and they were on their way. "Thanks for driving me," Emily said.

"It's my job. And I love it."

"You get paid to do this?"

"I get paid to keep people safe and stop them from killing each other. Great job, ay?"

"I don't know how you can do it and keep your sanity."

"That's what everyone says. I keep a lot of secrets, but, if you have a million buried in your yard, no promises!"

That actually brought a giggle. "I don't have two dollars," Emily said. "That's why this keeps happening."

"Lots of us are poor, Emily, but we don't hit each other," Grace said and searched Emily's face for some understanding. "This isn't your fault."

"Yes, it is." It was quiet for a moment as the old Jeep ratted down the mountain. Emily looked away and said, "You don't know. I never know when to shut up."

"If that was the case," Grace said laughing, "I'd have been dead years ago."

"I keep thinking if I'd just do things better, this," Emily said, pointing at her forehead, "wouldn't happen. Or, maybe if he didn't drink. He was drinking, you know?" Emily explained, sounding hopeful, like drinking would make it all right.

"A lot of people drink and don't hit their spouses," Grace said, "Let me ask you a few questions, okay?"

Emily turned and looked skeptically at Grace.

"Is Berk controlling sometimes?" Grace asked.

"Ha!" Emily let out a sarcastic laugh.

"I'll take that as a yes. Is he jealous?" Grace asked, looking at Emily. "Not just of other men, but of the attention you give the children or friends or family?" Emily sat silently, eyes ahead, expressionless. Going on, Grace asked. "Does he blame everyone else for all his problems?"

"No, just me, it's always my fault. Well, I guess he also blames Amber and Greta. I can't convince him that he's Greta's father," she said quietly.

"Was that what you were arguing about?" Grace asked.

"No," Emily lied, looking away.

Grace decided to avoid the subject for now. She asked, "Does he isolate you?"

"No, I can do whatever I want, but if I go to my mother's in California, it causes problems, so I don't. I don't like to fight."

"Emily, from what you're telling me, Berk has a problem that is not going to be fixed by you or anything you do. Only Berk can change Berk." Grace watched Emily look at the floor. Emily crossed her legs and folded her arms, silent for a moment.

"I keep thinking I can help him change. If I spent less money, everything would be okay; or maybe if he made more."

"A lot of people fight about money, Emily. They don't all hit each other."

"I know, but he's not like this all the time." Looking intently at Grace, she said, "I push his buttons." Sitting back, she waited for Grace to judge her. "How many women do you see like me, like that?"

"The national statistic this year is one in four women have domestic violence issues."

"Wow, so many?" Emily mumbled, shaking her head.

Grace pulled up to the curb by the emergency room and parked. "We're here. Let's go in."

"Wait, I don't want you to think I'm weak. I'm not, you know."

Turning in her seat, Grace saw Emily's eyes glisten in the dim parking lot light. Sniffing loudly, Emily wiped her eyes and nose on her sleeve and said, "I just, I just love him."

"I know," Grace said, turning the car off and smiling at Emily, hoping her smile didn't look as sad as it felt. "Once, I heard a speaker say that most men who abuse their spouses have very low self-esteem and a tremendous fear of abandonment. They attach themselves to very strong women that have traits they would like to have or exploit, then we call those women victims."

Grace gave Emily a minute to take in what she was saying. Emily nodded almost to herself, and Grace went on, "Most of the victims I've worked with are really great people." Emily wiped the tears on her cheek and then wiped her nose with the back of her hand. "Emily, you're a survivor and that takes strength. You'll figure this out."

Grace looked for the light of understanding in Emily's eyes, knowing she was rushing to get information to Emily in case they never spoke again. *At least Emily stayed in the car*, Grace thought. Wanting to validate Emily's experience, Grace needed to show Emily that she could trust her, a total stranger, with her deepest, darkest secrets.

Grace sighed as she swung open her car door. Emily would be home soon, and Berk would be doing all the talking. Some nights it all felt just a little hopeless.

CHAPTER 5

SECRETS

KELLY LAY IN BED WITH HER EYES CLOSED, SENSING everything around her. Her husband's breathing was regular. The house was dark and still. Her mind was churning, unwilling or unable to stop thinking, wondering, worrying. Slowly, she opened her eyes and let them adjust to the dark room. Clean white cotton sheets in the spotless bedroom smelled freshly laundered, felt crisp, and were noisy from any movement. Luckily, her husband wasn't touching her anywhere. Slowly, she tried to slide out of her side of the bed and from in between the rustling sheets. Every sound seemed to be magnified.

Moving smoothly, her feet found the cold hardwood floor. Her light cotton nightgown seemed to make more noise than usual. *Less starch*, she thought.

Skipping the third floorboard from the bed, a squeaker, she softly made her way down the hall toward the bathroom. The door was ajar. Like a ghost, she slid around it.

He had removed the knob. At first, the empty hole had been a slap in the face. But now it was just a fact of life. Carefully, she lifted the toilet lid like she was going to use it, in case he was listening. Sometimes she was sure he had superhuman senses.

Both knee joints popped as she knelt by the clawfoot tub. The moon shone through the stained glass window, and the spotless brass fixtures reflected in her tired eyes. Momentarily, she found herself scanning the fixtures for fingerprints. Then she shook it off and began her silent prayer.

God, she prayed silently, *everything is so hard. Thank you for my beautiful Hazel and little Sam, but I am so worried. Please God, save us,* she begged, letting her desperation pour out.

She sensed him before she heard or saw him. He was there, on the other side of the door, standing silently, angrily in the dark. Peeking out of one eye, she saw his clenched hand in the light of a moonbeam shining through the hole in the door. Her heart began pounding. Her mind was racing. What excuse?

As she began to get up, he violently slammed the door open with his fist, smashing her ear. The pain burst like white hot light in the dark, while the loud, hollow sound of the wooden door hitting her broke through the quiet of the night. She bent over, clutching her ear. Trying not to show him how bad it hurt, she checked for blood.

"I'm sorry, Sam, I'm sorry. I just had to go to the bathroom," she whispered desperately, holding her hands up protectively in front of her face.

"On your knees? Just like my pious mother. Praying?"

It was no use. She was a lousy liar. "I was just praying for Hazel. She's too thin; it scares me, Sam. I'm sorry."

"I was thin. She's my kid."

Shuffling backward, she tried to move around him toward the door. "I'm sorry, Sam." He clenched his fists. In the dark, his eyes were two empty holes. His face was so dark she wanted to turn the light on. "Don't wake the kids, Sam."

Suddenly he was in her face, spit blowing in her eyes. Afraid it would anger him, she didn't dare move. "Don't you love me?" he asked, then without waiting for an answer said, "There is no God. Are you trying to leave me? You're going to leave, aren't you?"

"No, Sam, I love you." Forcing herself to reach out, she touched his face. Taking her in his arms, he collapsed against her. *Was he crying? He was so injured, so abused.*

Anguished, she felt so sorry for him. *It's my fault*, she thought. *Poor Sam.* After all, she knew he had been forced to pray for hours as a child. She felt thoughtless and selfish.

"Come to bed, Sam," she whispered, taking his hand and gently leading him to their room.

———

Grace held Emily's hand while the doctor stitched her forehead together, the fine line creating a permanent reminder of the night. Emily's fingers dug into Grace's flesh as silent tears cut paths through her bloody face. Between stitches and a trip to get an x-ray, Grace heard more of Emily's story.

Emily had been married for a short time to someone else before Berk. Compared to her first husband, who was now in prison, she believed Berk was a great guy.

When Emily met Berk, she was still married to her first husband, and her daughter Amber was small. Even though he had rescued her, he didn't trust her. She didn't blame him because she had cheated on her first husband with Berk.

Emily's parents had fought all the time too, so this was just the way life was. Berk took good care of them. They had a big house, and after all, he wasn't a monster all the time. Emily was sure Grace couldn't possibly understand.

"You don't know," Emily said.

"Maybe I do," was all that Grace offered.

Emily looked at Grace and studied her face. Then her eyebrows raised and she had that look. They exchanged the look of understanding and recognition.

"I've been single for almost five years," Grace offered.

"Oh," Emily said knowingly. Grace knew that Emily was busy making assumptions and she let her.

Grace's marriage was the experience that drove her to want to change the world and go out at all hours of the night. Her ex-husband was truly evil, controlling, manipulative, abusive, and luckily, history.

It was easy to leave her ex when she saw his angry storm head in the children's direction. It was okay to hurt her, but not her children. The first time she recognized his darkness, she was out the door. Her ex was capable of hurting children and then wanting to love her like nothing had happened. Over time, her feelings went from anger and hurt to pity. Eventually, she even prayed for him. But she was the exception, and not everything was as black and white as her marriage had been.

Surprised that her thoughts about the past were still so charged with pain and shame, she still felt lucky to be alive. *Earth to Grace,* she thought, *come back to now.*

"You seem so normal," Emily said, interrupting her thoughts.

"Way too normal. Messy, loud, and definite proof that happily ever after comes with stained laundry and big bills." Laughing, Grace was glad to leave the memory of her ex-husband in the past, happy to keep him as far away from her as possible.

Emily smiled warmly at Grace and they continued talking, finally sharing the truth.

CHAPTER 6

MABEL

MABEL WOKE TO THE SOUND OF THE ALARM CLOCK reminding her she was in Grace's room. It was five thirty in the morning. Slamming the snooze button, Mabel rolled onto her back with her eyes closed.

Mabel dreaded this time of day for many reasons. One reason involved cranky, sleepy, and opinionated teenagers coming together to argue about whose turn it was to pray. Then, one by one, they would remember that they needed money or something important right that second.

Mabel, barely sixty, felt too young to be a grandma and too old to be a mother. *I should be surfing*, she thought, *in Mexico . . .* She never got to finish the thought. Something slapped her on the forehead.

"Wake up! It's the Prayer Fairy! Time for family prayer!"

Cracking open one eye, she saw her six-year-old granddaughter, Mary, in red-and-white-striped footy pajamas with a button-flap bottom and a pair of cartoon underwear she had pulled over the top of them. A towel was tied around her neck. A blue-feathered opera mask and a magic wand completed the look. Mary smacked Mabel on the forehead again with her wand.

"Wake up, sleepy head!"

"Ouch! I'm up." She couldn't keep from grinning.

Mary smiled back with a huge toothy grin that would shame the Cheshire cat, showing a hole where one tooth was missing, and she was out of the room. High-pitched complaints came from her sister Esther's room.

"Mary!" Esther yelled. A pillow made its way into the hall right before the fairy came out of Esther's room. Mabel sat up in time to see Mary cross the hall at a dead run back to Esther's room, landing on Esther's bed with both feet. The leg of the bed broke. The whole thing listed to one side, but the fairy never lost her footing as Esther chased her back across the upstairs landing of the James home and into Grace's bedroom. The door hit the wall with a bang at the same time as the complaining began.

"Nana! Mary broke my bed!"

"Prayer time!" Mabel replied.

"Make her stop!"

The fairy was making her second run around the room when Mabel caught her and tucked her under her arm. Skinny, striped legs and arms went limp as the fairy continued to giggle. Hauling her onto the landing, Mabel dumped her onto the old oriental rug at her seventeen-year-old son Nephi's feet.

Nephi pointed at Mary. "You say the prayer!"

Not long after the prayer, Mable made a to-do list and passed out various amounts of money and one check. Later, Mabel was back in bed, listening to the kids fight over the bathroom. Oh, how she wanted to go back to sleep. *Just ten minutes,* Mabel thought as she dropped back off to sleep.

Grace had encouraged Emily to go into safe housing or a hotel, but Emily couldn't imagine taking her kids to a shelter or sleeping in a motel. She just wanted her own bed and her own pillow.

Grace dropped Emily at the neighbor's house so she could pick up her kids. So Emily could reach her, Grace gave her a business card with the twenty-four-hour crisis line number and an invitation to call her any time, day or night. An officer sat in a parked police car across the street. Grace waved at the dark figure as she left, and it waved back.

———

Greta slept soundly, breathing softly, rhythmically. Both Emily and Amber had tucked her tightly into bed and kissed her good night. Then Emily carried Bjorn into his room and laid him in his crib. Amber carefully pulled the blankets out from around him without waking him. Standing side by side, they watched his pursed lips suck on a dream bottle. Amber leaned over and kissed his forehead, then they quietly backed out of the room, pulled the door almost closed, and looked through the opening at Bjorn's crib.

Amber turned to her mother and whispered vehemently, "Look, Mom, I had to do it. I thought he'd killed you!"

Deflated, Emily's arms dropped to her side, and she gingerly touched the stitches on her head as she turned. Walking softly to Amber's bedroom, she turned the light on. She put both hands on the end of Amber's bed and leaned forward with her eyes closed. Amber held her breath and waited. Without opening her eyes, Emily said flatly, "He loves us, Amber. He doesn't mean it. He's just a drunk. He can't help it."

Amber had heard it all before, over and over again. Feeling guilty, she even believed some of it. He was a drunk. He did love them, and she loved him at some level. She was just sick of it. Since she'd been in high school she'd realized that not everyone had parents that hit each other. There was an ache deep in her gut. Emily walked past Amber as if in a trance and disappeared like a shadow into her own bedroom.

Emily turned the light on and stood silently at the large window. Reflected in the glass, she saw the curve of stitches on her forehead and the emerging black eyes. *I won't be going anywhere public for a while,* she thought. Mechanically, she brushed her teeth, changed into a clean nightgown, and climbed into her empty bed alone. She reached over and hugged Berk's pillow, collapsing into sobs. She missed him.

———

Three minutes after Mabel closed her eyes, the front door closed loudly, waking her. She listened to Grace plod up the stairs. Jumping up, she was straightening the bedspread when Grace came in.

"Good grief, Mom, you didn't go back to bed, did you?" She raised one eyebrow and looked at Mabel.

Amazing, Mabel thought, *how does she do that with one eyebrow?* She tried to match the face.

Grace didn't wait for the answer to her question. "I need a shower. I have to get ready for work."

CHAPTER 7

NECANICUM

EMILY FELT LIKE HER HEAD HADN'T BEEN ON THE PILLOW for more than a second when she heard a rustling sound outside her window. Checking the clock, she realized it was morning already.

"He's back," she whispered to herself. Her heart pumped with the usual adrenaline. He was going to be angry this time. She knew she wouldn't call for help. It would have made things worse if she had gone to a hotel like that woman Grace wanted. Shaking, she went to the window and opened it.

Berk was hanging inside the branches of the pine tree growing next to the second-story window. Perched on a branch, he let go of the tree, caught the windowsill, pulled his muscular body over the frame, and dropped into the room. Rising, he stood a full half a foot taller than her.

"I didn't say a thing, honey," she insisted.

His arm shot out and he took her by the throat, his face never changing expression. He smelled of sweat, dirt, and the outdoors, and he had small bloody scratches covering his cheeks; sticks and dead leaves were woven in his course hair. His Carhartt pants had dried mud on them, and his flannel shirt had a cut by his logger suspenders. His breathing never changed. He looked directly into her eyes, his eyes narrowing.

25

No light—empty, lifeless eyes, flat like black holes, she thought. Then he began to squeeze. Tiny points of light flashed in her eyes. She clawed at his hand. He was squeezing hard enough she couldn't breathe. Her vision began closing, going black. Air, she had to have air. Frantic, she could hear her own pulse slow as he closed off her arteries.

"I'm sorry, I'm sorry," she mouthed, but nothing was coming out.

He threw her back, releasing her throat. She landed halfway on the bed and slid to the floor coughing, hands shaking, feeling her neck while she gasped for air and felt her blood begin pumping again.

"Where is she?" he asked.

Knowing he was asking about Amber, she kept her head down. Amber had called the police and betrayed them.

"She's gone to school early," she lied, without making eye contact.

Stomping out of the room, he went to Amber's room. Emily was still mad at Amber for calling the police and making their lives even worse than they already were. She had ruined everything, but that didn't mean Emily wanted Amber to get hurt. Running after him, she tried to get between him and the door to Amber's room. He kicked the door open.

A cold breeze fluttered through the eyelet curtains hanging over the open window.

Amber let her car roll silently down the hill. The classic Bug was light and easily picked up speed. She popped the clutch and started it two blocks away from the intersection. Seeing the officer parked across the street from the house watch her leave, she wondered what he thought. Would her sister be okay? Mom was too busy with Berk to take care of them. Ever since she was old enough to hate him more than she loved him, she had called Berk by his first name, knowing it annoyed her mother.

She pictured seven-year-old Greta lying silently in her bed with that blank look on her face. Her mousy brown hair, spread on her pillow, looked thin and dry, unlike anyone else's in the family. The strands looked like withered brown leaves ready to blow away in the wind. Why did her father hate Greta so much?

Little nine-month-old Bjorn still cried, but it was a fruitless endeavor when Berk was home. Bjorn and Greta were both so thin it infuriated Amber. She had to make sure they ate. Mom was just too busy keeping Berk happy. Someone had to do it. What would happen if she left home for real?

She decided to take the scenic route through town. Arriving this early at school would make her look geekier than she already did. The houses gradually gave way to the quaint, nautical down-town shops, which lined Broadway, Main Street, and all the way to the Pacific Ocean. Her mind turned to the ocean and its sound, a rhythm that seemed to calm her like a drug.

It was autumn. The tourists were going home and kids were back in school. Driving over the ornate cement bridge that crossed the Necanicum River, she slowed the VW Bug down and finally stopped. The sandy beach, with its waving grass and rugged rocky cove, was empty as far as she could see in either direction. It was like she and the seagulls were alone in the world.

Letting the car idle, Amber rolled down her window, closed her eyes, and took a deep breath of fresh sea air, loving the brisk saltwa-ter smell of fish, sand, and aging wood. She listened to the rhythm of the ocean until someone behind her honked. She jumped, look-ing in the rearview mirror and saw the city truck; she was stopping traffic. Sighing, she put the car in gear and gave in to the day that was upon her.

━━━

Amber's car was the only one in the Necanicum High School park-ing lot. She looked in the rearview mirror and tried to comb her greasy hair. No chance for a shower today. Someone was going to notice she was wearing the same clothes she had on yesterday. Man, she stunk. Luckily, her school bag was still in the car. Pulling her book bag into the front seat, she tried to finish her math assignment before class started.

———

Kelly had made Sam breakfast, packed his lunch, and kissed him goodbye as if nothing had happened the night before. She hadn't given it much thought. When she heard his car drive away, she realized she hadn't been breathing. She took a deep breath and let it out long and slow and felt her bruised head.

She looked around her immaculate kitchen. She really loved it. She knew she needed to leave him and her beautiful home, but wished she could take the gorgeous woodwork, granite countertops, carved island, and antique furniture with her. Sam was a lot of things, including a great carpenter and contractor. He was brilliant with wood. The floors shone; the pickled beadboard was perfect. Everything looked like a professional decorator had been hard at work. She found herself scanning for dust, looking for things she knew would set Sam off.

She went to the bedroom and crawled on the floor. There was a dime under his dresser. Going to the laundry room, she checked the dryer and found another few pieces of change. Taking the money she found last night from underneath the plastic lining of the drawer where she kept the tinfoil, she slipped into her flip-flops, stepped out the back door, and crossed the lawn to her garden. Moving the pumpkin by the big rock, she dug up a jar and put the change in it along with the other money she had collected. She figured she was up to about two hundred dollars. It wouldn't take much more for bus tickets, if that was the way she decided to go.

CHAPTER 8

BAY TOWN

GRACE'S OFFICE AT THE FAMILY CRISIS CENTER WAS IN AN old cannery on the pier in Bay Town, Oregon, about thirty minutes north of Necanicum on Highway 101. As she crossed the Youngs Bay Bridge and emerged from the fog, Grace was again struck by the beauty of Bay Town. It was a melancholy piece of ghostly history that seemed to hang onto sliding land at the mouth of the mighty Columbia River. Nineteenth-century Victorian homes perched precariously on streets that steeply climbed the peninsula. She never tired of the unique view.

Traveling the main road through the narrow Bay Town streets, she eventually turned left onto a gravel road ending at the pier. Stopping long enough to check for oncoming traffic on the narrow plank, she slowly eased onto the old boards. Running only a few miles per hour, her Jeep began crossing the single-lane plank structure, bumping and bouncing, the hollow sound of the wood making butterflies in her stomach. She hated that narrow little bridge. The pier widened enough for parking and an old cannery, which was now remodeled into offices, restaurants, and a coffee shop. The river ebbed and flowed under the pier and around barnacled-covered mossy posts sunk into its muddy bottom, creating constant movement with the tide.

At five after nine, Grace slid open the heavy antique main door. Half old wood and half wavy ancient glass, it rolled open on a rusty track. She ran up the wide stairs to the second story where professional offices lined a hallway. Wall-size windows in the offices on the riverside of the building allowed people to watch the ships go by and see the sea lions up close and personal.

The furniture in their office was donated. It was eclectic, funky junk trying to be homey and welcoming. Grace entered the reception room calling, "Hi, all. Honey, I'm home!" No one answered. Wondering if she was the first one in, she picked up the phone, collected messages, and let the answering service go for the day.

Grace's office was a reflection of Grace. It had yellow sunny walls to chase away the damp, foggy Bay Town gloom with baby-blue-and-white-striped overstuffed chairs facing the fantastic view. Her desk was turned to the wall so that when she spoke to clients her chair was facing them in an open setting instead of across the desk. The clutter of a busy life was everywhere.

Next to Grace's office was another petite but plump advocate named Karen. She was the exact opposite of everything Grace was. In her home life there were no kids, all pets, no serious relationships, all fun. When Grace went nuts over babies, Karen just rolled her eyes and called them little party poopers. While Grace ran and ate health food, Karen ate burgers and fries for lunch and smoked like a train.

Karen came into Grace's office and sat down with her shirt cut low and her skirt rising high. That's why Grace was surprised to see Karen wearing a CTR ring.

"Karen?" said Grace, pointing at the ring. "Do you know what that stands for?"

"Can't think right?"

"No," Grace laughed, "It's a Mormon thing. The letters stand for 'choose the right.'"

"So? I stole it from my college roommate years ago."

"No way!"

Karen was laughing. "You better take it. It might melt on me."

"No, I think you should keep it. Maybe you will think twice about stealing."

"Or choose the right card," Karen mused.

"Very funny."

"No, seriously, you take it. I have a lot of rings," Karen said, taking it off, smiling and holding it out toward Grace.

"Thanks, that's sweet. I've always wanted one."

"Why haven't you had one?"

"I've bought many . . . for my girls and relatives, not me. You know how it goes. Mom is always last on the list." Grace sighed as she slipped the ring on.

"Well . . . see . . . It was meant to be. We're staffing at nine fifteen. See you there."

Karen left Grace to ponder the ring. It looked old. Amazingly, it fit. Grace had large knuckles. Rings never fit. It was the only ring on her hands.

Chapter 9

The Path

KELLY PUT THREE-YEAR-OLD LITTLE SAM, WITH HIS FATHER'S blond curly hair, and eighteen-month-old Hazel, with her matching strawberry-blond ringlets, in front of the television and turned on cartoons. *They are always so good*, she thought. Too good, too quiet, it just wasn't normal. They were calmer when their father was at work. When their father was home, they were clingy, silent, wary, and different. She wished she had a friend or someone else to watch them, give her a reality check, and tell her what they thought.

Sam was an independent contractor, so she never knew when he might turn up at the house. It made for an atmosphere of tension. It hadn't always been that way, and she longed for things to return to the way they'd been in the beginning.

Kelly was the oldest of seven children and had been raised in a strong Latter-day Saint, or Mormon, household. Her family had been really great. Why hadn't she realized how great it was until it was too late? Everything was always chaos. She'd hated that at the time. Everyone always wanted her attention, making her feel like she didn't have any room to breathe. Now she realized they'd just loved her.

Her mother babysat more kids than her own seven. Consequently, the house was less than organized. Although it wasn't filthy, everything had been torn, broken, chipped, or cracked. Her mother had just laughed and said why waste money on furniture when they could spend it on a trip to the beach.

Every year they had taken the family to Necanicum, Oregon, with extended family. They would rent a large house, fill it with cousins, and visit for two weeks. It was a special place to Kelly before . . . before things got so hard.

Kelly went to her bedroom and began making her bed and laying out her clothes. Drawing a bath, she felt the hot water, adjusted the temperature, and added bath salts. She gently parted her hair on the side of her head and examined her scalp in the mirror. At least he always hurt her where no one could see.

Kelly dated Sam against her mother's wishes. The fighting with her parents had begun, the drinking and parties took over, and her grades fell by the wayside.

Sam's house was often empty. His parents had always been at work or away together. As soon as she could, she moved into their house.

Sam's family had attended another local Christian church that she had liked at first. His parents prayed a lot, loud and long, but then used religion as a tool in their arguments. They often gave long lectures or forced Sam to pray. It was confusing for Amber to hear them use the scriptures like weapons one minute and then watch them ignore commandments like chastity or Christlike love of others the next.

In the beginning, she and Sam had fought off and on, but she had yelled as much as he had. When she'd moved into his parent's home, she realized that his mom and dad fought a lot. Then the fighting between her and Sam got worse. She was too proud to go back home. Soon she was pregnant, so they quickly married. She had thought if they could get away from both their parents, things would be better, and they wouldn't fight so much. She was all for the move. It was her idea to go to Necanicum, far away from his family and hers. They saved their money and moved to Necanicum.

Kelly had been sure that distance was the magic answer. She remembered that every time they'd fought, his mother had asked her what she'd done to make him mad at her or what she did that made him hit her. Nothing was ever his fault, and everything was always her fault according to his parents and according to Sam.

Things were better after they moved to the coast. Locals loved his work, and he was making good money. For a while they had fought less, though the fights were bloodier and she was lonely and isolated.

She used to think they wouldn't fight so much if she could find a way to just let things go or be a better wife. But she couldn't. It was hurting their children. She had a constant inner struggle going on—to stay or go. Knowing her children shouldn't watch Sam hit her, she still wrestled with the hope there was a way to fix things and that she should stay. After all, no one knew Sam better than she did, and he knew her better than anyone else could.

Kelly dried herself off and dressed in plain sweats, nothing fancy. Calling attention to herself would upset Sam. She combed her wet hair into a tight ponytail and put on her wedding ring and the CTR ring her parents had sent her for Christmas. Sam had made fun of the ring, but this was a fight that Kelly had won.

CHAPTER 10

CONNECTIONS

OFFICER HART WAS FINALLY READY TO LEAVE THE STATION. He was tired, but not too tired to give Ironpot a hard time. He had noticed something while they worked, and Hart had waited all day to make fun of his partner.

Ironpot was putting his things in a locker when Hart found him. "Quite a night, huh," Hart said.

"Ya, I wish we'd have found Berk. Day shift will watch."

"So I noticed something tonight," Hart said innocently.

"Ya?"

Hart pointed to Ironpot's finger.

"Nice ring," Hart said with a smile.

"You making fun of my jewelry and accessories? My wife dresses me. You'll have to answer to her."

"CTR ring. 'Corrupt the righteous' or 'choose the right'?"

"How did you know?"

"I used to be a Mormon," Hart said sheepishly.

"How does that work? Used to be?" Ironpot sarcastically retorted.

"Well, I went to Primary with a friend for years. The missionaries even taught me the lessons at my house, but I outgrew it when I went to junior high."

"Baptized?"

"Yes."

"You're kidding?"

"Why is that so hard to believe?"

"It's not, it's just that I don't think baptisms wear off, so I think you're still a member of the secret club. So, where's your ring?"

"Very funny."

"No, I think it's great," Ironpot slapped Hart on the back.

"My girlfriend had me baptized in her church. She says the Mormon Church isn't real."

"It's the Church of Jesus Christ of Latter-day Saints, and the millions of members are going to be upset to find that out."

"Funny again."

"I can't help it. It's a gift."

With that, Hart left the building.

———

Watching Hart leave, Ironpot found himself wondering at the turn of events. He had put his daughter's ring on his pinky when he found it on the driveway on his way to work. At the time he'd complained to himself that his kids were messy and irresponsible. This was a nice ring. He was sick of picking up after them. Now he was pondering.

———

Hart thought about Ironpot on his way home. Ironpot had a great family, cute kids, and he seemed to love his wife.

Hart hadn't told Ironpot, but he and his girlfriend had split. The breakup had created an ache and an empty place in his stomach, but he knew it wasn't from the break up. He'd known she was wrong from the beginning. She was way too loud, too drunk, and too fun to be wife material. Her blue eyelids got on his nerves. Everyone else loved her at a party, but day after day . . . that was another matter. Every night it was a few beers before dinner, and her volume went up. She hung all over everyone and thought everything was funny. At least he'd never let her move in or get that close.

She had gone to a community church. The only reason she went to church was because her Harley-riding buddies did, and they had a weekly after-service ride. Church ended with a ride, barbecue, and more beer.

But she had looked great on the back of his bike. Maybe he'd sell the bike.

Hart used to feel invincible, but not lately. Now he felt old. He had a house. It was a real man's house, a log home kit put together by a company that specialized in log homes. He had done most of the finish work himself including building his own shaker-style cabinets. The kitchen had cement countertops with impressions of ferns pressed into the back splash. It was a real work of art that blue eyelids had not appreciated.

He pulled up his long gravel drive, past the berry bushes, and into the pines. The pines created a barrier that made him feel like he were miles away from anyone. When they opened, there was his home, his project. It sat on a small rise in a clearing beside the river. Behind it, the river ran shallow this time of year. The rise kept him safe during spring runoff, but now he could see brown, blue, and gray rocks through the clear, sparking water. It was a perfect river to fish.

A few days ago, he had finished his latest addition: a tire swing he had hung on the big tree in the front of the cabin. *Funny*, he thought. He didn't have kids, but he couldn't resist. It just belonged there.

Hart parked his Jeep Cherokee and looked at the empty house. It needed something.

Suddenly it hit him. What's the point without someone to share it with? The tire swing swung in the autumn breeze, and Hart imagined a little boy swinging and waiting for Dad.

CHAPTER 11

RULES

BERK LAY IN THE BACK OF EMILY'S SUV AS SHE BACKED OUT of the garage and onto the street. A blanket was thrown over him. Waving at the officer parked next door, she drove down the hill. Greta and Bjorn were buckled into car seats. Greta's feet were resting on Berk.

The baby started to scream. Emily tensed and looked at the officer in her rearview mirror.

"Shut him up!" Berk growled.

Emily was afraid that Berk would try to discipline the baby. He always complained that she was too soft on the kids. She looked at Greta over her shoulder.

"Greta, take care of your brother," Emily directed.

Greta pulled a bottle out of the bag and put it in the baby's mouth. He sucked hungrily. Emily's body relaxed when the crying stopped. Remembering he hadn't been fed for hours, she realized he was probably starving.

Emily did exactly as Berk told her, dropping him in the trees a half-mile from his father's logging company down Old Highway 30. Fingering her stitches, she watched him in her rearview mirror retreat in the distance. Suddenly, she became aware the baby was crying again. He would have to wait. She had to get farther down the road.

———

Berk pulled out his cell and called his father. "Dad? Did you hear?"

"Of course I heard. What did she do now?" His father, Edward Anderson, sounded angry.

"It wasn't Emily; it was Amber who called the cops on me."

"That girl is out of control. You need to step up to the plate and take charge. How many times do I have to tell you to be a man?"

Berk felt stupid. One hand on his hip, head down, he kicked a rock in the road.

His father sighed, exasperated. "Well, what's done is done. Where are you now?" his father demanded.

"Half a mile down the road from your office." He paused while he tried to find a good way to put it to his father. There was no good way. "They're looking for me, Dad."

His father swore. "I can't believe this! Do they know who you are?"

Berk's shoulders slumped. *Here we go*, he thought. He checked out while he waited for his father to finish his diatribe about his name and how important he was and how the whole county should be grateful he kept people employed.

"I'll call Tom," his father said. "I'm coming to get you."

"Then what?" Berk asked.

"Tom's a good lawyer. He'll know what to do."

———

Mr. White watched the sea of kids flow loudly down the hallway of the small high school. His lanky body leaned against the cold brick wall while he twisted his CTR spinner ring without thinking. Something was nagging at him. What was it? He high-fived a few of his favorite kids and exchanged words with a few more, all the time trying to tune inward and figure out what was bothering him.

The skin prickled on the back of his neck as he saw the tiny girl with her hood on, obviously avoiding him. Everything else seemed to go away, and for a moment the hall was empty and silent except for the retreating back of her head. He peeled himself off the wall and began to follow Amber.

———

Amber was almost there. Shoulders hunched, hoodie up, sleeves pulled over her hands, books clutched against her chest, she spotted the door to the math classroom through her lowered eyelashes. It was open. Slipping through, she headed to the back of the room.

"Amber," Mr. White said. Whipping around, she snapped to attention and her heart stopped. "I need to see you in my office." He didn't know why he needed her; he just knew it was important enough for a still small voice in his head to shout a little.

Amber's mind raced. Had something happened to her mother, did he listen to a police scanner, did one of the kids tell him, how did he know? Panicked, she simultaneously wanted him to tell her right this second and didn't want him to tell her at all. She felt like a deer in the headlights whose legs were on automatic.

———

The Family Crisis Center met around a kitchen table. Grace's boss, Eunice, was a thin, energetic woman without a family. Her husband, love of her life, had been gone for ten years—as in left for Vegas with another woman. A wry sense of humor and sarcasm covered her major brain and deep mean streak. The woman was a genius with grant writing and money. Her whole life was her job, and she was good at it. Grace wasn't sure she ever went home.

Eunice had a nose for people and could spot a manipulating client at a thousand paces. However, she didn't recognize it when staff was buttering her up.

"Grace had a domestic *all night*," Eunice said. "Someone has to follow up. Grace, tell us about it."

Grace gave the group a short, fast version of Emily's assault, the family, and her work with them.

"What does the victim want to do?" Karen asked.

"She wants to stay. He has all the money and resources. She believes he would win the kids in court. His family isn't a name I recognize, but I guess they are known locally, run a small, but very profitable business and can afford an attorney. She has no friends or family she feels she can turn to."

"What about the kids?"

"I don't think she understands the impact the abuse is having on them. Are all the children his?" Eunice asked.

"Amber isn't, but he has been her only father figure most of her life, and he could sue for psychological parenting. With the right lawyer, he'd win."

"Is this the first incident?" Mindy asked.

"No. Just the first reported incident," Grace answered Mindy and then went on. "The kids seem unfazed, which says to me that this happens a lot. It seems Amber is the parent. Emily is too distracted by Berk to parent. The police will forward their report to the Department of Child Welfare, and I think in this case we should work to help Emily through the Child Welfare process. I know we don't have to, but I'm sure this won't be the last assault, and the kids will continue to be exposed to it. There will be more reports to the state."

"What kind of mother lets that happen?" Mindy shook her head.

"Grace," Eunice interrupted her thoughts, "you had better type your report now, and then get some sleep. It's not safe to call the victim if the perpetrator is still at large. We can't risk having him pick up or see us on caller ID. We'll have to hope she calls us or wait to do a follow-up contact when he's picked up."

CHAPTER 12

PRIVILEGE

BERK AND HIS FATHER WALKED INTO THE ATTORNEY TOM Potter's office. Tom stood and shook Ed's hand. "Ed."

"Tom, you remember my son, Berk? You represented him in Juvenile Court after a fight."

"I had hoped to never see him again," Tom said with an affectionate pat on Berk's shoulder.

"Have a seat," Tom pointed. "Would you like coffee, water?" Tom smelled money. Berk was a mess and looked like he'd been up all night. This was going to cost his father a pretty penny.

Filling Tom in on the story, he finished with a long list of Amber's faults. Tom sat back and tried to look like he was thinking. He already knew what needed to be done.

"Berk, did your wife mention to you that someone from DSAT came to your house with the police?"

"Yes, she said a blonde lady came. But she said she didn't tell them anything."

Tom knew that wasn't true. They all talked. He almost always received discovery or paperwork from the district attorney following a domestic assault, which included signed release forms and a DSAT report with statements from the victim. He also knew that blonde woman was Grace. He'd had her on the stand before. If Berk's wife wanted out, it was just another nail in his client's coffin.

Tom leaned back in his chair and rubbed his thinning hair. Wearily, he asked Berk, "What did the officers look like?"

Berk explained that he hadn't seen much from the woods. "At one point I was up in a tree and two officers were down below me. I left for the bar in town before the dogs came." He described Officers Hart and Ironpot.

Tom recognized the officers Berk was describing. In a small town like Necanicum, he had faced all of the local officers many times in court and regularly in local restaurants and bars. Hart and Ironpot were both good officers and not easily rattled during a trial. The evidence was probably good. He scribbled on a legal pad, and then without looking up he asked, "Did anyone take pictures, or did she go to a doctor to document her injuries?"

"I don't know about pictures, but she went to the emergency room with that woman," Berk said.

Tom shook his head and said, "That woman is an expert witness in court, as is a doctor, and photos tell the whole story."

All the color drained from Berk's face. "So you're saying I'm going to jail?"

"Probably not, because I'm good," Tom said, trying to sound more confident than he felt.

Ed stood up, pacing the room. "What do we do, Tom?"

"He needs to turn himself in, with me at his side, so that we can go in front of the judge. We'll ask the judge to put your son on a release agreement that releases him to your care. The nature of the injuries, as well as possible photographic evidence included in the police body-camera footage, may worry the judge, so we will offer to put him on the electronic monitoring system. You'll have to commit to keep him with you or your wife at all times."

"No problem."

"We need to talk money."

"I'll do what it takes," Ed offered.

Amber waited her turn. Three more kids were now lined up behind her waiting for an interview with his eminence, Mr. White. They all sat without a sound, heads down, waiting to find out how much trouble they were in. At least she wasn't the only miserable person. The secretary was calling their mothers. One of the little geeks started crying so hard, snot was running down his face. *Get a real problem*, Amber thought, and looked down at her shoes.

A large shadow covered Amber's shoes.

"Amber," said an unusually gentle voice.

A shudder ran through Amber. She could take anything but kindness. Feeling her hard shell shake, and threatening to crack, she walked the long four steps into his office.

"Amber," he began again, "How are you?" Asking the open-ended question, he let the silence sit heavy in the air.

Squirming in her seat, she felt the oppressive weight of the loaded question. *Is he just baiting me? Is this a test?* It wasn't like talking with Berk where she had learned to predict his meanness. This was like dancing with a cobra, and she wasn't sure where he was going to strike. But she was sure he would strike. They always strike; everyone strikes.

Eyes on her, he waited. *Why does he just sit there?* Amber thought. What could she tell him that would get him off her back?

"I'm getting sick," she whispered.

"What are your symptoms?" he asked casually. He inched his chair back like he was afraid she was going to infect him.

"Sore throat," she whispered, breathing out long and hard in his direction.

He visibly leaned back. "Oh . . . well . . . call your mother and let's have her pick you up."

"I can drive myself home."

"Call her anyway."

"Okay." Shuffling out, she smirked into her hoodie. Picking up the receptionist's phone, she dialed nothing, and then tapped the button on the phone, making the dial tone buzz in her ear. She breathed hard on the phone and coughed loudly all over it a few times.

"Hi, Mom," she said to no one, while wiping her nose with her free hand, and then shifting and holding the handset with that hand. She coughed again loudly all over the receiver. The receptionist's head jerked up and her eyes grew large.

"I'm sick . . . sore throat . . . fever . . . you want to talk to whom? She wants to talk to you." Amber held the phone out to the receptionist, who backed away, shaking her head.

"I'm . . . busy."

"She can't talk, Mom. I'm coming home, okay? Okay, see you then." Amber hung up the phone and lumbered weakly toward the exit.

The receptionist sprayed the phone with disinfectant and was wiping it vigorously as Amber left the office.

Home is worse than school right now, Amber thought. She didn't want to go home. She'd go to the Cove, watch the surfers, and study.

———

Amber drove through the narrow Necanicum streets across town. The view opened up, and on her right were the crashing waves of the west coast's best-kept secret, the Cove. Waves, perfect for surfing, beat against large boulders and roared in her ears, depositing long twisted logs on the rocky inlet. Tall evergreens covered the side of Tillamook Head, which jutted out to sea on the south side of the cove. Parked cars faced the rolling surf. Seagulls called and fought for scraps. The sun sprinkled light on the water.

Vans were opened at the back. Local, tan surfers with towels wrapped tightly around their waists changed in public, slipping out of their work clothes and into wet suits. Every other car, truck, or van had a surfboard on top or in it. Amber parked her vintage Volkswagen Beetle facing the ocean, opened the windows and the sunroof, and laid her seat back. She breathed in the salty ocean air, closed her eyes, and listened to seagulls call out, begging tourists to feed them. The rhythmic crashing waves seemed to pull the tension from her body. She pulled off her hood, grabbed a blanket off the back seat, and covered up.

The weight returned to her chest, and her eyes threatened to flood over and ruin her thick mascara. She covered her head with the blanket, rolled on her side, and began to quietly cry herself to sleep.

CHAPTER 13

PATTERNS

KELLY HAD HAZEL IN HER LAP AND SAM JR. SITTING NEXT TO her on the plush rug in the family room off her kitchen. Books were strewn around them on the floor as she read the book Sam Jr. had picked out.

A shadow fell across them and she jumped. *He is so quiet,* she thought. Slowly, she looked up at her husband's angry face.

He kicked the books across the floor. Hazel jumped up, chasing the books.

"Honey, you're home," Kelly said with a smile.

"Is this what you do when I'm working hard? I'm out sweating, working for you and you're playing!"

Trying to get the focus off the kids, she stood and was roughly pushed by Sam.

She snapped. "What do you think I do all day, Sam!" she asked as she headed away from the children to the bedroom.

"Well, let's just see!" Striding past her and taking the bait, he said, "Let's see what you do all day!" He yanked back their bedspread. "What are these?" he said, without even looking at her. She knew he was talking about the way she tucked in the corners of the sheets. This was a ritual they had done before. Violently, he pulled off the bedspread, sheets, and blanket, sweeping everything off her nightstand and onto the floor. When he moved on to checking her drawers, Kelly turned from him to see Sam Jr. and Hazel watching wide-eyed. Slowly, she shut the bedroom door.

―――

Tom Potter called the District Attorney, hoping to arrange for Berk to turn himself in and pay bail so he could be released. If he were released, he would get a later date for an arraignment, and that would give the victim time to recant.

Bill Masterson, the District Attorney, was a serious older man who wore an old hat, cowboy boots, and a bow tie.

"Look, Tom," Bill said into the phone, "I plan to take this case to Grand Jury as soon as possible. You know the felony law. The kid's a witness, and it's a felony."

Tom shot back, "This is a family that's lived here forever. He's not going anywhere. He's committed to stay with his parents, go on electronic monitoring, and pay bail. Have you met Ed? Ed is a great guy."

"I don't care who his father is. If he screws up and contacts my victims or witnesses, I'm going to ask for no bail and no release," Bill spit into the phone.

"I'll have a talk with him, I promise. I think we can get this resolved."

―――

Berk sat on the bench in the jail booking room waiting his turn, looking at the brick walls. They were just like the walls in Juvenile Detention. He'd been in Juvenile as a teenager for a few short stays over fights he'd had and drunken brawls outside local bars he wasn't supposed to be drinking in. Strutting, he'd gone into Juvenile cocky and had been well-rewarded. When his father bought his way out, he was placed in a cushy drug and alcohol treatment facility in the mountains of Idaho. It was like a long extended stay at camp. He was positive he wasn't an alcoholic or drug addict. It was just anger. It wasn't his fault; he couldn't help himself.

He was always sure his father would find a way out. The rules still didn't apply to him.

They photographed and fingerprinted him, and now they were putting an electronic bracelet on his ankle. It was supposed to track him. He was sure there was a way around it, and he intended to find it.

"Mr. Anderson," the deputy said, interrupting his thoughts, "do you understand your release agreement?" Without waiting for Berk's answer, he continued to read from the paper in front of him, "You may not have any contact, first or third party, with Emily Anderson, your victim." The deputy looked at him, and Berk realized he was supposed to agree.

"Sure." Berk leaned back in the chair and folded his arms.

"Do you realize and understand that you are not to be within five hundred feet of your previous residence?"

"Yes."

"Do you understand that you cannot contact any witnesses listed in your case, including Amber Anderson, or you will be in violation of your release agreement?"

"Hey, wait a minute, she's my stepkid."

The deputy ignored Berk and continued to read in his monotone voice, "If you violate this release agreement, you will be returned to jail, possibly for the duration of the time until your trial."

"How long is that usually?"

"It varies case by case. If you violate this release agreement, you will forfeit any money paid on bail, and you will owe the remainder of your bail."

Berk thought whatever bail there was, his Dad would be able to pay bail again, or find another way out.

Not long afterward, Berk walked out of jail a free man with a new ankle bracelet. His father drove him to his parent's home on the mountain where his mother, Anna, was barbecuing his favorite cut of steak.

"Dad, which car can I borrow?"

"Take the old pickup."

"Thanks."

CHAPTER 14

CHOICES

VICE PRINCIPAL WHITE SPOTTED ALAN, A HEAD TALLER THAN any other senior in school, laughing and coming his way. *Alan looks great*, he thought, marveling at the glow that had emanated from Alan's face since his recent baptism into the LDS Church. Just this last summer, after going to his third scout camp with his friend Jake, Alan chose baptism. It was amazing. Alan was the only member of the Church in his large family.

"Alan!" Mr. White called.

Alan crossed the crowd to Mr. White, grinning from ear to ear, and grabbed Mr. White's right hand in a serious missionary hand-shake, then they bumped chests.

"You going to church ball tonight?" Mr. White asked.

"I don't know. I have this huge urge to go surfing."

"Surfing? Why would you want to surf and miss a blood sport like church ball?"

"Now, now, Mr. Vice Principal. That's not very Christian of you," Alan teased.

"All right, I'll play nice . . . you know I'm always a good example."

"Ha!" Alan let out a belly laugh. Everyone knew the vice prin-cipal was a ruthless basketball cheater who'd knock you down and then hug you, after he scraped you off the floor.

"I still feel like I should surf."

"But you're wearing a basketball T-shirt and a CTR ring. Choose the right, man, come to church ball."

Alan shook his head, smiled, and reentered the stream of students flowing out into the sunlight, and got into his little soft-top Jeep.

Mr. White gathered his things to go home. After logging off his computer, he locked the office. He was looking around one last time when his thoughts were interrupted by a thought out of place, *Go to the Cove.*

What? he thought, and began arguing with himself.

"Why would I go to the Cove?" he said to himself.

Go to the Cove. If he did go to the Cove, he could talk Alan into playing ball.

"It's church ball night and I need to eat and mow the lawn before the game," he argued with himself.

Go to the Cove.

CHAPTER 15

THE COVE

TOWEL, DON'T FAIL ME NOW, ALAN THOUGHT. ALAN STOOD next to the Jeep with a towel tied tightly around his waist. He had his wet suit all prepared as he quickly dropped his jeans and slipped into the suit. Once it was zipped past his waist, he breathed a sigh of relief, took off the towel, put his arms in the sleeves, and finished pulling the zipper closed. Bending over to put on his booties, he heard yelling and pounding.

Looking over the top of his Jeep, he saw a really large man pounding on an old Volkswagen Beetle. He recognized the car. It belonged to a girl in his class at school. What was her name?

The man shouted, "Amber! Open this door!" The girl had the window up and was huddled in the middle of the car between the seats.

"You're supposed to be home!" the man roared as he reached in the sunroof. Still yelling, he took a hold of her hood and began trying to pull her through the roof. "You turned me in, you little . . ." He started swearing.

Without thinking, Alan began to move, not noticing the gravel on his bare feet. He didn't have a plan of action. He didn't notice the massive amounts of adrenaline pumping through his system as he grabbed the man by both arms from behind and pulled him away from the car and off his feet. "Let go!" Alan demanded.

The man wheeled on Alan and slammed him into the hood of the car. Alan hung on, climbing higher on the man's back. Clutching, twisting the girl's sweatshirt, the man still had her hair with his left hand. Alan saw the shirt was choking the girl. Without thinking, Alan moved his arms around the man's throat and began choking him out. The man finally let go of the girl's shirt and hair and repeatedly tried to bang Alan into the hood of the car to scrape him off. As the man's legs began to buckle, Alan saw Mr. White running toward him across the long narrow parking lot with a cell phone to his ear.

"Alan, Alan!" Mr. White yelled as he pocketed the phone. "Let go!"

Alan's tunnel vision seemed to widen, and he realized the man was limp. Dropping him to the ground, Alan staggered back, hoping he hadn't killed him. He looked wild-eyed at the girl who sat silently in her car with her hands over her mouth and a look of horror frozen on her face.

Coughing, the man rolled onto his knees. Alan, relieved and panting, felt like he was going to throw up. Blood pumped in his ears and rushed like a waterfall. Onlookers ran to Alan who was only catching every other word everyone said. A crowd gathered of half-dressed surfers and small-town faces, all talking and looking confused.

Sirens cut through his fog, and his face whipped around, looking for Mr. White. He'd never been so relieved to see a friendly face.

———

Officer Hart and Ironpot had only been back on duty for a little over an hour when the call came in.

"600 units, I've just received a 911 for a physical altercation in progress at the Cove."

Ironpot radioed the station with his badge number and said, "Copy, in route," then turned his squad car toward the cove. He heard Hart on the radio say, "Copy, in route Code 3." Code 3 meant driving top speed, lights and sirens clearing traffic.

Both squad cars pulled into the parking area, sliding on loose gravel. In front of them, a man was on his knees on the ground. A surfer in a wet suit and with a bloody nose was bent over and vomiting on the rocks. For some strange reason, the high school vice principal, Mr. White, was patting the puker on the back.

When they got out, Hart realized that Amber was locked in her Volkswagen, crying. Hair was sticking up around a messy ponytail; she looked like she hadn't been home since the incident the previous evening.

Berk saw the officers coming. Standing up, he put both hands in front of him as if to ward them off. "Hey, guys! I turned myself in today. I'm on a release agreement. I ran into Amber, and her boyfriend just attacked me!"

It was clear to Hart. This was Berk Anderson, their suspect in the assault last night. He looked at Ironpot and quiet understanding passed between them.

"What!" Alan interrupted, wiping his mouth, and headed back to take another swing at Berk. Ironpot held him back with one arm, putting himself in between them.

"It's my word against his. Tell him, Amber," Berk demanded.

"No, it's not," said Mr. White calmly. "I saw the whole thing. Alan was protecting Amber."

Ironpot cuffed Berk. Hart assisted Ironpot in putting Berk in the patrol car.

Berk looked arrogantly at Ironpot through the window, and when Ironpot got in the patrol car, he began trying to explain. "Look, Officer, I was just trying to be a good father. She's out of control. She was supposed to be home hours ago. The school secretary called to see how she was. My wife didn't tell the school Amber wasn't even home. I volunteered to go look for her because I'm a good father." Ironpot shook his head and put his hand up. Berk took the hint and stopped talking.

"Before you say anything else about talking to your wife, I have to notify you I am recording this, and I have something to read to you." He unbuttoned his shirt pocket and pulled out a laminated card and read, "You have the right to remain silent. Anything you say can, and will, be used against you in a court of law. You have the right to an attorney. If you wish to speak to an attorney and cannot afford one, one will be appointed to you at no cost to you." He put the card away. "So," Ironpot said, "do you understand these rights? Also, I have video cameras and recorders on the front of my squad car and in my squad car mounted both here and here. I have been and will continue filming you." He smiled and asked, "Are you supposed to have contact with your daughter?" and waited for Berk to respond.

"My lawyer is Tom Potter," was all Berk had to say.

———

Vice Principal White tapped on the glass of the Volkswagen door.

"Amber, Amber?" the vice principal softly called.

Hart and Alan had been talking. They both stopped and watched Mr. White tap on the car window. Amber was inside, completely covered by a blanket, unresponsive and rocking. They were mesmerized.

"Amber," he said gently. "You're safe now . . . It's okay to come out . . . Amber?"

Amber didn't feel safe. They couldn't stop him. He'd be back, and it would be worse than ever.

Alan joined Mr. White at the car window while Hart continued to stand back and watch. Alan used his long arm to reach in the sunroof and unlock the door to the car. Amber flinched when his arm came in the roof, but when the door was open, she and her blanket burst out of the door and fell into his arms, still sobbing. She and Alan collapsed onto the gravel, and Mr. White knelt, gathering them in his arms, tears running down his own cheeks.

When Amber could finally talk, she whispered breathlessly. Still gulping for air, she said, "Thank you," and she looked up into Alan's concerned dark blue eyes.

"Man," Alan said smiling, cracking the drying blood smeared on his handsome face, "it's a good thing I'm wearing a wet suit, because you're leaking."

Amber was surprised when a laugh slipped out of her lips. She couldn't remember the last time she'd laughed.

Alan looked at Mr. White and said, "This is way bloodier than church ball." They all laughed together as the tension washed away.

Mr. White helped Amber to her feet. Alan began massaging sore muscles while rubbing the back of his head, checking for injuries.

"Why don't we get you home?" Mr. White offered to Amber. He felt her whole body twitch. Officer Hart stepped in.

"Actually, I need to invite you all to come down to the station to make statements. I have a recorder and camera there and I'd like to record your statements."

Amber looked concerned, but he was a police officer and it didn't occur to her to question his authority. Even though she knew she would be punished for telling the truth, she also knew it was time.

"Sure," Alan said. "Amber, are you okay to drive? I could drive you."

"Thanks," Amber said and woodenly walked to the Jeep.

"First, let me step into my dressing room and change out of my rubber wrestling suit." He had her smiling again.

Hart looked at Mr. White, "Nice ring," he said. "Another member of the secret club?"

Mr. White looked down at his hands, saw his wedding ring next to his CTR ring, and said, "Yeah, I've been married a long time."

CHAPTER 16

FAMILIES

HART SETTLED HIS WITNESSES IN THE SMALL INTERVIEW room at the Necanicum police station. He excused himself and went out to talk to Ironpot about calling out DSAT.

Ironpot and Sergeant Henry had already brought Berk Anderson into the booking room. They had removed the cuffs, taken booking photos, and fingerprinted him. Ironpot took all of Berk's property including his belt and shoes and put them in a property locker. He looked at the electronic monitoring ankle bracelet. *A lot of good it did*, he thought. It was put on by the jail and was supposed to signal the system when he left his home or designated areas.

All through the process, Berk arrogantly demanded his phone call. Finally, before putting him in the cell, Ironpot offered him the phone. He dialed Berk's attorney for him and waited while he was forced to leave a message on an answering machine. Being generous, Ironpot let him call his father. The foul language bounced out of the phone and circled the room. Ironpot put his finger on the button and hung up. Berk looked like a beaten puppy. Ironpot led him into the holding cell to await transport to the county jail and then he met Hart in the hall by dispatch.

"Judy, watch him for suicide," Ironpot told the dispatcher. "He's pretty down."

"I think he's way too stupid and selfish to do us that favor," Hart said.

"Watch it, cynic. You'll get what you asked for. Believe me, you don't want it on your watch."

Hart smiled sheepishly, knowing Ironpot was right; he was a cynic. "Do you think we should call DSAT?" Hart said.

"It's not a typical domestic."

"Yes, but it's the same victim as last night. I don't know if Grace got too far with our victim, Emily, other than getting her to go in for stitches. It would give her a second chance to talk to Emily when Amber has to go home."

"I've been thinking we need to call Child Welfare and get a child protective services investigator on this, even though they don't do much for teens."

"But we have a nine-month-old and a seven-year-old in the home."

"That's true."

———

Grace was doing the dinner dishes when, "Bye, Mom!" was called loudly as everyone left for church ball. *At last*, she thought as she had a quiet moment at the sink doing dishes. She'd had about two hours sleep before everyone came home. Even though she loved being here with her family, every once in a while she loved a good book or time to paint. Right now she was looking forward to both. An unfinished painting was on the easel in the living room, and a book on tape called her name like chocolate cake.

Work broke into her thoughts, and she found herself thinking about Emily. Drying her hands, she checked her pocket to make sure she had her cell with her. It rang and all the wind went out of her sails.

"This is Grace."

"NPD has requested a DSAT worker meet officers at the station."

"All right," she sighed, "I'm there. Thanks."

Ending the call, she walked toward the door, looking longingly at the canvas on the easel as she slipped on her shoes.

———

The call from the Child Welfare worker came soon after they were paged. Hart stopped interviewing and went to the squad room to answer the phone.

"Hello. This is Child Welfare, whom am I speaking with?"

"This is Officer Hart of the Necanicum Police Department."

"Officer Hart, you called? This is Reesa."

"Oh, hi Reesa." Hart knew Reesa. She was fifty, married without children. She wasn't a soft touch.

"Last night, officers responded to a domestic at—"

"The Anderson house. The district attorney sent us reports. We staffed it this morning and put it on a five-day response."

"Meaning?"

"Meaning our investigator will meet with the family in five days."

"Well, we've had another incident involving the seventeen-year-old daughter, Amber, tonight."

"You know we don't do much with teens?" she asked him like he was an idiot.

Hart knew the policy was that teens could defend themselves, call police, or run away. Foster care rarely worked, and kids usually ran if they were not in care voluntarily. "I know, but tonight he assaulted Amber."

"Is she an unruly teen? What did Amber do?"

"Does it matter?"

"Yes, it changes everything."

"No, she's not unruly. She seems almost meek."

"So, you don't know."

"Not yet."

"Did you arrest him?"

"Yes. Not only on the assault, but on a violation of his release agreement."

"Perfect. He's not going anywhere. We'll staff it in the morning. Forward me your report."

Hart hung up and turned to Ironpot, who was in his cubical typing reports. "Ironpot, you were right."

"Child Welfare?" he asked, pointing at the phone.

"Yes."

"They going to do anything?" Ironpot cocked his eyebrows and smiled as if in anticipation.

"All right, you were right. It's a big fat promise to staff it."

"Well, that's something," Ironpot said.

A speaker interrupted their conversation. It was Judy in dispatch. "DSAT to meet with officers."

They looked at each other.

"I hope its Grace," Ironpot said. "It's not that I don't like the others, but she knows the case."

Hart buzzed the lobby's magnetic door locks. When Hart saw Grace open the door, he broke into a grin. "Miss us, honey?" Hart asked.

"I've been calling people all day trying to get them to beat each other up on your shift so we could spend more time together. I am your biggest fan." *If only he knew*, she thought, and a smile spread across her face.

"Do I need a stalking order?"

"You'll have to come see me tomorrow so I can help you fill it out."

"It's a plan."

"So, what brings me out on my broom again?"

"Amber Anderson," Hart said, his face becoming serious.

"Amber?" Grace couldn't place the name, but it sounded familiar.

"Berk and Emily's daughter."

"Oh!" The puzzle pieces began moving toward each other. She knit her brows and asked, "What happened?"

Hart filled Grace in.

"Is the surfer okay?" Grace asked.

"Yeah. He has bloody nose, bumps, and scrapes."

"You got photos?"

He nodded. "We're in the middle of a taped interview."

"Oh, I can just listen and do my work when you're done."

"I called Child Welfare." He looked at her to see what she would think.

"Good. What did they say?"

"It's a five-dayer."

Grace just shook her head in disbelief. "I hate the thought of those kids in that house if he bails out again."

"I don't think he can, but you know our jail's release system."

"That's an even scarier thought," Grace said. They looked at each other and both shook their heads. Due to overcrowding, when the jail hit capacity, usually two or three inmates were let out early per day.

Hart led Grace to the interrogation room. She expected to see Amber, but was thrown by seeing Brother White and Alan. They both went to her church. Ignoring them for a minute, she held her hand out to Amber, who looked up with wary eyes. "Hi, Amber. I am so sorry. I'm Grace. I met with your mom last night. I understand you've had a bad day, or is that an understatement?"

"Do you have to call my mom?"

Grace looked over her shoulder at Hart.

Hart sat down facing Amber and said, "As I told you, Amber, because you're a minor, I have to notify your mother. We'll wait a minute though if that's all right. I'd like to finish the interview."

Amber nodded. Grace turned to White and Alan. "You're missing church ball, and you must be the surfer hero, Alan, because it can't be Brother White."

Brother? Hart thought. He hadn't heard someone called that since he was a kid. Alan must be a member too. "You know each other?" Hart asked Grace.

She made a deadpan face, "Never saw them before in my life." Amber actually laughed, and Alan stood up and gave Grace a hug as she held her arms out to him.

"Hi, Grace," he said.

Hart looked surprised.

"Alan just lives at my house with my brother and Esther sometimes. Whenever there's pizza or water in the hot tub. We go to the same church and he's the same age as my bratty brother."

"Not you too. Let me see your hands, all of you," Hart said seriously. They all held out their hands. "Three rings . . ." Hart shook his head. "Do you have a decoder for those?"

Amber looked confused.

"I'll explain later," Alan said to her.

"Time to get back to work," Hart reined them in.

Grace looked at Hart's handsome face and wondered if now that he knew she was a nice churchgoing girl his interest in her would fade away.

———

Vice Principal White had finished his interview first and gone home. When Ironpot was done calling their parents, he joined Hart, Alan, Amber, and Grace in the interview room. Amber was just signing her written statement when Ironpot returned.

"Alan, I called your parents and they wanted to come down. They are on their way," Ironpot told Alan. Amber visibly tensed.

"What about my mom?" Amber asked.

"She said it was okay for you to drive yourself home. She said the baby was asleep and she didn't have a sitter. Your neighbor Martha wasn't home."

"Oh," Amber said, looking worried. "I left my car at the Cove."

"I can take Amber back to her car," Alan quickly volunteered.

"You better talk to your folks first, Alan," Ironpot told him.

"I can take you home, Amber," Grace offered.

"Thanks, but if Alan could that would be great." Amber looked down at the floor, and Grace realized by the color in her cheeks her choice of drivers was about more than the ride.

"How about if you go with Alan and I go talk to your mom before you get there?" Grace offered.

"She's going to be mad at me for getting my stepdad in trouble again."

"Maybe I can help. You didn't do anything wrong." Grace looked at Amber, wishing somehow Amber would trust her.

"She'll think it's my fault."

"I know," Grace agreed, surprising Amber, "but I am sure it's not your fault, and I really want to talk to her."

"Okay," Amber reluctantly agreed.

Hart stood up. "I'll check to see if your parents are in the lobby, Alan." Hart left the interview room and then came back with a smile on his face.

"Alan, your fan club is in the lobby," he said with a smile.

"Thanks. Come on Amber, I'll introduce you to my parents."

"Oh, I don't know," Amber said. Alan ignored her response, took her hand, and led her out. Grace followed.

The lobby was filled with children and two adults, who all called Alan's name and gathered round him like a brood of chicks around a mother hen. Alan took the baby out of his mother's arms like it was natural. Everyone was talking at once. His mother was really short, Grace noticed. She shined like Alan. She had a pretty, freckled, round face with sunny light brown hair and was wearing what looked like gardening clothes. His dad was tall like Alan. They looked a lot alike: handsome, dark hair, clear skin, blue eyes, and long, lean muscles. His dad was definitely a workingman and was covered with sawdust. Without saying a word, he walked over to Alan, wrapped his arms around him, and patted him on the back and began leading him and the brood toward the door. Alan stopped his father and turned toward Amber while the baby pulled his hair.

"Dad, Mom, this is Amber," he said, while his mother examined his nose and a few scratches on his face, clucking her tongue over the blood on his shirt.

Everyone's attention turned to Amber, who stood frozen with her hands pulled back in her sleeves and her hood over her messy hair. Her eyes were filled with anxiety, looking like a frightened bird ready to fly.

"Oh, Amber, I am so sorry to hear what happened," Alan's mother said while she naturally put her arm around Amber, touched her face, and began to examine her.

"Are you hurt?" she asked Amber.

"No, Mrs. . . ."

"You can call me Clareen."

Grace was pretty sure that would be hard for Amber. Grace interrupted and introduced herself.

"Mrs. Johnson, I'm Grace, I work at the Family Crisis Center, and I go to church with Alan. I just wanted to tell you that your son is a real-life hero," Grace said as she took Mrs. Johnson's hand and shook it. Alan's neck and face flushed patchy red. Mr. Johnson's eyebrows rose, and the rest of the children actually stopped talking to listen.

"Mmm?" Mr. Johnson said, being interpreted as "tell me more."

Grace looked at him. "Mr. Johnson, Amber was in the process of being assaulted when Alan stepped in to protect her. You have a lot to be proud of." Mrs. Johnson was beaming. Alan looked at the floor, and Amber still hadn't moved.

"Mmm," Mr. Johnson answered, being interpreted as agreement and pride.

Grace turned to Alan. "Alan, you were very lucky today. Next time, call the police, but thank you. I know I'll see you around. Call me if you need anything." She handed Mr. Johnson her card.

Turning to look at Amber, Grace said, "Remember what I told you, Amber. This is not your fault." With that, Grace squeezed Amber's thin arms and excused herself to drive to Emily's house.

CHAPTER 17

REACHING OUT

GRACE PULLED UP IN FRONT OF EMILY ANDERSON'S HOUSE. Taking a deep breath and letting it out slowly, she worked at relaxing. Knowing this might be a difficult conversation, she tried to put on a positive attitude.

"Here goes nothing," she said to herself, getting out of the Jeep. Walking across the beautiful lawn to the tall front door, she noticed all the curtains were closed, but one was moving. Smiling, she rang the doorbell.

Waiting, she strained to hear if anything was moving in the house. It was silent. She rang the doorbell and knocked again. A baby began crying on the other side of the door. Emily must be looking out the peephole and holding the baby. Grace laughed to herself. Busted!

Emily pulled the door open but stood in it defiantly with the baby on her hip.

"Hi, Emily," Grace said cheerfully. "I just thought I'd come by and tell you that Amber is fine. She got a ride back to her car with the young man that was at the assault."

"She shouldn't have lied to the school. This never would have happened if she hadn't pretended to be sick. The secretary called to see how she was, and I had no idea what she was talking about.

Then she didn't come home. What were we supposed to do?" Emily said angrily.

"I know teenagers are hard. I also know you love your husband, and I'm sorry this happened."

Emily deflated like an empty balloon and tears threatened to flow. "She just knows how to push his buttons," she said. Looking down, she gently wiped the corners of her bruised eyes, wincing as her stitches pulled.

"Teenagers are pros at button-pushing. Emily, I know you love him, and I'm sorry he's going to jail again. Would you like to talk about what that means for your family?" Grace asked.

Without looking up, Emily opened the door wider and Grace went in.

———

Alan had explained to his parents that he needed to take Amber back to her car. Two of his brothers had insisted on riding with Alan. After making sure his brothers were properly buckled into the Jeep's back seat and Amber was comfortable, Alan pulled out of the police station.

"Alan, did you get the guy bad?" Bradley asked as soon as they were away from the rest of the family.

Alan looked self-consciously at Amber. "Ah . . . the guy is Amber's father," he said, trying to clue Bradley in. Bradley wasn't dissuaded.

"Yeah, but did you get him?"

Jack joined in. "I'd have given him a right, a left, and then a hi-!" he said, demonstrating every move all over Bradley. Pretty quick there was an out-of-control brawl in the back seat.

Alan looked at Amber, who was looking straight ahead without any expression on her face. *Obviously she isn't used to little brothers,* he thought.

"Hey, Amber," he shouted over the boys, "how about I take them home first?" Amber smiled as she turned toward Alan, and Alan smiled back. "All right," he said, "it's a plan."

Grace and Emily sat talking in Emily's quiet living room. Grace could tell by looking at the house that a man lived there. It was full of antlers, mounted fish, and plaid. It was Early Northwest Outdoorsman at its best. The house was quiet, and the lights were dim.

They shared small talk, updated each other, and discussed the huge headache that Emily had. Commiserating, they talked about how difficult it was to raise a teenager who couldn't be turned off and put away at night. Now it was time to talk the truth. Grace could feel Emily working around the heart of the issue, talking lightly about things that had little importance. Finally, there was a pause in the conversation. Instead of filling it with small talk, Grace waited.

Emily looked at the plaid quilt on her lap and played with the yarn. Her eyebrows met in deep thought. After two or three breaths, she began to say something, but pulled back.

Finally, Grace watched her take a deep breath and take the plunge. Speaking softly, looking down at her nervous hands, she started, "I've never really been alone. I've never paid my own bills. I don't know how I can do this without Berk." The words came tumbling out, and all Grace had to do was nod and add an occasional "uh huh" for them to continue. "Berk is a good father who takes care of us, and his family is really respected, you know? They have money and they can help when things go wrong. They're really angry that Amber called the police. Berk can't help himself. He doesn't mean to do the things he does. It's just that me and the kids can be so irritating, and he's under so much pressure, and he drinks. If we'd just be more supportive, and he stopped drinking, things like this wouldn't happen."

"Emily," Grace cut in, "I know you love Berk, but nothing you or Amber did excuses his behavior or . . . that," Grace said, pointing at the long bruising wound on Emily's forehead.

Emily reached up and gently touched the stitches like she'd forgotten the injury. "He knows he's done something wrong. At least he says he's sorry."

"I believe he is sorry. But then he does it again, doesn't he?"

"But he doesn't want to," Emily said, sounding unconvinced.

"He needs help, Emily. No one knows Berk better than you. It's not my job to tell you how to live your life, but I'm afraid for Amber and the kids, Greta and Bjorn. You're an adult. You get to do what you want. Don't you think they deserve to be safe?"

Emily looked down, shaking her head, "I always thought when I was married it would be like when I was a kid. My family was great, except my Dad worked a lot."

"We all want the best for our families," Grace said. "We all want white picket fences and sunny days, but sometimes bad things happen to good people. My job is to help you make a safety plan to protect your children and yourself and to hopefully prevent a homicide."

Emily rubbed her face with her hand. "How can anything good come out of this?" she asked.

"Well, for one thing, Berk could be mandated into treatment for alcoholism or therapy if he's found guilty. And maybe therapy will make a difference. It's hard to tell. The statistics aren't very good, but you never know."

"Do you think he could change?" Emily asked, finally looking into Grace's eyes.

"I don't know. The only way to find out is to try it. The only real thing we have control over is ourselves. You can't make Berk change," Grace said, studying Emily's face. Emily nodded, looking like she was trying to put the pieces of a puzzle together. Grace continued, "He has to want it. Sometimes when we love someone, we have to allow them to hit bottom and be forced to look at themselves. I know you want to rescue him, but—"

"I know," Emily interrupted, "Sometimes I feel like all I do is take care of him. I want my kids to have a dad who is there for them. I don't want to be divorced."

"That's not a decision you have to make today. Today we just have to worry about how to protect your children and how to make your ends meet."

Emily looked back down at the yarn on the quilt, but she finally nodded. "I know you're right. It's just that I love him and I'm afraid to be alone. How will I make it?"

"With help. You don't have to do it all alone. The Family Crisis Center is supposed to help you problem-solve, so tomorrow let's start with the easy stuff, money," Grace said sarcastically with a smile. "Tell me what you think your immediate financial needs are. I'll tell you all the resources I know. We'll set some goals and make a plan of action. Okay?"

"Okay . . ." Emily looked uncertain.

CHAPTER 18

HYDRANGEAS AND SAWDUST

A FEW SHORT BLOCKS FROM THE COVE, IN THE NECANICUM avenues, Alan and Amber pulled in front of an old craftsman house. It was set back from the curb. Lights placed strategically in the yard lit it up like someone was having a party. The Necanicum River ran dark and slow a hundred feet behind it. A white picket fence bordered the entire property. An ugly little dog barked along the front fence, running and jumping in and out of flowerbeds.

Flowers were everywhere. The house may have been old, but because of the abundant blossoms, it didn't seem old. Flowers climbed the fence and the arbor over the gate, trailed along the porch, and seemed to fill the night air with sweet summer's scent. Amber thought it was like a fairyland or a picture out of a magazine. Complicated scrolled wood cutouts were placed along the porch and in the eves of the house. A beautiful gazebo, unlike anything she had ever seen, sat off to one side of the front yard, and a girl sat in it reading a book.

The boys bailed out of the Jeep and headed for a large brightly lit garage that sat down the driveway to the side of the property and a little behind the house.

"It's beautiful!" Amber said in awe. Without thinking, she got out of the Jeep and began walking to the fence to get a closer look. All the furniture in the gazebo and on the porch was wooden.

Adirondacks stained with paintings on their backs and matching foot rests, carved tables with polished driftwood legs, and a porch swing made of wood decorated the long well-lit front porch.

"Isn't it great?" Alan said in her ear, making her jump. Totally captivated, she hadn't even noticed him coming up behind her. "My dad is a pretty good carpenter. He doesn't talk a lot, but he is really good with wood. My mom is into gardening, and she did the paintings on the chairs."

"He's good. You must be rich," Amber said, without taking her eyes off the yard.

Alan laughed. "Hardly. Didn't you see the size of our family? Besides, he doesn't do it for a living. He drives a log truck."

A shiver went down Amber's spine. "For who?" she asked.

"Anderson logging. You probably haven't heard of them. It's a small company."

The blood started pumping in Amber's ears, and her stomach felt like lead. She was suddenly sick.

"I better get home," Amber said quietly.

Amber was silent for the rest of the drive. Alan occasionally glanced her way. Although he liked it, he wasn't used to the quiet, except for when he was working alone with his father. *She's a complicated girl*, he thought, *and smart*. Everyone at school knew that. What he hadn't noticed before was how pretty she was. It surprised him how protective he felt.

Amber's VW was one of two or three cars sitting in the Cove parking lot in the dark. Alan automatically jumped out of the Jeep to open Amber's door. Amber, who was already getting out, looked up in surprise when she realized what he was doing. No one had done that for her before. But then, she had never been on a date.

Alan walked her to her car. They both reached for her car's door handle at the same time, hands brushing each other. Surprised, she pulled her hand back as if it was on fire.

"Amber," he said. She looked up at him. "Amber," he began again. "I'm around if you need me." And then without thinking about it, he gave her a hug. Electricity tickled its way down their spines. They both jumped back.

Fumbling with the door, Amber got into the car mumbling, "Thanks," and drove away.

Standing in the parking lot, Alan watched her taillights as she drove away.

CHAPTER 19

LONG NIGHTS

"THANKS!" AMBER SAID OUT LOUD IN HER CAR. "THANKS! IS that the best you could do?" she said to her empty car. What just happened? *What a mess*, she thought. Mom was going to kill her, and Alan's father worked for Grandpa Anderson with Berk. She tried not to implode. Home was the last place she wanted to be, but she hadn't had a shower in two days, and the need for soap and water was overriding her sense of self-preservation.

Making her way up the hill, she spotted Grace, the blonde woman from the Family Crisis Center, pulling away from her house. Grace drove past her as she pulled up to the street and into the driveway. She didn't look forward to talking to her mother.

Amber had long ago given up hoping that her mother would leave Berk. Any future plans ended with her feeling it was her duty to protect her mother, Greta, and Bjorn.

"Greta!" she said out loud to the car, realizing she'd been gone too long. Greta had to be frantic. Hopefully Mom wouldn't want to talk too much. Maybe she wouldn't say anything.

Amber unloaded her heavy school bags so she could do homework, went to the dark front porch, and used her key to get in. Her mom had turned all the lights off and was beginning to climb the stairs when Amber came through the door.

Emily turned and looked at Amber. The light from the stairwell shone on her angry face. Folding her arms, Emily angrily snapped, "This is all your fault. He wouldn't be back in jail if you had just gone to school."

"I did."

"Why couldn't you stay there and keep your mouth shut? What happens at home stays at home!"

"I didn't say a thing."

"Then why is your father alone in jail?" Emily started to cry as she fisted her hands at her side. "Someone is going to hurt him!"

Amber reeled. She had never thought of that. Standing with her back to the door, clutching her school bags to her chest, she couldn't breathe.

Emily turned around and ran up the last of the stairs. A door slammed, and Amber stood frozen in the dark. The living room clock, with pinecones that swung to keep time, ticked. Turning, she looked at it, but couldn't read the face. Tears were blurring her vision, washing over her cheeks. Slowly, she let the air escape her lips. Her bags were so heavy. She whispered, "He's not my father," to nobody.

Amber climbed the stairs and cracked Greta's door gently. It squeaked again, waking memories. Greta was rolled in a ball in the corner of her bed with her back to the wall. No fewer than ten stuffed animals surrounded her. Light from the street shone on her small form. After watching her breathe for a moment, Amber relaxed, then, when she was sure Greta was all right, backed out of the room.

Leaving her things on the floor, she crossed the hall to Bjorn's door. Opening the door slowly, she tiptoed inside his room, across the soft carpet, and up to his crib.

He was still dressed and wrapped in a loose blanket. Amber carefully slid the blanket out from around him and left him alone in an empty crib, sleeping on his back. She knew the crib was supposed to be empty to avoid sudden infant death syndrome. Next she looked at the baby monitor. It was off. She turned it on and put the listening end of the monitor in her sweatshirt pocket. Reaching into the crib, she touched his pants. They were wet. In the light from the street lamp, she could see that his nose was crusted and he wasn't sleeping soundly. Restless, he kept making little sobbing sounds and jerking in his sleep; so much for her shower.

Gently, Amber tried to change him and clean him up without waking him, but by the time she was putting the clean sheet on the crib mattress, Bjorn finally had enough and woke up clawing for her with a sleepy cry. Expertly, she wiped his face. Then she settled into a large wooden chair and began to rock him back to sleep.

How, she wondered, was she ever going to go to college? Slowly, she rocked him, tears tracing well-worn paths down her cheeks, dreaming about belonging to a family that lived happily ever after in a garden full of flowers and beautifully carved furniture. Shaking off the wish, she was sure that she would be the poison that would kill the garden and end the happily ever after.

CHAPTER 20

ISOLATION

HAZEL'S CURLS, DAMP WITH SWEAT, WERE PLASTERED TO Kelly's chest as she rocked Hazel in her dark, quiet bedroom. Hazel had been asleep for a while, but Kelly had been avoiding going to bed. Rocking, she was a million miles away in Utah at her parent's home and wondering about all the birthday parties she'd missed. There were a few September birthdays. She hadn't talked to her parents since their summer visit.

Her heart hurt when she thought about it. Wanting to forget, she tried to put it out of her mind. The memory of Sam shouting at her father on the front porch while her mother sat in the van crying could not be easily sent away. The vivid image of her father slowly backing down the cement stairs as she watched from behind the living room window curtains carried her away in time. Sam yelled things like "judgmental busybodies" until her father slowly turned, head down, and walked to the van. Hope had driven away with her parents. How would they ever forgive her? Would they ever want to see her again? She should have done something.

A giant sigh escaped her lips and Hazel stirred. Slowly, Kelly stood and took Hazel to her princess toddler bed.

Her knees cracked as she rose from her bedside. Stopping, she waited to see if it woke Hazel. Hazel's breath stayed deep and regular. Carefully, she folded the lap blanket on the rocker and checked the room to make sure it was in good order and wasn't going to upset Sam. She crept out of the room.

Sam was still in his office. Usually she would just go to bed and hope he kept working, but they were out of milk. She knew it was time to negotiate. If she were really lucky, he would let her go to the store alone or maybe even give her money to go. She had some cans stashed and wanted to recycle them for money without him knowing.

Anxious, she went down the stairs and looked into his partially opened office door. His laptop was on the desk, but no paper. It was obvious he was really into whatever he was doing. Slowly, she opened the door.

"Sam," she said quietly.

"What!" Swiftly, he closed the laptop but didn't get up from behind his desk. He was instantly rolling in anger. Black hate emanated from him so clearly she thought she could see light leaving the room. Walking toward him, she knew this was the wrong time to ask for anything.

"I'm going to bed, honey." She kissed him on the cheek.

"So go to bed already!"

That was odd, she thought. "Okay. Good night." Smiling, she backed out of the room wondering.

As she went to their bedroom, on the first floor near the kitchen, she speculated about what he had been doing. Always on that laptop or BlackBerry, nonstop lately. He said he was making a website for his business, but he was sure typing a lot and fast. She shook her head. Whatever it was, he still had time to monitor her. That reminded her, she had left the baby monitors upstairs.

Taking off her CTR ring, she dressed for bed before heading back toward the stairs. The house was quiet and dark. Light spilled out from under the closed office door. Kelly stopped at the end of the hall and listened. Was he laughing? Who was he talking to? She could hear computer keys clicking. *It's eleven o'clock*, she thought. What is he doing? Oh well, at least he wasn't bothering her. He was probably talking to one of the guys.

Exhausted, Grace and Mabel sat in the hot tub. They had all the lights out in the yard. They could see every star that chose to venture out from behind the silver-lined clouds. They floated in the hot water and talked about everything they should be doing instead of relaxing. Finally, it was quiet and Grace felt all the day melt into the water. Her lids became heavy. "I need to sleep."

"Go ahead. I'll put the lid on," Mabel said.

"How come you're so energetic?"

"My new diet. I'm thinking about making an infomercial, as long as I don't have to wear spandex. I could market it."

"Ha, ha. See you upstairs." Grace's body felt like it weighed a thousand pounds as she pulled it out of the water. Her cell phone rang. "Ahhh," Grace cried.

"Oh no," Mabel groaned. They both froze, looking at it vibrating on the little table by the lawn chair.

Grace took a deep breath and answered it. "This is Grace."

"Thought you were going to sleep?" the dispatcher asked.

"Hi, Sue." Shivering, she tried to put her robe on without getting the phone wet and talk coherently, all at the same time. Finally, she threw the robe over her shoulders and the water dripped onto the deck. "Put 'em through," she told Sue. The line clicked. "Hello, this is Grace," she said. There was silence, a pause, and then gurgling noise.

"Grace," the caller sobbed, "This is Emily. I can't sleep."

"Oh, Emily, I know it's hard. I'm here, what's going on?"

Mabel put the top on the hot tub, dried off, and gently pushed Grace as she continued to talk. Hands on her shoulders, Mabel walked her into the kitchen, through the house, and upstairs to hopefully sleep.

Thirty minutes later, Emily ended the call with a promise to talk later. Grace dressed in a warm, clean, oversized T-shirt and knelt on the soft area rug at her bedside and began to say her prayers. Suddenly, she felt she needed firewood.

Firewood? she thought. Then she remembered. They had burned a whole cord of wood this summer on the beach and given wood to visiting families and the ward for youth bonfires. The kids had also burned a lot in their metal fire pit on the deck, leaving them out of wood, and winter was coming. She began to have an odd sense of urgency.

Ending her prayer, Grace climbed into bed and started listing off what they did and didn't have stored. She wondered how old their seventy-two-hour kits were.

I can't believe it, she thought. *I don't drink caffeine. Why am I still awake? Please*, she screamed inside her own head, *someone turn my brain off.*

Rolling over, she tried to forget wood. She realized her CTR ring was still on. Twisting it, she pulled it off and laid it on the bedside table.

CHAPTER 21

BELIEVE

SOMEWHERE DEEP IN THE NIGHT, GRACE BEGAN DREAMING. Fitfully, she twitched and kicked her legs.

The ocean was vast and she was floating in it with her daughter. Mary's skinny little body kept slipping below the water. A wild storm was raging all around them. The waves swept them up and then they would slide into a trough surrounded by gray salty water. Black clouds rolled out thunder and crackled with sheet lightning. She could taste the salt as the wind blew frigid rain into her eyes. Grace kicked and struggled to hold onto Mary. Cold water surged under her feet; something was different. Then the ocean opened up beneath her and she slid into baleen, through the black, and found herself clutching Mary in the mouth of a whale. Coughing up seawater, she felt soft tongue tissue with her hands. Mary clutched Grace's clothes and cried. Grace wrapped her right arm around Mary and pulled her underneath her, protecting her with her body. She cried out, "All right, I'll buy wood! I'm sorry. I should have listened!"

She sat up drenched in sweat and breathing hard. "We're buying firewood."

===

In Grace's office, the sun filtered in through the windows, reflecting on the water, making rusty ships look regal as they made their way up and down the river. Sea lions barked from below the dock, and birds roosted on rotting pilings. Grace sat at her desk, drinking in the smell of the river through her open window and wishing she were outside running or kayaking on a lake. The office pager beeped, and a voice cut into her daydreams.

"Grace, line one."

Grace smiled and picked up the handset, "This is Grace. Can I help you?"

"Hi, Grace. It's Adrian."

"Hey, Adrian." Adrian was a Child Protective Services worker at the local Department of Human Services. "Long time no see. How are you?" Grace could picture Adrian. She always looked the same. Wild gray hair caught in a loose bun with a pencil or pen in it and black reading glasses on the tip of her nose. She was a meaty woman who looked like she should have wings and be singing to Cinderella.

"Good, well . . . Bill and I are done dating. You met him when we drove to that training, didn't you? He works for Bay Town Police. Remember?"

"Yes, I'm sorry. I liked him."

"I'm not."

"Well, then congratulations?"

Adrian laughed. "I don't know. Well, whatever. It's that training I'm calling about. Remember how we talked about meeting state statutes for reasonable efforts by doing joint home visits while investigating cases?"

"Yes," Grace said tentatively, wondering where this was going.

"We got the report on the Anderson family from Officers Hart and Ironpot. I need to go see Emily Anderson today and wondered if you or someone from your office could go with me. I also have to interview her daughter Amber. I'd like to do it while he's still in jail and hopefully they feel safe enough to talk."

"I can if we go around three this afternoon. Would that work for you?"

"Sure. I would rather go before the kids are home and have a moment alone with the mother, but I'm fine with three. Since he's still in custody, we don't need an officer, but I may take one anyway. You never know when he might be released.

"Great," Grace answered. "I'll meet you at the corner by her house."

Grace shut her office door, pulled out her lunch, and began to make calls. She called the first number on her list. "Hello, wood doctor?"

"Hey," a rough voice said. "If you're calling for wood, I am sold out."

"Oh, thanks."

Every call seemed to be the same. There wasn't any wood at the usual places in the county. Frustrated, she tried to remember the name of the drunk guy she bought wood from last year. His greasy card was posted on the wall at the local gas station. He would deliver, hopefully sober. She looked up the Gitty Up N Go gas station and food mart and called the number listed.

"Gitty Up N Go," a husky women's voice said.

"Maxine?" Grace asked. "This is Grace James. I need firewood and there is a guy's phone number pinned on your bulletin board. I think it's Gordy?"

"Jordy, I'll get it. Hold on," Maxine said, coughing.

A few minutes later, Grace heard Maxine ringing up cigarettes and selling a lottery ticket and then she was back. Coughing, she gave Grace the number. Grace dialed Jordy. "Hi, Jordy, this is Grace, I live in Necanicum and I . . ."

"I know, need wood," Jordy finished the sentence for her. "I ain't got none. Sold the last of it last week. I am going to go out again and cut some 'cause there's been a call fer it."

"Can I give you my number?" Grace asked. Jordy took her number and Grace hung up. Maybe there was no wood. Nonsense, she told herself. Then she logged onto a local sales website. She sent a few emails to wood sellers and then went back to her paperwork. It had been a wasted lunch.

Amber thought about skipping lunch and taking a nap in her car, but she hadn't eaten in a while. In fact, she couldn't remember the last time she'd eaten, except for the banana she'd eaten on the way to school. She hoped she had money in her lunch account.

Head down, she made her way alone in the river of kids chatting in pairs. She was numb to the noise of the never-ending teenage conversation that stayed at a level high enough to cause most of them to talk louder and louder to be heard over the din.

Clutching her science book, she made her way around to the lunch line without looking up. She didn't see Alan Johnson until she bumped into him, her book hitting his chest.

Startled, she realized that Alan had stopped dead in front of her in the lunch line and was giving her a smile that could have sold teeth-whitening products. Amber felt her heart wake up.

"So," Alan asked, "must be a good book." Then he took it from her hands and turned it around. "But you're reading it upside down."

Self-conscious, she realized she was smiling back and was surprised to hear herself laugh.

"Eat lunch with us?" Alan asked. Then Amber noticed there were three really pretty girls, Esther, Gayle, and Connie, standing behind him with the geek Douglas and a good-looking football player who had a weird name she couldn't remember. They all turned one by one and smiled or gawked at her. She felt the color rising in her cheeks. Would he keep her secret?

"Come on," Alan begged. "We'll be nice."

"Please, please, please," the three girls broke into dramatic pleading with their hands clasped, looking heavenward, standing behind Alan making fun of him.

"You're mocking me," he scolded and laughed at the same time. Esther gave him a shove. He looked at Amber and asked, "Do you know the guys?"

"Sure," she lied.

"Guys, this is Amber."

"Hi, Amber," said the boy with the funny name, stepping in front of Alan. "How does this loser know someone as smart as you?"

"Nephi," Alan said protectively, making a face in Nephi's direction. Alan put his arm around Amber, and she felt herself try to shrink. Then she realized it felt good, in fact, she liked it. It was . . . comfortable. He just kept talking like it was an everyday occurrence. "Amber's a nice girl and isn't used to eating with a bunch of baboons."

Immediately, Nephi and Douglas began acting like baboons. Amber wondered what hippie had come up with the name Nephi.

"Nephi!" Esther yelled at the baboon. "Alan, you started this. Make him stop before someone realizes we're related!"

Amber was frozen, waiting for Alan to give away her secret. Her heart beat fast in her ears. She realized she wasn't hungry at all.

"Amber is my friend! Be nice," Alan said, still standing with his arm draped around her shoulders. Pretty rapidly the others seemed to lose interest and began torturing each other. They turned to conversations among themselves. Alan looked down at Amber with his clear blue eyes, pushed his hair back with his free hand, and continued to just smile.

It was their turn to pay the lunch lady. A rather large, hairy woman wearing a white apron and hairnet sat on a stool with a cash box and computer. "Name."

"Amber Anderson."

"No credit left. That will be two seventy-five." The woman said without looking up. Amber shrank. She didn't have any money. Alan laid the money on the table without a word and pulled her on in the flow, heading toward the trays and silverware. Amber looked up, feeling tears rise and threaten to leak.

"Hey, we have this end-of-summer bonfire tonight. I mean, I know summer's past, but the winter's coming, you know?" Alan was talking to her, and she realized he wasn't going to say anything about the money. Not knowing what to do, she slid her tray down the metal ramp, looking down at it, embarrassed. "Well? You wanna go?" he continued. "I could pick you up or you could meet us there."

Amber had never been on a date. Berk would never have allowed it. She opened her mouth to begin to say no, when Alan went on. "I know the timing is bad, but we won't bite. I promise. And Esther has a hot tub and firewood. Douglas's dad works at Safeway and he'll bring the s'more stuff and I promise there won't be any drinking. We're a bunch of Mormons, you know?" They moved their trays down the metal ramp, with their plates being filled by lunch helpers as they moved.

Amber's mind spun. Berk was in jail. Why shouldn't she go? Her mom ought to be able to take care of the kids. After all, Amber was seventeen. It was about time she had a date. Asking Mom would be hard, but . . . Her stomach growled loudly. Embarrassed, she looked at Alan, but he didn't seem to notice.

"Bring a towel and suit for the hot tub. Esther has extra suits too. If it rains, we'll probably watch a video and use Nephi and Esther's fireplace."

She would do it. She was excited. Who cared what Mom said? Berk wasn't home. It was about time. "Okay. I'd love to go."

CHAPTER 22

Small Parts

THE DOORBELL CUT THROUGH KELLY'S THOUGHTS. SHE WAS watching little Sam try to read to Hazel. Habitually, she ignored the bell. She never answered the door. If Sam was watching, it just caused too many problems. Little Sam was actually sounding pretty good.

"De ugwy duckwing," little Sam read.

The bell rang again. *They're persistent*, she thought as she went to the curtains and peeked out the crack, trying not to move them. Her breath caught in her throat. Two Mormon missionaries stood on her porch. One was ringing her bell, and the other was balancing two bikes on the sidewalk. She immediately thought about her brother and wondered if he was going on a mission. She hadn't talked to her parents forever. The tall, lean, brown-haired, freckle-faced missionary walked back down the steps and was saying something to the other one. What were they talking about?

———

Elder Oscarson was a farm boy from Idaho. His light brown hair matched his eyes and freckles. *Man*, he thought, *the whole morning of knocking on doors has been a waste.*

His companion, Elder Sappenfield, never wanted to waste a minute: push, push, push. He walked back down the steps to Elder

Sappenfield. "No one's home," he said and began pulling on his bike gloves.

Elder Sappenfield was squinting at the house with his pale blue eyes. Elder Oscarson had to look up at him now that he was down off the porch. Elder Sappenfield was tall and lean, pale and blond. "Elder," Sappenfield said to Oscarson, "the curtains moved."

Oscarson turned and looked over his shoulder, "So? They don't want to talk to us." He started to take his bike from Sappenfield, but Sappenfield hung on. Then Sappenfield handed him his bike and began rummaging in his bag.

"I've been saving this Book of Mormon that Sister Simons wrote in. We need to leave it here."

Oscarson groaned, "Are you sure?"

Sappenfield didn't hesitate. He never did when his mind was made up. "Do you have one of those pass-along cards with the picture of the Savior on it?" he asked.

"I don't know. Does it have to be that one?"

"Yes."

Frustrated, Oscarson knew it was pointless to question Sappenfield. When they finally found the exact card Sappenfield wanted, he put it in the Book of Mormon and walked back up to the house, leaving the book on the porch.

Oscarson felt good about it, but hoped that they hadn't wasted the signed Book of Mormon. They walked their bikes toward the next house. "Sappenfield, you promised that was the last house. I'm starved. Let's go find something at the Farmer's Market for lunch."

"Lead the way, Elder."

They got on their bikes, buckled their helmets, and rode away. The curtains in the window fell together.

——

Kelly's blood was rushing in her ears. She ran to the side window in her bedroom and checked the street for Sam's van. She shut her door and knelt behind it.

"Thank you," she prayed. Tears overflowed her eyes. She had been craving the scriptures. Now all she had to do was get them off the porch and hidden before Sam found them.

Feeling a sense of urgency, Kelly went to the front door, cracked it open, and looked both ways. No Sam. She knelt low and reached out, taking the book and hastily bringing it in. She stood behind the door and just felt the cover. Something stirred in her as she remembered reading with her family as a child. What was this feeling? She felt good, alive, hopeful—things she hadn't felt in a long time. Smiling, she cracked the new book, smelling the familiar pages and glue. She loved the smell of a new book. Taking the card out, she turned it over. It was a picture of the Savior and it was beautiful. Her heart was so full. Tears broke through her lashes and ran down her cheeks.

Kelly loved this picture. Her parents had one just like it hanging in their living room. Amused, she remembered thinking it was cheesy. Now she realized she missed it. No, she craved it. Sitting down on the hardwood floor behind the door, she opened the front of the book. There was a picture of a heavy woman, a bald man, and a lot of kids. She had to smile through the tears. Complete with dog, it was definitely a Mormon family. Inside, in neat cursive that looked like a woman's hand, was written:

To Whom it May Concern,

In this book are the answers to the questions: why are we here, who are we, and where are we going? I am so grateful for the gospel. Many times in my life I found myself feeling totally alone, without hope, and afraid that I couldn't go on. I often felt overwhelmed by my inadequacy and weakness.

Kelly stopped reading and looked back at the woman's picture. *She looks so happy*, she thought, and read on.

I found my answers in this book. I found a personal relationship with my Savior and an understanding of who I am, why I am here, and where I am going by reading this book, praying, and asking if it was true.

You are a child of God. He loves you and He wants you to have the answers to your questions. Those answers are contained in this book and in the Bible. I have a testimony of the Savior, His love for us, and His wish to help you and me through His gift of the Atonement.

Sincerely, Sister Simons

Kelly's heart warmed. She was surprised at how this woman's testimony made her feel. Did the Savior remember her even though she had made mistakes? Many times she didn't feel worthy of anyone's love. Lately, she had been thinking about repenting. She had been thinking about the Atonement as a gift that could finally bring her the peace she needed.

Unexpectedly, the sure knowledge it was time to go home settled in her bones. There was no question in her mind anymore. She didn't belong here. Looking around the cozy living room in her beautiful home and at her babies, she knew it was time for them to leave.

She wasn't sure how, but she was going to find her way home. Silently, she said a prayer and thought maybe it was time to reconnect with her family. It was time to call her mother.

Kelly looked up to see her husband, Sam, watching her from the open front door like rolling thunder, a dark cloud coming her way.

CHAPTER 23

PROMISES

HART AND IRONPOT HAD FINALLY SWITCHED TO DAY SHIFT for the next three months. Today was the first day of the change, and Hart could feel it as he yawned. They had a lull in their calls and called in Code 7, or lunch, driving to Sub Sandwiches where they could watch their food being made. At least at Sub Sandwiches they could be sure that no one spit in their sandwiches. Ironpot ordered a large soda.

"I thought you were giving that stuff up before we have to take our test?" Hart asked. Once a year they had to run one and a half miles in fourteen minutes and do push-ups and sit-ups to prove they were still fit for duty. Sit-ups were hard with a paunch.

"Yes, but today I need caffeine. Dr. Pepper to be exact."

"Hey," Hart teased Ironpot, "I thought Mormons weren't supposed to drink coffee and stuff."

"We're not. But this isn't coffee, and they don't ask about soda in the interview." Ironpot looked at him over the top of his glasses like a father looking at an annoying child.

Hart knew he had him now. "Sinning, are we? Well, I think I've got a camera in the patrol car. Maybe I should call your bishop?"

"Why, so he can have lunch with us? I'd buy him one too."

"You're a little defensive. I think you feel guilty."

Ironpot ignored him and filled up his cup at the soda machine. Hart took his tray to their table. Ironpot joined him, "You sure know a lot about the Church for a used-to-be member."

"I liked the Word of Wisdom stuff," Hart said, setting his tray on a table. "Doesn't Grace go to your church?" he asked casually.

Ironpot didn't even register the question. "Hmm, how did you like the family home evening stuff?" he asked Hart.

"Family home evening?"

"Remember, where a family gets together once a week and plays games or does something as a family to build love and unity?"

"You mean with a lesson?" Hart bit off some of his sandwich.

"You just gave yourself away as a previous family home evening attendee."

"So what if I am, Officer? Are you going to arrest me?" Hart asked with his mouth full.

"No, I'm going to invite you to the Ironpot annual fishing family home evening this Saturday morning. We are going fishing at Lost Lake on Saturday. Want to join us?"

"I don't know. Won't I be sort of a fifth wheel? What will Karen think?"

"She'll be grateful there is someone else around to help bait the kids' hooks."

"Are you trying to assimilate me back into the hive?"

"Yes."

Hart had no answer for that. Maybe he wanted to be back in the hive, but he was pretty sure the hive wouldn't want him. He had broken a few of the top ten commandments, and Ironpot knew he liked an occasional beer. But, it was just fishing. "Okay. I'll meet you at the lake," he said, thinking this way he could back out if he wanted to.

———

"It's just a Book of Mormon! And I want to keep it!" Kelly shouted at Sam. She was usually afraid to shout, but this time it was important. She didn't care if Sam Jr. heard, or Hazel. He was not taking the book.

Trembling, she held onto one end of the book with both hands. The card was sticking out and Sam had the other end of the book with one hand. They fought toe-to-toe and nose-to-nose over the book in the living room by the closed front door. So far he was only holding it. Kelly knew if he pulled he would win.

"You know how I feel about it, Kelly!" Sam shouted back at her. "This church makes you feel like an outsider. My parents hate it!"

"Your parents aren't here. Your mother still runs our lives from eight hundred miles away. When do I get to do what I want? When do I matter more than your mother?" Kelly shouted back at Sam.

He heaved her into the door, the back of her head hitting it as her feet slid out from underneath her. Sam Jr. started to cry and sat down on the floor next to Hazel. Sam yanked the book out of her hands and headed for the kitchen.

"Sam! Sam! Give it back to me! Sam!" Kelly cried, following him.

Opening the lid on the trash, he stuffed the book deep inside with the eggs and coffee grounds. He slammed the lid and looked at her, like he dared her to move or breathe. She went toward the can. His arm shot out and his fist hit her chest. Her feet slid on the floor as he shoved her back.

"Kelly, I know what's best," he said loudly but calmly.

It irritated her that he could be so calm. How dare he? She lost it. "You're not my father! You're not my zookeeper! I feel like an animal trapped in a cage! I am so sick of this! If I want that book, I can have that book!" She started again for the can. Somewhere in the back of her mind she knew this was not like her, but she couldn't stop herself.

———

Hart had just filled his mouth with Italian meatballs, cheese, and parmesan onion bread when his radio went off in his earpiece.

Dispatch said, "600 units, I've just received a 911 for a verbal dispute at 2729 Edgewood."

"Lunch is over," Ironpot said as he heard the same report. They wrapped their sandwiches, grabbed their drinks, and trotted to their cars.

———

Kelly headed for the garbage can again. Sam elbowed her in the stomach. Kelly doubled over as the pain surprised her. "Stop it, Sam!" she said as she struggled to get past him. He had elbowed her before. It wouldn't even leave a mark.

"You . . ." Sam swore at her. He called her a string of names. His cell phone fell out of his shirt pocket and broke into plastic pieces as it hit the hard kitchen floor. He swore loudly, shoving her with both hands into the refrigerator. She went for the garbage can again. *This time*, she thought, *he isn't going to win*. This was it, she had truly had it. She was done.

Sam stooped to pick up the pieces of his cell and rammed her in the belly with his shoulder as she tried to get past him. "Knock it off, Kelly! You . . ." he reeled off another string of ugly names. This time he added some new ones. Her fury rose. Determined, she tried to get around him again, but he just put his arm out. He was too strong for her.

Kelly planted her feet and screamed, "Sam! Get out of my way! I'm done letting you tell me what to do!"

Something in Sam snapped, and he looked at her with a rage she had never seen before. His eyes were dark in the daylight. There was nothing there but blackness, and it rolled off of him in waves. When he spoke, he yelled, growled, and sounded like an animal. "I am the master of this house." It was a statement of power and he expected her to cower, but this time, she knew she didn't belong in his house.

"I am leaving you, Sam!" she yelled back at him.

"You're not taking my kids! You go ahead and go, but I have all the money, and I will have the best attorney. You won't take my kids! Everyone in town knows you're crazy! Look at you!"

The reality of his words hit her. She had spent so much time trying to look bad so other men wouldn't talk to her, that all people saw was this crazy woman in gray sweats with no makeup and who never looked up. Sam was handsome and everyone liked him. Horror cut through her with searing pain.

"I will take your children. I will take your home! You go ahead and go back to Utah, you ugly fat pig, and see if anybody else will ever want a woman who abandoned her family!"

Kelly backed up until she felt the cold stainless steel of the refrigerator on her back.

"I'll hunt you down. I will make your life a living hell. I don't need you. You need me!" he went on. "Get out! Walk out that door, but you're not taking anything with you. Everything is mine! The house is mine! The cars are in my name! Your name isn't even on the bank account! What judge in his right mind is going to give a crazy mess like you kids?"

She put her hands over her face and sank to the floor. *Make him stop, make him stop!* she thought. *He's right. What am I thinking? I can't leave.*

"Mommy?" Little Sam touched her hair. She put her arms around him and rolled into a ball, tears streaming down her face mixing with snot and wetting his shirt.

Someone was banging on the kitchen door. "Police, open up!"

Everything stopped. Time stood still. She couldn't breathe.

Sam's whole demeanor changed. He opened a drawer and put the broken cell phone in it. Calmly, he walked to the door and opened it.

"Hello, Officers," he said calmly. "I'm sorry, but my wife is mentally ill and we were arguing." He turned sideways so they could see Kelly on the floor.

Oh my gosh, she thought, *I look like a nut case!* Her hair was sticking out of her ponytail because she had been rubbing her head with her hands. Snot and tears were all over her and her child. Her eyes had to be bloodshot, and her face must be a mottled mess. Her clothes were twisted and she realized both Sam Jr. and Hazel were crying.

"I do the best I can, Officer," Sam was saying. He looked down and played the part of the poor husband. "You understand, Officer, I just lost it. It's been going on so long. I came home for lunch and the kids hadn't even had breakfast."

Kelly couldn't believe it. She couldn't speak. The officer in the door was tall, handsome, and so put together. He must think she was a fat, ugly, raving, lunatic.

He said something quietly in his radio that Kelly couldn't hear over little Sam's cries. Then he turned to her husband and said, "Sir, will you step outside with my partner? Can I speak to your wife alone?"

"All right, but please don't upset her any more than she is. I don't have any paid help, and I need to get back to work today if possible. I have a job due and could be out all night if I don't get back soon."

"We'll do the best we can, sir," the officer said.

Kelly saw another officer come around from the front of the house and stand in the driveway. Sam went out to talk to him. She knew he would probably give him the same story.

The tall, good-looking officer let himself in the house, came over to Kelly, and offered her a hand up. "I'm Officer Hart," he introduced himself. He gently pulled her to her feet.

"I'm Kelly Finch," she said, picking up little Sam.

———

Hart stepped back and leaned on the counter, pulling a notebook out of a pocket on the side of his pants. He flipped open the notebook and took a pen out of his pocket. Kelly balanced Sam Jr. on her hip. Hazel came into the kitchen and attached herself to Kelly's other leg, gulping and hiccupping for air while rubbing her nose on Kelly's sweatpants.

Kelly instinctually whispered words of comfort to Sam while lifting Hazel to sit on her other hip and reaching for a dishtowel to wipe her face. Hart watched her carefully.

Hart thought the children looked healthy and well cared for. The house was clean. She looked sober, like she didn't do drugs. But looks could be deceiving. He wrote her name and then took another look at this tiny, thin woman holding both of the children as if they weighed nothing. Her striking eyes were tearful but crystal clear. He stood tall over her dark glossy hair caught up in a messy bun with escaping strands. She absentmindedly pushed the strands out of her face. He checked himself, stopping his train of thought, reminding himself he was on the job and to stay alert.

He looked out the window at his partner. He and the male half of the family were laughing and joking. *Good job, Ironpot,* he thought. He surveyed the room and saw a place in the family room where she could sit and he could still see out the kitchen window to watch his partner. "Let's sit down," he offered, pointing at the antique rocker near the kitchen table. He turned it toward the table with the rocker back to the window so he could look over her shoulder while they talked. Then he perched on an armless kitchen chair that would put him eye to eye with her. Hart had too much equipment on his duty belt to get really comfortable.

Kelly turned on cartoons with the volume turned low, picked up a blanket folded on the couch, sat back in the rocker, and wrapped the kids in the blanket in her lap. Automatically, she began rocking, and the children watched the television.

"Kelly," Hart continued, "what's your date of birth?" She gave it to him and he realized how young she was, twenty-three. He called in the name and date of birth to dispatch. They would run a background check on her while he made notes listing her address, phone number, and the kids' names and dates of birth. Dispatch radioed into his earpiece that she was clear or without a record, wants, or warrants.

"Can you tell me what happened before we came, Kelly?" Hart asked.

"We were arguing. It was my fault. I should have just let it go. Our marriage is not going well. I've decided I'm not going to stay, but I don't want him to go to jail. He's not, is he? He'll lose business and we'll lose the house."

"I don't know," he said, looking her directly in the eye. "What were you arguing about?"

Kelly thought for a minute and wondered if she should be truthful. She was going to leave, but putting Sam in jail would only make him angrier, and he would carry out his threat to take the children with an attorney. It could be done with money, and she certainly didn't have money for an attorney. She wondered if she would be trapped alone in Oregon forever because she refused to leave her children. She decided to tell part of the truth.

"We were fighting over . . . here, I'll show you," she began. She stood, taking the children who had calmed down and placing them on the couch. She walked over to the garbage can and dug in it. Hart stood and took a defensive stance, not knowing what she would pull out of the garbage can. It could be a gun or drugs.

After rummaging in the garbage can for a minute, she turned and showed him a Book of Mormon.

"A Book of Mormon?" Hart asked.

"Yes, I used to be a member of the Church of Jesus Christ of Latter-day Saints."

"Used to be?" he asked, surprised, taking the book. "Me too," Hart said smiling. "Nice ring," he noted, pointing at her hand. She looked down at her CTR ring and her hands. She remembered all the times Sam told her how ugly her torn and short nails were. She hid her hands.

Carefully, Hart thumbed through the book. It was stained now and had a crumpled picture of the Savior in it. He realized that he felt something. He handed it back to her. "Why were you fighting over the Book of Mormon?"

"The missionaries left it on the porch. Sam hates the Church. I wanted to keep it." He believed her. She stopped talking and wiped off the book with a dishtowel. When she was done, she looked out the kitchen window at Sam talking with the officer. She turned her back to the window, hiding the book. Hart watched her slip the book into a ziplock bag. Then she put it in the dishwasher.

"Are you going to wash the Book of Mormon?" he asked. She smiled. *Wow*, he thought, *that was distracting*.

"No, he never does the dishes. He won't find it in here," she said and went back over and sat down in the rocker.

Hart joined her. "So Kelly, this isn't the first time you've fought." She nodded her head, admitting it wasn't. Hart leaned toward her and asked, "Did he hit you or push you today?"

She looked at him, long and hard, and then she shook her head no. He knew she was lying and that she didn't do it very often. She was lousy at it.

"Has he hit you before?" Hart asked almost in a whisper. She didn't move.

———

Hart came out of the kitchen door and walked over to his partner in the driveway. Ironpot and the person he was now sure was a suspect, were laughing and talking about fishing. Hart knew that Ironpot was actually interviewing a very angry, calculating man by making him comfortable. Ironpot gave him a knowing look and said, "Mr. Finch, would you sit in my vehicle while my partner and I talk?"

"Am I under arrest?"

"No, we just need to keep things calm for a minute more," Ironpot said, smiling. He patted Sam on the back, walking him to the patrol car. Sam sat in the car. Hart and Ironpot stepped far enough away to see both the house and car, while talking quietly without being heard.

"What have you got?" Ironpot asked.

"She's the primary victim. I know we heard her yelling when we pulled up, but I'd bet that's rare. I'd also bet there's been physical violence, but she won't admit to it. She says they were fighting over a Book of Mormon. She even pulled it out of the trash and showed me. It's such a screwy story I believe it. She says the

98

Mormon missionaries left it on her porch today, and he was making her throw it away because he hates Mormons."

Ironpot smiled and Hart smiled back.

"Wonder how he'd feel about a Mormon cop?" Ironpot said, laughing.

"He hates you."

"No way! He's my new buddy."

"Well, she says that she used to be a Mormon, and wants to leave him and go back home to her parents in Utah with the kids, and back to church, but doesn't think he'll let her."

"There you go again with that 'used to be' crap." Ironpot looked over his glasses at Hart.

"You know what I mean," Hart said, "I radioed for DSAT. Grace said she'd come. If we don't arrest, we'll have to stay while Grace's here and babysit her in case your new pal causes more trouble."

"Let's just send him back to work. He'll stay. He's my buddy."

"I don't know . . ."

"He says she's crazy, never takes care of the kids. He has to do everything. She is always after other men . . ."

"Her?" Hart cut in. "No way! I don't believe it. She's smart, pretty, and one of the nicest . . ."

"Hart?"

Hart realized Ironpot knew he wasn't feeling very objective. He took a breath, shook his head, and willed the feelings away. "You're right. Anyway, I think he's full of it, and she doesn't want him to go to jail. She just wants to leave him."

Sam heard the word *leave* and his head snapped up. He began carefully watching the officers.

Hart went on, "We've got nothing, no injuries, no witness to an assault and no reported assault. We have no reason to arrest. Did the neighbor that called say they saw anything?"

"No." Ironpot looked back at Sam who immediately looked down. "I think he's listening." He lowered his voice, "Look, let's get him out of here, and I'll stay here while Grace's here in case he comes back."

Hart nodded in agreement. Ironpot went over to the car to send the suspect back to work.

———

Kelly watched the officers closely from behind the kitchen curtains. They were telling Sam he had to leave and go to work. She knew he would be back first chance he got and that she was going to pay for this. Her heart was pounding. Somehow she had to move, leave, and get out with the kids. There was no long distance on the house phone. He checked the caller ID and always checked the redial list. If she was careful to load the redial feature on their phone with fake numbers maybe she could get a collect call out to her parents and they could meet her somewhere. Then she remembered the broken cell phone.

Quickly, she put the case together over the shattered glass. She pressed the power key and it turned on. She punched in her parent's number and waited, watching Sam and the officers through the curtain. Finally it started ringing.

After the forth ring the answering machine came on. "Hi, you have reached the Robinsons," said the cheerful voice of her mother. Then the family voices began listing off names, "Nancy, Jack, Joseph, Kendra, Katie, Joel, Jacob," and then the cheerful little girl's voice, "and Jenny!" Her mother's voice again, "We're not home now, so leave your name and number and," then the whole family together said, "we'll bring you Jell-O!"

Kelly's eyes teared and her heart felt ready to burst as she heard their voices, but when she heard the word *Jell-O* she laughed. Her mother made interesting Jell-O for all church events. She was notorious for her Jell-O.

Kelly heard the beep. Suddenly she didn't know what to say. Taking a jagged breath, tears overwhelming her, she tried but couldn't get air in or words out for a minute. Finally she said, "Mom, Dad." The machine beeped again and a voice came on, "If you're satisfied with your message press one, if you'd like to erase and rerecord press two."

She pressed end.

Grace pulled up at the Finches' house on Edgewood. She saw Ironpot parked in front of the house.

"Hi, Grace," he said with a smile.

"Brother Ironpot."

"That's Officer to you."

"What do we have, Officer?"

"Well," he flipped open his small notebook. Grace pulled out her pad and pen. "We believe the victim in this case is Kelly Finch, and the suspect is her husband, Sam Finch. We responded to a verbal altercation reported by their neighbor. We could hear them arguing, but as you can see," he said pointing to the house, "there are curtains on all the windows and we couldn't see what was happening. Neither party reports physical abuse. They both say it's only verbal, but I don't buy it. Hart didn't either when he was here. We have no reason to arrest at this point. The victim, however, would like to go home to her parents in Utah."

"Utah?"

"Yes, she 'used' to be Mormon," Ironpot said, making quotation marks in the air.

"How does that work, used to be? Was she excommunicated?"

"Did you know Hart 'used,'" he made quotation marks again, "to be Mormon?"

"Shut up! I'm not surprised."

"Yes, you are!"

"No, he's shiny. So, what are you going to do about Hart, Brother Ironpot?"

"I'm going to become a fisher of men."

Grace smiled. "Well fisherman, don't leave me here alone, okay?"

"I warned him. Sam Finch is not coming back," Ironpot said with conviction.

"Wanna bet?"

"I'm a Mormon, we don't gamble."

"No, but we do service. I'll volunteer to take all your extra zucchini this year if he doesn't drive by."

"You're offering too much. Do you own a truck?"

"Take it or leave it."

"Take it." They shook hands and Grace went in.

CHAPTER 24

THE BIGGER PICTURE

SAM FINCH HAD ALREADY BEEN BY HIS LAWYER'S WHEN HE went to the phone store in Gearhart. There was a beautiful, thin brunette behind the counter and a guy in a Hawaiian shirt. He went to the woman. "I need a new phone."

Grace noticed someone watching her from an opening in the curtains. The door opened before she knocked. She introduced herself to Kelly Finch.

"Hi, Kelly. Officer Ironpot sent me to help you. My name is Grace. I work for the Family Crisis Center." Grace gave her spiel quickly. She looked at Kelly, a small but very pretty woman, and waited for her response.

Kelly studied Grace and wondered what she should tell her. After an uncomfortable minute of silence, she motioned to two wingbacked chairs on either side of the fireplace. They sat down facing each other. Grace perched on the edge of the chair and leaned toward Kelly. Without trying, she mimicked Kelly's body language.

"Kelly," Grace said, "Ironpot says that you want to go home to your family in Utah. I want to tell you that if that's what I'm helping with, I won't write about your plans in my report or alert anyone. I won't share it with your husband. We have the resources to help you with that."

Kelly looked unsure. She studied Grace's face and finally said, "If he finds out, he'll keep my children from me. He'll find a way. He's very smart."

"Yes, but he isn't God, and he can't read your mind. If you decide that you need to leave to be safe, we have the resources to pay for bus tickets, train tickets, and other forms of transportation. We can also arrange shelter with sister agencies across the country. I can put you in a hotel tonight, and you could be heading home tomorrow if you want."

Kelly looked around the house. "What about the kids' things? What about our stuff?"

"I can't help you with stuff. If you take the bus you are allowed to carry two bags. If you drive you can take what you carry. We recommend that you pack important items like birth certificates, social security cards, and immunization records for sure. Then add other items like medication or things that you can't immediately replace and must have."

Kelly's head dropped as she thought about returning to Utah. She took a deep breath and slowly blew out. She took a long look around her home and then at her feet, letting her shoulders slump and tightly folding her arms.

"What if my parents don't want me?" Kelly asked. Tears started silently running down the same trails they had cut on her cheeks before. Grace looked at her and wanted to gather her up in her arms and say that of course they would want her. How could they not? But Grace had seen worse things happen. She had been in the hospital with a fifteen-year-old rape victim and had a mother refuse to come to the emergency room because her daughter probably did something to cause the rape. She knew better than to promise Kelly anything.

"Do you think they wouldn't want you?" Grace quietly asked.

Kelly turned toward the fireplace, covered her mouth, and thought. Grace gave her time. Finally Kelly said, "I don't know. I've caused them a lot of grief and shame. I've embarrassed them."

"How do they feel about their grandkids?"

"I honestly don't know. My husband never got along with them. He said my family just caused problems. So, we haven't spent a lot of time together since I moved to Oregon."

"Would you like to call them to find out?"

"I started to earlier."

"You can use my phone."

"I have one."

———

Ironpot spotted the expensive Ford work truck turn the corner at the end of the block about forty-five minutes after Grace went into the Finch house. "Crud," he said out loud. He thought Grace and Kelly had been talking a long time. He wondered if they had lost track of time or if Grace had forgotten her appointment on the hill. Besides, he was ready to call it a day. His shift was almost over.

Ironpot had just started toward the door to check with Grace when Sam's truck came blatantly down the street. Sam, his new buddy, waved and went on.

———

Kelly stood and thanked Grace for stopping by. They had discussed several options: Grace paying her way home, Kelly staying and working on a divorce and custody, Kelly going someplace safe for just a day or two while things cooled down, Kelly going into safe housing while she decided whether to stay in Oregon or go back to Utah, and more.

Kelly was amazed at all the choices she had, but she stayed fairly silent. She kept thinking about Sam's threat to take her children. Believing him, she knew she had to think things out and make sure she did just the right thing. Sam had all the money.

Kelly walked Grace to the door and they hugged as Grace said goodbye.

"I mean it, Kelly," Grace said, handing Kelly a business card. "No matter what time, day or night, you call the crisis line and tell us what you decide. Whatever it is we'll be there to support you."

"Thanks," Kelly said. Smiling, she took the card and watched Grace walk down the steps to the patrol car and talk to the officer for a few minutes. She couldn't hear what they were saying, but Grace looked concerned. Grace turned and looked at Kelly. Ironpot got out of the car and called her name.

"Mrs. Finch," he said as he approached the porch. "I just wanted to let you know that Sam drove by, even after we asked him to leave." Kelly's mouth opened and her stomach dropped. Ironpot continued, "Why don't you leave with Grace and come back later to get your stuff?"

Kelly turned and looked behind her at her home. True, it was her prison, but it was also her sanctuary. The world beyond her windows looked mean and unpredictable. At least she knew this one. She wasn't leaving without her money or stuff. Shaking her head, she quietly said, "No, thank you," as she shut the door.

Kelly quickly made her way into the kitchen, where she turned the cell phone back on and called her parents again. This time when she put it to her ear there was a recorded message that this phone was not in service and she should go to her phone store for help. It was too late. He had changed the service.

Looking down at the phone, she panicked. She tried to erase any evidence that she had dialed anything. Frantic, she took it back apart and then tried to remember how it had laid in the drawer when she opened it.

She took the Book of Mormon out of the dishwasher and ran out the back door to her garden.

Across the street, a shiny, black extended-cab Ford truck with tinted windows sat idling.

——

The deputy at the Coho County Jail looked at the computer screen with disbelief. He knew there was a motorcycle club in town and a few other events, but it must be more crowded than he thought. The roster was almost full. They couldn't hold more than seventy-nine prisoners safely. He'd have to start letting prisoners out that were in for assault if it didn't slow down. They could only hold so many.

CHAPTER 25

GOOD OLD BOYS

EDWARD ANDERSON, OWNER OF ANDERSON LOGGING AND Berk's father, was clutching the phone, watching his wife, Anna Berk Anderson, cry her eyes out. He was having a hard time hearing his attorney Potter explain their game plan over the sobbing.

"So you see," Potter said, "because your son violated the no contact order, my job is a lot tougher. The chances of his getting out just went down measurably, and you may have forfeited the amount you put up for bail."

Ed Anderson swore. "I'm not made of money!"

"I know. I'll talk to the courts and see what I can do. In the meantime, I think I've been able to work out a diversion plan with the DA. It seems that your son had more of a drinking problem than you may have realized. He's pretty sick in jail. They don't want to deal with the detox situation. I've set up a deal that provides if you can pay for a bed in detox, and then the drug and alcohol treatment facility in Necanicum, the DA will agree to release him. They will drop the felony if he agrees to plead guilty to misdemeanor assault and—"

"I don't want anything on his record. I told you," Ed said, beginning another diatribe. Anna's sobs escalated when she heard the word "record."

"Hold on!" Potter interrupted. "Remember I said 'diversion.' That means he pleads guilty and agrees to complete a plan. If he completes the plan or agreement his record is wiped clean. Because he hasn't had a criminal record as an adult, he's eligible.

"What kind of plan?"

"The plan includes completing drug and alcohol treatment, batterers' treatment, and continuing to have no contact with his wife and children, staying with you as supervisor and the rest of the usual requirements."

"Such as?"

"No going into bars, no drinking, no probation, no fines, and no fees. I can give you the list."

"What do we need to do?"

"You set up the drug and alcohol detox and treatment. I'll give you the numbers."

"All right," he said. "Whatever it takes. My boy is not the same as all the lowlifes in that crappy little jail. I want him out now."

―――――

Amber's Volkswagen chugged up the hill toward home, carrying piles of homework, which she loved. She looked forward to seeing Greta and Bjorn at home. It had been a great day, and tonight she was going to the bonfire with Alan. He smelled so good. She didn't even mind his goofy friends like Nephi. Smiling to herself, she wondered what Nephi's parents were like. They probably made their own granola, didn't shave anything, and wore organic cotton. At the thought of clothes, a wave of panic shot through her. What would she wear? What do people wear to a bonfire? Her family didn't do fun. She'd never been to one before.

Inventorying her clothes in her mind, Amber turned up her own street. Then she stopped. There were a lot of cars at her house. They never had visitors, except for Grandma and Grandpa Anderson. One of the cars was a Necanicum Police Department patrol car. The sound of her own pulse pumped in her ears, blood rushing from her head as tater tots threatened to reemerge onto her lap.

She parked down the block. Her hands shook as she turned off the car and took her keys out of the ignition, grabbed her heavy bag, and quickly walked up the hill. She decided to go in through the side door to the garage so she could hopefully see what was happening before they saw her.

Quickly, she walked to the east side of the house, around the garage to a door that entered the large garage. She used her house key to open it. It was dark, but she knew her way around. Her step-father had set the back of the spacious garage up as his own bar, with a large flat-screen television, a reclining chair, and a refrigerator stocked with his favorite local brew.

She went around the fridge, walking quietly between the easy chair and her mom's Explorer. Noiselessly, she slipped her shoes off before she took the three stairs to the kitchen door, cautiously and quietly.

Slowly, she turned the knob on the door leading to the house and carefully pulled it open. She was sure someone would hear the rubber sweep on the bottom, or the escape of air as she broke the seal. Before she went in, she stood at the door and tried to listen. Muffled voices came from the living room.

She slid through the door and into the mudroom. She looked out the already open door, down the short hall toward the living room. Her mother was sitting in the living room on a chair by the fireplace, and she looked mad. Grace, the blonde lady, was back and sitting on the couch facing her mother. There was a police officer standing across the fireplace from her mother with his arms resting on his duty belt. This one was icky. His belly hung over his belt. Even though the house was dimly lit, he had his aviator sunglasses on and his short black hair was greased into a fifties thing. There was another woman on the couch she didn't recognize. Funny, she looked like the fairy godmother in Cinderella, but she had an official badge on a lanyard hanging around her neck. Amber couldn't tell if the woman was from a state agency, since she couldn't read the words from this distance.

Amber was an expert at sensing people's moods. For years, she had watched Berk's every nuance. It was how she survived. The room was filled with anger rolling from her mother, dark tension from the annoyed officer, frustration from the fairy godmother, and strangely, hope from the blonde lady.

Greta was hiding at the top of the stairs. Amber only had to glimpse her out of the corner of her eye to know she was there, tensely waiting and listening.

"Listen," said the fairy godmother, "there is no negotiating. I can only tell you what Child Protective Services plans to do at this point. The only way to keep us out of your life and home is to protect these children and make a safety plan with Grace that works." The fairy godmother pointed at Grace, who sat perched on the edge of the couch next to her. "That's why I asked Grace to come. When you've put a safety plan together, then we, as an agency, will make our decision. This investigation will be opened for thirty days or until we have determined the safety of the children."

"You're going to take my children! So just take them! I can't take care of them without Berk anyway," Emily barked, leaning forward on her chair. "How am I going to pay my bills or buy food? I'm out of everything right now!"

Amber's thoughts began to race. What was her mother talking about? Were they going to take Greta and Bjorn and put them in foster care? They couldn't be separated. Greta would die! Her mother would rather have her father than them. Amber wasn't surprised. She just felt out of control.

"Emily," Grace said, interrupting Amber's thoughts. "I told you that we would help find ways to help you provide for your family. Let's start with a list of needs and we can work on it."

"Mom," Amber entered the room, "I can make money! We don't need Berk!"

She turned to the women on the couch. "She'll go back to him. She always takes him back. But I can take care of the kids. I can work . . ."

The fairy godmother held out a hand and stood, interrupting Amber, "You must be Amber." Without thinking, Amber took her hand and shook it. "My name is Adrian. I'm from Child Welfare. We are not here to put you in foster care. Your mom and I were just talking. I would like to talk to you next."

Amber looked at her mom and felt like she was caught between a rock and a hard place for just a moment. If she spoke to this woman, her mother would hate her. She had always taught her what happened at home stayed at home. But, if she didn't talk to this woman, her mom might give them away and she could be separated from Greta.

"If you could have a seat, Amber, I would like to finish talking to your mom."

Amber sat on the bottom step of the spiral staircase and watched through the rail as the conversation continued.

"Now, as I was saying," Adrian continued, "Berk is not to have contact with the children or to be on the premises or at the school. He is being charged with child abuse among other things and Amber is his victim. If he has contact, we will intervene."

Feeling things spin out of control, Amber jumped to her feet and tried to take it all back, erase it, and make it go away. "It's okay! I don't want to charge him," she cried out. "He can come home if we can stay!" The thought of losing her little sister or brother was more than she could tolerate.

"No, Amber," Adrian stopped her again, "he can't, even if he's not prosecuted. We can't allow you to get hurt again. He needs help before he can spend time with you without supervision." She turned back to Emily and went on, "So, what that means is that you need to show us a plan that provides for the safety of the children so that we don't need to place them in care. We don't want to put your children in care. We want you to succeed and we're all willing to help."

Her mother put her face in her hands and shook her head.

"Look, you don't have to make any decisions right now. We certainly don't want you to give us your kids. I know this is a lot to take in. We're going to leave, but before I do I want to schedule an appointment for you in my office."

"Emily," Grace said, "can we talk while Adrian is talking to Amber?" Emily nodded.

Adrian got up and led Amber into the kitchen. Adrian motioned for Amber to sit down at the table. Amber looked at the table, but couldn't imagine just sitting down. Energy was pulsing through her; she had to do something, anything. She turned to Adrian, "I need to check on Bjorn."

"Okay, can I help you?"

Amber's mind raced. Was it clean upstairs? Had her mother kept it up? Did she want this woman to see it? She couldn't be sure, but now she had said something, so it was too late. She took a deep breath and made a sweeping gesture indicating the woman could go up the stairs first.

Amber began following Adrian's large frame as she rounded the spiral staircase. As they neared the top, she could hear Greta scrambling down the hall toward hers and Bjorn's rooms. A door slammed.

At the top of the stairs, Amber waited patiently while Adrian caught her breath and rearranged wild strands of escaping hair. "It's this way," Amber said as she squeezed around Adrian's ample girth and headed down the hallway. She held her breath and crossed her hidden fingers as she opened the door.

Greta froze. She was straddling Bjorn on the floor. She had his diaper off and a bottle of powder in her hands. She had one hand on Bjorn who was flailing like crazy. Just as she looked up at Amber, like a kid caught with a hand in the cookie jar, Bjorn let it fly and pee ran up the front of her and into her open mouth. Greta screamed as she jumped up and ran from the room spilling the powder as she threw it to the floor. Bjorn laughed viciously and rolled over and began wiggling in their direction. Amber's hands flew to her mouth, her stomach flipped. "Oh no!" was all she could say as she spun in place to look at Adrian. This was going to be a disaster.

Adrian let out a belly laugh and then bent over, holding her belly and crossing her legs. Amber's brows raised. She looked back and saw the scene differently and then laughed while tiny tears escaped from the corners of her eyes.

She went to Bjorn and rolled him over. In one smooth motion, she picked up the diaper Greta had left behind, sat down indian style, lifted Bjorn's legs with one hand, slid the diaper in place, and had him set in seconds. If it had been a rodeo, she would have been the winner.

Adrian who was still laughing made a note to herself—Amber does this a lot. Amber stood up and then hoisted Bjorn's weight onto her hip and spoke as she crossed the hall to the bathroom to check on Greta. "My mom won't leave Berk. I can take care of Greta and Bjorn."

Greta had her whole little head in the sink. Her skinny arms were vigorously scrubbing shampoo into her hair. Amber closed the toilet, sat Bjorn down on the floor, and began helping her sister wash her hair. "We can't be separated," she said to Adrian, who had followed her across the hall.

Adrian watched Bjorn sit and try to figure out how to pull himself over. Amber had taken a cup off the counter and was rinsing Greta's hair.

"I believe you can take care of your brother and sister. I can see how much you love them. I also believe that being a teenager is an important job. I believe your Mom can be a good mother and can keep you safe. I'm going to encourage her to do just that. She loves you, Amber."

Amber made a face, twisting her brows together, deep in thought, as she reached for a towel. Covering Greta's head, she towel-dried her hair, stopping only to keep Bjorn from reeling more toilet paper off the roll that hung within his reach.

"Can you tell me what happened here the other night?" Adrian asked quietly.

"No, I didn't see it."

"But you called the police."

"I'm not telling anything if it means I'm going to foster care."

"It doesn't mean that. No one wants to take you away. We just want your mom to keep you safe. When you tell the truth it helps us."

Amber studied her. Could she trust her? "What if I don't tell you?"

"Then nothing. We still have the police reports."

"Oh."

"We know that you probably love your stepdad. We also know that he needs help. If he goes to court, the judge might make him do counseling and stop drinking."

Greta looked excited. "Really?" Greta said.

Amber looked at Greta's face and realized she was old enough to understand. "Greta, go play in your room."

"Oh." Greta's arms fell to her side and her shoulders slumped as she trudged toward the bathroom door.

"I mean what I said," Adrian told Amber. "Think about it."

———

"I should just sign away my kids! I lose everything. Nothing ever goes right!" Emily still hadn't looked up. She was spiraling into her own personal despair festival.

"Emily," Grace said firmly but with kindness, "Emily!"

The second one caught Emily's attention, and she stopped making noises and looked up from her hands from under her eyebrows at Grace. "What?"

"You don't have to be a victim. You can be a survivor. You have choices!"

"What choices? To lose my kids or my husband or everything I own!"

"I mean that this is an opportunity for change. It could be the best thing that ever happened to him and your family. This is a chance for your husband to choose to do something different. The hard part is that it is his choice and you can't control him. The only thing you have control over is yourself and your children. Wouldn't you love to have a safe home for them as you learn new things?"

"I can't."

"I believe in you, Emily. You also have a daughter who needs to know that you believe in her and that she's important to you."

Emily looked upstairs and took a deep breath, letting it out slowly. "I know. I should be a better mother."

"Just choose to be a mother and don't give your children away. Let's make a plan that will keep Adrian and Child Welfare out of your life. How about it?"

"How though?"

"Let's start talking about safety."

———

Kelly had buried the Book of Mormon next to her jar of money. The jar looked pathetic now. What was she thinking? She sat in the rocker in her family room, rocking rapidly back and forth. The kids were quietly eating macaroni and cheese, watching television in the family room.

Of course he would hire a lawyer. Of course he would keep the kids. Here she was planning on leaving and had never thought about his ability to bring the children back. If he kept the children, she could never leave. She would suffer forever.

Closing her eyes, she felt forever looming out into the distance, dark and hopeless. The weight of the wretched future pressed her head and heart deeper into the chair. Tears began tickling their way along the edges of her closed eyes. Afraid to allow herself to unravel, she scolded herself for being weak, pushed herself harshly into a sitting position and then out of the chair.

Refusing to give into the sadness, she began pacing the kitchen and looking out of the kitchen window and scolding herself. There was no point in sinking into dark nothingness. She was not going to give up. She would do something. There was a God, and with His help she would do something. "Snap out of it!" she said to herself and then she went to the front window and checked the view. Where was he? What could she do?

That woman, Grace, she had some ideas. Kelly should call her and talk some more. After all, she had to trust someone sometime. She really wanted to talk to her mother. She found herself standing at the island in the kitchen looking at the drawer.

Slowly, she pulled the drawer open. The cell phone . . . why did he love this thing so much? He was constantly on it. It was like he was working 24/7. Suddenly, her heartbeat was present in her mouth and ears. Her hands shook and she found herself checking over her shoulders like a naughty child as she picked it up.

She turned on the phone. It said Sam had four calls missed. The banner notice listed a name she didn't recognize, Candy Kisses. The sound of water began rushing in her ears, her vision tunneled, and her knees felt weak. She began to sit down, but without a chair, she found herself sitting hard on the cold hardwood floor. Her mouth and eyes opened wide as she tried to figure out how to work the phone.

━━

Adrian slowly made her way down the spiral staircase, clutching the metal rail, each step heavy and metal sounding. She paused halfway down to adjust her girdle and push her glasses back on her nose. Grace looked up and smiled. Amused, Emily suppressed a giggle.

Adrian looked at Emily's light face and stopped again. "Well, it looks like you feel better!"

"I do. Grace is going to help me set up a plan to make it. We called my in-laws whose names are on the house, and they agreed to continue to pay the bills on the house and utilities until everything is resolved. They still love us and will send the kids money if we need it, and they gave me the name of their lawyer in case I need to get a message to Berk in an emergency. They are sure he is going to get well. All I have to do is let them visit the kids. And they don't want me to testify against Berk."

Grace shrugged and looked a little sheepish at the mention of the lawyer. "We also have a safety plan," she offered. "Emily is going to create a fire drill for her and the kids to get the kids out of the house if he shows up. They are going to use a code word, and when the kids hear it, they will evacuate the house. Also, she is going to allow the sheriff to remove Berk's guns and take them to her father-in-law's business for safekeeping. She is going to hide the knives or anything else that can be used as a weapon, and she plans to change the locks. There's more, but the most exciting thing is that she is coming up to a support group at our office."

"Wow, I was only gone thirty minutes!"

"Emily loves her kids. She's a good mom, and she's willing to do what it takes to make their lives happy and healthy."

Adrian peered up the stairs and saw Amber looking surprised, standing at the top of the stairs. "Are you sure, Mom?" she asked.

"I thought you'd be happy, baby!"

"I am, Mom. Do you think we can do it? 'Cause I can help."

"I know."

Grace stood up. "Well, it's about five, and my kids are waiting for me. So, I'm going to go, but Emily, how about if we meet at my office tomorrow at ten before the support group? Bring Bjorn with you. We have childcare during the group."

"I don't have much gas."

"I can help with gas for your car."

CHAPTER 26

HOPE

AMBER WAVED AT GRACE AND SHUT THE DOOR. SHE TURNED to her mother who stood behind her. "I'm sorry for being mean earlier, Mom."

"It's all right, I deserved it. Sometimes I'm such a baby. I get so overwhelmed. I forget I've got you on my team."

"Mom," Amber looked down and wrung her hands. She took a deep breath, looked up at her mom's face, and then took the plunge, "Mom, I want to go out with a boy tonight. He's taking me to a bonfire and his friend's house."

Emily stepped back. She was startled by the idea. "You have a date?"

"Sort of. It's a group of kids that go to church together. They're really nice," she said rapidly, "and I promise that I will call you and come home if anything goes wrong. I'm old enough. Everyone I know goes on dates."

"I know you're old enough. It's just that I know your father would never allow it."

It was Amber's turn to be startled. "But he's not here."

"I know, it's just, I . . ."

"Mom, we don't have to ask permission. You could go out with your friend Martha from next door and it would be okay."

"I . . . we . . ." Emily took a step back, hitting the plant that was behind her, and it fell into the couch. Amber thought she could almost see her mother's brain reboot. "Well . . . what . . ."

"I'll be home by eleven."

"A curfew?"

"Yeah, Mom, lots of kids have one. Do you think that's too late?"

"No. It's fine."

"Can you put the kids to bed?" Amber asked.

"Sure."

Amber left Emily with her mouth open and went upstairs to work on the question of the universe. What does one wear on a first date?

———

Alan knocked on Amber's front door. A really big dog barked inside the house and then hit the door. Stepping back, he looked at the house number and then realized it didn't match the one she had given him.

He looked across the road and then up the street; it was the last house on the hill. Embarrassed, he got back in his car and pulled into the right driveway. All the curtains were closed. He hoped this was it. He rang the doorbell. This was the toughest part, meeting the parents. Fidgeting, he ran his fingers through his long hair and wished he had cut it, kicked the edge of the doormat, and pushed his hands into his pockets. A woman as beautiful as Amber opened the door. Surprised, he wiped his sweaty hands on his jeans and reached out, offering to shake her hand. Apprehensively, she held the door open for him without saying a word.

Still holding out his hand, he said, "Hi, I'm Alan Johnson, I'm here to pick up Amber."

She realized he wanted to shake her hand. Tentatively, she held hers out. His handshake was firm if not seriously vigorous and damp.

Alan went on rapidly, "It's nice to meet you. I promise to have her home on time. It's just a group of my friends from church going to a bonfire and then to a hot tub."

"Hot tub?"

"Fully clothed with adult chaperones!" he blurted out.

"Ah." Emily said, sizing him up. "Amber," she called up the stairs, "Your . . . Alan is here." She looked up the spiral staircase. She and Amber had giggled as they practiced the entrance several times. Now she waited.

Nothing. Where was she? Then she came and stood at the top of the stairs, as they had planned for effect, to let her date take in her long, glossy dark hair, jeans, and clean, warm sweater with a matching scarf and hat.

"Nice hat. I mean, ah. Nice. You look," Alan said. "Ah, I mean, you look nice."

"Thank you," Amber said as she began walking slowly down the stairs, trying not to fall.

Emily knew this was her cue. "Have fun, but be in by eleven." She tried to look stern, but caring.

"Of course, Mom, aren't I always?" Amber winked at her mother as she and Alan walked out into the crisp evening air.

———

Kelly realized Sam had been texting a woman for months. Not just texts, but pictures too. Some of the pictures were graphic, and so were some of his responses. Kelly was still sitting on the kitchen floor, hands shaking, reading them. The kids had long since gotten down from the table and moved into their own rooms to play.

Kelly was lost in time. She wasn't breathing. She wasn't thinking. Her brain was going a million miles an hour. Thousands of thought puzzle pieces coming together to form a picture that gradually made sense.

All the late nights on the job recently, all the texting, all the computer work he was doing. Here he was always accusing her of cheating or looking at someone, and all the time it was him. He had been cheating on her.

At first she tried to deny it. She kept reading the texts with hope that nothing had really happened. Now she realized that she had been incredibly naive.

"Mommy?" Little Sam interrupted her thoughts, touching her hair with macaroni-and-cheese fingers.

Kelly let the phone drop into her lap. Shattered, she leaned back against the cupboard door, took a deep breath, and realized how cramped she was. Her foot was asleep. Unfolding her stiff legs, she pulled herself to a standing position. She wiped her face and realized that the tears had long ago dried up, leaving behind a hollow feeling and a knot in her stomach.

Kelly looked around the kitchen. The table still had the dirty dishes on it. The counters and stove were still a mess. Sam would be mad. Then it went through her like a bolt of lightning. Everything had changed. She couldn't predict anything. Everything spread out around her, a widening frightening world of emptiness, need, responsibilities, and panic. Oh how she wished nothing had happened today, nothing had changed. She didn't want him back; she just wanted the comfort of knowing her own problems back. The chasm of the unknown was frightening.

Habitually, she started to clean up. "Mommy," little Sam said as he pulled on her sweatpants.

"Oh, sorry, honey. Get Hazel. It's time for bed."

———

Alan parked the Jeep in the Twelfth Avenue parking lot and opened Amber's door for her. Amber could smell the smoke of bonfires coming off the beach. The sun had already set when he took her hand. Amber felt it all the way to her toes.

"Nephi! Esther!" Alan called as he turned to see them pushing a wheelbarrow of wood, paper, and other things up the road in their direction. They crossed the parking lot and headed toward the beach access road.

"Come help!" Esther yelled.

They saw other people coming up the road carrying things like lawn chairs and roaster wires. Letting go of her hand, Alan went to a woman carrying a stack of chairs and took half, revealing a woman behind the stack. "Hi, Alan. Thanks," she said smiling.

A woman handed Amber a bag of food she had balanced on top of a cooler she was carrying. Together, they started down the sandy beach toward the ocean.

"Sister Lee, this is my friend, Amber," Alan said, introducing her.

"Hi," Amber said to the short sister carrying plastic lawn chairs.

"Hi, Amber, I'm Sister Keys," said the woman carrying the heavy cooler.

"Would you like me to take one side of that?" Amber offered.

"Thanks!" Sister Keys beamed in her direction.

Alan walked alongside her. The sand was soft and took energy to walk in. Soon Sister Keys was huffing and puffing. Amber slowed her pace and they fell behind.

"So," Sister Keys began, "how did you meet Alan?"

"We go to school together." She didn't know what to say.

"I'm glad you came. We never have enough girls."

Amber looked at her questioningly.

"At youth activities I mean."

"Oh." She thought for a moment. "Why do you need more girls?"

Sister Keys laughed. "Right now, as you will see, we have a large number of young men."

"I see," Amber said. They were silent for the next one hundred feet. Then they rounded a sand dune covered in beach grass, and Amber could see a big group of very large kids standing around a raging bonfire.

Mr. White stood with them. He spotted Amber, smiled at her, and gave her a friendly wave. Amber found herself waving shyly back at the vice principal.

"Brother White!" Sister Lee called, "Isn't there a fire ordinance in this town?"

"There is. I checked it out and this fire is within regulation." Mr. White called back to her.

"Brother?" Amber asked Sister Keys.

"They're not brother and sister as in a family," Sister Keys said. "It's what we call each other at church. We're all brothers and sisters in the gospel."

"I see," she said, but she didn't see at all.

Large shadows were silhouetted against the fire. Amber and Sister Keys set the cooler down. Alan was placing chairs in a circle about ten feet away from the melting heat of the fire. Everyone was talking and laughing and all looked like they had known each other forever. Alan fit right in. Two of the largest silhouettes turned and she realized they were Brad and Doug, football players at the school. Then she realized that almost the entire starting lineup was there.

Amber had heard kids at school call some of the team the Mormon Mayhem, but she hadn't realized how many of the really great athletes playing football were Mormon. Berk didn't allow her to go to the games.

"All right, everyone," Mr. White said loudly, raising his hands. The noisy group became silent. The fire crackled, the wood snapped and popped, and smoke hung heavy in the air, stinging Amber's eyes. When she tried to move out of the smoke, Alan took her hand, led her to a plastic chair, and sat beside her.

"Jared is going to say the opening prayer," Mr. White announced. Amber was surprised. Jared looked like he ate small children for breakfast.

Jared brought his big frame around until he was facing the bulk of the group with his back to the fire. Everyone folded their arms, bowed their heads, and closed their eyes. Amber watched. Then Jared began to speak.

The prayer was simple and not too long, but it was sweet and there was a pleasant feeling in the air. Amber was astonished that a feeling like that, and such a humble prayer, had come from a football player.

"Amen," Jared said. Joseph knocked him over, just missing the fire, yelling, "I get the first hot dog!" as he jumped over Jared's downed body.

Jared raised. "Not so fast!" It was a brawl. No one paid any attention until they got to Sister Lee, who was calmly pulling food out of the cooler.

"Ah, ah, boys. Ladies first," she said without even looking up. Calmly, she stuck a hot dog on a long wire roasting stick.

Girls lined up. There was Esther, Gayle, and Connie, the girls she had met at lunch, and also two little thin girls that looked like they were in junior high. Sister Farmer gave the first hot dog to one of the girls. The girl was really lanky and had a big toothy grin. She promptly turned around and held it up high in the air. "What am I bid for the hot dog!" she yelled.

"I'll give you a dollar!" Jared yelled back and fell to his knees at her feet. It was all over. The bidding was quickly turning into a second wrestling and laughing match.

Sister Lee calmly kept handing out hot dogs.

Amber was in heaven.

——

The fire died down to warm embers. Gradually, all the testosterone settled down. Everyone watched the flames while singing. Brother Douglas accompanied them on guitar. They made songs up; they ruined perfectly good songs with silly words and laughed until Mr. White held his hands up again and announced it was time for a closing prayer.

This time Amber, who was full of hot dogs and had s'more chocolate smeared on her sleeve, knew what to do. She folded her arms, bowed her head, and listened while Alan prayed.

"Please bless that we all go home safely," Alan said and then closed the prayer. Everyone said amen. Amber watched while everyone's eyes were closed. She had never heard anyone pray like that before. They prayed like they were talking to God and He would listen.

Alan stacked the chairs. Without being asked, everyone policed the area and carried things back to the parking lot.

When the last of the items were loaded, Alan, Nephi, Esther, and Amber stood together under the streetlight.

"It's only eight thirty. Let's get our suits," Alan said.

"We'll meet you at the house," Nephi said. Nephi walked with Esther down the street back toward town. Amber and Alan got into the Jeep and he pulled it around the block and down the hill.

They pulled in next to four or five cars in front of an old Victorian. It sat on the corner, a block off the beach. The house's small yard had a tall fence, making it private from street traffic. Amber got her plain blue one-piece bathing suit out of her bag while Alan came around to let her out of the Jeep. She saw that Douglas, Gayle, and Connie were already there. She wondered if they would notice her old suit was worn out.

"Hi, guys," Alan said as they walked up to the door and let themselves in.

Amber was nervous to see the blonde woman, Grace, come into the entryway. She stepped back, feeling for the door handle. She didn't want Alan to know about all of her secrets, about Child Welfare coming to her house. She felt like a trapped rat. Her shoulders rose and her hands clenched as tension began working from her neck down.

"Hey, Alan," Grace said and gave him a quick hug. She winked at Amber, but didn't say anything else. "Hi, guys! I knew you were coming so I made popcorn. There are movies or the hot tub." Everyone acted like Amber had always been there. The tension released from her shoulders.

"Hot tub!" they all said in unison. Alan led Amber through the house. Nephi and Esther were already on the back deck taking the lid off a large hot tub.

"You can change first," Alan said. "The bathroom is this way." He led her back through the kitchen and utility room and into a large bathroom with a clawfoot tub and antique dresser with a sink on it.

"I'll change upstairs," Alan offered. "See you outside."

Amber changed and was just coming out of the bathroom when she found herself alone in the kitchen with Grace.

"I won't say anything," Grace whispered. "I don't usually have people from work at home. And I promise you I never talk about work at home. So, if you need me, you're going to have to call the crisis line. Otherwise, while you're here, I'm going to pretend we just met."

"Your kids don't know?"

"Not a thing."

Amber let out a rush of air. "Thanks."

Grace winked again and then smiled. "Cookie?"

"No, thanks."

"You're awfully thin. We Mormons like to grow 'em big. You met the boys?"

"Do you feed them something special?"

"It's what we don't feed them. No alcohol, cigarettes, coffee, or tea. Jell-O and ice cream are our last and final vices."

———

The hot tub felt wonderful in the cold evening air. Amber slipped into the water, feeling out of place, but loving the sensation of the jets pulsing on her back and legs.

"Thanks for coming over, Amber," Esther said.

Amber was surprised to be thanked. "Thank you. I've loved this."

The wooden screen door on the deck slammed, and Amber looked up to see the smaller girl that Alan had whispered to at the fire. She was dressed in a one-piece suit and had goggles and a snorkel on her head and flippers on her feet. "Cannon ball!" she yelled, racing toward the tub.

"Mary!" Nephi shouted as he stood and waded to the side of the tub she was racing toward. "Grace!" Nephi caught Mary in his arms, hoisted her over his head, and balanced her on his shoulder as he stood in the tub. Her legs were kicking and her arms were pointing, dive fashion, toward the water.

From somewhere in the house Mabel's and Grace's voices said, "Mary!" Then Grace appeared in the doorway. She smiled, crossed the deck, and removed the flippers. "No flippers. The water stays in the tub."

From under Nephi's arm, Mary went limp and looked at her mother through the dive mask, while breathing through the snorkel. She started laughing. Nephi dumped her off his shoulder into the tub, letting her fall headfirst until she was completely submerged. She emerged and posed like a bathing beauty posing for a picture. "Grace, can't she stay inside with you and Mom?" Nephi begged.

"Enjoy guys," Grace said. "Fire's warm and popcorn is popped when you're done." She returned to the house.

Esther smiled at Amber and said, "Watch this. Shut up, guys! Guys!"

They all looked at Esther but kept talking. She reached over the side of the tub and seemed to be fiddling with some knobs. The lights went out and the water stopped bubbling. Esther slipped back in the tub in the dark. Amber got nervous. Her heart started to race. What were they doing?

"Look," Esther said, and Amber could see her silhouette point up. Amber's eyes followed her direction and she gasped. Stars. Thousands of stars everywhere in the crisp night sky. She could see a satellite track rapidly across the sky and then a shooting star. She leaned back deep in the warm water. Alan moved over next to her. They all sat silently for a few minutes.

"Don't you love it?" Esther whispered to her.

"It's amazing," Amber said, and she meant it.

"I can't believe some people don't believe in God," Alan said quietly.

"I believe in God," Amber said.

"You do?" Doug asked.

"Doug, you idiot!" Gayle whispered loudly.

"I don't know," Amber answered honestly. "I just always felt . . .
I . . . I don't know."

CHAPTER 27

CHANGES

EMILY LOOKED IN ON GRETA. SHE WAS COMPLETELY ASLEEP, snuggled in with every stuffed animal she owned, and that was a lot.

She went into Bjorn's room and found him looking up at her from the crib with the streetlight spilling in through the window. He smiled. Her heart felt it would burst with love. How did she get such a beautiful baby? When was the last time she had noticed how cute he was, she thought with a tinge of guilt. She reached into the crib and pulled Bjorn to her. He grabbed a handful of her hair, pulled it, and nuzzled into her neck. His little body was so warm.

She took Bjorn to the rocker and began rocking him to sleep. His breathing became deep and regular and then finally she was able to detangle his fingers from her hair.

Silently, she rocked with a heart full of love as she examined his perfect little face, long lashes, and his pursed lips that sucked as he dreamed of bottles of milk. How long had it been since she'd had a moment like this? Where had the time gone?

Pain fractured her heart; the time had gone to Berk. She had been so wrapped up in Berk—saving Berk, protecting Berk, keeping Berk happy—the time had slipped away, and there was no way to bring it back. Pulling Bjorn's warm body to her, she let tears drop on his soft baby hair.

"I promise not to waste one more minute," she said out loud. Then another thought pierced her broken heart. She could lose Bjorn. They would take him away if she couldn't get her life in order. Resolve started to grow, filling the empty spaces with purpose. She would do whatever it took to keep her little family together, Berk or no Berk. It looked like she didn't have a choice—it was no Berk.

She heard a noise downstairs. She looked at her watch. It was ten fifty-five. She smiled to herself. Amber was home.

———

All the kids had gone home. Mabel was in the backyard putting chemicals in the hot tub and topping it off with the hose. Nephi and Esther had gone to bed. She was glad the next morning was Saturday and she could sleep in.

Grace turned off all the lights in the kitchen and started the dishwasher. Today, she had stopped on her way home to get groceries. For some reason, she hadn't been able to leave the store without about a hundred dollars in batteries, flashlights, matches, propane, candles, bottled water, and a serious case of spaghetti sauce. She had a major urge to check the seventy-two-hour packs.

The funny thing was that she ran into about half the church on the same aisle as the propane and bottled water and they were all doing the same thing. Sister Howard was there. She said that she was repacking her seventy-two-hour kits and was including cash. After the store, she said she was also going to fill her gas cans. She had a feeling something was coming.

Grace's phone alerted her to a new email. She had sent out about fifteen emails to people online who were advertising firewood within a hundred miles. So far she hadn't found any locally.

Her email opened. She finally had a hit. It was from a man in Tillamook. He must have just sent it. He had firewood for 180 dollars a cord. It was a steal. She would have to pick it up herself. He couldn't deliver.

She replied, asking if she could come tomorrow morning at eight. She had a full plate and wanted to get it done early.

He immediately responded, saying she could come and then had written his address. It was forty-two miles away, about an hour's drive on the winding coastal Highway 101.

"Mom," she called, "I found firewood." No answer. She went to look for her. They would get gas in the cans on the way down.

"Mom, lets reload the water storage," she said as she went out on the deck. "I found firewood. Isn't that great! It's in Tillamook. We have to take the little truck. We can get it in the morning at eight."

"So much for sleeping in. You want me to do the water tonight?"

"Yes, I have this feeling."

Mabel looked at her knowingly. "Let's rinse and refill the water tank tonight," she said. She knew about Grace and her feelings.

———

The house was quiet. Lights were on here and there as Grace finished washing her face and headed for bed.

She opened her bedroom door and realized how alone she was. Looking down at the CTR ring on her finger, she smiled as she thought about Hart going to her church. "Interesting," she said to the empty room. Changing into her flannel nightgown, catching herself in the mirror, she criticized her reflection, "Right, like he would be interested in you and your insane family."

The door opened. "I want to snuggle." Mary stood in the light in full-body zipper pajamas and a large lower lip. Without waiting for an answer, she threw herself onto the bed. Burrowing in, she held her arms out, begging for a hug. "Nephi hates me."

"No, he doesn't," Grace said.

"He never wants me around his friends."

"He's just trying to be cool," offered Grace.

"Esther says I'm immature and so did Greg at school."

"I think you're just right. There's no hurry to grow up. Being a grown-up is overrated," Grace said as she squeezed Mary again.

Grace and Mary continued to talk softly. Then Grace realized that Mary had stopped talking, and she could hear quiet snoring. Grace drifted off to sleep.

CHAPTER 28

LIVING

EMILY LAY IN BED, AMAZED AT THE DAY. WHAT HAD BEGUN AS one of the worst days in her life had ended as one of the best. She and Amber had stayed up past midnight talking and laughing over cups of hot chocolate.

She couldn't remember ever having a conversation like that with Amber. Amber was always looking at her so judgmentally, or complaining about her. Tonight, they were almost friends. Amber had actually asked her advice and had wondered about her dating experiences. She hadn't reminded Amber that she had made bad choices, and Amber hadn't reminded her. They talked about things like having a boy hold the door open for you and what it meant if they held your hand.

It dawned on her that Amber hadn't had her first kiss yet. It felt good to know that she would be a part of Amber's life when that happened. It was a good day. As her mind tried to quiet, she heard the ticking of her clock. The house creaked and her worries bubbled to the surface.

How was she going to pay the bills? What if someone broke in? She heard a door squeak. She sat straight up in bed, her heart racing. Carefully, she slid silently out of bed and walked down the hall in the dark. In the shadows, she saw Amber's form at Bjorn's door. She came up behind her. Amber looked back, seeing her coming, and smiled in the muted light coming through the window.

"He's beautiful, isn't he?" Amber said.

"Yes."

They both stood and watched Bjorn sleep for a minute and then went their separate ways, finally a team, joined together in one goal—to keep their tiny family safe.

———

The kids had been in bed for hours. Wide awake, Kelly still waited, gently rocking in the rocking chair, watching the back door by the kitchen. The door Sam usually used. The clock in the kitchen ticked loudly. It was four in the morning and Sam still wasn't here. She knew now.

Every cell in her body ached. It seemed such a useless pain. She had hated him. She had wanted to leave him. But she still loved him and couldn't bear the thought of him with someone else.

This would have been so much easier if he had been a monster every minute of every day. Looking back, she remembered him building little Sam's racetrack Christmas morning. She remembered him rubbing her pregnant belly. There had been good moments. They just seemed so long ago.

There was no point dwelling in the past. Looking down at the broken phone, she wondered what his voice mail said. Consumed, she began to fiddle again, torturing herself. She was still there when Sam came home.

Hearing the truck pull into the driveway, she stopped breathing. Blood pumping in her ears, she waited. The door opened and there stood Sam, a stranger. Feeling broken, beyond anguish, she was caught between a reality that threatened to annihilate her and oblivious denial that would allow her to remain functioning in hell.

He threw papers at her.

"Paper?" she said. Her hands shook as she took the large stack of stapled paper from her lap and tried to focus on it. There was an official seal. "Dissolution."

"It means divorce, you fat pig. I'm moving on. The kids are going with me and this house went on the market yesterday at four p.m."

Kelly felt something snap. It wasn't loud. It was silent. It wasn't a small snap. It was the twang of a heart, heavy as stone, fracturing in two in a single moment of frigid ugliness beyond all bearing. What was fright became fight. She lifted her heavy soul out of the rocker and flew at Sam with the papers. She hit him square in the chest with her fist full of dissolution orders. Paper rained everywhere.

"Read them if you can," he said. "I get the kids. You might as well sign them. None of this is yours. They saw you today. They know how crazy you are. No one will believe you."

He was right. No one would believe her. Desperation replaced anger. She turned and ran toward the stairs and the kids' room.

"I know about your jar and I filed papers. I will call the cops!" he yelled.

She stopped dead in her tracks. That jar was all she had. She spun around with a wild look in her eye.

"I saw you bury the book. I'm taking it with us." He was taunting her while he went back out the open door.

She chased him. All reason had left her. That money and that book was all she had in the world. Rain dropped heavy and loud in the dark. Finding him on his hands and knees, digging in her garden in the dark, she began pounding on his back. "Stop it! It's mine! Stop it! Stop it!"

Suddenly, he whirled on her, grabbed her by the throat with one hand, and pulled her down to the wet ground. The back of her head hit a rock, but she didn't feel it, or the rocks that bordered the flowers digging into her back. All she could feel was his hands on her throat. She had to have air. Rain pelted her eyes, filled her mouth and nose. He laid his forearm over her neck and spit in her face. Desperate to get him off, she scratched his face with her dirty nails. He laughed harder. She pulled his wet hair, knowing she was losing and was going to black out soon. Feeling around in the dirty mud, she found a rock and came up harder than she expected, catching him full in the eye.

He screamed, "You . . ." and swore at her, but took his arm off her neck. Gasping for air, she swung again and again and again. He covered his head with his hands.

"Police! Stop!"

She didn't hear. She was screaming and swinging.

She was standing over Sam when she saw the officer with his gun drawn.

Behind the officer, in the pouring rain, stood her mother, father, brothers, sisters, and the barking family dog. Her mother started running toward Kelly when the officer clotheslined her with his arm and stopped her.

Officer Olson ordered Kelly in a loud voice to roll over onto her stomach with her hands and feet extended. He shouted, "Face down! Face down! Put your arms out to your sides! Arms out to your sides!" The rain was so loud he was straining his voice to be heard. Kelly seemed to wake from a deep sleep to see the wind whipping the trees above her head. She knelt on the rocks and lay spread eagle with her face in the wet dirt and grass. Someone grunted and knelt beside her. They pulled her arms together behind her and put handcuffs on her. She felt like she was living a nightmare and any moment she would realize this couldn't possibly be happening. Then she remembered.

"My kids! My kids! I can't leave my kids!" Kelly screamed and began to struggle to get to her feet. One of the officers took her firmly by the elbow, cuffs cutting her wrists, and helped her to her feet.

"Settle down! Your kids are fine," the officer said.

"Mom! Mom! Get the kids!" Kelly cried.

"The kids are coming with me!" Sam bellowed in her direction and then swung around and headed into the house. A short fat officer took Kelly by the other elbow, and Officer Olson followed Sam into the house.

"You have the right to remain silent," the officer began. Kelly stopped listening.

"Mom, don't let Sam take the kids! Help, Dad! Daddy!"

Her mother slumped against her father and then Kelly realized her father was sobbing. As the rain washed down his face, he wiped tears from under his glasses, wiping his wet face with wet hands. Her brothers and sisters were all standing with their mouths open, holding back their barking dog.

As each one realized what was happening, their faces folded into tears and they held onto their mother or father. Her twelve-year-old sister, Jenny, had her arms around the yellow lab that was barking viciously at the officer. Her brother Joseph had the leash.

Seeing Joseph made her feel surreal. Wasn't he supposed to be on a mission? Kelly felt like the world was folding in on itself and darkness began coloring the corners of her vision. Her knees buckled and the officer, who was still talking, callously escorted her stumbling, weak, wet body through the rain and across the lawn.

—————

Officer Olson stood in the quiet, clean family room talking to the victim of the assault. Sam sat on the edge of the couch with his head in his hands, crying, holding a ziplock bag of ice wrapped in a clean washcloth on his eye.

"I don't know when it started to get so bad, Officer. She's always been different, but I loved her. You know? I've tried and tried to help her, but she won't take any medicine or go to a shrink. I offered to go with her if that would help, but she wouldn't. Even her family hasn't seen her for over a year. She won't talk to anyone. She just stays holed up in the house talking to God like he's real."

Sam went on, "I think it's because she's paranoid. You can see that she kicked my office door in. It looks like she was going through my computer and phone. She probably found something that made her mad."

"Can I examine the phone?"

"Yes, but I need it for work. I can't give it to you for evidence."

"Oh, well we don't want to impact your business. I don't really need it."

"It's been so hard to go to work and leave the kids with her when she's so crazy." Sam let out a little sob and then stood to pace.

"I know you're upset, Mr. Finch, but I need to get some information. Can you tell me what happened?"

Sam sat back down without looking at the officer. He thought for a moment. "We had a fight yesterday. The police came because she was so loud one of the neighbors called the police. I realized I just couldn't do it anymore." He paused and took a deep breath. He rubbed the back of his neck as he let his breath out slowly. "I have a new bookkeeper. I called the bookkeeper and asked who their attorney was. It turned out I had done some work for him before. I decided it wasn't safe to come home. I didn't think she'd hurt the kids, so I left them here and went to the attorney's."

"The attorney wrote up dissolution papers, giving me the kids because she's so unstable. I didn't want to put her out on the street, so I wrote them so that she could stay here while she looked for a job and a place of her own. I'm a nice guy. I didn't wish her any harm. Anyway, I slept in my truck for a while. Finally, it got cold and I decided it was probably safe to come home."

"When I got here she was up waiting and still mad. I made the mistake of letting her see the divorce papers. She chased me out into the yard. I slipped on the wet lawn. You saw the rest. I tried to stop her by holding her down. I hope I didn't hurt her." He broke into renewed sobs.

Officer Olson slicked back his greasy dark hair. He sat his pinch book down on the counter and tucked in his shirt after smoothing it over his large belly and pulling down his bulletproof vest. He thought for a moment, while pulling a cellophane-wrapped toothpick out of his pocket, opening it and picking his teeth. "My aunt's crazy. She almost killed my uncle. She got him with a pitchfork. He lived, but he never could have children."

"So you understand?"

"I'm supposed to call DSAT for you, but you probably don't want them."

"DSAT?"

"It's that women's group at the Family Crisis Center. They've got this broad that comes out and helps you. You don't want to talk to a man-hating woman, do you?"

"What I need is a beer and the guys at Darrell's bar, not a broad."

The officer laughed. "I'll see you there tomorrow night when I'm off duty. Want to smoke? We can go outside."

"No thanks. I better just pack the kids up and go to my friends."

"What about your in-laws?"

"What about them? They hate me. I guess they can stay here. I'm a nice guy, you know."

"You're nicer than I am. I would have told them to hit the road."

"She needs them. I love her, you know. I just can't live with her."

"That's what I told my ex. Now it's just my beer, my motorcycle, my dog, and me. It's the life, I tell ya."

Outside, the rain and wind blew Kelly's mother's words away. She began to sob.

"What?" yelled Officer Nelson.

"How can we get our little girl out of jail?" shouted Kelly's father, trying to stay calm as he put his arm around his wife and pulled her anguished form to him.

"After she's at county, you can pay her bail," Officer Nelson said.

"We don't have money."

Officer Nelson shrugged and turned to get in his car.

"Wait, Officer, what about the kids?"

"You'll have to ask Mr. Finch," Officer Nelson barked and then got in his car and drove away.

———

Kelly's father, Jack Robinson, wiped his bald head with one hand, as was his habit. He searched for his wife Nancy's hand with his other hand. The rain made him blind, so he used a finger to wipe his glasses. They looked at each other and then turned to see their stunned children behind them.

"Go to the car, kids," his wife yelled over the storm.

Jack and his wife headed toward the house. When they opened the back door, they found Sam holding a sleeping Hazel and carrying a suitcase. Sam Jr. was in the officer's arms, looking sleepy and lost.

"Where's Mama?" Sam Jr. asked.

Sam looked at Nancy Robinson and Jack. He said coolly, "Jack, Nancy, make yourselves at home. I'll be back tomorrow for more of the kids' things at eleven in the morning. I'd appreciate it if you were gone when I was here. You can stay here while you're here. Leave your cell number on the counter and we'll talk tomorrow."

He and the officer went out into the rain. Nancy sat down hard at the table and looked at Jack. "Honey, it's time to pray."

CHAPTER 29

PLACES

THE SUN WAS RISING WHEN OFFICERS HART AND IRONPOT escorted Kelly out of the Necanicum temporary holding cell, through the booking room, and out to the sheriff deputy's car. Deputies would take her to another city and the Coho County Jail.

Kelly was still in her sweats, but a female officer had removed the string from the waistband so she wouldn't hang herself. She was cuffed in the front, with a chain that went around her waist, back to the cuffs, and down to her ankles. Her loose pants began falling off her narrow hips, so she held them up and shuffled in bare feet. The deputy, Jim Jones, followed her with everything she owned: a CTR ring in a paper bag with an inventory sheet stapled to it.

The ground was frosted. She could see her breath in the cold air. Shivering, she looked up at the sky of red and purple through her mud-crusted hair. The deputy opened the car door and turned her so her back was to the seat. He placed his gloved hand on her head and protected it from hitting the door as she lowered herself onto the hard plastic seat. She turned to face forward, racking her knees on the metal cage between the front and back seats. When she finally looked up, she caught her reflection in the rearview mirror.

Mud, streaked with tears, covered her face. Dead, flat eyes, looked through stringy, dirt-encrusted hair. Surprised, she noticed there were funny purple marks around her eyes. She took a deep

141

breath and let it out, looking away from the mirror to the deputy as he buckled himself in and radioed dispatch.

As he pulled away, he looked at the frightened small woman in the back of his car.

When they arrived at the Coho County Jail, the deputy opened the door for Kelly and helped her out of the car. Kelly shuffled across the cold cement floor, heavy chains jingling; she watched her feet move. Instinctually, Kelly flinched as Deputy Jones reached out to gently lead her by the elbow to a door. She heard a buzzer and a series of clicks as an unseen jailer tripped the electric lock and the door to the jail opened. A jail deputy met them at the door.

Deputy Jones handed over her property, and it was inventoried again. Kelly's photo, prints, and information were taken, and she was put in a small holding cell with a telephone. She wanted to call her parents but didn't know their cell phone numbers or where they were. Time dragged by.

When the jail deputy returned, she was strip-searched by a female deputy. The female deputy had her change into a black-and-white striped, loose-fitting jumpsuit. It looked like something out of a silent movie.

The deputy began explaining the rules and how the jail worked. Electric locks were triggered. Automatic doors slid open, then shut, and Kelly went deeper and deeper into hell. After wandering in a warren of corridors, they ended at a door with a thick-tempered glass window next to it. Two women argued loudly on the other side. The deputy looked at the camera in the ceiling and asked the camera to open the door to the women's dorm.

Electric locks clicked, the door swung open, and eight women stopped what they were doing to stare at Kelly. Kelly's pulse was flat. Too sad to be scared and too numb to feel nervous, Kelly shuffled into the room.

The female deputy turned to a woman sitting on the side of a bunk and said, "Take care of her, will you, Angela?" The cuffs and chains were removed, and suddenly the female deputy was gone.

"Hi, I'm Angela," said the woman. She looked like she was sixty, until you looked closer. Most of her teeth were missing. Her hair was dark at the roots and blonde on the chin-length ends. It looked like a yellow Brillo pad. Her skin was pitted; her eyes were watery blue in a puddle of yellow. She smelled pickled with day-old tobacco breath. "I'll take care of you, honey," she said with a raspy smoker's voice, grunting as she got up off the bunk and made her way in Kelly's direction.

———

Grace had been up since six in the morning, jogging on the beach. The moon still hung in the morning sky. She could see her breath. She couldn't see any cloud cover over the ocean. The damp sand crunched under her feet. It was so blissfully quiet.

So why, Grace wondered, *do I have a feeling of impending doom lately?* What was the urgency to get the wood? The trip to Tillamook was going to eat up the whole day, and they had a family birthday party for dinner tomorrow. She had to make a cake, shop, and clean.

Her cousin was coming home down from Fort Lewis, and her sister Sarah, was joining them for Nephi's birthday.

Nephi would be eighteen. He and Esther were less than a year apart. Poor Nephi hadn't had the title of baby of Mabel's family for more than ten and a half months when Esther had arrived and made him an uncle. He and Esther were close, and he was pretty good to her, considering. For Grace, that meant making sure that he knew how special he was.

She wished she could do more for his eighteenth birthday. He hadn't wanted much. He'd only asked for movie tickets for him and his friends and money for pizza.

She finally slowed to a stop and took in a deep breath of fresh morning air, and smelled the salt water, almost tasting it, watching her breath form a cloud as she breathed out. Another runner, a tall man with a fast stride, came out of the dunes and onto the beach, passing her. She wondered what Hart did in the mornings. He probably had a girlfriend. *Forget it, Grace*, she thought. Turning on thumping music, she sprinted toward home, deep in her own thoughts.

━━

Hart gathered his gear and followed a worn path in the grass, walking on three-leaf clovers and rich, bark-covered soil. The forest opened to Hidden Lake. The morning sun was shining brilliantly on the glassy water. The lake was surrounded and hidden, like the name, by an old-growth forest of ancient pines standing, draped with moss and mushrooms. A blue heron posed for Hart as two bald eagles circled the lake, looking for breakfast.

Following the narrow path to the left, he didn't go far before he heard Ironpot's family and saw stones skipping across the placid lake.

"Peter! You're scaring the fish!" Ironpot's firm voice carried and Hart followed it around the next bend in the shore. Little giggles echoed, and Hart found himself smiling and wondering why he thought he'd catch anything today.

"Well, well, it's sleepyhead." Ironpot said when he spotted Hart. Three folding canvas chairs, a dutch oven, cooler, and other campstools lined the shore. Karen's round frame lay back with her legs outstretched in one of the chairs next to Ironpot.

Hart caught a whiff of bug repellent and sunscreen as Ironpot's six-year-old son, Peter, bumped into him, heading for Ironpot. Elizabeth, Ironpot's seven-year-old daughter, was trying her luck at climbing a tree that grew over the lake while hanging onto her pink fishing pole.

"Give me a worm, Dad!" said Peter loud enough to ensure the safety of all fish in the vicinity.

"We're not using worms. We're using stinky cheese." Ironpot grunted as he pulled himself upright and got into his tackle box. Peter's Snoopy pole and hook were making Hart nervous every time they came close to Ironpot's face, but Ironpot didn't seem to notice. Hart sat down in the chair next to Ironpot and laid his gear on the ground.

"Morning," he said quietly.

"Want a breakfast burrito?" Karen asked Hart. Before he could answer, she had the lid off the dutch and a tinfoil-wrapped hot tube was placed on a paper towel and she was handing it to him. She opened the cooler and gave him orange juice in a box with a little straw to poke in the hole. He loved Karen. Not only was she was the best cook ever, she was the one woman that gave him hope for marriages everywhere.

Hart sat down the orange juice and peeled open the tinfoil. On the first bite his mouth was filled with sharp cheddar, eggs, sausage, and salsa wrapped in a steamy soft tortilla.

"Ahhh, now that's heaven. Thanks, Karen." He smiled at her and she smiled as she lay back and tried to sleep.

"No cell service up here," Ironpot told him.

"Perfect," Hart whispered. He didn't know this was an ambush and Ironpot wanted to talk religion.

CHAPTER 30

ANGELS

KELLY DIDN'T WANT TO EAT EVER AGAIN AFTER WATCHING Angela chew at the small table in jail. With the teeth she had left, Angela gummed a power bar, food escaping down the front of her.

"You gonna eat that?" Angela asked.

"No, you can have it."

"Thanks."

Angela took Kelly's power bar and started to work on it. "Listen, honey, don't be scared. All of us are here for different reasons, but most of the girls are nice, even Bear. What are you in for?"

Kelly thought maybe she should say murder so everyone would leave her alone, but she decided the truth was bad enough. "I was arrested for hitting my husband."

Angela started to laugh. She threw her head back, mouth full, and let out a cackle that had crumbs flying. She covered her mouth with her hands and said through her fingers, "Listen up, girls, my friend, honey here, beat her old man!"

There were a few cheers and applause. Bear actually smiled.

"I don't think it's funny," Kelly protested. "I was defending myself. He was choking me!" The laughter got louder. Kelly turned her back on Angela.

"Oh, listen now, don't get upset. I'm in for the same thing. Well, sort of."

Kelly turned back toward Angela with her mouth open and an incredulous look on her face.

"Don't look at me like that, miss high and mighty. We ain't so different. My original charge was domestic violence four. And I was defending myself against that . . ." She let off a string of descriptive words. "He had broken my collarbone. See," Angela said as she pulled her striped pajamas over to show Kelly bones that stuck up at a funny angle under her skin. "He broke my leg a few months before." She pulled up her pant leg and showed Kelly a long scar that still showed evidence of being stitched shut. "I think he broke my hand too." She held up a hand that was still swollen, the skin black and blue. The pinky finger had healed at a funny angle to the rest of the fingers. "I'd just had enough. I waited until he was asleep, and I got him across the privates with a bat. The problem was, I was drunk."

Angela went on, "I took his truck. I drove down the mountain and made it as far as the gas station. I got out of jail, but I kept drinking. I lived in a shelter, but couldn't stay because they don't allow drinking; but if I don't drink I have bad dreams and my shoulder hurts. I can't stop drinking, so they keep violating me."

"Violating you?"

"It's a probation violation to drink."

"Oh."

The electronic lock sounded on the door and all the conversations in the room stopped. "Finch, you got a visitor."

"Me?" Kelly said and then looked at Angela to see what to do.

"It's okay, honey. Someone come to see you." She smiled as if someone had just won the lottery. "It's your lucky day."

Kelly was put in cuffs that went from her ankles to her waist and then her wrists. Shuffling in her ankle chains, she followed directions as the deputy moved her through the jail. Finally, he opened a door and pointed.

There was a long narrow room with a glass wall. On Kelly's side were cubicles with phones attached to the sidewall. Matching cubicles were on the other side of the glass in a large open room. There were several guards and prisoners.

Her mother was seated at one phone with her father standing anxiously behind her. She quickly sat across from her mother and picked up the phone.

"Mom, how did you know I needed you?"

"We got a call on caller ID from Oregon. All we could hear were sobs. I knew it was your number. I knew it had to be you. Your brother traced it back to a Necanicum number. I just had this terrible feeling and we had to come."

Her father leaned over and took the phone. "Your mom called me at work. We had everyone in the car in the hour and we came. We didn't even have time to find a sitter for the dog. We should have been here sooner. This never would have happened."

"Daddy," Kelly started to cry. The dam had broken and the flood was threatening to overcome her. She had to have help. *Grace*, she thought. She would have her parents ask Grace for help.

"Kelly, honey, it's going to be okay." Her mother sounded sure. "We're going to try to find a way to pay your bail and get you out of here. We're not leaving without you."

"Mom, there was a woman," Kelly said between big gulping efforts at breathing. "Mom, she can help, I think. She came to the house with the police. Her name is Grace. Call the police. They'll know how to reach her."

Her mother started digging through her purse, looking for paper and a pen. Taking the phone, her father said. "Honey, he took the kids with him. Is he safe with them?"

"He's never hurt the kids."

She could see that her father didn't believe her. "Every time he hurt you he hurt the kids!" he snapped.

She started to cry again. Her mother snatched the phone from her father, giving him an angry look. She put her hand over the receiver. Kelly could see her fiery little mother was lecturing her father, but couldn't hear a word she said. She felt a laugh creep up and over her lip.

"I'm sorry, honey," her mom said. "The last thing you need is a lecture or more to worry about. Now, what was that woman's name?"

———

Kelly shuffled with the guard back to the cell. When she entered Angela beamed. "Hurry," Angela said, "look out the window."

Kelly looked out the window and saw her whole family headed across the parking lot. She saw her dad open the van and the dog try to get out. She savored every move, every moment like a fine dessert.

"Thank you," she grinned at Angela.

"You are so lucky to have family. You look exhausted. Why don't you sleep on your cot and I'll watch over you. You don't need to worry about nothing," Angela offered.

Kelly hugged the bony, smelly woman, grateful for her guardian angel.

———

Mabel was driving her little pickup with its extended cab down Highway 101. Grace was in the passenger seat reading a book. The Beach Boys played on the radio.

"How can you do that without throwing up?" Mabel asked her.

"Huh?" she said without looking up.

"I said," Mabel said loudly, "how can you do that without throwing up?"

"I should have been an astronaut," she answered with a smile.

"You're missing some great scenery."

She sighed deeply and closed the book, giving up. "What are you thinking about?"

"Nothing," Mabel answered. "Isn't it great?"

Grace's phone rang. She turned down the radio and answered it, "This is Grace."

"Grace, this is the answering service. We have a call from a woman that says she has to talk to you. It's an emergency," the dispatcher said.

"Did you try to put her through to the on-call crisis worker?"

"She said it has to be you."

This happened a lot. "Tell her to talk to the on-call worker, and they will call me if they need me. But get her name and number first in case she hangs up and then I'll call her. I might be in a dead zone. I'm on the road to Tillamook."

"Tillamook? Are you going to tour the cheese factory?"

"Nope, we're going cow tipping."

"All right!" Mabel laughed.

Grace gave her a look, hung up, and looked out at the ocean. The Pacific Coast Highway followed the coastline winding in and out, along cliffs, and down near beaches. Today, the sky was blue and the air was unseasonably warm, and rather than playing on the beach, she was going to spend her last dollars on firewood, and the gas to pick it up.

She turned on Van Morrison "Brown Eyed Girl" and rolled down the window, letting the fresh sea air in. Her cell phone rang again. She sighed, "This is Grace."

"Grace, this is Jackie, the on-call crisis line worker, we have a call from a woman named Nancy. She says you worked with her daughter the other day and now her daughter's in jail."

"What's the daughter's name?" Grace began ticking through the filing cabinet in her brain, wondering who it was.

"Kelly Finch."

"Crap! Did she say what happened?"

"No, she wouldn't talk to me. She said her daughter said she had to talk to you. Could you give it a try? I can do the leg work."

"I'll call. Give me the number."

Grace called the number that Jackie had given her. "Hello, this is Grace, you called?" she said to Kelly's mother.

"Hi, I'm Nancy, Kelly Finch's mother."

"Hi, Nancy. How can I help you?"

"They arrested her for assaulting Sam. She didn't do it. I know my girl. She is not violent. She says she was defending herself, and I believe her."

"Kelly was the victim." Grace said assuredly. "I can't talk to you about Kelly's case without a release from Kelly, but I can call the jail and go see her."

"We have to get her out." Nancy sounded desperate.

"Where are the kids?"

"He has them. They went somewhere with him. I am so worried. I just have this feeling, you know?"

"I'll call the jail, promise."

"Thank you. She trusts you. Please help her."

She peeked at Mabel out of one eye and asked, "When we're done in Tillamook, you feel like going to the wholesale grocery store by way of the jail?"

Mabel gave her the knowing look. "Sure, any time with you is a good time. Just a couple of wild single chicks out on the town squeezing melons."

She closed her eyes again. "There's nothing like a Saturday in jail. Besides, it's by the Tug Boater, and they have the best fish-and-chips ever."

"Life is good!"

━━

Ironpot's son, Peter, had several small fish of questionable size in a creel and was looking at them with wonder and awe. Ironpot's daughter, Elizabeth, had finally fallen in the lake and was wrapped in a blanket while Ironpot dug around in the truck for a pair of sweats. Karen, who had just given Hart a diet pop, was rummaging in her cooler. Hart couldn't remember the last time he'd had this much fun. Life was good.

"Wrap?" Karen asked Hart.

"Another one?"

"It's chicken, cheese, and grapes. At church we had a class called '101 Tasty Tortilla Treats or Life's a Wrap.'"

"Ah, that explains it. What's for dinner?"

"Fajitas."

Ironpot came back with an oversized sweatshirt and dressed Elizabeth. He sat down next to Hart and rolled up Elizabeth's sleeves. "Elizabeth is getting baptized next week."

Elizabeth beamed and turned to Hart. "Yes! Mr. Hart, you want to come?"

"Sure, but you better call me Joe. I'm Joe Hart."

"So you coming Mr. Joe?" she asked.

"If it's okay with your dad."

Ironpot had the look of a cat that had a mouse cornered. "Uncle Joe can come. In fact, I brought Uncle Joe a special book to help him get ready for it."

Hart smelled a trap. He knew he should protest, but he was ready to be trapped. He didn't mind one bit. Ironpot pulled out a Book of Mormon and smiled as he handed it to Hart.

Hart took it in both hands and felt something. A memory maybe? He thought, *maybe I just recognize it from before.* But there was something rising in his stomach, traveling though his heart and coming up his throat and threatening to pour with tears from his eyes. It was a powerful, warm feeling. He looked out over the water and just felt it for a minute. The intensity of it surprised him.

Elizabeth started patting his shoulder, interrupting his thoughts, "Uncle Joe, Uncle Joe, I have a book too. Except mine is old. It's not as nice as yours."

Hart knew she was working him over and wanted him to give her the book. "Do you want this one?"

Ironpot stood up. "No! Elizabeth, you'll get a new one . . . someday. This one is for Uncle Joe."

Hart's eyebrows rose and he opened the book. In the front there was a picture of Ironpot in a suit with his one hair slicked over. Standing next to him were Karen and the kids in their Sunday best. Ironpot had written in it.

"Ironpot, you autographed it!" Hart said. "My, what a lovely photo. You look . . . you look . . . like that 1970s leisure suit is a little tight! I'm touched."

"Give me that!" Ironpot reached for the book.

"No, it's a gift!" Hart grinned and put it inside his flannel shirt and buttoned all the buttons, trapping it out of Ironpot's reach.

CHAPTER 31

NEW OLD HABITS

UNCLE JOE HART SMILED AND LAUGHED OUT LOUD AS HE drove off the mountain, bumping all the way home. It was time to go back to church. Thoughts about church had crossed his mind off and on for years, but now it felt right. It occurred to him that he had felt wonderful ever since he'd taken a hold of the book. Smiling, he decided he was going to surprise old Iron britches and go to church tomorrow. He'd have to call someone to find out what time it started. Who could he call? After thinking about it for a minute, a smile spread across his face.

———

Elder Sappenfield felt his cell vibrate in his pocket as he bicycled alongside his companion toward the neighborhood they had decided to tract. He stopped at the side of the road and answered it. "The Mormon missionaries, this is Elder Sappenfield."

"Hi, Elder. My name is Joe Hart. I used to be a member, and I think I might want to come back to church. I wondered if you could tell me what time the meeting is in Necanicum."

"Sure we can." Sappenfield began gesturing thumbs up excitedly at his companion. He pulled a pen and little notebook out of his coat pocket. "The meeting is at ten in the morning. If you would like, we could come by tonight and meet you. Then when you go to the meeting, you would be welcome to sit with us."

"That would be great."

Elder Sappenfield made the touchdown sign, and Elder Oscarson pulled closer to listen into the conversation on the phone as Elder Sappenfield took down Joe Hart's information.

CHAPTER 32

POSSIBILITIES

AMBER AND HER MOTHER HAD CLEANED THE ENTIRE HOUSE, dressed Bjorn, listened to Greta—who was developing an appetite—wish for cereal instead of eggs for breakfast, and were now sitting alone in the kitchen.

"So, now what?" Emily said.

"Now we get to do whatever we want," Amber said, smiling.

"I can't seem to stop worrying. I'm supposed to meet with Grace Monday and solve money problems, but the cupboards are getting low and I'm afraid that I don't have any money."

"Don't you have a credit card?"

"All the accounts or cards were in your dad's name."

"I guess I better go get a job."

"Not yet." Emily sipped her coffee thoughtfully. "I've been thinking. This house was bought in the name of the company or something like that for a write off. I think they may have something to do with his truck and my car too. I know Grandma and Grandpa loaned your dad a big down payment. I'm sure they don't want to lose it in a foreclosure. I think I'm going to call them."

"Then what do we owe them?"

"Oh," Emily said, looking pensive. "I never thought about that. It doesn't matter though. You're their grandkids. Why wouldn't they want to help?"

"Help with a catch," Amber said with conviction.

They sat and watched the clock tick for a minute. Emily got up and went to her room to use the phone.

Amber looked around the house, realizing she had never really thought about how much it costs to take care of a family. All this time she had just wanted her mother to get out. Now Berk was out and they were faced with the very real problem of hunger or having the lights turned off.

Bjorn was in his high chair, gumming baby cookies to death. Drool and cookies were everywhere. Amber began wiping his face and the tray. She almost had it all out of his hair when Emily came down the spiral staircase. Amber stopped moving and stared at her mother. She looked relaxed.

"I was surprised when they said of course they would help. They are going to continue to pay his salary. I'm eventually going to have to figure out how to pay all the bills except the house payment. They will pay that, and they'll also loan us some more money for a while. They will deposit the balance of the money in an account in my name at the credit union on Monday. I can go in and sign the signature card in the afternoon."

"What's the catch, Mom?" Amber asked skeptically.

She deflated. "They think I'm not going to testify against Berk and that I'm going to take him back as soon as I can. They also want visits with you kids every other weekend."

"No! We're not going!"

"You don't have to go, Amber. But, you know your grandparents love you. They wouldn't hurt you!"

"He's there. I'm not going and neither are Greta or Bjorn." Amber pulled Bjorn out of the high chair and balanced him on her hip.

"We don't have a choice. But, he's not there. They say he's in an inpatient treatment facility down here in town somewhere."

"Oh." Amber sat down, bouncing Bjorn on her knee, thinking. "Well . . . then Greta and Bjorn can visit. I'm not."

"That's up to you. Now, back to what are we going to do today. I'm so used to Berk telling me what to do that I don't know what to do with myself."

"Anything you want," Amber said, smiling again.

"I've never thought about it. What do I want?"

<hr>

Grace was back in cell service. She had Hart's personal cell number from a previous call. There were a lot of reasons she wanted to talk to Hart. She felt her color rise.

"Are you okay?" Mabel asked.

"Yes, why?"

"You look like you're having a hot flash." Mabel continued driving but kept glancing her way. A giggle escaped Grace's lips before she could stop it. Her hand flew to her mouth and she covered it, turning her head to the window. She felt ridiculous, like a little girl with a crush. Lately, he kept popping into her thoughts. Grace took a deep breath and tried to gain her composure.

"What is wrong with you?" Mabel asked. Grace continued to dial.

"Nothing."

"You are such a liar!" Mabel laughed.

Grace was breaking a personal rule and calling him while he was off duty. It was a great excuse. *Shame on me*, she thought.

"Hello?" Hart answered.

"Hello, Hart, this is Grace." Mabel snickered and shook her head. Grace turned her whole body to the window and hoped the noisy truck would cover her mother's laughter.

"Oh, hi, Grace. Is everything okay?"

"Fine, I'm fine, it's great. How are you?" She winced.

"Great. You sure you're okay?" he probed.

"I was hoping you could help me." There was a long pause as she held her breath.

"Sure, what can I do you for?"

"You remember Kelly Finch, the verbal from the other day that was more than a verbal?"

"Yes, the cute one."

Great. Grace you are such an idiot. You're too old for him, Grace thought. "Did you know that Olson arrested her last night?"

"What! That . . . ! He is such a . . . I'm sorry, there is no way she's the perp! Olson is . . . well, he's Olson."

"I know, I think I'm going to have to go to the jail to see her."

"Let me know what you think," Hart said sincerely. "I really liked her. She was nice, and I think she was definitely the victim."

"Sure, I'll call you." Grace smiled.

———

Alan Johnson was raking the lawn. Autumn leaves were everywhere. Just as he got his pile of leaves arranged and was going to go for a wheelbarrow, the wind picked up and began blowing all his work onto the front porch. He threw the rake down in disgust.

His father's rusty old pickup truck pulled into the gravel driveway. Alan was surprised. It was Saturday. Every good log truck driver took care of his rig on Saturday. There was no way he was done by now. The truck engine rattled and then was silent, his father sitting in it, not moving.

Something was wrong. It wasn't the wind or the weather that gave Alan a sense of foreboding, it was the forward slope of his father's shoulders. Alan didn't know what to do.

Finally, his father opened the door to the truck. Without looking up or at Alan, he got out of the truck and began walking like his feet were made of lead and the air was as thick as water, passing Alan without acknowledging him.

"Dad?" Alan said softly. No answer.

"Dad, is every . . ." The wooden screen door creaked as it opened and then his father was inside. Alan stood for a moment and then followed his father into the house.

The vacuum was running, but no one was touching it. His mother stood in the middle of the living room staring at his father walking up the stairs. Without turning off the vacuum, she ran after his father. Turning off the vacuum, Alan stood silently. The television was playing cartoons in the family room. He crept up the stairs quietly after his parents and stood silently outside their door.

He heard something he had never heard before. He heard his father cry. He knew it was his father because he could hear his mother comforting him. His heart sank, his knees wanted to give way, and his eyes closed. Worried, he wanted to go in and find out what was happening.

"Mom, Dad?" he asked quietly as he put his hand on the door-knob and softly knocked. His dad's crying paused and his mother's voice stopped. Footsteps approached the door. He stepped back.

Clareen Johnson cracked the door open and slid out. Registering the look on Alan's face, she took him in her arms. "It's all right. Nothing to worry about. Your Dad just lost his job. He'll get another one."

"He's been there all my life! Is this because of me and that guy's son?"

"It's nothing personal. Don't you take it to heart. Mr. Anderson just says that since you're a witness against Berk, your dad can't work there until this is resolved in court."

"It is my fault!"

"No, it's not." Clareen said evenly. "It's Mr. Anderson's. Your dad hasn't been treated right there for years anyway. It's a good time to look for work. Now I've got to take care of your dad. You go down and keep the kids quiet, okay?"

"I'm sorry, Mom."

"Don't you ever say that again. I'm proud of you. You did the right thing."

———

Grace and Mabel pulled up at the Coho County Jail. They parked alongside the curb. Visiting hours were over, but the deputies knew her.

Leaving Mabel in the car, she went to the heavy metal door and pushed the button by a speaker. A voice came out of the intercom system, "How can we help you?"

"I'm Grace from the Family Crisis Center. I'm here to see Kelly Finch. Can I visit her? I hope to have her sign a release form." She held up the form to the camera lens. She knew this would get her into the room the lawyers used to speak to prisoners. It had a slot for passing papers back and forth.

There was a buzz and she pulled on the door as the electro-magnetic lock opened. She entered the waiting area and waited for several minutes.

Finally, Grace heard a series of locks opening, and a deputy led Kelly Finch into the cubicle on the other side of the glass. She looked terrible. She had tiny pinpoint red dots, or petechiae, which Grace knew could be caused by strangulation bursting tiny blood vessels around her eyes. Her shiny hair was tangled. Her beautiful eyes were dull. She looked exhausted. Her bony body swam in the large black-and-white striped suit. She was wearing shackles. At the sight of Grace, tears welled up and spilled out onto her cheeks. Kelly tried to wipe them with her manacled hands. She sat down and they both picked up the telephone handsets to talk.

"Kelly, your mom called me."

"I asked her to."

"You look like it was a long night. I have to warn you before you talk that they will tape our conversation."

"That's okay. I was defending myself. He was choking me."

"I can see that," Grace said, looking at the telltale bruising. Kelly's hand went to her neck. Grace turned the release over and started taking notes on the back. She continued, "Not on your neck, but around your eyes. You have bruising around them. I bet you have it around your ears too. Can you pull your hair back and let me see?"

Kelly pulled her hair away from her right ear. Dark bruising was emerging behind it.

"Kelly, do you have any bruising on your neck or chest?"

"I don't know. Let me look." She pulled the neck to her giant striped shirt down and tried to look down at her chest. She gasped as she saw a dark, almost black line surrounded by a green hue that ran down from behind her neck down onto her chest and back around behind her neck like a giant necklace.

"Sometimes the injuries don't show the first night. Those will get darker. They are just emerging," Grace explained. "Listen, you're going to get a court-appointed attorney if you are arraigned. When they arraign you, they take you to court, read the charges, and ask you how you plead, guilty or not guilty. If you stay in jail, you'll be arraigned soon. I'm not a lawyer, so I can't give you legal advice, but I would really like to call the district attorney and give him an earful. Let me take pictures with my phone."

"Anything. I just want my kids back," Kelly said, still examining the bruising.

"What happened to the kids?"

"He threw divorce papers at me. That's what started this," Kelly looked at Grace with renewed horror on her face as she remembered. "He said he had custody of the kids and he was taking them. Then he went out to steal the little bit of money I had buried in the yard. I tried to stop him, but he choked me. I was hitting him with a rock trying to get him to stop when the police came."

"Who called the police?"

"I don't know. Probably my neighbor. At first I was mad, but now I think it probably saved my life. I felt like I was going to suffocate. I panicked."

Grace said, "Strangulation is the easiest and quickest way to kill someone. You're lucky to be alive. You have the right to defend yourself."

"I shouldn't have hit him, but I didn't know what to do."

"So he has the kids?"

"Yes."

"Do you think that's safe?"

"He'd never hurt them."

"Are you sure?"

"Yes."

"Could you have predicted he would divorce you?"

Kelly looked down. "No."

"Kelly, you could ask Child Welfare to check and help you. I don't think he's a good father. I am pretty sure he's abused you in front of the kids before, hasn't he?"

"Yes. But I try not to let them see," Kelly said softly, feeling ashamed. "Ask anyone to help, even Child Welfare."

"Kelly, you're a good mother," Grace reassured her. "I could tell when I watched you the other day. Let me ask you this though, do you still love him? Do you want him back?"

"I just want my kids to have a dad. But I haven't had any feelings for him for a while. Besides, he says we're divorced."

"Did you sign the papers?"

"No."

"Then it's not final. You have the right to contest it or the custody."

"I don't mind the divorce. I just want my kids," Kelly said, looking directly into Grace's eyes.

Grace knew she meant it. She smiled and said, "Well, first things first. If you will sign this release, I can talk to the district attorney, Child Welfare, and the police. I want to try to get you out of here."

Grace slipped the paper through the slot. Kelly clumsily used the pen attached to the table on the other side to sign the form and initial the places Grace showed her.

"Kelly, how many women are in your cell?"

"I think about nine."

"Good, that means the jail is pretty full. There is a chance you'll get matrixed out."

"What does that mean?"

"It means they can only legally hold so many prisoners in here and then, because the county refuses to build a bigger jail, they have to let someone out."

"I hope I get out. I want to see my family while they're here."

"Where are they staying?"

"At my house."

"I'll add your mom to the release form and have you initial it. I'll keep in touch. Okay?"

"I'll be fine. Some of the girls aren't so bad."

"Tell them hi from Grace."

———

Grace decided that today must be a rule-breaking day as she listening to the district attorney's personal phone ringing. Mabel was eating fish-and-chips at a picnic table while Grace was pacing in the park. Seagulls stood by, waiting for Mabel to drop a crumb.

"Hello?"

"Bill? This is Grace. I am so sorry to bother you on your day off, but I have a client in crisis I need your help with."

"Oh, hi, Grace. Sorry it took me a minute to answer, I was out shoveling poop on my lawn."

"Sorry to interrupt."

"No, I'm grateful," Bill Masterson laughed.

"I've got more poop for you. Yesterday I responded to a domestic in Necanicum. I met a true victim—power, control, the whole bit. This morning, at about four a.m., her husband gave her divorce papers and said he was taking the kids, then went out in the yard to dig up the change she had been collecting and burying. She followed him and they got into a scuffle. He was strangling her when she used a rock to try and make him stop."

"Does she have injuries?"

"Yes, serious strangulation injuries. I can send photos. Although she hasn't had any medical care yet, she probably should have. The thing is, I don't think her injuries were visible last night. So officers arrested her. But she was defending herself."

"Who was the officer?"

"Olson."

There was a long pause on the line and then the district attorney said, "I see. Who was over at the verbal?"

"Hart and Ironpot. Hart knows she's a victim and he's the perp."

"I believe you. You know your stuff. What kind of injuries did the male have?"

"She said his face was cut and bruised from the rock she was hitting him with while he strangled her. I didn't see him."

"Do you think his injuries are worse than hers?"

"I don't know about that. I just know my client looks terrible and needs medical attention. Also, if she is put on a no-contact order with her children it will be detrimental to them."

"Did they witness?"

"She says they didn't."

"I'm coming into town to do paperwork. I'll come by the jail and review the charging instrument. If I feel the case is weak, I'll decline to prosecute and she can leave. If she has to stay, I'll get a nurse to look at her. Either way, I'll have them photograph and document her injuries."

"Thanks, Bill. You're the best. I owe you."

"No you don't. This is better than the county being sued for a poorly handled case or a prisoner dying in jail from her injuries."

Grace sat down to cold, greasy fish-and-chips.

CHAPTER 33

UNEXPECTED GRACE

KELLY SLEPT ON THE COT. SHE WAS AMAZED. AT FIRST SHE had kept opening her eyes and looking up to see Angela watching over her, then finally she had given in and slept. She slept soundly and deeply. Waking up, she actually felt refreshed.

"How long was I out?" she asked Angela.

"Just a few hours," Angela replied.

"Thank you, Angela."

The electronic lock sounded and Kelly looked up to see the jail matron at the door.

"Finch!" the matron called.

"Yes?"

"You're going home."

She couldn't believe it. She jumped up and started for the door. She turned and looked at Angela, beaming.

"Good luck, honey!" Angela called as if she were sending her off on a cruise ship, waving her hands and smiling.

Kelly went back and once again gave the small woman a hug. "Good luck to you, Angela. Thank you for helping me."

"No contact with Mr. Finch," the matron said. "You can be charged with tampering with a witness."

"So can the court attorney decide to charge me later?"

"He could. If you try to assault Mr. Finch again, he could tack these charges on as well, but I can't give you legal advice, so you should go see a lawyer."

Kelly smiled as she dressed. Then it occurred to her that she didn't have a way to get back to Necanicum. "Can I make a phone call for a ride?"

"Sure."

"I don't know the number. I need to call my mom. I don't know her cell number. Her house number is long distance."

"I can't help you there. Local calls only, unless you call collect."

Kelly walked out of the small room and over to the booking phone. She thought for a moment. "Do you have the number to Grace at the Family Crisis Center?"

"Yes."

The matron gave her the number and she called it.

"Hello, Grace?" Kelly said hopefully.

"Yes, is this Kelly?"

"Yes, they're letting me go!"

"They're not going to prosecute you, or are you being let out because of overcrowding?" Grace asked.

"They said they're declining to prosecute."

"That's great!"

"I'm trying to reach someone for a ride home."

"I have your mom's cell number. Would you like me to call her?"

"Could you?"

"Sure, I'll call you back."

———

Grace let Kelly know her family was picking her up. Kelly was let outside the jail. She didn't have a coat. It was cold and crisp and the sun was setting.

One by one the streetlights came on and then the family van pulled up. Kelly's parents and her entire family poured out and surrounded her, hugging and holding her. Only two small things were missing, Sam Jr. and Hazel.

Kelly turned to her mother and asked, "Mom, have you seen the kids?"

"No. Sam said we could stay at the house, but he took the kids with him."

"I have to call him and see if I can see the kids, but I don't want to have contact with him. They said I shouldn't."

Kelly's dad offered, "I'll call him, Kelly. I'll explain that we're in town for just a short time and want to visit the kids."

"Thanks, Dad."

"Let's get in the van first and get warm," her mother said, putting her arm around Kelly's shivering shoulders. They all got in and her father started the motor to let the heat run. He took out his cell phone and got Sam's number from Kelly. He dialed the number.

"Hello?" Sam said.

"Hello, Sam, this is Kelly's father, Jack." The line was silent. "Listen, Sam, we are only in town for a few days and we would sure like to see the kids." Kelly leaned into her father and listened.

"I don't know, Jack," Sam said.

"Kelly is with us, and she would also like to see the kids. It would be good for them."

"The kids are fine, Jack."

Jack waited. He let the silence work for him. Finally Sam spoke, "All right. I guess, if you pick them up. And I want them back here by seven on Sunday. If Kelly reads the divorce papers, it will tell her when visitation happens and how. This can be her first weekend. You can pick the kids up at my girlfriend's."

Kelly felt the word *girlfriend* go through her like a hot poker. She didn't know why it bothered her. After the papers in her face and jail she shouldn't have any feeling for him, and yet it hurt. Why did it hurt?

Her father took the directions for the house. It was a new subdivision on the east side of Bay Town, across the highway from the Camp Richmond area. She felt again like her whole world had been built on lies. The foundation had definitely cracked. Everything she had believed was untrue. Even though knowing the truth explained a lot about her life with Sam, it left even more unanswered questions.

An affair explained the late nights away, the long phone calls, and the constant texting and online time, but it didn't explain why he had still tried to control her and keep her under his thumb. Why would he want the children? He never played with them. They were more like property than people he cared about.

She tried to make sense of it all as her father pulled away from the jail and the van drove south on Highway 101.

She began to emerge from her fog as they turned off the highway onto Parker Road and then followed it around twists and turns, taking the first right they could. Then on the left a long driveway pulled up and off the main road. A brick mailbox marked it. Kelly could see the house from the road at the end of the gradual rise and next to the circular driveway. The house was huge. It had a main portion in an A-frame shape with windows covering the west end of it. Two wings went north and south off of the house, both two stories tall. Lights shone from every window. There was a fountain in the middle of the circular driveway with statues of two full-size horses on their hind legs in spraying water. A full-sized red-and-white barn was also on the property, facing south. It was clean and tidy looking. A pristine red Humvee and Jeep CJ-7 were parked in front of the house next to her husband's truck. The house and cars made Sam's beautiful truck look old and small.

Now Kelly understood why Sam would treat her the way he had. A tall, very thin blonde dressed in tight jeans and riding boots brought out little Sam and Hazel.

Little Sam saw his mom and lit up like Christmas morning. Hazel only clung tighter to the blonde. When Kelly reached for her she pulled back. The blonde looked down her nose at Kelly and finally pried Hazel off.

"I'm Sabrina. You must be Kelly."

Kelly just looked at her. It was too much to take in. Robotically, she took Hazel, who started to cry, from Sabrina and pulled little Sam in the van.

The woman asked her another question, but Kelly didn't take it in. "What?" Kelly asked.

"Do you want their car seats?"

"Oh. Yes."

Finally the kids were buckled in and her father was driving the van down the driveway. "She's a looker," her brother said and then ducked as Nancy took a swing at him.

"Joseph!" Nancy said and then looked at Kelly with tender eyes.

"Don't look at me like that, Mom. It's no wonder he left me. I can't compete with that."

"Kelly Anne Robinson Finch, how dare you compare yourself to that home-wrecker!" Her mother gave her a stern look.

The absurdity of the words *home-wrecker* tickled something in Kelly and she let out an inappropriate giggle.

"I'm sure Sam had something to do with it, Mom."

"Mom, Kelly," Joseph, her brother, interrupted, looking out the back window of the van at the house receding behind them. "Who's that?"

Another tall blonde had come out of the house and was standing next to Sabrina. She looked like a younger, prettier version of the woman.

"I don't know," Kelly answered softly, confused. "She must have a daughter. They look alike."

"Well you pay them no mind," her mother said as she brushed imaginary crumbs from her lap. "Just brush them off. Now, how are my grandkids! Who wants to go for ice cream?"

CHAPTER 34

SIBLINGS

KELLY HAD TAKEN A LONG, HOT BATH AND PUT ON FRESH, clean pajamas. The kids were asleep and everyone was sitting quietly in the family room discussing what the next step should be when Kelly called the crisis line again.

The crisis worker came on the line. "I'm sorry, Grace is off duty right now, but if this is Kelly, she said to have you come into the office first thing Monday morning."

"Okay. Can I have the address again?"

Kelly wrote down the address and then turned to her family who sat watching her. "Grace is not in so I guess I'm on my own until Monday," she announced, smiling nervously.

"Then let's make the best of our visit with the kids and we'll work on it again on Monday," her mother said, stretching and yawning.

"Don't you all have to get back home?"

"Honey." Her dad walked over to her and put his arms around her. "Nothing is more important than you right now. Everything else can wait."

Kelly's brothers started laughing. It was so out of place in the somber little home that she and her parents stopped and stared.

"What's so funny?" her mother asked.

"We've decided that we should invite Sam to have some Mormon punch," Joel said, sending Joseph into a fit of laughter.

"Maybe he needs to be 'blessed by a laying on of hands,'" Joseph offered, sending Joel into a laughing and snorting fit. The snorting started Kelly laughing.

"Shh, the kids will hear," she said. "He is their father."

"Sorry, we just thought he might need to 'choose the right' and I could show him an 'iron rod,'" Joel said.

"Yeah," Joseph said. "WWPRD."

"What?" Kelly asked.

"What Would Porter Rockwell Do?"

Kelly's mother interrupted, "All right, you goofballs, remember to pray for your enemies . . ."

"I'm praying for him all right!" Joel smirked.

"Come on, you know what I mean."

The jokes got worse, the laughter getting louder until one by one they giggled their way out of the room and found a place to sleep.

CHAPTER 35

DAY OF REST

"I LOVE SUNDAY," GRACE SAID OUT LOUD TO NO ONE. SHE stretched in the luxury of clean sheets and rolled over to check the clock and then sat up quickly. "Oh no! It's eight thirty! I can't believe it. We're going to be late again. Esther, Mary! Are you up?"

Grace put on her robe and opened Mary's door. "Time to get up! It's eight thirty." A whiff of dirty socks assaulted her. *Something has definitely passed the expiration date in here*, Grace thought. Mary's bed was empty. Padding down the stairs, Grace headed for the kitchen.

Mary was at the table in the large country kitchen wearing a leather flight hat and goggles while eating cereal. Someone was on FaceTime laughing while Mary talked with her mouth full.

"Mary, it's too early to be calling people."

"No worries, Mom. It's my friend from school, Emerson."

"Hi, Emerson." Grace leaned over so she could see the screen and waved.

"Hi, Mom," the phone said back.

Grace was just about to pour herself a bowl of cereal when she heard someone pounding on the bathroom door upstairs. It was Esther.

"Nephi, get out! Mom!"

———

Kelly woke to the smell of sausage, or was it bacon? Wondering, she went to the kitchen to find her mother cooking a huge breakfast. She couldn't remember the last time she had been hungry. Her stomach rumbled. She heard the kids laughing. Laughing? It was a wonderful sound.

Her father was teasing little Sam and Hazel. They would run up to him and he would clap his hands in their faces, telling them he was going to get them. But he never got up to chase them. Screaming and giggling, they would run away and then come back for more.

Heaven, Kelly thought, *this must be what heaven is.* A lump rose in her throat as she realized that once she had thought this was stupid and had been glad to run away. Now she knew. All this—this was exactly what she wanted.

Her mother was flipping pancakes. Looking up, she smiled at Kelly. "Hi, honey." Reaching out, she pulled Kelly into a hug. "You better eat and get going. Church starts at ten."

Church? Kelly hadn't been to church since they lived in Necanicum. Sam wouldn't want her to go to church. And then it occurred to her. Who cared what Sam wanted? Surprised, she realized, she could do whatever she wanted. Did she want to go to church? Yes! And she wanted to pray out loud and in front of everyone.

"Mom, let's have a prayer over the food. I'll say it."

———

Joe Hart had thought church was a great idea, but now that the sun had risen on a perfect day at the beach, and he actually had to get out of bed and go, his feet felt awfully cold. He rolled onto his back, put his hands behind his head, and stared at the ceiling.

The cabinets in the master bathroom weren't finished yet. He had a laundry list of things to do and shopping that he hadn't done yet this week. Maybe he was jumping the gun. Three hours was a long time to spend sitting when he had so many important things to do.

———

Berk Anderson woke up on the cold tile floor next to the toilet in the detox center. He had been throwing up for what felt like forever. Every nerve in his body was raw and all he could think about was how to get out of here and get a beer. That little . . . Amber. She had done this to him. It was all her fault. He wouldn't be here if she had just done what he said.

After all, he was a man. The room began to spin and bile rose in his throat again. His hands shook uncontrollably as he pulled himself up to sit on the seat and laid his face on the cold porcelain sink. Dry heaving, he thought about how he'd be at home with his beer and Sunday sports right now if it hadn't been for Amber. Emily was so weak. She'd probably already found another man, a sugar daddy, to pay her bills. He could just see her now, sitting in the bar, looking for Mr. Gotbucks to replace him. That little tramp.

———

Amber pulled the picnic basket out of the Explorer. The air was cool and crisp. The beach was almost empty. They'd had their pick of spots. Her mother had driven the car skillfully down onto the beach near Fort Stevens, a well-known campground that ran along the ocean. She could see the wreck of the Peter Iredale, or what was left of it, not far north. "Mom, you're right. It's a perfect day for this. It's a little cool, but the view is great, and I'm going to build the best fire ever."

"Come on, Amber, I can see five whole sand dollars from here!" Her mother laughed like a girl. Beaming, she gave Amber and Greta bread sacks to feed the seagulls and then hoisted Bjorn onto her hip. The tide was out, the sun was shining, and her eyes were bright as she turned and walked toward the water. It was going to be a perfect day.

Alan set up the sacrament table on autopilot with the teachers and then took his place, ready to bless it. Esther came in early to sit on the stand for her talk. Alan ignored her. His whole world felt gray. Repeatedly glancing his way, Esther finally got up and walked over to the table. The chapel was still relatively empty. People were just now filing in, and the bishopric wasn't entirely seated yet.

"Alan," Esther whispered. "What is wrong with you?"

"Nothing."

"Liar." She looked sternly into his eyes, challenging him.

He let out air like a leaky tire and looked down. "Look, I don't want to talk about it."

She just stood and stared. Alan looked around frantically. "Esther, go sit down."

She just stood there.

"Esther!"

"Fine. Don't you leave after sacrament. We're talking."

"Fine!" Exasperated, he glared at her.

CHAPTER 36

RISKS

JOE HART HAD SAT IN THE PARKING LOT FOR FIFTEEN minutes. Finally, he decided the meeting must be starting and he could just slip in the back. Getting out of his SUV, he headed for the doors to the Necanicum chapel. It was a small neat and tidy building. The parking lot was full. He had seen many families and even a few single people go in. Following the sidewalk, he went around to what he thought was the back door; it was locked.

He had to go in the front. As he entered, he saw Grace from the Family Crisis Center sitting on the back row. Smiling, she stood up to meet him and threw her arms around him and said, "Hey! Wow! Nice to see you!"

"Grace, I've come to join the club. Where's my decoder ring?"

"You want to wear my CTR ring? You just made my day."

Hart smiled shyly. Ironpot walked up to Hart and gave him a man hug. Standing side by side with Hart, he put his arm around his shoulder, gave him a quick man shake and slap on the back and moved on.

Grace said, "Hart, this is my Mabel. I mean my mom, Mabel" They shook hands. Grace was still grinning when a woman approached her and hugged her, the woman's back to Hart. Grace's expression went from confused to surprised and then back to smiling. Hart couldn't tell who it was, except that she had beautiful dark hair and a pretty figure. When they stopped hugging, Grace said, "Kelly! Welcome to the Necanicum Ward."

"Kelly?" Hart said.

Kelly Finch turned around and Hart felt goose bumps rise on his arms and the hair rise on his neck. She was stunning.

"Officer Hart?" she said.

"Ah, ah, no business at church. You're going to have to call him, Brother Hart," Grace said. "So are you going to introduce us to your gang?"

Kelly turned around and saw her family smiling expectantly, and the happy reunion continued.

———

"So, I have a testimony of tithing," Esther said to the congregation as she finished her talk. Alan wondered if paying his tithing would help his family. What if his dad didn't pay tithing? Would they still be blessed?

"And," Esther went on, "I want my family to know how much I love them. Nephi is the best uncle ever." Beginning to cry, she wiped her eyes and continued. "I hope that I am a good example for Mary, who is like my best friend."

Grace sat with her mouth open. She looked at Mabel who had bowed her head and had her face covered with her hands. *She's laughing*, Grace thought. She looked back at Esther. Who knew she felt that way? She seemed sincere. If only she acted like that when vying for the bathroom.

What a morning, Grace thought. Casually, she turned to see Hart looking at Kelly.

———

People gathered in the chapel for Sunday School. Kelly sat quietly. The size of the crowd made her nervous. She hadn't been out of the house and with people for a long time. They all seemed so comfortable, chatting and visiting with each other. Kelly's hands started to sweat. She looked down at them when someone sat next to her. Out of the corner of her eye, she saw Hart smiling at her, and relief flooded through her body. She found herself smiling back. He smelled so good.

Like her, he looked around the room, the he leaned toward her and whispered, "I'm almost embarrassed to have this loaner Book of Mormon."

Kelly smiled sheepishly, leaned down, and pulled her tattered copy out of her purse and sheepishly showed it to him. Hart remembered her Book of Mormon, and where he had seen it the first time. His eyes softened. He reached over, gave her free hand a quick squeeze, and whispered, "Yours is . . . priceless."

After the meeting was over, Alan, with his head down, started to leave the chapel. He wasn't fast enough. Esther had him by the shoulder. "Alan, what is going on? You look like someone ate your birthday cake."

Sighing, he shifted his weight from one foot to the other. He looked at her long and hard. "Esther, promise not to tell anyone?"

"Of course."

"My dad got fired because of what I did to his boss's son. You know the guy who was beating up Amber, Amber's dad?"

"Alan! No! You have to tell someone. What about Brother White?"

"Esther! You promised." But Esther was already pulling him by the hand through the crowd toward Brother White who had his back turned to them.

"Brother White! Brother White!" Esther called.

When they got to Brother White, Alan finally yanked his hand free and said, "Esther! You promised!"

"Don't be stupid, Alan. Tell him."

Brother White turned toward Alan. Alan felt responsible. He was sure it was his fault that his father lost his job. Esther nudged him. "Go on. Tell him, Alan." He gave Esther a sharp look.

"All right, Esther," Brother White said. "Cut him some slack. Come on, Alan, let's go out in the hall where it's quiet." Brother

White opened a door to the hall and Alan went through. Esther followed. Standing with her arms folded, she looked down her nose at him. Alan sighed again. "Well, you remember that guy that was beating up Amber, Amber's dad, Berk Anderson?"

"Yes?" Brother White said expectantly.

"Well, his dad was my dad's boss."

"Oh." Brother White said, as the pieces began to fall dreadfully into place.

"He fired my dad yesterday, saying it was a conflict of interest for my dad to work for him when I was a witness against his son."

Brother White closed his eyes, put one hand on Alan's shoulder, and rubbed his face and head vigorously with the other as if he were wishing to erase everything Alan had just said.

Brother White looked at Alan for a minute. The wheels in his mind were obviously turning. Patting Alan's shoulder, he said, "Alan, don't worry." He walked away and left Alan wondering just how was he supposed to stop worrying.

———

After Sunday School, Grace wandered the halls, wondering if Hart was still in the building.

"Sister James?" a woman asked behind Grace. Grace turned to see Kelly's mother's concerned face.

"Yes," Grace answered guardedly.

"I just wanted to thank you for helping Kelly. I am glad you're here for her."

"I am happy to be of any assistance I can be," Grace smiled sincerely, "but if you don't mind, can we wait to talk until Monday? I need to make sure Kelly is with us when we talk, you know?" Grace searched her face for understanding. "I have to be careful not to breach her confidentiality or break her trust."

Kelly's mother looked embarrassed. "Oh. I'm sorry, of course. You're not at work."

"Please know I want to help Kelly. Can you come see me Monday?"

"Sure," she said and smiled. "I'll be seeing you Monday." Watching her walk away, Grace felt terrible. She wanted to stop the world and get off.

CHAPTER 37

ENTITLED

BERK ANDERSON REACHED FOR THE SODA POP ON THE table in his room at the New World Detox and Rehabilitation Center. Hands shaking, he knocked it to the floor. He swore. Laughter floated down the hall and scratched his remaining nerves. He swore some more. Visitors met with patients in the group room and family rooms.

Berk wasn't allowed visitors yet. It was like being back in Juvenile, having some idiot in a uniform telling him what to do. His anger rose and fell, but never left him. All he could think about was drinking. His hands shook, making him clumsy and unable to do the simplest of things like hold a glass of water.

A man and woman walked across the back lawn below his window holding hands. He wondered whose hands Emily was holding.

He could walk out of here any time he wanted to. There weren't any bars on the windows, and then he would show her.

━━

Kelly's mother pulled a roast turkey breast from the oven. Mashed potatoes, green beans, dinner rolls, and Jell-O salad decorated the table. *My mother is amazing*, she thought as she took in the smell.

She carefully set the table, while watching little Sam and Hazel play with their uncles on the floor.

The giggles were out of control. The boys were on their hands and knees making whinnying and neighing sounds while the kids rode them. It was a rodeo of laughter.

This was the way life was supposed to be. She felt it in every fiber of her being. And yet, while peace reigned all around her, the clock ticked on and she felt seven o'clock coming like a black cloud of oppressive horror. Seven o'clock and it was time to return the children to Sam.

Later, Kelly loaded the children into her parents' van. Lovingly, she had packed overnight bags for the children and written out directions on how to care for them. Holding both their hands, she sat stoically while her parents drove the little family to their father's new home.

Kelly felt a new pain wrap around her heart. She wondered if it would become a permanent part of her body. It kept her from being hungry and kept her awake at night. Now, it made it hard to smile, but she wanted little Sam and Hazel to see her face smiling before they left her.

———

Kelly's father pulled up the gravel drive and into the circular turn around. He stopped in front of the front door. He turned silently to look at Kelly. She didn't move. He got out of the van and knocked on the front door of the large home.

A blonde teenage girl opened the door sullenly. Without saying anything to Kelly's father, she turned around and yelled back into the house, "Mom, they're back."

Kelly mechanically unbuckled the kids. Sam appeared at the door in jeans with an opened shirt. Sabrina was in sweats but still looked beautiful. Striding to the van, Sam took Hazel in his arms and little Sam by the hand. Turning, he began walking toward the front door. Without talking to her, Kelly mechanically gave Sabrina the children's small bags.

As Sam got to the door of the house, Kelly could see Hazel's face suddenly realize that Kelly wasn't coming. She twisted in Sam's arms and reached out to Kelly, her little chubby hands opening and closing as she began to scream. Red-faced, with water running from her eyes, Hazel wailed as Sam went into the house. Little Sam looked over his shoulder at his mother, hung onto his father's hands, and toddled into the house.

―――

"Mom?" Grace said to Mabel, who was asleep facedown on the couch. A movie was playing on the television. Nephi and Esther were watching the movie and eating popcorn. Grace put her book down and listened to Mabel snore.

"Mom," she whispered and poked her. "Are you asleep?"

She rolled on her side and wiped the drool off her chin. "No."

"Mom."

"Yeah."

"I think I have a problem."

She tried to sit up unsuccessfully and then rolled on her back and rubbed her face. "What's wrong?"

"I'm not supposed to talk to people I work with about religion, unless they bring it up. We are also not supposed to work with friends, and we have to keep healthy boundaries between home and work. Our policy is to pass a client to another case manager if we are friends with our clients or see them outside work. I should refer one of my clients to another advocate, because I think we will be seeing each other a lot at church. I worry about upsetting her by referring her to someone else. I think it will bother her. She trusts someone for the first time. I don't want to rock the boat. You know?"

Grace could tell Mabel had no idea. "Yes."

"Oh well. I'll worry about it Monday." Grace sat back and opened her book again. Mabel lay down on her face again.

CHAPTER 38

TENDER MERCIES

HART NOTICED IT WAS STAYING DARK LONGER. THE MORNING air was crisp and damp. He walked across the parking lot next to the small police station, head down in the light drizzle. Gravel crunched as Ironpot pulled in, but Hart didn't look up. He knew what was coming. The car door slammed.

"Hey, Mormon boy!" Ironpot called out.

Hart didn't answer him. With one eyebrow raised, he looked sideways at Ironpot who trotted to catch up to him.

"Glad to see you chose the right. I brought you a sticker," Ironpot said laughingly as he stuck a sticker on Hart's chest. Hart peeled the sticker off and read it out loud.

"'I was good in Primary'?" Hart shoved Ironpot and laughed. "Yeah, laugh it up, old man. That was some suit. Did you buy that in 1979 or was it '78? Were those polyester pants?"

"Mr. Mac's for my mission. Still going strong too."

"Doesn't your wife love you?"

"She tried to donate it, but I went down and made the place give it back. You can throw that suit on the floor, pick it up, and the wrinkles fall right out. Swedish knit wears like iron."

"It looks like you leave it on the floor a lot."

"Smart aleck."

"What'd you think of Kelly Finch and her family?" Hart asked.

185

"I think she's still married."

━━

Alan's father was already out in the shop when Alan left early Monday morning. Mr. Johnson had been working in the shop since Saturday night almost nonstop. Alan's mother had taken food out to him, but it sat uneaten on the shop bench. This morning she had decided it was time to take action.

"Mr. Wilson Johnson! You eat these eggs! We are not wasting any more food." Clareen held a plate of cold eggs and ham underneath Mr. Johnson's nose. He turned off the lathe he was working on and took the plate.

"Enough is enough, Wilson. You need to take care of yourself."

"Mmm," he said, while giving the food a disgusted look.

"Wilson." She stood firm, hands on hips, waiting.

He took the fork and poked at the cold eggs. Then he took a bite of the ham.

Both the Johnsons heard tires on the gravel driveway and looked toward the shop door. Clareen wiped her hands on her apron and Wilson Johnson gladly put down his cold eggs as they looked through the open shop door at a new expensive extended-cab truck with "Swedish Construction" printed on the doors. The truck driver's side door opened and a round balding man wearing a cowboy hat and aviator glasses got out. He stood for a minute in the driveway and looked around the yard at the home's hand-made, wooden, Victorian gingerbread trim and the long front porch with its wooden furniture and trim. Then he walked toward the Johnsons in the shop.

He held out his hand and Wilson took it. "You Wilson Johnson?" the man asked.

"Yes."

"I'm Brother Richton. Brother White called me. I go to church with Alan."

"I see."

"You do all that?" He pointed out at the yard.

"Yep."

"This your shop?"

"Yes."

"Do anything else?"

"Why yes, he does," Clareen cut in. Briskly, she shook Brother Richton's hand. "I'm Clareen Johnson, Mr. Richton. My husband, Wilson, is the finest carpenter there is. If you'll follow me, I'll show you some of his work. Now keep in mind, we have a lot of kids and they've done some damage to his work, but the work is fine." Clareen whisked the silent Brother Richton into her home and spent the next hour showing him every single piece of work Mr. Johnson had ever done.

When Clareen finally ran out of things to show him, she took him out to the shop where Mr. Johnson was quietly working on the lathe again. She tapped him on the shoulder and he turned off the lathe, removed his safety goggles, and turned to look at Brother Richton, who was beaming.

Brother Richton's smile would have wrapped around his head if his ears had not gotten in the way. "Mr. Johnson, I've been looking for a finish carpenter and a cabinet maker. I've got more work than I can keep up with. I'd like to offer you a job."

"Really?"

"But I don't pay much to start. If you're fast enough, I'll raise your wage to thirty an hour quick. But first I've got to see you work. So, if you're interested, you could start tomorrow."

"Mmm, I guess I could."

CHAPTER 39

PAPERS AND PROMISES

GRACE SAT AT HER DESK, SURROUNDED BY FILES AND HALF-finished projects. She had someone in the overstuffed chair waiting for her while she finished talking to someone who had called to ask how to find money for prescriptions. The client in her chair was working quietly on a restraining order.

"So," Grace said, "let's see how you're doing." She held her hand out, and the fifty-year-old woman gave her the paperwork.

"Do you think the judge will believe me?" the woman, Marta, asked.

Grace looked at her. The client was impeccably dressed in plain clothes with a no-nonsense haircut and glasses. Fidgeting nervously, she seemed to have a permanent look of worry worn into her face. Grace smiled at her in an attempt to put her at ease.

Marta composed herself as Grace read. Finally Grace finished.

"Marta, this is great. I can tell you teach school," she said, smiling. Marta smiled back. "I'm going to get our favorite volunteer Joanne to take you over to the courthouse to file this. It should be heard today after lunch. After it's filed, I need you to come back and we'll make a really solid safety plan. Okay?"

Marta nodded and Grace got up and went to the reception desk in the front of the office.

Joanne was sitting at her desk holding Bjorn. Emily was seated across from her on the couch holding a cup of coffee and laughing at something Joanne was saying. Bjorn looked at Joanne's face with fascination. Joanne bounced him and patted him on the back.

"And so my three-year-old granddaughter put her hands in the air, and said the mess was 'beautiful chaos.'" Joanne said, demonstrating and laughing at the same time. Emily and Joanne laughed heartily, and Grace marveled at Emily's changed mood.

"Emily! You look great!" Grace said.

"I had a great weekend. Amber and I did whatever we wanted, whenever we wanted. It was great!"

"Wow! I don't even get to do that."

"It's a first for us."

Grace introduced Marta to Joanne and took Emily back to her office.

CHAPTER 40

BIGGER PLANS

AMBER SAW ALAN COMING TOWARD HER IN THE HALL DURING a break between classes. Something was wrong with him. She could tell by just looking at him. He wasn't talking to anyone, his head was down, and he walked like a zombie. She stopped, clutching her usual stack of books and waited for him to get to her.

"Alan?" Amber said. He didn't seem to hear her. He was deep in his own thoughts. Turning, she watched as he passed her and then saw Esther coming his way.

Esther called to him, "Alan!" He didn't look up at her either. Esther was not to be ignored. She grabbed his arm. Slowly, he looked up vacantly.

"Oh, hi, Esther."

"Are you coming to lunch with us?"

"No, I'm going home. I want to check on Dad."

Esther let Alan's arm drop, looking at him with worry on her face. "You want to come over for family home evening?" Esther asked him.

"No thanks. The missionaries were supposed to come to my house. But I think I'm going to cancel. Dad isn't in the mood."

Amber wanted to go over and ask just what was going on. But she had spent years trying to be invisible, and today she was too afraid to emerge. Pulling her hood over her head, she walked to class.

———

"That sounds like a solid plan," Grace said. "Your in-laws pay while they are able. You apply for benefits from the state, apply for jobs, and apply for energy assistance and the rest of the list so that when they stop you're covered."

"I also need formula and diapers."

"I'll call WIC. That stands for Women, Infants, and Children. It's a program that supplies mothers with formula and nutritional guidance as well as food. It's a great program. The local Crisis Nursery not only does crisis day care for court and things, but they also have a diaper and baby store. You can take one parenting class and get a pass to their store once a month. I have some diapers I can load you up with too."

"You know, I've never had a real job."

"Well, you have a couple of options. We have an agency in town that helps with résumés and job training, like for medical reception work. Or, we also have a program at the local college for housewives that are at moments of change in their lives. It's called Changing Places. It is supposed to help you choose a direction and get enrolled in college."

"I'd like to do a medical reception job." Emily smiled. "Thanks, Grace. I feel like maybe we can make it."

"It's not going to be easy. All these referrals mean you have to ask for help."

"That's the hardest part."

"I know. But people have to stick together and work together. This community is full of people who have been in situations similar to yours who now volunteer and give back daily. Someday it will be your turn to give back. Now it's your turn to graciously receive."

Emily nodded. Bjorn reached up and grabbed a handful of hair and began pulling.

———

Kelly and her mother stood on her front porch and waved goodbye as the rest of her family left for Utah. Both women had a sense of melancholy, tears cresting in their eyes. Kelly's mother put her arm around Kelly, and Kelly leaned into her mother. When the van was finally out of sight, they turned and went into the house.

Kelly was still surprised at how different the house felt. It was brighter. All the curtains were open and the smell of homemade muffins still hung in the air. It had a different spirit with her mother here. But it was so empty without the kids. She heard so many noises she had never noticed before. Even now, the clock ticked, reminding her that time was passing—passing without little Sam and Hazel.

"I guess we better find you a lawyer," her mother said.

"I think I'd like to call Grace first."

"Okay. I have her number in my cell phone."

Kelly went into the kitchen and dialed the number her mother read her.

"Family Crisis Center. This is Karen, can I help you?"

"This is Kelly Finch. I'm calling for Grace."

"Grace is in with a client." Kelly felt a stab of disappointment and the usual anxiety rise. "But she's expecting you. Let me see if she can break away for a minute."

Kelly felt better. After knowing Grace for just a short time, she had quickly become a lifeline to sanity.

"Kelly?"

"Hi, Grace."

"Kelly, we need to meet. Can you come up after lunch at about one?"

"Sure. How do I get there?" With a sense of relief, Kelly took directions to Grace's office.

———

Amber had taken her lunch off the tray and carried it outside to the back door of the gym. A bench was bolted to the cement by the doors. It was cool and breezy outside, but the bench was in a protected area.

Two seagulls landed in the parking lot and began inching their way toward her. She tried eating the two fish sticks she had wrapped in a napkin. They were limp, cold, and nasty. Disgusted, she thought about throwing them to the birds, but she was too hungry. She put the fish sticks down and tried opening her milk.

The milk carton opened, but her icy hands slipped on the waxed cardboard and she spilled milk on her hoodie. Irritated, she put the milk down and was brushing milk off her clothes when she saw Alan's Jeep pulling into the parking lot.

"Great," Amber said out loud. She already couldn't get him off her mind. He probably thought she was a real geek; and here she was with spilled milk and broken fish sticks, hiding behind the gym. Embarrassed, she decided to make her escape.

Amber took the milk to the garbage can next to the gym door and threw it away. When she turned around to head back to the bench to get her books, she saw two seagulls perched on her books fighting over her fish sticks.

"Crap! Shoo, shoo!" she said as she ran back to her books. The birds lifted off and flew away. But not before depositing a gift of bird poop on her English book.

"Amber!" Alan called from the parking lot.

Now what, Amber thought as she went back to the garbage can to fish out a napkin. She looked warily at Alan. For so many years everything had always been her fault. Now, for some reason, she was sure that Alan's foul mood was her fault.

Alan was smiling and waving with both arms. He started running in her direction. With her mouth open, Amber froze, astonished by the change in his demeanor.

She hadn't made it two steps in his direction before he had her by the shoulders, hugging her, arms pinned to her sides, her eyes wide opened in shock.

"Amber, you're never going to guess what happened! Today is the greatest, the best!"

"I . . ."

"My dad got a new job!"

"He . . ."

"Yeah, he got fired because of me hitting your dad and the assault and everything, but Brother Richton saw him, and now he's got the job of his dreams!"

"Fired?"

"Isn't it great? I am so glad! If your dad hadn't hit you, and I hadn't been there, my dad would still be driving a log truck; now he gets to be a carpenter and build cabinets and do everything he's always wanted to for more money!"

"That's . . ."

"I know, it's so great! Listen, I want you to come to my house tonight. Tonight's the night. I've been looking for ways to have my folks have family home evening and this is the day. I already called the missionaries, and they'll do it. Oh, you don't know them."

"I . . ."

"I know, but if you'll try it, you'll love them. So what do you think?"

Amber was still three sentences behind, trying to catch up, when it dawned on her that he was asking her to go someplace with him again.

"I'd love to."

CHAPTER 41

HOPE

KELLY AND HER MOTHER WAITED IN THE RECEPTION AREA OF the Family Crisis Center. The homey room was empty but smelled of fresh coffee. The coffee was tempting—she was so tired—but having her mother with her made her embarrassed to drink it. Mormons didn't drink coffee, and she was done disappointing her parents.

"Mom, I just wanted to thank you for staying with me."

"Nonsense, it's what mothers are made to do. I wouldn't be anyplace else. My favorite place to be is anywhere my children need me."

As Grace entered the reception area, both Kelly and her mother stood up. "Hi, Kelly, Nancy. Sorry for the delay. I was trying to scarf some lunch down."

Kelly smiled. "We didn't wait long."

"Let's go back to my office," Grace said, pointing the way. Grace led Kelly and her mother down the hall to her office. "Kelly, there is something I need to tell you."

Kelly felt immediately apprehensive. Grace continued, "Because we go to church together, I feel it would be better if you worked with someone else in my office. That way you and I can be friends and talk about things at church."

"I don't mind that we go to church together. I've really felt safe with you, Grace," she said, sounding desperate.

"I know. I also know that you are going to love Karen. Karen and I do things almost exactly the same. The difference is that she is here every day and doesn't do crisis work, so she will actually have more time to work with you and will probably do a better job. This way, you can call me at home anytime you need to about church and family, but Karen can help you with the divorce, custody, safety, and other issues."

"Sure," Kelly said with a faint smile. Inside she was panicking. Hart said she could trust Grace, and she didn't want to talk to anyone else. But, she had been trained for years to not argue. "Will I have to tell her my whole story again?" Kelly asked.

"No, I already filled her in this morning. We'll meet together the first time. Can you follow me?" Grace stood up.

"Wait," Nancy said. "Is this because I talked to you at church?"

Grace shook her head, "No. It's because I have to avoid conflicts of interest when I am being paid to do my work and allocating funds to victims. I already would rather be Kelly's friend than her advocate."

The room was silent while they all took it in. Grace showed them the way farther down the hall into Karen's office.

Kelly was surprised at the difference in offices. They both had a spectacular view, but this office was painted a deep red with gold rolled over the red paint. The desk and furniture were black. The curtains were black and red. A short round woman, who had a curvy figure stuffed into a tight knit black dress, sat at the desk. She had short, black, straight, bobbed hair. When she turned around, Kelly smiled at her black cat eyeglasses with red rhinestones on the frames.

The woman smiled, stood up, and extended her hand. "Hi. You must be Kelly. Grace told me all about you. I'm Karen."

Over the next hour, Kelly got to know Karen and share the details of her story. Grace quietly slipped out and left Karen in charge.

Karen began, "Kelly, after hearing what Grace had to say, I feel strongly that our first step is to get you to an attorney who can look at your divorce papers and give you some advice about your criminal charges. I know that the district attorney has decided not to charge you criminally, but being arrested and the pictures and evidence may play a part in your divorce."

Kelly felt a jolt of panic. She had tried not to think about any of this while visiting with the kids. Talking about it was like peeling off a scab. She leaned forward and anxiously said, "I took care of the kids most of the time. I don't think Sam ever even changed Hazel's diapers once."

"I know," Karen said. "Did you ever call the police or report any violence to anyone with authority?"

"No."

"Did you ever tell your family?"

"No."

Kelly's mother leaned forward and said, "We had no idea. We knew Sam didn't like us, that he was controlling and that we didn't like him. But we had no idea he was hitting her."

"Did you tell any friends?"

"No. I haven't really connected with anyone since we moved to Oregon."

"That's typical of a serious victim. Part of the abuse pattern is to isolate victims from friends and family so that you feel like you have nowhere to turn."

"I loved him. I didn't want anything bad to happen to him. I think I was trying to protect him, and now look what he's done to me."

"Well," Karen said, "Let's get the phone book out and see if we can get you an appointment with an attorney."

———

Kelly and her mother sat on the dock outside the Family Support Center looking at the to-do list that Karen had helped them put together. It looked overwhelming.

Kelly's mom called her father on the cell phone. "Hello, Jack? Yes. Listen, Jack, where are you?" She turned to Kelly and said, "They are in Idaho already. They are stopping for lunch in Boise." Her mother talked loudly into the cell phone, "Listen, Jack, we just went to see that Grace woman. They assigned Kelly to another gal who got her an appointment with a local attorney who agreed to give her a free consultation. Yes. I know that's good. But I think she is going to need some money for attorneys."

Nancy nodded and listened to her father on the cell phone while Kelly waited. Hanging up, she turned to Kelly again. "Your father says that he has a retirement account that he can probably borrow from."

"Mom, I don't want you to have to do that."

"Kelly, would you do it for Hazel?"

Kelly hesitated. She knew she would. Her mother smiled.

CHAPTER 42

UPHILL

ELDER OSCARSON AND ELDER SAPPENFIELD PEDALED THEIR bikes up the steep hill. Elder Oscarson's legs felt like they were on fire. "I can feel the burn, Elder. In fact, I'm burning up. You want to go higher?"

Elder Sappenfield joyfully waved his arms at the mountain. "Elder, I've got a feeling our golden contact is on this hill."

"I've got a feeling lunch is going to come back up and I'm going to leave it on this hill." Elder Oscarson had gone far enough. He hit his brakes to keep the bike from rolling back and then got off the bike and let it fall to the grassy strip by the road. Winded, he bent over, hands on his knees, and gasped for air. Unbuckling his helmet, he stood up, breathing like a freight train.

"Elder!"

Elder Sappenfield looked back and realized his companion wasn't within arm's length anymore. Stopping, he turned around to see Oscarson's chest heaving and his face beet red from the strain. Sappenfield got off his bike and walked back down the hill to Elder Oscarson. "Elder, are you all right?"

"No! I am done with this hill. I say we start here at the bottom."

"But, Elder, I told you I have a feeling . . ."

"Feelings shmeelings. I feel like I'm gonna die. We can come back later when we have the car," Elder Oscarson snarled at his companion.

Elder Sappenfield didn't hear the last of the sentence. A classic Volkswagen Beetle went around them. Its engine was so loud he missed what his companion had to say. "What was that, Elder?"

"I said let's start here. I've had enough!"

Elder Sappenfield watched the beetle go up the hill and stop at a house about three blocks from where they stood. A pretty girl in a hoodie opened the door.

"Lock up your heart, Elder," Elder Oscarson said to Elder Sappenfield, slapping him on the back.

Elder Sappenfield sighed. "I guess we better start here." He and Elder Oscarson walked their bikes to the nearest door and away from the pretty girl.

———

"Mom, I'm home!" Amber called to the house.

"We're up here!" Her mother's voice came from upstairs.

Amber dropped her books on the kitchen table, smiling because no one was there to yell at her to pick them up. Running up the stairs, she called again, "Mom?"

"In here," came her mother's voice from Greta's room. Amber followed it into Greta's bedroom. There was a giant tent in the middle of the floor made out of sheets. She looked under what appeared to be the tent door opening and saw Greta, Bjorn, and her mother in the middle of a pile of what seemed to be every toy in the house. Greta started to giggle and her mother joined her.

"Mom?"

"Come in and have cookies and punch with us."

"Mom, this is a mess. We're not supposed to eat in our bedrooms."

"Says who?"

Amber started to say her stepfather's name and then realized the enforcer was gone.

"Come on, Amber, sit down!" her mother said as if she were scolding her. "Don't be a party pooper and ruin our mood."

Amber realized that her whole body was filled with tension. Terrified, she said, "I don't know, Mom. It just really stresses me out."

"Why, because you're afraid we're going to get in trouble?"

"Yes."

Emily's eyes looked sad. "Has it really been that bad and that long?"

"Yes, all my life," Amber said, crawling into the tent next to her mother.

Her mother took her in her arms and began rubbing her back. "Breathe, baby, breathe," her mother whispered in her ear. Amber breathed out and tears mixed with sobs came out of her and rained down on her mother's shoulder. Her mother whispered, "No one's here to hurt you."

"Amber?" Greta asked. "Are you sad?"

Amber started to laugh; relief came as the tears went. "No, sweetie, I'm not sad. I am so happy."

"Let's play," her mother said. And they had punch in tiny tea-cups and ate cookies on little plates.

CHAPTER 43

SYSTEMS

KELLY FINCH AND HER MOTHER PULLED INTO THE PARKING lot of the Law Offices of Olson, Andersen, and Svenson. It sat on the riverfront in an expensive-looking building. There was a small parking lot across the riverwalk. The building was covered in cedar shingles with white trim. A bell hung from the apex in the front of the building.

The smell of leather mixed with the fishy smell of the river in the reception area. A lemony-looking woman with gray-and-yellow hair looked at them over the top of gold reading glasses.

"Do you have an appointment?"

"Yes, I'm Kelly Finch."

"The pro bono. Have a seat."

As the woman stood up, Kelly realized she was tall as well as thin and pinched. She had a sweater over her shoulders clipped on with tiny clips and a gold chain. Kelly hadn't seen anything like it since her grandmother was alive. The woman walked down a hall to the left of her desk.

Kelly and her mother sat on a leather couch and looked at old black-and-white photos of ships on violent seas hanging on the plank walls."

"Uff da!" Kelly said, "I saw it once on a bumper sticker. Sam said it's Scandinavian for something like 'holy cow.'"

The lemony woman was back. "Ms. Olson is still in court."
They sat back to wait.

⸻

Bjorn had fallen asleep dressed as a princess, with chocolate chips smeared on his fat little cheeks. Amber and her mother were leaning against a stack of pillows and Greta was downstairs getting more punch when Amber remembered her date.

"Mom!"

"What?" Emily sat up concerned.

"I have a date!" Amber turned to her mother with a look of panic on her face.

"When?" Emily asked. Amber looked down at her watch and stood up, sending the tent crashing down around her.

"In ten minutes!" Amber cried. "I've been crying. I look awful. I have chocolate smeared on my clothes, and my hair is all messy from the tent."

"Amber, Amber, calm down. Part of the fine art of dating is making the date wait. You get ready and I'll grill him at the door."

Amber fled from the bedroom and Emily struggled to get out of the tent and pick up Bjorn's weighty little body. Then she followed Amber to her room.

Amber was in her drawers looking for a shirt to wear. Emily sat on the bed. "So, who is the date with?" Emily asked facetiously.

"Alan."

"Isn't that the same boy that took you to that church bonfire before?"

"Yes." Amber found a few T-shirts to layer and a clean hoodie. Next, she began to dig for pants and clean socks.

"What are you going to do?"

"We're going to his house for dinner and something he wants to do with his parents with some missionaries. He's a Mormon."

"Mormon?" Emily said, alarmed. "What does that mean? Aren't they the ones who can't dance or listen to music?"

"I don't know. I'll have to ask him if he's not allowed to dance. He just joined last year. That lady, Grace, that came over goes to church with him."

"I don't know, Amber. I've heard some really strange things about the Mormons."

"Well, Mom, I'll ask the missionaries lots of questions, and I'll find out. All I know is that Alan has been really nice, he smells great, and I love looking at him."

"Ah, I see. The important stuff, nice and smell."

The doorbell rang and Emily left to answer it. Amber ran down the hall to the bathroom to try to drag a brush through her tangled hair.

———

The lemony woman was turning off her computer and cleaning up like she was ready to leave. Kelly's mom had fallen asleep on the couch, and Kelly had been trying not to nod off while reading a magazine. The lemony woman turned off the lamp on her desk and looked out the window to see that the sun was setting.

The phone on the desk beeped once. Picking it up, she quietly said, "Yes." Hanging up, she looked at Kelly and said, "Ms. Olson will see you now."

Kelly woke her mom. They were led down the darkening hall, upstairs, and into another hall. At the end of the hall, they were led into an office with the lights on.

A bland-looking woman sat at the desk. She had on stylish glasses, but was rather nondescript. She was wearing a suit and the buttons on her jacket were buttoned crooked. A desk lamp shone on the stack of papers she was reading. Neat stacks of files and notebooks were piled everywhere.

Two wingback leather chairs like the chairs downstairs faced her desk. Her back was to the river and the evening sunset was glorious. She put her papers down and looked up.

"Kelly?"

"Yes."

"I'm Kristy Olson. My father is the 'Olson' in the law firm's name. I am a first-year attorney out of law school, so I agreed to see you and give you a free consultation."

"Thank you, Ms. Olson."

"Karen filled me in on a great deal of your story, but I would like to hear it from you." She took out a legal pad and pen.

Forty minutes later, Kristy Olson had heard the entire story and spoke to the district attorney's office. "Kelly, I think that your husband is an abusive jerk. You, however, are in a pickle.

"We don't have one shred of evidence of his abuse other than the day that the police responded to the verbal, and unfortunately in their report, they don't mention any violence. In fact, you went out of your way to protect him, you took all the responsibility, and they only heard you yelling. You haven't given me anything to work with.

"We also have the added issue of you not having an education or job that would provide support for the children.

"Mr. Finch has aligned himself with the daughter of a local wealthy and well-known family that can afford to hire him the best attorney in town and provide full-time care for your children while he works. When the judge sees their name, the judge will be impressed."

Kelly couldn't breathe. The weight of it all sank her deeper in the chair.

Kristy went on, "In looking over the paperwork, I have to say that he has offered almost joint custody. He only retains the right to make all the decisions around the children. A fact that does not surprise me, considering that he is abusive and that he will want to continue to maintain control, perhaps even of you.

"I hate to say it, but because you can't testify that he is a danger to the children, and because he has photographs and police evidence of the injuries you did to him while the children were in the house, my advice to you is to sign the papers and accept his offer. If you don't, you may end up with less than you already have."

Kelly felt her gut lurch. "But you don't understand," she said, "the kids are unhappy. They cried when they left me. I have always been with my children twenty-four hours a day. They've never even been left with a sitter. They're going to be miserable. And I was injured too! They took pictures of me!"

"Ms. Finch, can you support your children without working?"

Nancy broke in, "Kelly can come to live with us!"

"Mr. Finch's attorney has written in a stipulation that she can't leave the county or move more than half an hour away without Mr. Finch's permission. This is not unusual, and the courts will work to have the children remain close to both parents. I don't believe they will let her leave the state with the children." Kelly didn't notice the tears running down her face.

Kristy handed her a box of Kleenex and then asked her, "Kelly, wouldn't you have to leave them with a sitter if you went to work?"

"I guess so."

"Kelly, I think you are going to have to get used to the idea that divorce is ugly. Because you are in the middle of a divorce, the children are going to lose something. They are either going to have to be without you or their father or end up with a sitter at some point. Unfortunately, Mr. Finch states that he plans to remarry and that he has full-time care for the children in their new home and he has generously given you almost forty percent of their time for visits.

"According to this, in one year, if you complete a psych evaluation and are found fit, you can have the children for alternating weeks. This is a very generous offer."

Kelly said weakly, "It doesn't feel generous. It feels like torture."

"If you choose not to sign the divorce papers and go with the present plan, then you can pay a 5,000 dollar retainer and my hourly fee of 175 dollars to fight this in court. I can tell you though, that even if my father were your attorney, at 425 dollars an hour, I don't think you can get a better deal at this time.

"You are welcome to go get a second opinion of course. Also, Ms. Finch, if Mr. Finch should happen to show his true colors and you were courageous enough to report it to the police and to document his behavior, then we could go back to the courts and apply to modify the existing order."

"I see," Kelly said, quietly blinded by tears of hopelessness. "He's too smart for that." Her mother reached for her hand. Her touch made it worse. Kelly began to cry uncontrollably.

"I am so sorry, Mrs. Finch. I know this isn't what you wanted to hear," the attorney said coolly. Then trying to be sympathetic, Kristy said softly, "I know it won't make you feel any better, but I believe you. I can tell you're a good mother and I think you should have your children. If I thought there was another way, I would offer to fight him for free. But, I don't see another way."

Kelly and her mother stood up. Crying, Kelly couldn't see, and the more she tried not to cry the harder it was to breathe. Her mother led her blinded back down the dark stairs and out into the cold Oregon rain.

CHAPTER 44

MEETINGS

LIGHT RAIN FELL ON THE WINDSHIELD OF GRACE'S CAR. SHE hated coming home in the dark. Pulling in her driveway, she turned off the car, leaned back in the seat, and closed her eyes. Suddenly, someone was knocking on the driver's side window.

"Mom, Mom, I have a concert tonight," Mary said as she banged on the window with both hands.

The front door of the house opened, and Nephi came out and headed toward her car. "Grace, I need to borrow your car. I have to buy some supplies for a science project."

Grace pushed the button on her door and all the locks on the car engaged and she lay back and closed her eyes again. Her cell phone began to ring. Sighing, she fished in her purse for it. When she found it, she opened it and said, "This is Grace."

"Hi, honey." It was Mabel. "Have you left yet? We're out of milk. If you're stopping on . . ."

"I'm here, Mom."

"Oh. How was your day?"

"Same old, same old. Yours?"

"Nothing new. Laundry, toilets."

"What time is the concert?"

"Seven o'clock and we're supposed to pick up Anthony around the corner and bring cookies."

"All right. I'll go to the store and I'll be right back," Grace said. She rolled down the driver's side window. Mary's hands were still on it. Slowly, her hands lowered and her nose appeared above the glass.

"Mary, you want to go to the store with me?"

"Can I get some ice cream?"

"Sure. Nephi, you want a ride to the store?"

"No, I want to drive."

"I'm leaving and I am driving. If you want a ride, you can come now or walk later."

"All right," Nephi said and then he yelled, "shotgun!"

"Mom!" Mary said and then she began to race Nephi for the car door.

———

Amber loved the chaos of Alan's house. The entire Johnson family, plus Amber and the missionaries, were sitting at a long table with twelve chairs crowded around it. Clareen had made spaghetti. Baskets of garlic bread, salad, and juice were also on the table. The food was good enough that it kept everyone from talking at the same time. Periodically, someone would stand up and reach across the table. Clareen's hand seemed to come from nowhere to slap the offender's hand and then a short lecture would follow. But no one seemed to mind. Amber was amazed. It was like a cartoon concert.

"Mrs. Johnson, this spaghetti is amazing. Thank you," Elder Oscarson said.

"Yesh," Elder Sappenfield agreed with his mouth full while reaching for garlic bread.

One of Alan's brothers had his chin down to the plate while shoveling spaghetti in. Another sister had a fork full of spaghetti heading for her mouth while reaching for bread. Clareen had a running commentary on everyone's manners going.

"Amber," Clareen said, "I am so sorry. We usually don't have company. I never realized what animals these kids are."

"I love it, Mrs. Johnson," Amber said and she meant it. For years at her house, no one had spoken during dinner except her father. Her mother had sat like a nervous Chihuahua and watched his every move, jumping up and getting him things before he asked. "Thanks for having us, Mr. and Mrs. Johnson," Elder Sappenfield said.

"Mmm hmm," Mr. Johnson said.

"Dad, Mom, the missionaries would like to share a short message with us. Is that okay?" Alan asked his parents, looking tentatively across the table at his mother. Amber looked at Alan's mom who was looking at Alan's dad. Everyone around the table paused. Amber was surprised. She thought Alan's parents had known about the lesson. He had told her at school how excited he was. Her dad would have blown a fuse if she had surprised him like this.

The silence hung heavy in the air. Elders Sappenfield and Oscarson had both stopped chewing and were looking at Mr. Johnson.

"Okay, I guess," Mr. Johnson said.

Amber watched Alan grin and turn to his mom with a look of joy. His mother had her mouth open in shock. Finally, she leaned back, looked around the table, and said, "Mr. Oscarson and Sappenfield," Clareen started, "your church has been good for my Alan and the job your member offered my husband will be good for my family. If it makes Alan this happy, I better find out what it's all about."

———

Six of the Johnson family children gathered in the family room on the rug in front of the elders. Wilson sat by the woodburning stove on a plaid recliner next to Clareen. Alan had fought off his siblings to give Amber a seat beside him on the love seat.

"And so I want to also add my testimony to Elder Sappenfield's that our Father in Heaven cares about each of us and wants us to know about the restored gospel on the earth," Elder Oscarson said.

Amber was fascinated by Alan's face. She could see that he felt something. She felt something but wasn't sure what it was. Elder Sappenfield looked at her. The room was quiet save for the wood crackling in the old stove.

"We would invite you to find out for yourself if this is true by praying about it. If you feel a good feeling, warmth, or what some call a burning, you can know for yourself."

This was a new thought to Amber. She had felt strong feelings when she had prayed, but had never thought about being answered so quickly and directly.

"Thank you, Elders," Clareen said.

"Do you have any questions?" Elder Oscarson asked.

"Well, just one. Why did a nice young man like you choose to go on a mission?" Clareen asked.

"My mother always said that's how we know the Church is true," Elder Sappenfield said with a smile on his face. "If it wasn't, young missionaries like us would have made a mess of it long ago."

———

Berk Anderson looked around the room. *Losers*, he thought, *losers all of them.* He was already sick of this and he hadn't been here long.

"Berk?" The female counselor dressed in a black skirt and jacket shook him out of his thoughts.

"What?"

"Everyone has gone, are you ready to try?"

He dropped his head. He didn't want to talk. He wanted to growl and break something, but he didn't want to get thrown out yet.

"Hi, I'm Berk, and I'm an alcoholic. I drank every evening after work. I didn't drink at work because I was happy. I drank when I had to be home with that war witch, my wife. She drove me to drink."

"We don't make victim-blaming statements," the counselor said. "We take accountability for our actions here."

Berk threw himself back in his chair, slunk down, and folded his arms. He was done talking. He was done trying. They did not understand the pressure he was under.

CHAPTER 45

FORWARD

ESTHER HAD NOT STOPPED TALKING SINCE THEY HAD LEFT the school concert. Grace and her family pulled into the driveway. "So if all twelve of us go it's not a date, we can each pay our own way," Esther hadn't taken a breath yet. "She says she has a new best friend that is better than me because she is more mature. They are both going to go without dressing up. They don't think the seniors will dress up."

"Maturity is overrated," Mabel said as she opened the front door.

"Anyway, I . . ." Esther began. Mabel held up her hand to signal Esther to stop talking and turned to Grace.

"Honey, let's skip family home evening and sleep. I'm exhausted."

"Can't. For some reason, I am so stressed out about this winter I can't sleep. Tonight we repack the seventy-two hour kits. I bought all the stuff at the store earlier," Grace said while she walked to the entryway closet. She began to pull backpacks off pegs hanging behind coats and threw them in the hall. "Nephi, Mary, Esther! Time for family night!" Grace called.

===

The house was dark. Kelly had tossed and turned until she finally gave up. She passed Hazel's room, looking at the empty bed in the clean room. She stopped and looked in on little Sam's dark room

212

and rearranged the trains on the wooden track still set up on the floor. Then she slipped barefoot into the bathroom. *Funny,* she thought, *I'm all alone and I still come here to pray.* She crossed the cold floor and knelt by the clawfoot tub and poured her heart out. Finally, she felt peace.

Kelly got up, went to the kitchen, turned on the light, and found a pen. She found the divorce papers, turned to the last page, and signed them.

CHAPTER 46

NOVEMBER

WINTER WEATHER HAD ARRIVED WHEN GRACE WENT TO THE table in the Relief Society room and arranged her papers on the mini pulpit. She felt inadequate. She hadn't made thirty or forty little loaves of bread, candy, or any cute treat or refrigerator magnets to send home. But she was prepared. She had thought about this every day for a month.

She looked out at the familiar faces. Older sisters gathered in one section, widows sat in the front, and single sisters and young mothers gathered in another section. Over the past two months, Kelly Finch had become a regular, bonding with Jana, a new sister in the ward.

Grace worried about which sister might be triggered by what she had to say. Scanning the room, she looked at Kelly again, so comfortable and actually laughing with her friend. Sitting together, the older sisters visited while Grace wondered if any of them had grown up in violent homes.

Grace began her lesson. "I had the privilege of attending the conference session during which President Hinckley spoke openly and plainly about how husbands should treat their wives. It gave me a lot to think about and I want to share my thoughts with you."

Grace shared her thoughts, sparking a discussion. After a few minutes, she wrapped up her enrichment night lesson. "As people, we all have an innate need to be free and to be able to make our own choices. Agency, or choice, is a gift we learn to exercise here on earth. The pattern of someone trying to control someone else, and people fighting for freedom, is as old as recorded time. In recent history, we have had the Civil War and World War II.

"The same battle is taking place in some of our homes. People are abusing their spouses physically or mentally, using abuse to control their partner's and children's behaviors and choices. The need for power and control is often the reason for abuse."

A young sister, who looked like a Barbie doll and was vigorously bouncing a baby boy on her knee, raised her hand. Grace pointed at her.

"Why would anyone stay where she is being hit?" the young sister asked.

"Research says the number one reason they stay is fear, but there are many reasons. Often when I meet with victims, they describe how they have slowly cut off ties with family and friends and that often they have moved far away from their support systems and found themselves very isolated.

"Isolation makes it harder for them to feel they have a choice about becoming self-sufficient. Or it may make them feel like they can't make it without the abuser."

Grace looked at Kelly Finch who was staring at her, but looked a million miles away. Her eyes were open, but no one was home.

The young sister who looked like Barbie seemed unsatisfied with Grace's answer. "I would just leave. Nothing would keep me there," the young sister arrogantly said. "Why don't they just leave?"

"Sisters, once again, we have the commandments to guide us, the freedom to choose and the wonderful power of prayer to help us find our answers. We can never tell a sister to get divorced, or to just leave, unless we are prepared to take the place of the abuser and take control of her life, move in, and pay her bills. She has to live with the consequences of her choices.

"It is important that we do not let our gospel sisters get isolated or feel alone. It's important that if a sister feels she is unsafe or if she must leave a relationship, that we don't judge her decisions or get caught up in gossip. Our job is to love and support each other in action and prayer."

Sisters in the room buzzed with opinion. A sister, who was also a schoolteacher, raised her hand in the back and asked, "Grace, can you teach some of the red flags to the young women?"

"Sure, I will also tell you that I have taught most of them in the local schools when I taught a dating violence prevention class."

After the lesson, refreshments were served. A bifold door on the east side of the Relief Society room was open, revealing a small kitchen, and strawberry cheese cake with chocolate sauce and whip cream was being dished up on the dividing counter. Grace was thinking about making herself sick with a second piece when she looked up to see Kelly standing quietly looking at her.

"Hi, Kelly. How are you?"

Kelly smiled politely. "Good! I'm getting some temporary spousal support and help looking for a good job. The house hasn't sold yet, thankfully."

"How are your kids?"

Kelly looked down at the uneaten cheesecake on her plate. Picking up her fork, she played with the strawberries but didn't take a bite. "They're fine. They're little, you know? They seem to really like my ex-husband's new girlfriend and daughter. I guess I have to be grateful for that. His girlfriend and I actually talk a little when I pick up and drop the kids off now."

"Wow, that's really lucky. How is Sam when you do the transfer?"

"He's not usually there. It's just as well. I like Sabrina, and Hazel has learned to love her. Little Sam likes her daughter, Candy."

"Are they nice women?"

"I think so. They don't swear and they seem to love the kids. She has a lot of money. Little Sam has his own pony."

"I'm glad the kids have a nice woman in the house, but a pony is hard to compete with. How does he do when he comes with you?"

"Great. But he keeps saying his pony's name. I feel inadequate, you know?"

"You give them something much more important than stuff. I see them come to Primary."

"I'm sure they'd rather be riding a pony."

"Kids are smart, Kelly. They'll grow up and see the truth."

"I hope so," she said with a long sigh. "I better go. Tonight was fun, but Jana and I are walking together in the early morning hours on the days I don't have the kids. Six a.m. comes really fast."

"Before you go, how is your mom?"

Kelly smiled and took a sip from her punch. "She's good. She's back in Utah, but we're on the phone a lot."

Mary and Esther came into the room with six or seven children running ahead of her. "Kids for sale! Cheap!" Mary announced loudly. "Oh, is that cheesecake!"

"Mary! Where is Nephi?"

"Still playing basketball."

Karen Anderson was standing by the door as Grace went out to find Nephi. "Be sure to add cash to your seventy-two hour kits," she said as Grace passed.

Grace stopped and looked at her, "Cash?"

"Yes, the ATMs won't work, you know. If you want to get out of here and go to Portland, you're going to need gas. You might end up paying five dollars a gallon."

"You think?"

"Remember the four-day ice storm last year?"

"Yes."

"I wanted to leave town, but I couldn't find anyone pumping gas except Earl's, and he wanted cash. He took my check because he knows me, but, if you don't know Earl, you want cash."

"Do you think there is going to be a storm this year?" Grace asked, concerned.

"I don't know. I just have this feeling, you know?"

Grace wove through the sisters and away from the noisy room, down the carpeted hall. The sound of a ball and tennis shoes squeaking on wooden floors got louder. The smell of sweat was leaking into the hallway, along with the questionable names the men were calling each other.

Alan passed the ball to Hart who knocked Ironpot down onto his posterior as he drove to the basket. Hart seemed to climb the air, hitting Nephi with his elbow as he dunked the ball.

"Fetch!" Ironpot said.

"Brother Ironpot! You'll bring a tsunami on us," Brother White said as he stood on the sidelines, grinning, getting ready to throw the ball back in.

The smell of sweat permeated the room. For a moment, Ironpot and Nephi stood bent over, hands on knees, heaving for air.

Nephi was laughing. "What, didn't your wife let you buy a motorcycle?"

"I had to buy a generator with my motorcycle money. You know, the funny thing is, I was at a garage sale with her when I saw two chain saws and she let me buy them both."

"Weird. Grace bought us wood."

"It is weird. White thinks it's going to be a bad winter."

"It's Necanicum, duh!" They both laughed until Alan's elbow found Nephi's gut and Ironpot ended up on the floor, with Hart using his backside as a launch pad for his next dunk.

CHAPTER 47

DECEMBER

GRACE FINISHED RUNNING AND WAS STRETCHING ON THE promenade along the ocean in the cold dark morning. Her cell phone began ringing from a ziplock bag in the innermost layer of her clothes.

She unzipped the raincoat, wrestled with the jacket, and reached into her sweatshirt and finally found her sports bra, pulling the phone out just in time to hear it stop ringing. It showed a missed call from Hart. She stopped noticing the cold and realized her hands were shaking. *You're ridiculous*, she thought. *He's probably calling about work.* The phone beeped, and she stuck it in her pocket and finished jogging home to hear Hart's message.

Grace let herself into the house and began peeling layers. Finally, unable to wait, she sat in the entryway on the rug and listened to his message.

"Hi, Grace. It's Joe. I am heading to a church single adult activity later, would you like to come? Anyway, if you want a ride, text me and I will pick you up on my way."

A slow smile spread across her face as she wondered if he was assigned to drive people or if he wanted to spend time with her. Hopefully it was the latter. Whichever it was, she at least had his for attention for the one-hour round-trip drive. Happily, she began wondering what she should wear, what she should do with her hair, and if she had any perfume left.

———

The empty nesters and singles were to meet at Diana Harrison's farmhouse out on Highway 26. Kelly hadn't planned on going, but it had fallen on a weekend without her kids. Her new friend, Jana, had pressured her and she gave in, but she knew Jana was up to something, she just didn't know what. After putting the finishing touches on her cheeseball platter, she covered it with tinfoil, set it on the table by the front door, and turned the porch light on.

Kelly had on jeans and a red T-shirt with snowmen on the front. It was the first piece of clothing she had ever purchased for herself with her own paycheck. After Jana had seen how clean Kelly's house was, she had suggested Kelly clean houses for a living. One of the sisters in the ward had hired her. That ward member had referred her to some of her friends at the Chamber of Commerce, and now she had six houses to clean and a business license that Jana had helped her with.

Housekeeping was the perfect job for her. She could clean on her own time when she didn't have the kids. Most of her clients were pretty flexible, unless they had a party or something special happening. So far, it had been great.

The doorbell interrupted Kelly's thoughts. *Why was Jana ringing the bell?* Kelly thought. "Come in!" she shouted. The bell rang again. Then Kelly got a knot in her stomach. What if it wasn't Jana? What if it was Sam?

"Snap out of it!" she said to the bathroom mirror. After she turned off the light, she headed for the front door. Sam wouldn't ring. The door was probably locked and Jana couldn't get in.

She looked through the open window to the lit porch. Officer Joe Hart stood there in jeans and a red flannel shirt. A white Jeep Cherokee was parked at the curb. *What was going on?* she thought.

Slowly opening the door, she asked, "Officer, is everything all right?"

"Oh, Hi. I mean, I . . . It's . . . ah." He stopped talking and looked at his shoes. The rear passenger door on the car opened and Jana leaned out.

"Kelly, come on!" Jana called.

"Oh." Kelly said and turned red. She put her hand over her face. "I am so embarrassed. Don't tell Jana how we met. I mean, I'm sure she knows, I told her, but I didn't tell her it was you that came to my house before, when . . . well, you know."

He smiled. "You're my favorite criminal," he said. "Now, if you won't come along willingly, I'm sure I can find my cuffs . . ." He started patting his pants pockets.

Kelly let out a belly laugh. "I don't think so. But I'm not sitting in back this time. I'll start having flashbacks."

"All right, but you'll have to tell Grace. And please call me 'Joe.' If you call me 'Officer' at the ward party, the members might feel the need to behave."

Kelly took her sweater off the hook by the door, picked up her cheeseball platter and her purse, and pulled the door shut and locked it behind her.

While they drove, Jana talked a steady stream about goats and chickens with Joe. Grace listened and tried not to feel so out of place.

"So, I should probably only start with one rooster?" Joe asked.

"Yes, I think they're violent. They never let the chickens rest."

"I just want eggs to eat, though," Joe said.

"You have enough room for chickens?" Kelly asked.

"I have a house on the river not too far from here." Joe explained, "It's a log home. There's plenty of land. I've been thinking about chickens and a garden."

"I love gardening," Kelly said.

"I don't love gardening. I love cooking and eating," Joe said, smiling.

"I am a fan of food." Kelly laughed.

"If you want to come out, I'd make you dinner," Joe offered. He looked at Kelly. She looked at the car door. He thought maybe she was going to jump.

"We'd love to come out, wouldn't we?" Jana said from the back.

"Grace, Kelly?" Joe asked.

Kelly smiled and leaned toward Joe. "If I don't have my kids. They are usually here on weekends."

"Sure. What about Monday? What do you think? Jana, how about it?" He looked in the rearview mirror. He caught Jana winking at him.

"Okay," Jana said, "but I have to come from work in Hillsborough, so, I'll meet you there."

"Grace?" Joe asked.

"Sure, why not. I work on Monday, but I can get there by six."

"It's a date," Joe said and then wished he hadn't. He could feel the panic coming in waves from Kelly. He wasn't trying to ask anyone out and now he thought he was probably scaring Kelly to death.

"Grace," he said in an effort to relax Kelly, "why don't you bring your kids? If you have yours, Kelly's can come too."

"I'll call Jack and Ernie. Maybe Abigail would like to come too," Jana said from the back. *Great*, Hart thought, *maybe this way Kelly would be more comfortable.*

———

Kelly hung onto the dashboard as Joe went down the steep bank of the creek, crossed the timber bridge, and then easily climbed the bank on the other side.

When they broke out of the trees into the clearing and she got her first look at the A-framed cabin the Harrisons lived in, her breath caught in her throat. "It's beautiful. Wouldn't it be great to live out here like this? It's like a little piece of heaven." Joe pulled up alongside an SUV and parked the Cherokee. He got out and opened Grace's door and then headed around to open Kelly's and Jana's doors.

Before Joe could, Kelly opened her own door. Then she went around to the back of the Jeep and got out the cheeseball platter. Getting her message loud and clear, he headed into the house.

Kelly stood and watched him go in. Her mind was racing. He was single and so handsome, but she had no interest in men right now. She was barely divorced. It was only final by about three weeks. Wasn't she supposed to wait for a year in mourning, or was that when someone died? She didn't want people to judge her.

Kelly walked toward the house. Catching up with Joe, she slowed her pace and walked beside him. A breeze caught his shirt and blew her hair off her face. *Oh my*, she thought, *he smells so good, but what is that other smell? Goats?*

━━

Grace hung back and watched Kelly smile up at Hart. He had his hands in his pockets and walked confidently while Kelly seemed to chatter away, hand gently on his arm. *Who I am kidding*, she thought. *I am older and he is out of my league. Thank heavens she is working with Karen and not me.*

━━

Grace had laughed so hard and long her face hurt. The group had gathered in the large living room in a circle around a game on the floor. Joe had sat next to her, but she had been having so much fun she forgot he was there.

Then her cell phone rang.

"Hello, Grace, it's Cheryl." Grace's heart sank. Cheryl was her DSAT volunteer covering the line.

"Hi, Cheryl, what's going on?"

"My kids have been throwing up, and now I am sure I have the bug."

"No problem, just give me time to get home." Grace sighed. Suddenly, the party was just noise swirling around her. Everybody made way for her to step outside.

She dialed her mother. "Hi, Mom, I have to take the line over. My volunteer is sick. Can you come get me?"

Before her mother could answer, Steven, another divorced empty nester, stepped out of the shadows and said, "I can take you."

Ugh, Grace thought, *better and better.* "Sure, Steven, thank you." *Be nice Grace,* she thought, scolding herself. He straightened his beard and snapped his logger suspenders. Grace's head dropped and she shuffled to his Ford truck.

―――

After laughing until she cried, Kelly had eaten dessert. Not just one dessert, but three. If she had lost any weight, she would gain it back tonight. As she was putting her third piece of peanut butter pie on her plate, she caught Joe Hart looking at her, smiling. She immediately became embarrassed. In her mind, she could hear Sam's voice oinking. She flashed back to him calling her a fat pig and following her around oinking. Her heart raced. Joe moved on to talk to someone else.

Later, Diana stood on the porch and waved as she, Joe, and Jana walked out to Joe's car. "Bye! Come again," Diana called. Kelly looked around the yard and took one more deep breath. Although it smelled of goats, it also smelled of fresh pine, wet grass, and smoke from the fireplace. The trees gently swayed in the evening breeze against the night sky and she thought this must be paradise.

"Kelly," Jana said, "Bill is going to drive me home."

Kelly looked at Jana in a panic. She whispered, hoping Joe wouldn't hear, "Are you kidding me?"

"Bill, you know." Janice kept jerking her head in the direction of a handsome older man with the passenger door of his large extended-cab truck open.

"Can I come with you?" Kelly whispered. Although she knew Jana wanted to be with Bill, she wasn't about to go home alone with Joe. She just wasn't ready.

"Kelly," Jana begged, "It's a truck. No room. You know. So . . . see ya!" She flounced off, saying something clever that made the man laugh as he helped her into the truck.

Holding her empty plate protectively against her chest, Kelly turned in the empty yard to see Joe holding the passenger door of his Jeep open.

Ready or not, she thought as she got in without a word.

They rode silently for several minutes. Joe fiddled with the radio and then finally turned it off. Kelly hadn't looked directly at him. Her right hand was on the door and her other hand was clutching the pan like it was a weapon.

"Storm's coming," Joe said.

"What?"

"Storm's coming."

"What makes you say that?"

"Saw it on the news," he said and smiled. She caught herself looking at him and quickly turned her face forward. "And I can smell it in the air. Here, smell." He rolled the window down a few inches.

"You're right. It smells . . . like wet pine."

"The wind is picking up a little. It shouldn't be bad. About fifty- or sixty-mile-an-hour winds. You know, the typical winter wind and rainstorm." He chuckled at his own sarcasm.

"Will it freeze like it did last year?"

"It looks like it's coming from the south. Luckily, it shouldn't freeze. I'm on patrol tomorrow, working for a friend."

"That's nice. I don't have to work until Monday."

"Do you want me to pick you up Monday, or do you want to come with Jana?"

She didn't say anything for a minute. The car bounced down the gravel road. It entered the river flooding over the road and then bounced out onto the dry road. Kelly took a deep breath and squared her shoulders.

"Listen, Joe, you're a nice guy, but . . ."

"Oh no . . ."

"No, it's not that."

"You want to be my friend."

"No, I don't want to . . . I mean, yes."

"Oh," he groaned.

She shook her head and tried again. "It's just that I'm barely divorced." She looked at Joe to see if he got the hint. He was silent and looking straight ahead. She went on, "I just, well, I . . . it was a bad marriage."

"Kelly, it's not a proposal. Just dinner. It's okay if you're not ready. But I want you to know that I . . ." The car bumped along for a minute more. They emerged from the blackberries and turned onto the highway. Kelly waited, wishing she could open the door and jump. Joe went on, "I . . . I just have to tell you that I think you're great and when you are ready to go out, I'll take you, if you will let me."

"Thank you." *Thank you!* she thought, *Thank you! I'm an idiot!* "I mean . . . well . . . I . . . ah . . . that's nice of you."

CHAPTER 48

PERSEVERANCE

ALAN HAD HELPED AMBER GET A JOB AT THE BIKE RENTAL shop in downtown Necanicum, where he worked. It was Saturday morning at eleven o'clock, and they had not rented a single bike or surrey yet. They both stood in the large open garage door looking out on the empty parking lot. No one was in town. The wind blew the rain in sheets across puddles in the black top. Trees swayed and the shop sign next door swung on its chain. The sky was gray and rolling, but it wasn't cold.

"No point in staying open," Alan said.

"Man, I could really use the hours," Amber answered. She sighed and turned toward the desk. Alan called the office and arranged to close.

He turned to Amber and shrugged. "They are closing everything. It seems Highway 101 is flooded at the campground and Highway 30 is closed because of an accident. The coast is entirely cut off. It's all over the news. Tourists can't get here. Everyplace is dead today." He put on his coat and handed Amber her hoodie. "You want a ride back to the office?"

"Sure."

"Why don't you come to my house and we can make a Christmas gift for your mom in the shop?"

"Really? What could we make?"

227

"I made my mom a curio cabinet last year."

"Wow. I don't know if I could do that."

"You could if I helped," he said with a grin. He put his arm around her, and they walked comfortably to his Jeep. They were together a lot these days. Nothing was spoken, he hadn't kissed her, but she loved moments like these. Leaning into him in the rain, she took a deep breath.

———

Saturday was almost over. Elder Oscarson pedaled up the hill, fifty yards behind Elder Sappenfield. The rain pelted him in the right side of his head. "Elder, Elder!" he shouted, but Sappenfield ignored him. "Elder!" Finally, he just stopped.

Elder Sappenfield stopped and turned back down the hill until he pulled alongside Elder Oscarson. "What?" he shouted over the rain.

"The sun is setting. I am cold and wet and I want to go home."

"You can't go back to Utah, Elder."

"You know what I mean. Back to the apartment."

"Elder, I keep having this feeling that we need to tract this hill, and every time, there is a reason we don't. I am going to tract this hill."

"You're going to have to do it alone."

"Let's pray about it and see what the Lord says."

"No fair, Elder. No fair," Elder Oscarson shouted into the wind as he remounted his bike and started pedaling again up the hill.

Finally at the top, Elder Sappenfield stopped. "We're here, Elder," Sappenfield said. He climbed off his bike and rang the doorbell. He and Elder Oscarson stepped back and looked at each other. The wind blew the rain onto their backs as they faced a heavy oak door. Every once in a while the wind picked up speed, gusted, and tried to topple them, but the Elders stood feet apart, braced, ready. They both straightened their ties and then looked expectantly at the door.

A scrawny seven-year-old pulled the door open, using both hands to get the heavy door open. "Hi," she said, putting one hand on the inside doorknob and one hand on the outside door knob and then pulling her knees up and swinging on the door using her feet to push it back and forth. Her shiny light brown ponytail was blowing in the wind.

"Hi," said Elder Sappenfield. "Is your dad home?"

"He doesn't live here." She made a frustrated look with her face and then dropped like a monkey to the floor. "Mom!" she called as she ran deeper into the house, leaving the door open, allowing the wind to knock about knickknacks and pictures inside.

The Elders stood waiting in the open door. The rain kept falling and the wind blew the door open wider. A woman came to the door. Her hair was pulled back in a tight ponytail and she had a white headband holding her bangs and stray hair back. There was a long white scar on her forehead. She had on blue rubber gloves like she had been cleaning.

She quickly took off the gloves and pulled off the headband and smoothed her bangs over the scar on her forehead. Elder Sappenfield extended his hand. Hesitantly, she stepped to the threshold, reached out, and took it.

"Hi, I'm Elder Sappenfield and this is Elder Oscarson, we're representatives of the Church of Jesus Christ of Latter-day Saints. We'd like to share a message with you."

"Which church?"

"The Church of Jesus Christ of Latter-day Saints. Some people call us the Mormons, but our real name is the Church of Jesus Christ of Latter-day Saints, ma'am. Can we share a message with you today?"

"Oh, the Mormons. My daughter dates a boy that's Mormon. Perhaps you know him? His name is Alan Johnson."

"Yes, ma'am, we do. Is your daughter Amber?"

"Why yes! She's not here right now, though. My name is Emily Anderson and this is Greta." A baby started to cry in the background. "Oh, that's Bjorn. I better go get him. Maybe some other time, Elders."

"Sure, can we leave you with this gift?"

"A gift?"

"It's a Book of Mormon and a picture of the Savior."

"Oh, well, I don't know if I'll ever have time to read it."

"That's okay, Ms. Anderson. You don't have to read it. We'd just like to leave it with you. May we come back sometime?"

"I don't know. I have to take care of my baby."

Elder Sappenfield pulled the book out of his bag. He handed it to her. She took it, waved, and closed the door.

"Well that was a waste of time," Elder Oscarson said.

"Elder! It was a golden contact!"

"You think?"

"I know so! Feel it, Elder?"

Elder Oscarson looked up at the sky, rain pelting him in the face. "I feel it, Elder, I feel it. Can we go home now?"

———

Emily sat with Bjorn, whose crying had become breathless sobs. She rocked back and forth frantically. The book was on the table by the chair. She looked at it. Greta came running up the stairs, shoes slapping at full speed. She put the bottle in Bjorn's open mouth and the screaming stopped. Greta giggled and held the bottle with both hands, making faces at Bjorn.

Emily used her free hand to pick up the book. There was a picture in the front. A thin woman in a sixties kind of dress sat primly on a chair. A thin man with large ears, black hair, and glasses, like a comic book Clark Kent from *Superman*, stood behind her. Five children gathered around them with an ugly black dog, tongue sticking out, finishing up the family.

"What's that, Mama?" Greta asked.

"A book, honey."

"Read it to me."

"You won't like it, honey, it's for grown-ups."

230

"I'm grown-up. Read it, Mama."

Emily smiled at her little mother feeding Bjorn. "All right." She shifted and took the book in her left hand. She took the bottle from Greta with her right hand. Greta leaned on her lap and looked at the picture.

"'To whom it may concern,'"

"What does that mean?"

"It means that they are saying hello to whoever is reading this book."

"That's us."

"That's right," Emily said with a smile. "'We want you to know how much we love this book. This book came into our lives many years ago. In it are the answers to all the questions we had ever asked about life. We want you to know that we know that the gospel of Jesus Christ is true.'"

"Godspel?"

"Gospel. I think that means that this book tells you a lot about Jesus," Emily guessed.

"Oh."

"'We hope that you read this book and learn to love the gospel as we have. Sincerely, the Pringle Family, Jeff, Bev, Sylvia, Scott, Stacy, James, and Sara.'"

"There's a lot of them."

"Yes, there are."

"Keep reading."

"Okay." Emily turned the pages to what looked like the start of the story. "'I, Nephi, having been born of goodly parents . . .'"

"What's *goodly*?"

CHAPTER 49

HIGH TIDE

LITTLE SAM WAS TUCKED IN THE RACECAR BED. SABRINA SAT next to the bed in a rocker with the book she had bought him today. Sabrina read the book, watching little Sam's eyelids struggling to stay open. Hazel slept in the pink princess castle bed across the large playroom.

Sabrina read softly, "'And then the lion made the mouse tea and they became fast friends. They lived happily ever after.'" Little Sam's eyes were closed. She gently closed the book and carefully laid it on the nightstand. She was standing up when his eyes fluttered open.

"Sabwina?"

"Yes," she whispered.

"I wanna say a pwayer."

Sabrina had learned "Samese" language long ago. He had often asked for a prayer at bedtime. "You're almost asleep, honey. Why don't you just go to sleep?"

"No, I wanna pway." Sam Jr. sat up and pushed the tightly tucked covers off.

"You can stay in bed, Sam," Sabrina said.

Little Sam shook his head while climbing out of the bed. He knelt next to it and folded his tiny arms. Sabrina knelt next to him and listened while he said his prayer.

"Now I way me down to sweep. Bwess me, bwess Mommy, bwess Hazel, Bwess Sabwina, bwess Candy, bwess Daddy. Amen." Sam finished his prayer and climbed into bed. Sabrina tucked the covers tightly around him, pulled his hair back, and gently kissed his forehead. He had made her so happy. Smiling, she turned on the baby monitor and shut off the light.

She looked up to see her daughter, Candy, standing in the doorway. Sabrina tiptoed toward the door, stopping to turn on a nightlight before she and Candy stepped out in the hall.

"He is so cute," Candy said. "It's a shame his old man is such a jerk."

"Candy, I wish you and he would try to get along better. I love him and I definitely love these kids. I want us to be a family."

"Weird family. Doesn't he give you the heebie-jeebies?"

"Candy, don't talk that way about Sam. Please."

Candy rolled her eyes and stalked across the hall to her bedroom and slammed the door. Sabrina's anxiety began to rise as she watched Candy with growing concern. Candy had begun wearing more and more black and dark colors and was losing weight, even though she was already thin. Lately, she had taken to wearing no makeup, big sweatshirts, and combing her hair so it covered her face. "I hope this stage passes soon," Sabrina said to herself.

━━

Sabrina walked down the long hallway past the master bedroom, down the stairs, and into the kitchen. Sam was sitting at the table with a drink. When he had first come into their lives, he had been so helpful. Now he watched her work while he had a beer in his hand.

Sabrina looked at the dishes still sitting on the counter by the sink, the little fingerprints smeared all over the table, and felt her age. Kids took energy, and she wasn't sure she had it anymore. Still, she found herself becoming attached to them in a deeper way than she had expected. "Sam, would you pick up the kids' toys while I finish cleaning up the kitchen?"

"I would, honey, but I have a bid I'm working on. I'll be in the den," Sam replied while standing up and walking toward her. She stood waiting for him to give her a hug like he used to, but he passed her and went to the refrigerator, pulled out a six-pack and left the kitchen. Disappointed, she leaned on the counter. Lately, he was always sitting in the dark in the den with his computer.

She had met Sam while he had been remodeling her house. He was so helpful. The chemistry was amazing. She loved the way he treated Candy, always willing to help her with the horses and the barn. Lately though, he had done less and less. Now it seemed the only thing he did was take care of the horses and help Candy in the barn.

She loved him for more than what he did around the house, so maybe it was okay. Maybe she was being too judgmental.

Sabrina set little Sam's baby monitor in the kitchen window. *This house is too big*, she thought. If it weren't for the monitors, she wouldn't hear the kids if they cried at night.

Scraping lasagna off plates, she thought about Sam, remembering the things he used to say about Kelly and his awful injuries when he first came to stay at her home. She had believed him when he said Kelly was mentally ill, but she also thought for being so crazy, Kelly had done a great job with the kids.

———

Kelly had tossed and turned. Just when she would drop off to sleep, the wind would pick up and rattle her vinyl windows. Periodically, hail would tinkle against the glass and then fade away. Once she thought she even heard thunder. Lightning was rare on the north coast.

Her mind spun, and when she did sleep, she had wild dreams. She wished her brain came with a shut-off switch. Her thoughts were as twisted as the wind that shifted and blew in all directions.

Why was she so afraid of Joe, or was it men in general? Look at what a mess she had made of her marriage. Maybe her picker was broken. If she had feelings for Joe, then there was probably something wrong with him.

Over and over she played the tapes in her head. She could hear Sam's voice telling her how stupid she was, how lazy she was, how no one else would want her but him.

Still, Grace seemed to like Joe, and she liked Grace and trusted her judgment. Why was she so afraid?

She finally threw the covers back and decided to make herself a cup of hot chocolate. She turned on lights as she went. The house was so big and so empty. The lights made her feel less alone at night.

The wind had been blowing hard. Opening the fridge to get milk to warm, she took a quick inventory. Once slice of cheese, a head of lettuce, salad dressing, two eggs, one cube of butter, the emptiness—all screamed that it was time to let loose and finally spend some money. Her appetite had increased with all the physical labor of her work. Thoughts still churning, she made toast and warm milk.

Kelly was enjoying her warm milk when the lights went out. Panic rose in her chest. The wind forced its way through the windows, calling in the dark and making the small hairs rise on the back of her neck. She froze, listening to the wind and the scraping of branches against the empty house.

Her eyes began to adjust to the dark. Standing, she felt her way out of the kitchen to the front room. When she pulled back the curtains, she saw that the entire city was in the dark. She saw something else that made her heart race. The ground in the empty lot across the street looked strange. In the dark it looked like glass until a strong gust of wind broke the surface and white caps spilled out of the lot onto the road. The road had waves like the ocean rising, spreading across her lawn. She went to the door and pulled it open, stepping out onto her porch in the black night.

It was the river. It had risen, covering the lots across the street, flowing over the road further than she'd ever seen it and was coming across her lawn. The wind gusts blew little ripples across the surface and violent white caps against her cement porch. She looked up and down the street. In the distance, the golf course clubhouse was three-quarters of the way underwater with trees down and floating on the course and nearby road. Her neighbor's ancient maple tree had pulled out of the wet ground and covered the road. Its entire root system was raised in the darkness like a round plate. Trees were down everywhere. She was trapped.

Kelly ran back through the house and out the sliding glass door in the family room onto the back deck. Branches, leaves, pine needles, and other debris covered the deck. The large pine in her back yard had a huge branch down across power lines that sparked in the dark. There was no chance of getting out this way either, and the river was rising fast.

She wanted to run, but where? There was no one to save her. There was no one to call for help except Jana, and what could she do? The mist and rain clung to Kelly's nightgown, and the weight of her wet clothes propelled her, like a sail flapping in the wind. The temperature had dropped, becoming cold enough to be miserable, but not low enough to freeze.

Worrying about little Sam and Hazel, she wondered if the storm was this bad at Sam and Sabrina's big house. She hoped they weren't somewhere in the dark, afraid.

She backed into the door and closed it. The house had begun to rattle and shake. The violence of the storm outside was trying to blast its way in.

Her cell phone didn't work. The battery was charged, but it didn't show any bars or service, making her wonder if the towers had blown down. Thankfully, she remembered her mother had packed an emergency bag for her. She pulled it out and sat on the floor with it, opened the zipper, and found the flashlight inside. She was in luck—it worked.

Carrying the flashlight, she opened the drapes in the living room so she could watch the city and wait for the lights to come back on. Remembering the fireplace, she tried to turn on the gas log, but it had an electric ignition, which she eventually gave up trying to figure out. Pulling a quilt from across the back of the couch, she wrapped herself up and lay down on the couch, listening to the wind and thinking about her children.

Sabrina lay in bed alone, tossing and turning. Twice she had gone downstairs and tried to get Sam to come to bed. It was like she didn't matter at all. The second time, she'd caught him looking at pornographic pictures of women online. She didn't know why that upset her so much; her mother had always told her it didn't matter who they looked at, as long as they come home to you. *Millions of men did it, didn't they?* she thought. For some reason, it mattered to her. She felt stupid for feeling this way. Guilt, shame, and pain mixed to make her mind spin and kept her awake.

She felt hurt, betrayed, rejected, and angry. Maybe she wasn't good enough. Taking inventory, she felt her flat stomach, ran her fingers through her hair, and wondered if she lost weight if it would make things better.

Anxious, she wanted Sam's comfort. The wind was blowing furiously; the house felt like it was reverberating. The windows rattled. Trees outside were creaking, groaning, and fighting to remain standing. The rope on the flagpole beat angrily, a tin sound against the empty metal pole. Shadows on the night wall were wild, dancing patterns of pine boughs and paned glass.

A small child coughed over the baby monitor. She rolled over, facing the nightstand and heard little Sam cry with Hazel's voice joining his. She picked up the monitor and turned the switch on the lamp on the nightstand. The light didn't go on. She rolled back over and crawled across the king-sized bed to the lamp on the other side. It didn't work either. Then she realized the clock on the nightstand was off. The power was out. Little Sam must be so afraid in the dark.

Feeling her way across the bedspread, she found her robe at the foot of the bed. She put it on and felt in the dark until she found a flashlight.

Using her flashlight, she ran out of her room and down the hall and into the kids' room. "Hazel, little Sam, Sabrina's here," she called as she gathered a sweaty little Hazel in her sleeper out of her bed. Drying Hazel's tears, she carried her over to the racecar bed and gathered little Sam up while sinking into the bed with them both. She rocked them back and forth as they hugged each other. *Their little bodies are like heaters*, she thought as their shivering sobs slowed down.

The light from the flashlight showed on Hazel's little pixie face. Her head lolled back with her eyes closed, long eyelashes on red cheeks. Her lips pursed and sucked like a baby with a bottle while little sobs occasionally rhythmically escaped, jolting her sleeping body.

The wind pummeled the stone house, but only found its way through the cracks in the vinyl windows, occasionally screaming like a banshee.

Sabrina felt little Sam's fingers reach up and find a lock of her hair and hang on. She loved these children. It reminded her of days when Candy still needed her. Slowly, her eyes closed, so tired, and she began to drop off to sleep.

She had just started to dream when she heard the first explosive crack.

━━

The James family slept peacefully. The house was dark and warm. The furnace ran softly. Mabel snored rhythmically, sleeping without moving. In Nephi's room the windows began to rattle. The small pine tree outside the living room window rubbed the glass and wood back and forth, back and forth. The numbers on Grace's old digital clock shone in the dark as they clicked through the night; and then they stopped.

Grace sat straight up in bed. It was too quiet. The windows rattled and the little pine scraped the house. The light was out on the clock. She pulled back the heavy covers and sat on the side of her bed.

She tiptoed on creaking, cold floorboards into the hall and listened to wind rattling the old windows in the night. *The furnace is off,* she realized, then she wondered how cold it was going to get as she padded down the stairs to the first floor.

Grace noticed the pattern of light and dark in the shape of pine boughs wildly flailing back and forth on the living room walls. Hypnotized, she walked into the living room. The sound of the wind was louder here. The older front windows with the tiny panes of glass shook as the wind rumbled.

Walking to the window, she looked out in the pitch-black night, trying to see the old pine tree across the street. It had been leaning toward her house for years. She couldn't make it out in the dark.

Her feet were icy and she shivered as she went to the front door. When she pulled on the door, the wind blew it the rest of the way in. The sound of the squall was like someone throwing rice on tin. As Grace stepped out on the porch, the wind roared fitfully, hitting her in the face, taking her breath away, forcing her back a step.

The road was entirely covered in dead pine needles blowing across the pavement. The pine trees gyrated as the wind blew in from the south. It wasn't as cold as she expected it, but it was wild. The old pine across the street was still there, still leaning, but it was dancing. She stepped back in, pulled the door closed, and went back up the stairs.

"Brrr," she said as she slid under the covers and pulled her cold feet under the down comforter. *If I lived in Florida, they would call this a hurricane,* she thought, *but in Necanicum it's just another winter day.*

The tsunami alarm went off. Grace sat up again. The weather radio system had a tsunami alarm on it. It was battery operated and sat on a charger downstairs. Running down the hall and down the stairs, she picked up the handheld transistor radio-sized alarm system. She pushed the button to hear the radio report and looked at the screen to see if it had a digital alert. Nothing showed on the digital alert. The recorded voice droned on and mentioned no tsunami alert, just high seas and safety alerts. Nephi caught up to her and they stood looking at the radio.

"What do we do?" Grace said to her brother.

"We go to high ground."

"What if it's a false alarm? I can't check it on the computer or anything without power."

"I'd call Earl Ironpot. He'll know what's up." Nephi picked up the phone and then realized his error. The phone wouldn't work without power, and it looked like the cell towers must be down. No one had any service. Grace had kept a heavy, ugly old-fashioned phone in the living room for just this occasion. He and Grace both ran for it. "What's the number?" he asked.

Grace had it memorized. She held the receiver and dialed. She put her finger in the eight hole, drug the dial around, and waited while it ticked its way around before she could dial the next number. It felt like forever.

The phone started to ring. "Hello?" Earl answered groggily.

"Hi, Earl, it's Grace. Do you have a weather radio tsunami alarm?"

"No. Why do you ask?"

"Well, ours went off. Have you heard anything on the scanner?"

"No, I didn't even know the power was out until you called. I have a landline by the bed for emergencies like this."

"Can you check at the station?"

"Listen, if the alarm went off, it's probably a malfunction from the storm, but just in case, why don't you come on up? We're in a safe zone on the hill."

"Okay. We'll see you in a minute."

"I'll unlock the door."

Grace hung up the phone. "He doesn't know anything. He says to come on up just in case." They sprinted for the stairs together. Grace woke Esther and Mary. Mary rolled over twice, and Grace had to make her sit up before she was awake enough to hear. "Mary, get up and get dressed."

"Why?"

"The tsunami alarm went off," Grace said. Mary's eyes popped open. She put on her robe and slippers. She grabbed four stuffed animals and her swim goggles and headed down the stairs, yawning.

The alarm continued to beep in the background. Grace threw on a pair of jeans and a sweatshirt. She flew down the stairs to find Mabel and the kids already getting into the car in the driveway. Nephi was yelling directions loud enough that his voice would carry in pieces on the wind. Kids and the dog were actually working together to get in the car. She grabbed her purse and keys and pulled the door shut behind her. Her mind reeled with what she should have gone back to the house to get, but it felt too late. Nephi held the passenger door open against the wind for her until she was in. Then he went around the back of the car to the passenger side and got in.

Grace backed out of the driveway and the car bounced over debris in the street. The headlights revealed a large branch of the old pine tree hanging down with the power lines wrapped through it and hanging below it. She drove carefully around them.

They drove the two blocks to the river. She stopped at the edge of the bridge, and they looked at the river lapping the bottom of the bridge, twenty feet higher than on a normal winter day. Mabel and Grace looked at each other. "Tide's high," Grace said. Mabel was silent, as were the kids and the dog, as they crossed the bridge.

The road went another block and then they passed through an intersection. Trees were down on the road ahead. Grace carefully went around them and watched for more downed lines. They went two more blocks before they got to the next river. This bridge was still dry, but the houses along the river had water lapping at their doors. She reached out and held Mabel's hand as they went over. Once they had passed both rivers, they collectively exhaled.

"Why don't we go to Alan's? His family wouldn't mind." Esther asked.

"Because Ironpot's house is out of the tsunami danger zone, we hope."

"We don't even know if there will be a tsunami. Why do we have to go? I don't see anyone else going."

Mabel said, "Because your mom said so. We're going to Ironpot's house. End of discussion."

Grace watched Esther throw herself against the back of the seat in a huff. She looked sourly at Grace who held the wheel with both hands. Every time a gust of wind hit the car, it rocked as it picked its way through the night. Three more blocks through a neighborhood with short scrubby trees and they pulled into Ironpot's house.

Tall trees stood behind the house and to the west in front of one of Ironpot's neighbors. Nephi opened his car door and the wind caught it, snapping it out of his hands. The large trees swayed and creaked while rain blew up, down, and sideways all at the same time. The house was dark, the street was dark, and the trees were inky black against a black-and-gray sky.

The door to the house opened, and Ironpot's body was silhouetted, dark against a dark night.

"Mom," Nephi shouted at Mabel. "Do you think I should go back for the seventy-two hour kits?"

"Oh," Grace slapped herself in the forehead. "I can't believe we left them."

The kids got out of the car. Mary's robe flapped. She leaned into the wind, carrying her stuffed animals, hair wild in the wind, and wearing swim goggles.

CHAPTER 50

POWER

THE LIGHTS HADN'T BEEN OUT LONG. BERK ONLY NOTICED IT because the wind had caused the tree in the front of the treatment center to go down. It had been creaking and groaning and then the roots had lifted out of the soft dirt. The tree had landed loudly on a staff member's pick-up truck. He had laughed.

He had been lying in his bed thinking about Emily. He knew she was cheating. His dad was right; he was a loser. Here he was and she was out with someone better. It was something he had thought about constantly while sitting in the group room, sleeping, puking, shaking, or feeling angry.

Self-pity, shame, anger, and a well-fed sense of entitlement simmered. Revenge began to grow. It started with rolling gut-wrenching anger at Amber, who betrayed him, and Emily, who was cheating on him, and grew into dark, bitter poisonous thoughts of revenge—ugly ways to make them pay. His obsessive, furious thoughts ran. Amber and Emily had planned this together. They wanted him to suffer so they could have some other man in his home. They had never wanted him. If he had to suffer they should suffer.

No one loved him. Emily loved Amber, Greta, and Bjorn more than she loved him. Greta didn't even look like him. Whose was she? What had that witch done?

What happened at home should have stayed at home. He was the master of his house, and they needed to be shown.

There was no light in the treatment center; there was no light in his soul. His anger rose and consumed him. He loved the dark. He belonged in the dark. He was master in the night. It was when he had been able to be everything that made him powerful and strong. Now the world was swallowed in darkness. It was a sign. He felt the power bring him out of bed and to his feet. Putting on his shoes and sweatshirt, he went to the door and listened. He could hear others. Gently, he opened his door.

It was quiet pandemonium in the halls. Berk stood casually in his doorway, watching the chaos. The staff was digging for flashlights and trying the phones. The phone system didn't work without power. Sleepy patients shuffled, staggered, and gathered in the group room. Berk smelled opportunity.

He followed the rail on the wall away from the voices in the dark. Flashlights started coming on about thirty feet down the hall. The beams of light crossed, looking in the opposite direction of Berk, swung around to the group room where residents applauded the light, and then down the hall, resting on Berk who smiled weakly and waved as they blinded him. They swept back away and he blinked and waited for his eyes to adjust again. Then he began following the rail again away from the voices.

In seconds, he reached the end of the hall and found the door. It had an alarm system that did not go off when he carefully slid it open and slithered out the narrow opening into the windy night.

———

Mabel and Grace had settled on Earl Ironpot's large sectional couch with recliners built in. Mary leaned on Grace, and Nephi lay on the recliner on the other end of the couch. Esther had the lazy boy. The woodstove in the corner was burning hot, and the house was filled with flickering light, a little smoke, and warmth. Earl's fat cat slept in the light of the fire. The wind rattled the old aluminum windows.

Mabel snored peacefully, but Grace couldn't sleep. She felt like she should be doing something. A beam from a flashlight cut the dark; she heard someone moving around and saw a flashlight coming down the hall. Earl Ironpot entered the room in his uniform.

"You going to work?" Grace whispered.

"Yes, if I can get out of the driveway," Earl whispered back, taking his keys from a table by the door. He opened a closet door and pulled out a police coat and baseball hat and put them on.

"Do you need our car moved?"

"No, the squad car is parked next to the house. I can get around you after I check for flying garbage cans or falling trees."

"Call me if you need me."

"You can be sure I will," Earl answered. He looked thoughtful for a moment. "Wonder if there will be domestics in this stuff?" Earl asked himself as much as Grace.

"It's a dark night, Earl. I wonder how many of my clients have dead cell phones . . . I can't get any service."

Earl shook his head and pulled the door open. The wind pushed the door hard back toward the house and fought Earl. He held onto his baseball hat as it tried to lift off, then he slipped out sideways, and he was gone.

Mary wiggled and tightened her grip on Grace's arm. "Go back to sleep, honey," Grace whispered while refluffing the stuffed bear Mary was using for a pillow.

═══

Kelly couldn't sleep. She had turned off the flashlight to save the batteries. Praying silently, she tossed and turned. Uneasy, she watched the water levels out the front window. When she finally couldn't stand it anymore, she threw back the blanket and rearranged the furniture, pushing the couch up against the front window so she could try to make out the river in the dark while staying warm in her blanket.

The wind had picked up. It blew wildly and seemed to be coming from every direction. Trees in the water lifted from the saturated soil and fell northeast toward the mountains. The roots on her neighbor's trees had held, but the top had snapped off, sounding like a gun blast when it broke. The nearby golf course was entirely under water. Kelly looked past the water and toward the mountains to the north where her children were with their father and wondered how the trees around that incredibly large home were holding up.

It was an astonishing show from inside the dry house. Anxiety rolled through her stomach. She sat up with her knees hugged tightly to her chest, her blanket wrapped around her shoulders, and prayed for her children.

Kelly put her hands together and opened a prayer, asking her Father in Heaven to help her have faith and to protect her children. Then she waited and listened. Warmth started in her belly, washing away the anxiety and spreading to her heart and up and out of her eyes, running in tears as comfort flowed through her body. She felt the children would be safe.

———

Berk loved the devastation he saw around him. The power of the wind, roaring like jet engines, propelled him forward. He felt powerful and untouchable walking against the wind while leaves and debris swirled around him. Trees strained until they snapped, and black clouds rolled across gray skies. Fallen trees lay on sparking power lines, making his adrenaline pump, feeding his black mood.

Berk turned into the wind. It caught his clothes and pushed him back. Leaning into it, he spread his arms and roared. The wind ate the sound. Hail stung his cheeks and his eyes watered. Debris blew in his path, caught in his hair, battered his body, and covered the road. A shingle caught him on the cheek, cutting his face. He made his way to the river. He was going home.

CHAPTER 51

CONTROL

ALAN AND HIS FAMILY GATHERED IN THE BACK OF THEIR house around the woodburning stove. Silently, they took turns pressing their faces to the glass, watching the river rise. When Alan could stand it no longer, he went to the phone to call Amber. Although it was late, he had a feeling something was wrong. Using the old landline, he dialed her number. It rang and rang, but no answer. It occurred to him that she probably didn't have a landline. Everything at her house was expensive and new. "Mom, I think I need to go check on Amber and her mom," he said as he hung up the phone.

His mother looked up at him and anxiously smiled. "Wilson? Should Alan go out in this? She is probably fine, home asleep and all tucked in. You are a good boy, Alan, to look after her, but are you sure?"

"You want company?" his father asked, indicating his approval.

Relieved, Alan smiled and nodded. Then he saw his mother looking out at the fast-moving black water in the dark night. "No, I'll be all right, Dad. You better stay with Mom and the kids."

Alan went to the back door and put on his coat in the mud-room, took his keys off the hook, and opened the door into the wind. He shoved hard against the door and then held it, trying not to let it slam as he left. With his back turned to the wind, he pulled his hood up and walked sideways in the blowing debris to the street. The front gate was swinging wildly and banging against the arbor. He tried to fasten it without any luck.

While climbing into the Jeep, he realized the neighbor's tree was lying across the street, over their fence, and into their yard. Trees were lying on their sides as far as the eye could see in all directions. Power lines lay in and out of the trees, but he didn't see sparks.

Nervous, he thought he could probably make it. The wind was so loud he couldn't hear his mother as she stood at the front door waving and trying to call him back. He started the Jeep, watching the soft-top shake and threaten to tear. The wipers wiped dirt, debris, and light swirling rain. The headlights showed pine needles, leaves, sticks, and shingles in shafts of light.

Making a tight right-turn, he backed onto the sidewalk and turned around, carefully going back and forth between trees until he had turned entirely around. Then, crossing the street, he went up onto the neighbor's lawn around the smaller tree.

Picking his way slowly between trees, he thought he might come through in the clear when his neighbor's sheet metal pole barn exploded. Large sheets of corrugated sheet metal flew through the air, cutting tree limbs and slicing open the soft-top on the back of the Jeep. A large piece of metal hit his mother's arbor and then the sharp steel caught the wind and cut two feet off her hydrangeas before blowing out of sight.

Alan turned in time to see another piece of the barn fly in his direction. He ducked as it hit the windshield and sheared another piece off the soft-top of the Jeep. Staying down, he tried to back around behind the tree to the front of his house.

When he pulled onto his own lawn, he saw his mother at the door. He turned off the Jeep and ran to his mother waiting with his family at the open front door.

Falling into the house and his mother's arms, he helped his father shut the door, trying to keep the roaring wind outside. Gasping for air, like he'd run a marathon, he listened to his heartbeat in his ears.

"That was so cool!" eight-year-old Bradley said, beaming.

"High five," Nathan said and raised his hands.

Alan didn't feel cool. He feebly slapped Nathan's palm and went to the back room again, putting both hands on the cool glass of the window and looking out at the river. He felt afraid. Terror like he had never felt before. Something was wrong and he knew it.

━━

Berk stood outside the east side of the garage and laughed as the trees snapped off one by one, exploding in the night, falling toward the mountain and away from his house. The world was exploding, and no one was going to come if Amber called. He lifted up the rock next to the side door of the garage and dug the key out of the mud. It was still there, the key to his kingdom.

He unlocked the door to the garage and opened it. "Daddy's home," he whispered to the dusty, cold, dark room. He pulled the door shut, softening the roaring wind, changing the roar to a whistle pressing through the cracks and crevasses. His eyes adjusted to the dark. This was his territory and nothing had changed.

Walking straight to the liquor cabinet, he said, "Hello, Jose," and pulled a bottle of tequila out. Unscrewing the lid, he took a long swig, liquid courage streaming fire down his throat, leaking out both sides of his mouth and running down his neck. Using his sleeve, he wiped his mouth, sat down hard in his easy chair, and began planning.

━━

Sam had finished all the beer in his six-pack. The power was still out. He threw the last can at the television screen. Swearing, he cursed the computer, wanting the pictures on it back. He swaggered to the window and looked out at the barn. No one was there. They were all in bed.

Fumbling, he found his way in the dark back to the kitchen, opened the refrigerator, and took out another beer. But his mind was obsessed about what he really wanted. All along he had been watching her. She had been watching him. She wanted him. He was sure.

He took another six-pack out of the refrigerator and went to look for his magazines. He had an appetite that had taken over his life and he liked it. Lately, the pictures weren't enough. Cracking open a can, he let the darkness flow down his throat and grow courage in his belly.

━━━

Feeling brilliant, Berk set the half-empty bottle down on the cement floor and got up to carry out his new plan. Buzzed, he knocked the bottle over as he lurched toward the door into the house. When he tripped over a hammer on the floor, he cursed, picked it up, and saw it as proof. There was another man here. Emily never fixed anything. Swinging the hammer, he smashed the windshield of Emily's Explorer. That ought to wake them up, his alcohol-soaked brain reasoned. She wasn't going anywhere.

Pulling open the door into the kitchen, he listened. The only thing he could hear was the wind shaking the house. Slowly, he crossed the cold linoleum and looked up the stairs. No light and no movement. They weren't home. They were out with someone else. He knew it.

Angrily, he took the spiral stairs one at a time. When he looked over the edge of the upper floor, he saw nothing but the dark, empty hall. He finished the stairs and made his way east down the hall to the master bedroom. The door was closed.

Slowly, he turned the knob. He knew she was with someone. He yanked opened the door to her dark room. The bed was empty. He knew he was right. His rage grew, tightening every muscle. Clenching his fists, he went to take what she loved best. He'd start with the child that looked like no one.

━━━

When the howling wind began shaking the house and knocking down trees, Emily and Amber had moved to Bjorn's bedroom on the west end of the house. Greta's room was the farthest away from the falling trees on the mountain, so Emily and Amber had left Greta in her own little bed, and they tried to sleep in Bjorn's room on an air mattress on the floor. They listened to the storm in the dark, hearing trees on the east side of the house explode. Glass in the windows bowed, mesmerizing Emily, who watched it, wondering if it would shatter.

"Do you think we should put something over the windows?" she said out loud to Amber.

"I don't know, but it looks like they're bending."

"They are."

"Did you hear that?" Amber asked, sitting up.

Emily stopped moving on the air mattress and tried to be very quiet. "I hear a lot," she answered.

"There it is again. Did you hear that?"

"The wind is so loud it's all I can hear besides the trees going down," Emily said over the noise. Her heart began to beat hard and fast. She didn't know what it was, but she felt something. The small hairs on her arms and neck began to rise and then she and Amber had the same thought at the same time. "Greta!"

"Mama!" Now they heard it loud and clear.

They got up and raced across the hall and flung her door open. Berk stood silhouetted against the gray night window with Greta wriggling in his arms. He had one arm around her and held a bottle in his free hand.

"Put her down!" Amber shouted, rushing toward him, arms outstretched for Greta. He swung the bottle, hitting her hard across the face, knocking her backward into the closet doors, ripping them off their hinges and onto her.

"Amber!" Greta screamed, arms outstretched, reaching for her as Berk began backing toward the door.

Emily had frozen but only for a second. "Berk, stop!" she cried, trying to get her hands on Greta. He pushed her back easily and carried Greta through the door and down the hall. Greta's little hands reached out and caught Emily's hair. Emily tried to get her hands between Greta and Berk's chest to pull Greta away. He smashed the bottle against the wall, making her jump back. Berk pointed the jagged glass and growled at her like a wild animal. She rushed him blindly, taking a hold of Greta. He headbutted her in the nose. Emily saw stars and felt blood gush from her nose as she tried to get her hands on Greta.

Amber struggled to get to her feet and out of the closet to get to Greta as Berk headbutted Emily again. This time she dropped to her knees. Momentarily, her vision went dark. She let go for just a second and heard him scramble down the stairs as her knees buckled underneath her and she lost consciousness.

Amber stopped long enough to check her mom's pulse. She was still alive. Amber raced down the stairs, out the front door barefoot, in her nightgown, into the rain. Desperately, she ran around the side of the house to the backyard. He was already crossing the back lawn.

"Greta!" she screamed uselessly into the wind as she ran. Berk made it to the edge of the woods. She was twenty feet behind him. He whirled around and put his arm around Greta's neck. Amber stopped, hands up. "You'll kill her!"

"I'm going to make you pay!" he roared. "I'm going to make you both pay. She's not mine! You tell your mother to make it all go away! Fix it or we're all done! Do you understand me? Fix it!" He pointed the glass bottle at her. Greta was hanging by her neck, eyes wide, frantically gasping and clawing at his arms.

"This isn't going to change anything. Stop it! She can't breathe!" Amber screamed over the roaring wind. Trees exploded all around him.

Greta kept uselessly trying to pull his arm away from her neck when he screamed into the wind, "You're all going to pay!" and whirled around, running into the woods.

Amber ran across the lawn and into the woods behind him. It was black. The wind blew at her back, pushing her forward. Rain soaked her and then she felt hail sting against her skin. She couldn't see anything. Trees continued to splinter. The thick ancient tree next to her snapped off, fifteen feet above her head, crashing to the ground nearby, while she closed her eyes and covered her head. The branches were snapping like matches. Their tops were falling toward the mountain, breaking around her in the roaring blackness.

Her hair snapped against her cheeks, and her wet nightgown clung to her legs as she stumbled over debris, bloodying her shins from crawling over fallen logs. She stopped for a moment, willing her eyes to adjust in the spinning winds, and watched a tree begin to lean, then felt the earth beneath her feet moving as it gave way. As the hundred-foot-tall trunk began to topple, it broke the branches of the trees around it. The earth beneath her feet rose, as the tree's roots were wrenched violently from the drenched soil, throwing her to the rising ground. She rolled over and grabbed at ferns as she began to slide and fall. The falling trunk caught on something in the dark and she hung at a forty-five degree angle on a giant plate of roots.

She gulped for air and reached with her toes in the shadows for flat ground below. She looked down. It was hard to tell in the dark. It seemed about ten feet down. She reached for a lower plant and slid on the rocks and muddy soil. The weak fern pulled out of the saturated soil and she felt her skin tear as she slid farther down to level earth.

"Greta!" she screamed, and the sound of another falling tree swallowed her words.

———

Alan had nodded off in an overstuffed chair when he dreamed he heard Amber screaming. He sat straight up, gulping air and wiping sweat from his face. He felt something was terribly wrong. Panic washed over him in waves. He tried to reason that she was well above the river and probably fine, but he couldn't calm himself.

He knew what he needed to do. Even if it meant walking the entire five miles to her house in the storm, it had to be done.

Looking around the family room, he saw his mother's sleeping form on the couch with his brothers and sisters piled around her. They looked so warm and comfortable, making him wish he could stay and sleep peacefully like they did. His father had pulled a chair up to the window and had a cup of coffee in his hand, sipping quietly, as he watched the river. "Dad," Alan whispered.

His father put down the coffee mug on the woodburning stove and turned to look at Alan. "Dad, I have to go," Alan said, while looking his father straight in the eye.

"Be careful," his father said, which is to be interpreted as meaning, "I know, son, but be careful. I love you and trust your judgment."

Alan just nodded and then left the room to get his rubber boots and rain gear back on. He packed a flashlight and extra batteries in his pocket.

CHAPTER 52

OUT OF TOUCH

HART AND IRONPOT STOOD IN DISPATCH AT THE NECANICUM police station with John Grahm from the ward. Grahm's bony back was turned to the police chief, officers, and dispatchers as he frantically worked with complicated-looking electronic equipment and a hopelessly complex mess of wires. "Okay, Ironpot, you're licensed, right?" Grahm asked.

"Right, but just because of boy scouts. I don't remember hardly anything."

"It'll come back to you," Grahm said without turning around. The station was running on a generator. The lights were on and Grahm was able to plug his equipment in, making random lights come on and a beep that sounded like life.

"How did you know we didn't have 911 operational?" the chief asked.

"I remembered when that meth addict cut the cable last year and the whole county didn't have 911 for two days." Grahm answered. "I also remembered our ice storm last year and how phone service didn't work. I tried to call my friend in the next town and, since my call didn't go through, I knew you didn't have 911."

The chief patted Grahm's shoulder. "We sure appreciate your help. Ironpot says we can trust you, and that's good enough for me."

"Great. Now, how will this work?"

255

"You have two officers licensed to use a ham radio. We have two handheld ham radios. We will be base. I suggest you put Ironpot and a partner on patrol and put one officer with the other handheld set at the hospital."

"That's a great idea. I've been worried about how people will access emergency health services. I'm worried that with all the falling trees we'll have a lot of injuries."

"I'm hoping," Grahm said, while turning knobs and testing his mike, "that my buddy in the Bay Town Ward is either at the police station like we talked about or at the hospital. Depending on what he could get to." Grahm used his call sign and radioed for his friend. A voice came over the radio and the room cheered. They had communication, and they could talk to Bay Town. The chief took the mike and asked the chief in Bay Town questions about their status and the tsunami alarms that kept going off. While they were talking, Grahm outfitted Ironpot with his radio and set it to the right stations.

"KE71EB, calling KE71EA. Sandy, do you copy?" Grahm said into the radio.

"Loud and clear, honey," Grahm's wife returned over the radio from their house on the hill.

"You're all set," Grahm said, handing the handheld radio to Ironpot. Ironpot signaled Hart and they left the dispatch area together.

"Let's take the expedition," Ironpot said to Hart as they checked keys out and left the station. "We are supposed to check the neighborhoods that border the water first. I think we should start at the cove. Every major storm, a huge log or boulder is thrown up on the road in front of the first row of houses. Remember when that log was thrown through that fellow's window?"

"I think we should check the golf course first and the old bridge on that end of town," Hart said into the wind as they crossed the parking lot.

Ironpot smiled in the dark. He knew what Joe wanted. "Nah, let's check the cove," Ironpot said, needling Hart as he opened the driver side door to the white Expedition. He waited for Joe's response while he and Joe buckled themselves in.

"I think that old bridge is a risk. You know the golf course floods first. I think we should check it first."

"Would this have anything to do with a certain young lady?"

"Yes, it would, and she's all alone. What of it?" Hart said defensively.

Ironpot smiled and laughed out loud. "All right, golf course it is."

———

Amber had screamed Greta's name so many times her voice was giving out. It started raining harder. Her torn, muddy nightgown clung to her legs. Wet hair stuck to her face and neck. Her hands were filthy, torn, and bloody, and her feet were numb from the cold. The night was so black she couldn't see far enough to find Berk and Greta in the woods. Finally, she sank down to the mossy ground and onto her knees.

Amber had prayed before, but never like this. She had never begged like she begged now. When she paused for just a moment, she had a feeling she should go back to her house and check on Bjorn and her mother. She pushed herself up from the muddy cold ground, realizing she wasn't even sure which way she had gone in the dark. The wind clawed at her, screaming, surrounding her in chaos. She turned around several times, wishing the light from the house would be there to show her the way home. There was no light, only darkness, wind, rain, and cold.

She was lost. Closing her eyes one more time in frustration, she cried out, "Help me!" She opened her eyes and started walking. Trees exploded and fell all around her. The storm raged on and on while she called and screamed for Greta.

CHaPTeR 53

LIQUID COURAGE

SAM HAD FINISHED OFF ALL THE BEER. HE HAD FOUND A flashlight in the kitchen drawer and had used up all the batteries reading his magazines. Finding himself in the dark again with nothing to do, he ruminated on what he wanted to do. After all, she wanted it too. And hadn't he had done a lot for them? She laughed at all his jokes, even the dumb ones. She paraded around in her pajamas to tease him. His alcohol-saturated brain reasoned that everyone wanted him.

A few sober brain cells reminded him that if he got caught, he might lose the other one. He better make sure he doesn't get caught. Needing more, he went to the wine cellar and looked for something to help him think. He had a plan to put together.

––––

Berk's inebriated brain began to clear. Greta silently hung from his muscular arm like a limp doll, legs swinging as he dragged her through the wet underbrush. Trees snapped like brittle sticks above his head as the violent, roaring wind gusted to 160 miles per hour, pounding adrenaline through his veins, forcing terror and reality to the surface. He'd dropped the broken bottle and was using his free arm to feel his way over fallen trees and tear apart chest-high drenched ferns while the wind blasted his senses to overload. He needed more Jose, more booze. He swung around as a massive tree's roots were torn from the earth and lifted before him.

There were so many broken branches and fallen trees that he was constantly climbing now. He was far too sober to be happy. Knowing it would be easier to go back for more without Greta's dead weight, he searched in the dark for a place to keep her. Spotting an enormous rotten stump with its shredded core alive with larvae spilling out an opening, he laughed. Stumbling, he felt the inside with his free arm. The opening was large enough for five of her. He shoved her limp body deep in the hole. Then, like an afterthought, he reached in once more and felt in the darkness for her face and mouth. She was still breathing; she would be okay. He would come back for her when they had learned their lesson. "Don't move!" he slurred through the wind into the hole. He didn't see any change in the dark recess.

Berk looked for a landmark. There was a large boulder next to the stump and a Sitka spruce that must have been well over a hundred years old next to that. Now for Jose. Staggering in the dark, he hadn't gotten far when he realized he didn't know where he was. He looked up at the sky, but the gray clouds rapidly blew across the black sky, concealing the moon. Muddled, he decided to go back to Greta. He turned to pick his way back.

He had gone too far. The wind swirled needles and leaves around him, twisting his mind. His clothes pulled at him in the wind, and he spun with them, realizing he had lost her. He had gone too far, he couldn't find the stump, didn't know where she was, or which way his stash of booze was.

CHAPTER 54

RIVER AND OCEAN

THE NECANICUM POLICE SUV ROCKED AS GUSTS OF WIND pummeled it. Its headlights cut through the dense night, revealing incredible destruction. The windows were broken in Jack's furniture store. The owner and his son were wrestling pieces of plywood into place. The streetlight at the only intersection downtown was dark and lifeless, swinging violently in the storm. Power lines were draped over trees, and park benches lay across the road.

They turned south after patrolling the empty Broadway shopping area and found their way back to Holladay drive. Holladay drive joined Highway 101, and even though they had gone a mile, they had yet to run into another vehicle.

"What time is it?" Ironpot asked while clutching the wheel with both hands, peering through the windshield with the wipers frantically beating.

Hart pushed a button on his watch. "Almost six thirty a.m. already."

"Time flies when you're scared to death," Ironpot laughed.

"Look out!" Hart said as a large piece of corrugated metal whirled across the headlights and then into the inky darkness.

"What was that?"

"I think it was your mother-in-law," Hart replied.

"No, she rides a bicycle and steals little girls' dogs."

"Hey, do you know why Oregon is so windy?"

"No, why?"

"Because Idaho sucks."

"Ha, ha, very funny. Not!" Ironpot slammed on the brakes.

"What was that?"

"I thought I saw something," Ironpot said, turning the spotlight to the east side of the road. The beam swung back and forth once and then started following a person walking. "I can't believe anyone is out in this," Ironpot exclaimed.

"Unless they're a drunk or a mental patient. You think we'll have looters?" Hart asked as he watched the figure go around a fallen tree. It was dressed in a yellow rain slicker and pants with rubber boots. The hood was pulled over its face.

"Hey, wait a minute . . ." Ironpot pulled down the outside loudspeaker mic and honked the horn. His voice boomed from the public address speaker system. "Police. Stop!"

The figure turned around and Ironpot and Hart stared in disbelief. The figure started to walk toward them.

"Is that Alan Johnson? What's he doing out here?" Hart asked.

"I think it is," Ironpot said as he rolled down his window. Immediately, the wind became so loud it was deafening. Ironpot and the inside of the SUV were immediately drenched.

"Alan!" Ironpot shouted in Alan's face, which was a foot from his. "What are you doing out here?"

Alan smiled. "Trying not to fly!"

"Get in the car!"

Alan pulled the back door open and climbed in onto the plastic seat. Ironpot rolled up his window. Hart and Ironpot turned around and slid open the thick clear Plexiglas window that separated prisoners from officers. "Are you crazy?" Hart asked him.

Alan pulled the car door shut, closing the worst of the storm out, quieting the interior of the car down to a dull roar. "I have to check on Amber. They won't answer the phone."

Ironpot shook his head. "No cell service, and phones aren't working except for local calls, and if you have a remote, you can't use it."

"I know," Alan said, still looking worried. "It's just that I have this feeling I can't shake, and I worry about them being up there by the woods all alone. Trees are going down everywhere."

"We noticed." Ironpot laughed.

"Listen," Hart said, "We're going over to check on Kelly from the ward. Why don't you go with us and then we'll go check on Amber and her family? Okay?"

"I really should hurry. Will it take long?"

"No, and if you ride with us, you're less likely to walk on a live power line when the lights come back on."

"Well, if you put it that way. I'm in," Alan smiled.

"Here we go," Ironpot said and headed in the direction of the old bridge.

———

Amber finally emerged from the woods across the street from her home in her neighbor's backyard. Although it was dark, she recognized it. She went around their house on a dead run in her bare feet and crossed the street, wind whipping what was left of her torn nightgown around her legs. Pulling her hair out of her eyes, she saw that the front door of her house still stood open.

"Mom!" she cried, her words swallowed in the rumbling screaming wind.

She went in the door and forced it shut against the wind gusts. The cold house shook and rattled, wind screaming through every place it could force its way in. Amber heard Bjorn's screams above the winds. The house was dark, but she knew her way. She took the stairs two at a time. Her mother lay in the hall on the floor unmoved from where she had left her. Stepping over her still form, she went into Bjorn's cold room. He sat in his crib in the cloudy moonlight coming through the window, screaming and red-faced. She snatched him up and felt his icy little body shudder, lost in his hysteria. Taking a blanket off the rocker, she wrapped him up, holding him against her chilled, shivering, wet body. It was getting cold enough she could see her breath.

Amber went back into the hall and knelt by her mother. Bjorn continued screaming in her ear. Her mother lay facedown on the carpet. Even though it was dark, Amber could see blood was pooled on the white carpet around Emily's head. Amber took her mother's arm and pulled her dead weight over her shoulder. The blood was coming from Emily's nose, dark against her pale skin. Dreading the worst, Amber felt her mother's throat until she found a pulse. Emily's skin was so very cold. Amber knew another head wound so soon after the last one could be fatal.

"Mom!" Amber yelled, shaking her mother while calling her name. "Mom! Can you hear me! Wake up, Mom!"

Emily groaned. Amber shook her more violently. "Mom!"

Emily's eyes opened and then she shut them rapidly and covered them with her hands. "Oh, my head hurts."

"Mom! Stay awake! I think you have a concussion. Greta's gone. Bjorn's cold. I'm cold. We've got to get him warm, Mom."

"It's freezing," Her mom said as she sat up.

"No, but it's cold. It's not cold enough to kill you, but cold enough to make Bjorn sick."

"The power's still off," Emily said. Amber could see her mother trying to think. She didn't look right. Shock maybe. Amber had an idea. She got up and went down the hall.

Amber went into the bathroom and turned on the tub. They should still have hot water. They had an old gas hot water tank. During the last storm, when they had lost power, they had kept their hot water. She put her hand in the water and waited. Finally it began to warm. She adjusted the taps until the water was hot. She went back out into the hall to her mother.

"Come on, Mom, let's get you and Bjorn into the tub."

"The tub?" Emily murmured.

"Come on Mom, ups-a-daisy." Amber had to put the still-crying Bjorn down, making him scream louder while he leaned on her leg. She helped her mother up. Her mother flinched and Amber looked closer at her face. Her nose was swollen but straight. Her eyes looked really dark. It was hard to tell in the darkness if she had black eyes. She helped her mother walk into the bathroom and leaned her up against the counter. When she went back for Bjorn, she found him crawling and screaming in their direction. Scooping him up, she carried him into the bathroom and sat him on the floor.

Amber found matches in a drawer and lit a candle that sat on the counter. She gasped. Her mother's eyes were both swollen and definitely going to be black. Tenderly, she helped her mother undress and get into the tub. Then she stripped Bjorn and put him in with her mother. The water was warm. Amber wanted to get in herself, but she went down the hall to her mother's room.

In her mother's room, she stacked a pair of soft sweats, a robe, warm socks, and underwear in a pile. In Bjorn's room, she also picked up a new diaper, sleeper, and a fleece blanket. Then she found little socks and brought two pairs, one for his cold little hands and one for his feet. Back in the bathroom, she found her mother was slumped up against the tub with Bjorn still screaming in her lap.

"Mom! Mom! Stay awake. Stay with me, Mom." Amber shook her mother awake again. She pulled Bjorn's warm body out of the tub and dried him with a fluffy towel and quickly dressed him. He sat against the side of the tub and seemed to be finally happy while she helped her mother out and dressed her as well. She carried Bjorn and supported her mother as they walked down the stairs into the living room. She put her mother and Bjorn in front of the fireplace on the couch and then wrapped them both in a quilt that she found.

Amber then ran up the stairs and took the fastest shower of her life. The water ran over her cold, sore body, washing blood, dirt, and salty tears down the drain. Little sticks and leaves joined the dirt and her tears in the bottom of the tub. She finally forced herself out of the warm shower.

She wiped the steamy mirror and looked at her dark reflection in the candlelight. The flickering light revealed a hundred tiny cuts on her legs and arms. A long jagged cut ran across her cheek, and she had a bruise emerging where her stepfather had hit her with the bottle. Tears made the image in the mirror go blurry, but she had no time to cry. Greta was still out there. So silent tears ran against her will while she quickly dried, dressed, and ran downstairs to wake her mother again.

"Mom, you've got to stay awake."

"I'm awake, honey," her Mom murmured in the stormy night.

"Mom, I need to go for help."

"Go next door to Martha, honey. Maybe she has a landline."

"I can't leave if you keep falling asleep. I took first aid, Mom. You have to stay awake."

CHAPTER 55

RAPIDS

HART, IRONPOT, AND ALAN STOPPED THE EXPEDITION AT the end of the old bridge. Even in the dark, the headlights made the situation clear. Large trees and dead heads had washed downriver piling against the bridge, damning the river, pilling higher than the rails, putting pressure on the wooden pilings driven into the river bed seventy years earlier. The water was already level with the road, spilling over the top of the pile and through the wreckage. It was running a few inches deep on the bridge. The river had spread out over the golf course. The only way they could tell it was the golf course was by the two feet of wall and roof showing above the water in the distance.

"The road is higher than the club house," Hart said hopefully.

"Can't tell how deep the water is in the dark."

"You wouldn't be able to tell in the light either," Alan pointed out.

"I know," Ironpot said, "But if we sink the chief's rig, we might as well drown with it."

"The citizens need us." Hart smiled.

"Let's go swimming. Alan, I'm rolling your window down so you can get out if we get stuck," Ironpot said as he and Hart rolled theirs down. It was one thing to get washed away, but he wasn't going to drown inside a car. "Here goes nothing," he shouted over

266

the din as he inched the Expedition forward. Suddenly, he stopped. "Hart, prayer time."

Alan held onto anything he could as Ironpot rolled onto the bridge slowly.

"Sure," Hart said over the wind. He prayed loudly, his voice raising and sinking in the howling wind. Hart finished and closed his prayer. He looked up and said loudly, "Amen!"

"Amen," Ironpot and Alan said.

"I feel better," Alan offered.

"Me too, kid," Ironpot shouted into the wind and kept driving.

The wheels inched across the bridge. It seemed stable, nothing moved. Once across the bridge they began going down the slope on the other side toward the ocean and the golf course. The water gradually rose and they slowly rolled west. Hart put his head out the window into the wind and watched the wheels as the water rose higher and higher.

"The wheels are under!" he yelled at Ironpot. Ironpot kept moving forward. "The water is at the top of the wheel well!" Hart shouted and looked at Ironpot. He looked back out the window. "It's halfway up the door!"

Ironpot didn't respond, he just kept inching ahead. The wheels broke loose from the pavement. The car started to drift with the flow of the river. Then the wheels found the ground again. And they inched slowly forward. The SUV gradually rose out of the river and emerge on the other side.

The water flowed at the level of the hubs. They rolled their windows up. Hart sat back and breathed a sigh of relief. "I think we're okay. Kelly's house is just ahead."

"I remember." They passed houses sticking out of the water and pulled in front of Kelly's house. "There's no light in the window," Ironpot noted.

"Power's out," Hart said seriously.

"Really?" Ironpot said in his most sarcastic voice.

"Funny," Hart said. He got out and went up the stairs. He knocked on the door. "Kelly!" He didn't have to wait long. The door opened. Kelly came out and wrapped her arms around his neck and squeezed him tight.

"I am so glad you're here!" she shouted into the wind.

"I am too," Hart said with a grin. Kelly pulled back and looked down sheepishly, hair whipping wildly in her face. Hart laughed out loud. "Most people don't hug their officers." She playfully hit him on the arm.

"Most people don't hit their police officers either."

"I thought I was going to drown here."

"It's past high tide. I don't think the water will get much deeper. I think it will go down, as a matter of fact."

"Don't leave me here to find out!"

Hart looked at Ironpot and Alan waiting in the car. "I can't take you with me while I'm working," he said, frustrated. "Just a minute." He waded out to Ironpot at the car. Ironpot rolled down his window. "She wants to go with us."

Ironpot rolled his eyes. "I don't think it's a good night for a ride along."

"We can't leave her here all alone like this."

Ironpot thought for a moment. He let out a deep breath. A gust of wind caught Hart's hat and he held it down waiting for Ironpot to think. "Okay," Ironpot said, "Why don't we take her to Grace? Grace's at my place because of the alarms. Grace said she'd help if we needed her."

"It's our duty."

"How much longer, guys?" Alan said from the back.

"You getting restless?" Ironpot asked.

"Yes, I'm really worried."

"We've still got to drop him off," Ironpot jerked his head in Alan's direction, reminding Hart.

"We'll make a big circle. We'll drop her at Grace's and then take Alan to Amber's."

"I feel like a taxi service," Ironpot said. "Grace's probably still at my house."

"I'll get Kelly."

Kelly put on a coat and rubber boots. She got her purse. Hart carried her piggyback over the water and out to the SUV.

"Let's take another road out of here. I don't want to go that deep again," Ironpot said.

"If we cross town we can go over the new bridge," Hart pointed north.

Ironpot turned the car around and began inching back through the water. He went farther west toward the ocean. Branches were down, trees lay across the road, and debris covered the pavement. They wove through the chaos and turned on a road that ran parallel to the ocean and headed north. A mile down they turned back onto Broadway and turned east. The downtown area had broken windows, downed power lines, and a plastic chair was stuck in a shrub. Not a soul was in sight.

They turned north again and then joined the road that ran parallel with the Necanicum River. The river was full and brimming on this end of town too, but still within its banks. The new bridge rose a few inches above the water. Ironpot crossed the river and followed the back roads towards his home.

A few minutes later, Ironpot pulled into his driveway. Grace's family was lying around the fireplace. Grace was just coming down the hall from the bathroom. Ironpot stood just inside the door.

"Hi, I heard the storm blow you in," she said.

"No one else did," Ironpot said, looking at the bodies on the couch.

"I did," Nephi said and sat up stretching.

"Sorry," Ironpot laughed. "Listen, I have Kelly Finch in the car. She was at her house all alone and scared. The water by the golf course is really rising. Can she stay at your house?"

"Sure," Grace answered.

"Is my wife up?"

"Not yet."

"Thanks. When she does get up, tell her I love her and came by. By the way, we have no way of checking if there is a tsunami, but we think it's a short in the system. We don't have any other evidence of a tsunami. But we're pretty cut off from the rest of the world. There are no phone lines or roads reaching out of the county. We have a ham radio operator with Brother Grahm working on it."

"You can't reach Portland?"

"Nope, and they can't reach us. We are totally isolated. Phone lines, cell towers, and power lines are all down. The power company is telling us it's serious. The large towers, rated for wind over two hundred miles an hour, appear to be down, crumpled like tinfoil. Both major highways are closed due to hundreds of downed trees"

"Wow, this sounds like we're going to be out of power for a while." Mabel said.

"They are estimating thirty days."

"You've got to be kidding!" Grace was shocked.

"No, I wish I was. It's a mess out there."

"We might as well go home," Mabel said and started to stand up, stretching. "No surfing the tsunami today."

"Yeah, I'm not sleeping," Grace said. "The kids can sleep anywhere. Why don't you let Kelly ride with us?" Ironpot went back out to the vehicle and helped Kelly out. Kelly waved goodbye to Hart and Alan and went in with Grace and her family.

Ironpot backed out of the driveway and headed back to a main road. The wind hadn't let up, and the morning sun was making a failed attempt to break through the rapidly moving storm clouds. He followed the east side of the river. Rain fell in sheets, filling the river, soaking the ground until water was squirting out of blown manhole covers a foot into the air and running back into the widening river. One manhole cover was entirely missing. The river lapped in small waves onto the edge of the road and across it in places. The city workers in their white trucks were already out clearing the streets. They were cutting trees that lay across the road and cutting down widowmakers or branches that hung broken above the road, waiting to fall on an unsuspecting passerby. The power company wasn't far down the road. A crew had the bucket truck with its boom extended at an odd angle. No one appeared hurt. Men stood around the truck talking while one of their members scaled a nearby pole the old fashioned way, with a belt wrapped around it and spiked climbing boots.

"Wow," Ironpot said as he slowed to a crawl. "There's one job you couldn't pay me to do."

Hart rolled down his window and leaned his head out and shouted to the crew near the truck. "Everything okay? You need a hand?" All the men wore rain gear. An older crewmember walked over to the patrol car and shook his head, already looking exhausted.

"No. Everyone's fine. Tried to put up the bucket, too windy! Blew it over! Help's on the way."

Hart nodded and waved, rolling up his window. Ironpot radioed in information on the truck to the station on the handheld ham radio. Slowly, they rolled past the men working.

Downed trees made direct travel impossible. Ironpot drove onto the lawn of a vacant lot and then back onto the sidewalk and then around another tree closer to the river, in and out of the water. Slowly they made their way south.

As they passed the church, Ironpot pulled to a stop. The sun was rising and the light was making the destruction clear and overwhelming.

"Oh my gosh!" Hart said, staring at the twenty or so hundred-foot pines stacked like Lincoln logs in the church parking lot. One of the trees was eight feet thick, balancing on a brick retaining wall and sticking out across the lot. The chain-link fence looked like crumpled lace.

"Not one of them hit the building," Alan noticed. "Or one of the tall lights."

"Are you surprised?" Hart said as he turned to Alan and smiled.

"No." Alan smiled back.

"Boys, we've got a mess to clean up," Ironpot shook his head.

"After work," Hart said and sat back. "Let's go."

Ironpot kept traveling. The main road up the hill was open. All the large trees had been pulled down during the latest construction. As the sun rose in the east over the hill, he gasped and stopped the car again. "Will you look at that?"

The entire hillside looked like a bomb had gone off. "It looks like Mount Saint Helens after the volcano blew," Hart said, shaking his head.

"It does! Look at the trees." Alan pointed at the mountain, "They are all laying in the same direction."

"Some of them have been pulled up by the roots," Ironpot added.

"Those trees are old-growth," Hart pointed out. "Maybe more than hundreds of years old."

Ironpot started to move again.

———

Sam made his way to her room; he'd waited long enough. No one would hear. He couldn't even hear himself think in the wind. He didn't want to think. He realized he was really drunk, but the thought passed. He wove his way down the hall to his bedroom and then past. Farther down the hall he stopped at the door and smiled. Tonight was finally her lucky night.

Sam tried the door. It was locked. That little witch. He'd show her. He threw his shoulder into the door. Nothing happened. He hit it again and again. Finally he leaned back and kicked it. The door swung open.

Candy bolted upright. "What do you want?" Candy asked flatly.

"You know what I want," Sam slurred and lurched into her room. She screamed again, louder. He took her by the hair, pushing her back onto her bed. "Shut up!" His foggy brain didn't want her mother to hear. "Shut up!" he bellowed. She wouldn't stop screaming. He slapped her face hard. That's when he heard the shot and felt the burning force of it throw him to the floor.

———

Greta was finally sure he was gone. She had waited, silent and still, heart beating in her ears, afraid to move for what felt like hours to her little mind. It was quieter in the hollow of the rotten stump.

She sat up and wiped her tears with her dirty nightgown. Feeling terribly alone, she thought for a minute and then got on her knees to pray. Amber had been talking to the missionaries and praying for help for their mother. Greta would pray for help. First, she folded her arms, bowed her tiny head, closed her eyes, and then began to beg out loud for help. When she opened her eyes, she felt warmer, but so tired. Lying back down, she looked at the light coming into the tree. It was bright and warm when she slipped away to sleep.

———

Amber had gone to her neighbor's house, carrying Bjorn wrapped in a blanket, and banged on the door until Martha answered. Martha had taken Bjorn and was rocking him to sleep while Amber tried to call 911. "It just rings busy," Amber told Martha. "Not a regular busy, but a fast one. What do you think it means?"

"The phone lines must be down," Martha whispered over Bjorn's head.

"I need to go back in the woods to look for Greta but can't leave my mother. She can't go to sleep."

"Frank is getting dressed to go to the police station and get help. I'd stay with your mother, but I'm too old to pick her up if she goes down. I'd be too worried to be alone with her. Besides, you can't go back out in this wind."

"Don't worry about me. I'm just glad Bjorn can stay with you," Amber said. She knew Martha was worried. She tried to reassure her. "Thank you so much. Do you think he'd drive Mom to the hospital when he gets back?"

"Absolutely. Anything for your mom," Martha said with a smile. "Don't worry, Amber, we'll find her."

"Berk was so angry and drunk," Amber said, her voice catching in her throat. "I've never seen him quite like this. I . . ." Unable to talk about it anymore, she shook her head, looking down at the floor while she put her coat back on. "Have Frank come over when he's back," she said and opened the door. Then she saw a police car pulling into her driveway.

"The police are here!" She called back to Martha and then went out the door and crossed the lawn yelling into the wind, "Hello?"

———

Alan got out of the back of the SUV and frantically rushed toward Amber. Amber's anguished form ran across the lawn and threw herself on him, holding onto him, and finally breaking down into sobbing tears. Then she saw the police car backing out of her driveway.

"Where are they going?" she asked Alan, stepping back and looking over his shoulder.

"They just dropped me off," he replied, looking perplexed at her as she let go of him and ran toward the large white police vehicle. "Wait! Wait! Don't go!" she yelled, waving at the officers while running toward them. Ironpot scowled as he rolled down his window. Amber ran into the vehicle and put both hands on the windowsill. "You have to help us," she said breathlessly. "He came back. He took Greta into the woods," she explained pointing in the direction of the mountain. "I tried to get her back, but I couldn't find her. Mom's been hurt. I think it's bad. I can't leave her to go back and look. I need help."

"Whoa, slow down," Ironpot said, holding his hands up.

"Slow down!" Amber's angry reaction surprised herself. "I can't slow down! Greta's out there with Berk and he's drunk and mad!"

"Which way did they go?" Alan asked. "I'll go . . ."

"Not alone you won't," Ironpot said firmly, increasing Amber's frustration. "Amber, we're going to find her, and we're going to help your mother, but you can't go off half-cocked and get yourself killed. Trees are going down everywhere. The woods are dangerous. I'm going to radio for help and we're going to do this right."

Amber felt rage coursing through her body. "I'm not waiting for you!" she said and started running toward the back of the house. Alan sprinted after her.

"Amber! Amber, slow down!" he shouted over the ever-present storm. She didn't stop. He ran harder and caught her by the arm, yanking her wet body around. "Amber, he's right. Let's get your mom to the hospital and get help. They've got dogs and people that are trained to do this."

"I'm not waiting!"

"Okay, fine!" he said, exasperated. "Then let's get your mom taken care of and I'll help you. I'll go with you."

Amber looked intently at the woods, the rainy wind blowing her hair into her eyes, pulling at her clothes. Alan took a hold of her hand. She looked down at his warm hand and then up into his serious eyes. She decided he meant it. He would help. "All right, but let's hurry," she said as she pulled him along to the house.

Martha stood on her porch, watching. The police car rocked in the wind while idling in the driveway. Amber took the steps two at a time and went through the open door. Ironpot was standing by Officer Hart who was kneeling next to her mother. Hart was looking into her eyes with a flashlight. He had one covered. "Your pupils are working, whatever that means," he said.

Ironpot turned to Amber, "I radioed the hospital, but your mom won't go."

"Mom, you have to go! I'll find Greta."

"I can't stand leaving you here. What if he comes back?"

"I'm staying," Hart said to Emily. "Amber won't be alone. I'll call Grace to stay with her. Let your neighbor take you. You were out for a long time."

Emily took a deep breath and let it out in a loud rush. She looked at Amber who was so anxious and looked back at the officer. "All right, but you have to promise to tell me if you find anything." Tears involuntarily ran down her face as her nose turned red. "Anything! Do you understand me?"

"I promise," Hart said to her very solemnly.

Amber couldn't breathe. She couldn't stop crying. Finally, calmly, she went to the closet and got a coat out for her mother. "Here, Mom, now go with Ironpot so I don't have to worry about you too."

Her mother stood unsteadily and put the coat on with Officer Ironpot's help. Frank, her sixty-year-old graying neighbor, put his arm around her shoulder and walked her gently out the door.

"I'm going to get my hiking boots and gear," Amber said to Alan.

"Amber," Ironpot looked her in the eyes. "I've called the sheriff's department. Search and rescue has a dog. He can find anything, even a body underwater, he's so good. The handler, Renee Fish, lives just outside of town. I've radioed the station. They are going to send someone to try and bring Renee and her dog here. I also radioed an officer that's going to get Grace to come up and stay with you."

"How long would we have to wait?" Amber asked.

"We'll know in fifteen minutes," Ironpot told her. "You can help by getting some of Greta's clothes. The dog will need a scent. Dirty is better."

Amber looked at Alan who nodded his approval and then looked back at Ironpot skeptically. She crossed her arms and said, "I'll give it fifteen minutes, and not a minute more." She let her arms drop and went to the staircase and started up.

"Amber, I'll help," Alan said. He wanted to talk to her alone. Alan followed her up the stairs. She didn't slow down or look back when she skirted a dark stain on the floor. Alan's eyes got bigger as he stopped long enough to realize it was dried blood. Going into Greta's room, she started picking up the broken closet doors and moving them. Seeing her struggle, Alan silently took the heavy doors easily out of her hands and put them up against the wall.

Amber went to the closet and looked at the clothes. She said out loud to herself, "Dirty clothes work better?"

"Definitely have a stronger smell," he smiled weakly at her. He picked up the sleeve on a dress hanging in the closet and sniffed it. "This smells like flowery fabric softener."

Amber rummaged in a hamper in the corner of the closet and came out with a handful of little T-shirts. Pressing them to her nose, she smelled Greta, breathing her in deeply, releasing tears, folding into herself and kneeling on the floor. "Alan," she finally managed to say.

He knelt next to her on the floor, gently pulling her hands away from her face and holding them in his. He bowed his head until his forehead touched hers and then with no shame for the tears, he cried as he silently begged God for Greta and Amber's family and for his own. Outside, the wind raged, the ocean left its bounds, and it seemed the world was ending.

CHAPTER 56

WEATHERING THE STORM

GRACE, MABEL, KELLY, AND THE KIDS HAD GONE BACK TO her house. Grace and Kelly sat next to each other on matching overstuffed wingback chairs in front of the fireplace. Grace's feet were up, and she was knitting a long scarf. The fireplace was lit and crackling. Mabel and Mary sat on the old hardwood floor working on s'mores. Mary had on pajama bottoms, covered by jeans, covered by sweats, two pairs of socks on her feet and hands, and several T-shirts topped with one of Grace's oversized sweatshirts. "Nana, I think I made the perfect marshmallow," she said, holding up a golden-brown marshmallow on the end of a homemade wire roaster.

"Here's the graham cracker," Mabel said, holding up an open graham cracker sandwich with squares of a chocolate bar resting on one side. "Gently, gently," she whispered. They looked more like they were performing surgery than making s'mores. When Mabel and Mary had the perfect s'more in Mary's sock hands, she shoved the entire thing through the hole in her ski mask in one bite. There was only one problem. Her mouth was bigger than the hole in the mask. Sticky marshmallow clung to the knit ski cap all around her mouth and all over her sock gloves.

"Mmm," Mary critiqued the s'more. "Next time I think it needs more chocolate."

Mabel nodded seriously. "All right, a four square s'more," she said and opened the chocolate while Mary skewered another marshmallow.

Nephi came in carrying a load of kindling and an axe. Esther followed him, carrying firewood.

"That's not enough!" Esther complained to Nephi. "The power is going to be out forever! Have you looked outside?"

"Well then you cut it. My hands are raw," Nephi retorted.

"I will. Anyone can do better than you, sissy boy," Esther said, taking the axe roughly from him.

"I'll do it. Give me the axe!" Nephi said, not wanting to lose sight of their new toy. He reached out for the axe.

"No, Nephi, I'm chopping it now!" Esther said back to him, holding it tight against her chest.

"Kids! Kids! Don't fight over the axe in front of our company!" Grace said. "Mom, you think they should be chopping wood unsupervised? Isn't it dangerous?"

Mabel looked at her and rolled her eyes. "You have an Eagle Scout and Girls Camp grad here. They been chopping and burning things for several years. Fire and guns are their favorite things."

"Mom, you're scaring Kelly," Grace said.

"No, you're not," Kelly said. "I used to hunt and camp with my folks. Let me show you how to chop wood," she said with a smile and took the axe from a surprised Esther and went out the back door.

Grace's surprise was interrupted by a knock on the door. She went to answer it. Officer Lynn Fish was there.

"Lynn, come in," she said, happy to see the officer. She extended her hand into the smoky living room, signaling Lynn to enter. The wind, several leaves, a handful of pine needles, and streaks of mud followed Lynn inside.

"Grace, Officer Ironpot asked me to come and get you. We have a domestic on the hill."

"Who is it?" Grace asked.

"Berk Anderson," Lynn told her.

Nephi dropped the last of the wood on the floor and looked shocked. "Is that Amber Anderson's dad?"

Officer Fish didn't answer Nephi. "Can you come?"

"Sure. Let me get my shoes and my coat." Grace slipped off her slippers and pulled a pair off suede fur-lined boots out of a basket by the door.

"Mom, I'm taking the Jeep. I don't know when I'll be back. You can put Kelly in the guest room down here, okay?"

Mabel crossed the room and kissed her goodbye.

"Perfect!" Mary said with chocolate teeth, smiling behind a marshmallow-smeared hole in a ski mask. Grace's heart ached at the thought of missing any moment with her family, but she knew she had to go. "What is Hart doing?" she asked Fish.

CHAPTER 57

INTO THE WIND

GRACE FOLLOWED THE OFFICER ONTO THE LARGE FRONT porch and into the noisy wind. She wondered how much longer it was going to blow like this. "This storm is bad!"

"We've clocked the wind at over a hundred miles for hours now," Officer Fish said. "I heard on the ham radio that someone across the river has recorded gusts over a hundred and fifty. There are a lot of fallen trees. I know a few clear roads so stay behind me."

"Can you tell me what the domestic is about?"

"Hart is the lead." Officer Fish filled Grace in with what she knew.

"Here we go." Grace stepped out of the protection of the porch and felt the wind hit her hard, trying to knock her off her feet. It gusted and grabbed her hair. Pulling her hood up and hanging onto it, she turned into the wind. It took her breath away. She began to realize the enormity of the storm as it continued to rage all around her.

CHAPTER 58

HIDING PLACE

GRETA HAD BURROWED UNDERNEATH THE LOOSE, ROTTING wood and bark inside the dark stump. She slept soundly, dreaming of pirate ships and storms at sea.

"Greta . . . Greta . . ." a soft voice woke her. It was like a whisper on her face. Stirring, she looked up. No one was there. Maybe she was dreaming. She shivered and felt her wet, dirty hair. It was starting to dry. She looked outside the opening, which let light in. It was daytime, but the wind was still howling and screaming. *At least it's not raining*, she thought. She lay back down and closed her eyes. "Greta . . . Greta . . ." She heard it again.

This time she sat up. Maybe it was Amber. Maybe she was calling her. Rolling over onto her knees in the soft rotting wood, she looked out of the opening. The wind caught her thin hair and battered her as the roar filled her ears. Squinting into the wind, she looked all around and saw no one. Nothing. She was alone. The forest looked different.

She pulled back into the stump and realized that something was wriggling under her hand. Hastily, she yanked her hand up and squealed, finding it covered in bark dust and larvae. Little worms were crawling in the wood, eating the rotten tree. "Ew, ew, ew!" she said, quickly standing and hitting her head.

"Greta . . . Greta . . ." There it was again, like a whisper in the roaring wind. She heard it all the way through her and down to her toes. The little hairs on her arms stood up and goose bumps rolled over her prickling her flesh. She shook herself. Amber, it had to be Amber.

Greta looked around and wondered where she was. How far had they gone? She almost hoped her father would come back for her.

"Daddy! Daddy!" she called. But every time she opened her mouth, a large gust of wind would swallow her words. She tried again and again, but always the biting wind picked up and she was sure no one would hear her. Cold, wet, and getting awfully hungry, she looked at the larvae and remembered a reality television show she had once seen.

"No way! I am not eating you!" she said out loud to no one. Finally, she made her decision; she would try to find her way home. But which way should she go?

She thought for a moment and then looked up at the boiling black and gray clouds blowing overhead. "Hello, God! It's me, it's Greta."

———

Grace's car rocked and swayed as the wind gusted while she navigated the debris-filled streets. Officer Fish had explained loudly over the wind what she knew had happened so far. The news wasn't good. Berk and Greta were somewhere on the mountain, in the woods, in the storm. Luckily, because the wind and weather was coming from the south, it wasn't cold enough to freeze anyone. It wasn't warm enough to be comfortable for a wet, frightened little girl though. She could get hypothermia. Emily was still at the hospital getting x-rays. The hospital was running on a generator, as was the sewage plant, and oddly enough, the lights on the Twelfth Avenue Bridge.

After weaving through town in the gray daylight, Grace started to realize the extent of the damage. It was mesmerizing. The wind continued raging; it was coming up from the southwest, blowing into the coast across town and against the mountain.

The mountain above Necanicum was covered in trees whose roots had held, but because the trees didn't bend far enough, had snapped off at about fifteen feet in the air, leaving the tops laying on the ground, all facing the same direction. Other trees were blown down, roots and all. The damage was in a pattern. It almost looked like the wind had blown in streams that followed the path of least resistance, laying trees down in a shape like water flowing.

Along a road that ran parallel with the river, several trees growing in the waterlogged earth beside the river had fallen, pulling their entire root system from the ground. They lay against each other in a row like toppled dominoes.

Here and there, windows were blown out, shingles and whole roofs were missing, or siding was torn away from homes. City trucks, the state department of transportation, and private contractors were cutting trees and clearing the roads. A power crew was on the road near the church. Grace gasped when she saw the church parking lot covered in downed trees stacked ten- and twenty-feet deep.

As she turned to travel up Emily Anderson's street, she saw that the beautiful mountain behind Emily's home was completely changed. Hundreds of trees were snapped off at about the same height, and stood with trunks stripped bare and jagged tops reaching above the piles of green treetops laying on the ground. Tangled massive, round root balls showed their bottom to the city like toppled toy soldiers.

Officer Hart and Amber were just leaving the house as Grace pulled in. Amber had on her usual jeans and a hoodie, but she also had hiking boots and a heavy jacket over her hoodie. She was carrying a large diaper bag and a pink suitcase. Hart smiled and waved. Grace smiled back as she pulled in the driveway.

Ironpot and Alan came out of the Anderson home. Alan ran to catch up with Amber while Ironpot stood on the porch, talking on the handheld ham radio, waiting for Grace.

"You're kidding me!" Grace heard Ironpot say in frustration as she joined him on the porch.

"No," Molly the dispatcher's voice said over the radio. "It's going to take a while to clear Highway 26. They say there are fifty-foot stacks of trees as far as the eye can see. I hear the curve near the egg farm had a mudslide, bringing the entire mountainside of pines down. We need major equipment."

"What about search and rescue?" Ironpot asked while rubbing his face in consternation.

"Have you looked at the hills? The cell towers are down. Crumpled like nothing. Dudley says they are supposed to withstand winds of 237 miles an hour. We can't page any of the search team. Cell phones and remote phones aren't working. I talked to the sheriff's department on the ham radio in Bay Town and most of his men live out of town on rural roads, which are completely closed. You're required to live out in the county if you're a deputy."

"How many men can you get me?" Ironpot asked.

"Ironpot, Chief wants you," Molly said. There was a rustling noise as the microphone changed hands.

The chief's voice came on. "John, from the fire department, wandered in here a while ago. If I send Officer Fish to find him, maybe he can scare up some locals, but they won't be a trained team. Is this fellow armed?"

Ironpot blew out a gust of air and dropped his free hand and head in frustration. "I don't know, Chief."

"We can't send a bunch of civilians up there with a dangerous man in this weather. We would be searching for more people than this kid. You and Hart are going to have to wait this out. I don't want to lose two good officers to this storm. When the wind stops and the trees stop falling, we'll find a qualified team of trained officers and send them up."

Ironpot was silent, seething with anxiety and frustration. He couldn't bring himself to give up. He knew this little girl. "Chief, let me go up with Hart. Have Fish stay with the family."

"No, do you hear me, Ironpot! This will cost you your job if you do! You're too close to the situation. Step back and think. I have to take everyone's safety into consideration, including yours!"

Ironpot paused. "Yes, sir. Ironpot K7PIG out" Ironpot looked at Grace. He almost looked embarrassed.

"I'm sorry," he said. Grace reached out and patted him on the arm.

He was so frustrated he swore, "Fetch!" He looked at her and raised his eyebrows and shrugged. "You heard him. We're stuck."

"Where are they?"

Ironpot didn't answer. Instead, he walked around the west end of the house and Grace followed, wind still blowing and violently slapping her hair in her face. They found themselves standing, blasted by wind, on the green back lawn, looking up at the cataclysmic destruction still happening on the hillside. "He took her up there. He's drunk, and on the last sighting, he had his arm across her throat and she looked like she couldn't breathe."

The picture he painted hit Grace square in the chest. She suddenly realized they might be looking at a homicide. The gale tangled her hair viciously while everything she knew about trauma recovery swam through her head. How would she ever help anyone who had suffered this much pain? "Why would he do that to his own child?" she shouted into the wind, more out of frustration and more to herself than as a question.

"Who knows? Amber said he was saying Greta wasn't his, and that that has been the source of arguments for years. It's all water under the bridge now." Ironpot raised his voice as a gust of wind picked his last words up and tried to take off his hat. "I can't go in there and tell that girl that no one is looking for her sister. She'll go up there herself."

"So would I," Grace spoke the truth they both felt as she scanned the mountainside, looking for any sign of the child.

"I can't stand this!" Ironpot yelled. "I want to be up that mountain, and I know Hart does too. I feel like she's right there! Like I can almost touch her! I know I could find her!"

"I know you could."

He shook his head and turned back in the direction of the house, shielding his eyes from debris. "I don't know what I'm going to tell Amber." They stood solemnly for a moment, worry creasing both their faces. "We decided to move them to the neighbor's for safety. I'd like to get them all out of here. Berk's a wild card that doesn't seem to give up. I have this feeling that when he starts to sober up he's going to come back for more alcohol and trouble."

"How did he get here?"

"We don't know. I suppose he walked away from treatment. He was right here in town. We think he got the alcohol in his own garage. The side door to the garage and the door into the house were open. It looked like he'd been there."

Grace knew they were just making small talk while they tried to figure out what to do. "I really should move them to a safer location," she said again, looking up at Ironpot's worried face.

"I don't think we're going to get them to budge. If the wind would just stop, I think we could search the hill. It can't go on much longer. It's been like this for over twelve hours."

———

Amber and Alan stood anxiously at the sliding glass door at the back of Martha's house, watching Ironpot and Grace walk toward them. Martha's and Emily's homes had spectacular views of the mountain in the back and the ocean in the front. Consequently, neither family had fenced their yards. Open lawns met the uncut forest. It had been a breathtaking sight, but now it was changed.

Amber opened the sliding glass door and let them and the storm in. The door slid shut, muffling the wind down to a constant howl, shaking the house. Ironpot and Grace wiped their feet on the welcome mat and entered the warm room. A woodburning stove glowed in the corner. Martha rocked Bjorn next to it in a padded recliner.

"Well?" Amber asked.

Ironpot took a deep breath and began, "Amber, the search and rescue team can't get to us. The roads are completely closed and the cell towers are down. No one can call any numbers except for those with their same prefix. So we can only call Necanicum phone numbers and most of the team lives out in the county at other prefixes."

"So we'll just have to search ourselves," Amber said.

"Amber," Ironpot said softly. "We can't go out there. It's too dangerous. Look at how cut up you got just trying last night."

"That was in the dark! It's light now! We can't leave her up there!" She fisted her hands by her side. "Please!"

Ironpot's shoulders slumped. Hart stood now, looking confused. Ironpot went on, "The chief is not allowing anyone up there to search until this thing dies down. It's just too dangerous."

"Well the chief can't tell me what to do!" Amber said and went out the back door. Alan quickly followed her.

"Amber! Amber!" Alan called above the wind.

She spun around. "What!" she growled in his face.

"Hey!" He held his hands up in surrender. "I'm on your side. But you can't just go up there without help. You'll get lost. It's not the old woods anymore. Look at it!"

He pointed at the mountain and she turned her back to the wind and looked at the hill. She began realizing again how complete the destruction was. As far as she could see in every direction, there were trees balancing on trees, snapped off broken trees, fallen trees with roots upended leaving huge holes, and pieces of everything flying in the wind. "I don't care, Alan! I can't just sit here while she's up there alone!"

"Okay, then let me go with you!" He reached out and took her hand. They started crossing the lawn hand in hand, heads down in the wind. When they reached the edge of the forest, they stopped and once more stood and looked.

The explosive sound of trees still breaking, falling, and whipping in the wind was deafening. Amber couldn't hear herself think. Alan pulled her close and yelled in her ear so she could hear him. "We'll find her, I know it!"

Amber nodded and once again they stood, eyes closed, heads together, and she felt warmth course through her, not from being close to Alan, but from something she was learning to recognize. It was something that she felt when she prayed. He gave her a quick hug and they both turned again, holding hands, and looked at the mountain.

"Maybe I should go back for bread crumbs?" Alan shouted. Amber smiled and they entered the woods.

"Greta! Greta!" Amber screamed into the wind, and Alan's voice joined hers. The hungry wind consumed their cries.

———

"I can't let them go alone," Grace said, going to the door.

"Seems like this is a day for getting in trouble with the boss," Ironpot said, giving her a look like a father reprimanding a child.

"I know it's not wise, but I don't know what else to do," she said and opened the door, letting the violent wind blow in as she went out. Once again, the wind caught Grace and tried to knock her off her feet. She crossed the lawn and saw Amber and Alan, heads together, eyes closed, and wondered what they were doing. She looked heavenward as she walked toward them. Alan and Amber entered the woods and Grace jogged to catch up.

"Amber! Amber!" The wind snatched her voice away. Knowing her boss wouldn't want her to do anything that put her in danger, she stood at the edge of the trees and hesitated for a moment. Watching Amber with her hand cupped around her mouth, she thought she must be shouting Greta's name, but she couldn't hear her above the wind. Greta would never be able to hear them.

———

"Greta! Greta!" Amber and Alan's voices were a chorus. Amber caught a flash of color moving in the brush to her right. Letting go of Alan, she frantically scrambled over a log.

Two little arms were reaching over the next log and then Amber saw Greta's dirty face beaming. Amber scrambled to push aside debris and reached the log as Greta was climbing over it. She snatched Greta up into her arms, burying her face in Greta's dirty hair. Tears fell. They laughed and screamed for joy together. "Alan!" she yelled in the storm as she turned around just in time to feel his arms circle both their bodies and hold them in a tear-filled, joyful embrace. "Greta!"

"I heard you call me," Greta shouted in Amber's ear. "I've walked ten hundred miles 'cause I heard you!"

Amber looked confused. "It was so windy, I didn't think you could hear me."

"Oh. Maybe it was Daddy?"

That thought made Amber look around in fear. She saw Grace running to join them.

"Greta!" Grace said, smiling as she reached them. "Listen, kids, we need to get out of here. Where's your daddy, Greta?"

"I don't know. I can't find him."

"Okay, kids, let's go!" Grace ordered and then she began herding them back down the trail over the logs and toward home. A fresh curtain of rain joined the howling wind. Greta remained wrapped around Amber, and Alan pushed and pulled the pair over the few logs they had to cross. It wasn't long before they emerged onto the open lawn and Martha's house burst open with Ironpot and Hart running across the lawn to meet them.

Ironpot was already radioing in Greta's safe return, and Hart was scanning the woods for Berk. Both officers had their holsters unsnapped and they put themselves between the kids and the woods as they backed across the lawn toward the house.

———

"Greta!" Martha exclaimed, waking Bjorn as they all entered her house. She opened her arms, and Greta let go of Amber and ran to Martha for a hug.

"Where's Mom?" Greta asked.

"She's at the doctors getting checked out," Amber told her. "She's fine. But I know she's going to want to see you. We better get you cleaned up."

"I don't know if we should wait to do that," Grace said to Amber. "I think the sooner we leave the area, the less likely we are to have more . . ." she made quotation marks in the air, "trouble."

A look of understanding crossed Amber's face. "What should we do? Do you think he'll come back?"

"I don't want Daddy to get hurt," Greta said seriously to Amber.

Amber rolled her eyes, but answered, "No one does, sweetie."

"Why don't I take you to see your mom and then we can find you a safe place to stay for the night?" Grace offered, looking at Greta but talking to Amber.

"Mommy! Let's go! I don't have any shoes," Greta said, looking down at her dirty feet.

"We'll take care of that. Let me talk to Amber and Officer Ironpot for a minute."

Grace, Amber, Ironpot, and Alan went into the kitchen together. Grace looked at Amber thoughtfully and shared her concerns, "I need to get you kids out of here, but all the hotels are closed. Your mom may not be well enough to go with you. I may need to bring you home with me."

"That's not necessary," Alan said. "I'll take care of Amber and her mom. They can stay with my family."

"Are you sure?" Amber asked.

"Of course," Alan said.

"I have to get permission from Emily. Maybe you should ask your folks," Grace said. "But if they say no, we'll work something out. Amber, what do you have in your suitcase? Could you be gone with your family for three days?"

"No, I have stuff for Bjorn and me, but not for Mom or Greta."

"I think we better get some clean clothes for Greta and make sure we have enough for your mom."

"Grace, will you come with me to pack for the family?" Ironpot asked. Grace knew it was risky because no one knew where Berk was. There was a chance he could be back in the house, but Ironpot was trained and he trusted Grace to follow him in and stay behind him. She trusted Ironpot.

"Of course."

"Thanks. That would be great. Amber, make me a floor plan and a list. You stay here with Martha and Officer Hart."

Amber drew a map and directions for how to find clothes for her mom and Greta. Martha got out plastic grocery bags to pack the clothes in. Grace and Ironpot went back out in the wind, always watching the mountain, and went over to the house to pack.

━━

Grace held escaping curls out of her eyes as she walked behind Officer Ironpot with the wind at her back, following him to the house. Ironpot was alert and scanning the hill. He opened the door to the house with his hand on his gun, still in the holster. He stopped and Grace ran into his back.

"Oof, sorry," Grace laughed into the wind.

"Wait here," Ironpot motioned seriously. Grace and Ironpot knew that Berk could have found his way back into the house. She had once been in a home with officers, only to learn later that the abuser had been hiding among pipes in a tiny cupboard under a sink in the kitchen the entire time.

Grace watched Ironpot pull his gun and begin to clear the house again, room by room. When Ironpot went into the garage, she heard a door slam, so she backed up against the wall by the door and out of sight. Ironpot was in the garage for what seemed like a long time. Thinking she could hear him come out, she peeked around the corner. It was Ironpot. She exhaled, realizing she hadn't been breathing.

"I heard a door slam."

"That was me. It was the door to the garage." She followed him through the garage and up the stairs into the house. The wind blew through the open front door, ruffling houseplants and playing with the tablecloth on the kitchen table.

Motioning to Grace to wait, Ironpot cleared the upstairs. After a few moments, he emerged at the top of the spiral stairs, looking decidedly more relaxed. "It's clear," he said and waved for her to come up. His gun was back in his holster. "Shut the door and lock it," he directed.

Grace closed and locked the front door and followed him up the stairs, where she packed clothes for Greta and her mother in black plastic sacks. She also took shoes, coats, shampoo, and a makeup bag that looked like it belonged to Emily.

"Has anyone told Emily we have Greta?" Grace asked.

"I radioed the station, but I don't know if anyone told the hospital. They were probably listening in. We're on ham radios using the same frequency,"

"I can take Greta over to her mother," Grace offered. "But don't you need to get a statement from her?"

"Yes. I wish I could wait for the experts, but I want to get a description of his clothes and as much information as I can so that as soon as this clears we can start a search and pick him up. I'll meet you at Alan's folks' and interview her there where she'll be safer."

"I can't imagine how frightened Greta was, and yet she still loves him," Grace said, shaking her head.

"Yeah. It's amazing isn't it? It doesn't matter how mean parents are, most kids still love them and want them. I've been on worse calls and had kids beg for parents when the state took them to foster care."

"I know. Well, I think this is enough. Let's get back."

"Follow me to the door," Ironpot directed.

"This storm is weird, isn't it?" Grace said, watching him.

"I can remember lots of wind storms, I just don't remember one that lasted this long and had gusts this strong, over and over."

"I know. Usually we get periodic strong gusts and heavy wind. This storm seems to be repeated strong gusts and a nonstop blow. I always worried about a tsunami, not a windstorm. Funny, isn't it?"

"I don't know. My wife had a feeling about this winter."

Grace knew what he meant. She was so grateful for the fire-wood she'd felt compelled to buy.

Ironpot went on, "Hart is the one I'm worried about."

"Why's that?"

"His place is deep in the woods along the river. If the flood-ing doesn't get him, the trees will. I don't think he can even get there tonight. I'm going to invite him to stay on my couch." Ironpot opened the door and the whistling wind became the roaring, howl-ing wind. He stepped out and Grace, locking the door behind her, followed him back across the lawn to Martha's.

CHAPTER 59

SPOONS

GRACE, ALAN, AND EMILY'S KIDS PULLED INTO THE PARKING lot at the hospital. "I don't know if your mom knows you're coming or not," Grace said, smiling at Greta. "This will be fun!"

Greta smiled back at Grace while unbuckling her belt. Amber was already out of the car and held the door open to let Greta out. Sure that Amber would catch her, Greta leapt out, bony legs and arms wrapping around her big sister like a monkey. Grace unbuckled Bjorn and carried him. They all walked across the parking lot, propelled by the wind to the door of the emergency room.

After they had waited for several minutes, Grace went to the security door, looked in the window, and knocked. It looked like the hospital was deserted. "They must be running on a skeleton crew," she told Alan. Finally, Dr. French came walking toward the door. His gray hair was standing on end and he was rubbing his head vigorously, looking exhausted. He was thin and had dark circles under his eyes.

Dr. French spotted Grace, smiled, and pulled open the door. Leaning down to face Greta, he said, "You're mother is waiting for you, young lady." Holding the door open for them, he announced. "It's been a long night. Winds have been blowing for over twelve hours now. We're running bare bones on generators."

"Have you been busy?" Grace asked.

295

"No. We've been lucky though, very few injuries. How are you doing?"

Grace smiled. "I'm about to have a lot of fun."

"Her mom's in room five. You know the way," he said, smiling back at her.

"Let's go, guys!" Grace smiled and led the way to room five. She turned to the kids and put a finger to her lips, motioning for them to be quiet. "Shh," she whispered, "Let's surprise her."

Greta grinned and clapped her hands. Amber put Greta down in front of the door. Grace cracked the door and peeked inside. Emily was sitting all alone, forlornly waiting in a hospital gown on the short exam bed with the back propped up. Grace motioned for Greta to go in and then opened the door. "Suwpwise!" Greta exclaimed and ran into the room to the bed and wrapping her arms around her surprised mother.

"Greta!" Emily exclaimed, hugging her close. Amber and Alan followed Greta in. Emily opened her other arm and they both went to her and became part of a group hug. Grace stood at the door, holding Bjorn and enjoying her job. "Greta," Emily asked, "What happened?"

"Daddy put me down to go find his friend Jose," Greta explained seriously. "I was in a stump. I slept for a while, but mostly I prayed like Amber taught me. Then I heard someone call me. They kept saying my name."

"Who was it?" Emily asked.

"I don't know. I thought it was Amber," Greta said, knitting her eyebrows and looking thoughtfully at Amber. "Maybe Daddy was looking for me."

"Maybe your prayer was answered," Alan said quietly.

"I know mine was," Emily said. "I don't remember praying harder ever in my life."

"Me too!" Greta said, throwing her hands out. "I was zausted, whew!" Everyone laughed. "It took fifty a hundred hours." She pulled a foot up with her hand and showed the bottom to her mother, "My feet are killing me!"

"Come here, baby," Emily said and picked Greta's light body up onto the bed with her.

"Emily," Grace said softly. Emily looked up. "I talked to the officer. It's not very safe at your house right now because we don't know . . ." Emily looked at Greta, who loved her dad, and then back at Emily. "We don't know where all the parties are and how safe it is. Understand?"

Emily nodded and looked at the kids. "I shouldn't have tried to stay there in the first place. I knew I was a sitting duck, but I didn't know what else to do. I don't have any money. Where can we go?"

Alan raised his hand. "I told Amber you could come with me."

"Oh, Alan, I couldn't do that to your family in December. Christmas is coming, and we're a lot of people."

"I promise my mom would love it," Alan said sincerely.

"Have you asked?" Grace said, talking to him like a naughty child.

Alan went to the phone hanging on the wall. It was a landline and had a dial tone. He punched in his number, grateful his parents had a landline. He stood for a moment and then said, "Hello, Mom. Yes, Mom. Yes, Mom. I'm fine, Mom. Yes, Mom. Mom, Emily's been hurt and Amber's dad came around. They're not safe at home. Berk doesn't know where we live so can they stay with us? Sure." He waited for a few minutes. "So it's all right? Great. I'm fine, Mom. Thanks, Mom."

Alan hung up and then turned to smile at everyone. "I told you so," he said proudly. "My mom loves everyone. She said she wouldn't have you stay anywhere else."

"I don't have anything to wear but this hospital gown," Emily said.

"We brought your clothes," Grace said.

"I don't have a car," Emily said.

"I do," Grace said. "But it's up to you. What do you want to do?"

"Mom!" Amber whined. "I'm not going back to that house, and Alan's family is nice!"

Emily thought for a moment and then looked at Amber, "All right, Amber, you win. But I don't know if they will let me out tonight."

"I'll ask," Grace said and went out to get the doctor.

———

Emily sat on a couch in Alan's mother's candlelit, cozy living room with a blanket wrapped around her legs. Both her eyes were black and her nose was swollen. She had a concussion and needed to stay awake. Alan's mother brought her tea and was fussing over her pillows when Ironpot rang the doorbell.

Grace was helping Greta and Amber set up two army cots in the family room by the fireplace.

"Wanna see my wooden train set?" eight-year-old John asked Greta.

"No, she wants to play walkie-talkie," five-year-old Jack said to John. Greta watched the volley, her head turning back and forth.

"We can play trains with the walkie-talkies." John offered.

"Okay!" Greta jumped in and got up to follow the boys.

"Greta," Alan's mother called from the doorway. "Officer Ironpot is here to see you."

"Hi, Greta," Ironpot said from the doorway. Greta looked at him like he was ruining her fun.

"Sorry, Jack, I gotta talk. Bwah, Bwah." she said, rolling her eyes. "Okay, c'mon," she said to Ironpot, leading him back into the living room with a large sigh.

"I am so sorry to bother you," Ironpot said sarcastically.

"It's all right." Greta threw herself onto a chair by her mother on the couch. "I don't mind." She sounded like she really minded.

"Greta, be nice," Emily said with a smile.

"Greta, I have to ask you a few questions. Can I tape our talk?"

Greta looked at her mother and then Grace. Both women smiled and nodded that it was okay. "Okay, I guess. But will this take a long time?"

"No, I promise," Ironpot said while taking a small tape recorder out of his inside jacket pocket. He turned it on and sat it on the table next to Greta. He stated the date into the recorder and then said, "Present in the room: Grace James of the DSAT team, Emily Anderson, and her seven-year-old daughter, Greta Anderson."

"Greta, can you tell me about what happened last night?"

"I was asweep. Daddy came and took me out of bed. He hit mommy with his head and made her bleed. He hit Amber with a bottle first."

"Then what happened?"

"It's a long story."

"I got time."

"He put his arm around my neck." She stood up and started acting it out for him. "I remembered the cartoon and played dead. Then he took me outside with the broken bottle and we got lost in the woods. The trees were breaking everywhere lots. Then he stuffed me in a hole in a tree stump with worms that got all over me. I prayed, and slept, and when I got up I prayed some more, after getting the worms off me. I heard a voice call my name, I thought. But it wasn't Amber, and I don't know who it was but they called for me. I found Amber and Alan." She smiled and took Emily's hand.

Ironpot turned off the tape player. "You were great. Thanks, Greta."

Greta sighed a dramatic sigh and slapped her forehead with her hands. "Can I play now? It's been a million billion years since I played."

"You can play," Emily said. Greta was out the door before Emily was done talking.

"Emily, I would rather she was interviewed by an expert," Ironpot said. "But because of the storm and time being of the essence, I want to get a search started with what statements we can get. I taped it, but you all will probably have to testify."

"I'm ready this time. I think I'm finally done," Emily said sadly. "It's just, where do we go from here?"

Kelly held one card in her hand and shouted, "I win!"

"Ahh! Again!" Mabel and Nephi said in unison. The entire James family sat around the kitchen table playing cards by the light of a kerosene lamp.

"We really should go to bed," Grace said. "It's midnight."

"Yeah, and the wind is still blowing," Mabel said, pointing out the window. "That makes over twenty-four hours."

Someone banged on the door. The entire family stopped and turned, wondering who it was at this time of night. "I'll get it!" Mary said, flying out the door. She slid on her socks as she rounded the corner and left the kitchen heading for the front door.

"Nephi, don't let her answer the door alone this late at night," Grace, the voice of reason, said.

"Sure," Nephi said, snapping out of his confused state. Nephi stood up and the entire family followed, leaving Mabel shuffling cards with Kelly at the table.

Mary slid to the front door, and, without checking out the window to see who was on the other side, took the handle in both hands and flung the door open wide. "Hi!" she said to Officer Hart.

"Hi, Mary . . . is that you in there?" he said. He lifted the mask she was still wearing, exposing a toothy grin. "Is your . . ." Hart looked up to see the entire family. "I didn't wake you?"

"No, Kelly was just creaming us at cards," Nephi said.

Hart smiled. "Oh, well, if I've come at a bad time."

"Nonsense," Grace said. "Get in here." She reached out and took him by the arm and pulled him in. "What can we do for you?" Grace asked, smiling.

"Well . . ." Hart looked embarrassed. "I can't get to my house."

"Oh," Grace said as she realized what he needed. "I am so sorry! I hope your house is okay. What happened to Ironpot?"

"He has the widow Sister Swinderten and her sister on his couch."

"The cat sisters?" Nephi asked.

"Nephi!" Grace reprimanded him.

"Anyway, it's a crowd," Hart said.

Grace looked at him, color rising. "You better stay with us. In fact, we were just about to give Kelly a run for her money. Someone besides Kelly has to win. How are you at playing Spoons?"

———

It was one in the morning. The candles were burning low, but the kerosene lamp was still bright. A circle of spoons was on the large wooden table in Grace's kitchen.

At that moment, someone turned up just the right card. Hart jumped up, bringing his fist down hard on the circle of spoons. Spoons flew everywhere while kids and adults dove after them, laughing and screaming, fighting to get one.

On the next go round, when the card came up, Hart jumped up and slammed his fist down hard on the spoons and the entire table broke in half. Everyone still dove for spoons while Hart stood looking sheepish. Grace snorted and Mabel howled with laughter.

"Game over!" Hart shouted triumphantly, dancing with a spoon raised in the air. Everyone was still laughing when Hart stopped dancing as he looked at the broken table. "I am so sorry! Really!"

"It was worth it! You should have seen your face," Mabel laughed. "Don't worry, I'll take it to Alan's dad to get it fixed."

"I'll pay for it. It's my fault."

"Are you kidding?" Grace said. "That was priceless. I only wish I'd caught it on tape."

Kelly reached out and patted him on the back. "You're a winner," she said, which brought a cheer from the entire family.

CHAPTER 60

TOGETHER

THE SUN ROSE BEHIND STEEL-GRAY CLOUDS. THE WIND HAD slowed. Grace stood in her kitchen, surveying the damage. Smoke poured out of the fireplace as Nephi and Hart tried to relight the fire. It was about nine in the morning, and the troops were finally dragging themselves out of bed. Grace watched Kelly laughing with Hart as he fanned the smoldering fire.

Grace was happy for Hart and Kelly, but her lonely heart ached just a little, and she wondered if anyone would ever look at her like Hart looked at Kelly. Hart was a smart man. He had probably invited the Swinderten sisters to sleep at Ironpot's. It was probably all part of his plan. Kelly stood near him. He stood up and casually put his arm around her, and she leaned into him.

"So," Grace said, suddenly a little uncomfortable, "I was going to go up to work today, but I heard on the radio that the roads are closed and they aren't allowing traffic on Highway 101." She looked at Hart's handsome face. Kelly leaned toward him.

"So, I repeat, what are we going to do today?" Grace said, smiling at Kelly and Hart.

"I have a chainsaw in the back of my rig," Hart said. "I thought about trying to get out and check on the Harrisons and their goats out in the woods. But if the roads are closed that won't work."

"How about we go around and check on church members in town and then work on the trees in the church parking lot?" Nephi said.

"That sounds brilliant," Grace said. "I'll get Esther and Mary to go. Mabel, can you take Kelly and Hart with you? We fill up a vehicle." *And,* Grace thought, *then I don't have to watch them.* Her head said she should be happy for them. After all, they were so happy together, a perfect match, but her heart still hurt like she was missing out on something wonderful. *Let it go,* she thought. *Envy isn't my color. Someday I will find my own happily ever after.*

"Sure," Mabel said, looking at Kelly who was smiling back. "If you want to go."

"I would love to. I only wish I had work gloves and better gear."

"I'll get you some," Grace offered. "First, let's eat."

Mary came running down the wooden stairs toward the front door. "Mary!" Grace yelled and then went after her. She was already out the door. She left the door standing open. Grace stopped dead in her tracks.

"Hey! Everyone listen!" Mary said, coming back in the room. Everyone stood and looked at her, confused.

"I don't hear anything," Nephi said sarcastically.

"Exactly!" Mary exclaimed and then went back out the door. Slowly it dawned on the rest of them.

"No wind!" Kelly shouted and threw her hands up in the air. "Hooray!" She went out the door with Mary. Soon they were all standing on the porch and looking up at blue sky peeking through the clouds.

The sun exposed the neighborhood damage. Pine needles blanketed everything. Trees were down here and there. City workers were at the end of the block cutting up a tree that was as thick as the workers were tall. One tree lay over a neighbor's brand-new car, smashing it flat. A broken branch, which hung by a torn piece of bark, was above the family Jeep.

"Nephi, you better move the car," Grace said, unable to take her eyes off the devastation.

"Let's get to work," Nephi said.

"Breakfast first," Grace said, and they went back in the house.

———

Two days later, Grace sat in the sun on the church steps making peanut butter sandwiches. The entire ward was pulling into the parking lot to join a few of the high priests that were cutting the fifteen tall, ancient pines that had fallen into the parking lot. Chainsaw sounds were in the air.

Grace was still amazed. They had not understood the magnitude of the storm while they were in it. It wasn't until it was over and they saw the damage and heard on the radio reports of massive flooding that they started to realize what they had survived.

Kelly emerged from the building with a stack of paper cups and a pitcher of water. "I wonder how long until they open Highway 30 so I can check on the kids," she said for the hundredth time.

"Let's try to drive out there again after dinner," Grace replied, worried for Kelly.

"I know Sabrina is taking good care of them and no injuries are being reported on the radio, but I can't help but worry. I haven't felt like anything was wrong. I just miss them."

Grace reassured her again. "I know. I would think that if anything were seriously wrong someone would know by now. They have ham radios. Hart has been able to get closer to his house, and the local loggers are cutting trees and clearing the roads as fast as they can."

"I know. I'll just won't be able to stop thinking about it until I see little Sam and Hazel."

"I don't blame you. I'd be going crazy."

"I would have if it wasn't for your family and Hart."

"Speak of the devils." Grace's family car pulled into the church parking lot. Nephi jumped out and smiled while he waved.

"The road's open!" he shouted. Cheers went up around the parking lot. "Make room! A truck's coming through!"

Everyone looked confused. They had heard on the radio that even the governor hadn't been able to fly over to survey the damage because the wind was still gusting unpredictably. The roads were covered, according to the radio, by hundreds of trees. They said it might take a week to dig out.

"Highway 26 is open and a truck is coming here. They're right behind us!" Nephi said again enthusiastically. Just then, a large semi with "The Church of Jesus Christ of Latter-day Saints" printed on the side blew its horn and pulled into the parking lot. Grace felt tears rise to her eyes.

"They must have started to load it the minute they heard we had a storm," Kelly said.

"I know. How could they get here so fast?" Grace said, looking at Kelly who had tears running down her face.

The brethren were shaking hands with the truck driver who smiled and was shaking their hands back. The back of the truck was opened and members, who were coming back to the church for lunch, pulled into the parking lot and helped unload the truck. It was filled with generators, cleaning supplies, food, water, blankets, batteries, and more.

Sister Babcock, one of the Relief Society counselors, had been calling people and was checking on all the ward families. She instructed the bishop on where to take the generators. Grace heard her say, "Sister Taylor is on dialysis. She gets the first generator."

Grace and Kelly helped carry cleaning kits in buckets into the church. After her tenth trip, she saw Officer Hart in his official police car and two county patrol cars pull into the parking lot. She looked over her shoulder and saw Kelly go into the church with a couple of buckets.

She turned and followed Kelly into the building, "Kelly, Hart is here."

Kelly smiled, stacked her buckets, and hurried out the door. Grace followed her to the parking lot.

Joe Hart was beaming. Kelly smiled back and he picked her up and squeezed her, twirling her around. "I have great news! Guess who we found?"

Hart put Kelly down and she covered her mouth as she gasped. Sabrina got out of the back of the county car carrying little Sam. Candy got out of the other door with Hazel.

"Sam! Hazel!" Kelly squealed, running to take her son from Sabrina's hands first and then pick up Hazel too. She had a child on each hip and was kissing both their necks while they were squeezing her back as hard as they could, both babbling to her.

"Oh, Sabrina. Thank you!" Kelly said. Then she looked at Sabrina and stopped and stood still. "What happened?"

Sabrina was a mess. Her hair was disheveled. She had dark circles under her eyes and bruises on her face. She looked a hundred years older than the last time Kelly had seen her. Candy looked totally different. She had on all black and looked twice as tired as Sabrina.

Sabrina looked down and started to sob, making little gulping noises, "Kelly, I am so sorry. I should never have believed him. You were right. You were so right." Kelly realized that her worst fears had happened. Sam had hurt someone else.

"Did the kids see?" Kelly asked.

"No!" Sabrina said, holding her hands up in surrender. "They slept through the night and all of it. It was amazing. I can't believe they never woke up. I am so grateful."

"What happened?" Kelly asked.

"I'll tell you what happened," Candy said angrily. "Your ex-old-man came into my room to . . ." She looked at little Sam and her voice trailed off. "My mom shot him, that's what happened!"

"Oh, Sabrina," Kelly looked shocked. "I am so sorry. Is he . . ." She looked at Hart, not wanting to say it out loud. "Is he . . . you know?"

"No," Hart said, putting his arm around Kelly and the children. "It was buckshot. He needs a new backside, but he'll live."

"Oh my goodness." Kelly said, trying to take it all in. "Are you all right?" She asked Sabrina again.

"Yes, the storm was happening, so we couldn't get any help—" Sabrina started to say.

"We didn't need it. We don't need anyone," Candy interrupted. "I tied him up and we locked him in the wine cellar until we could call the cops at the neighbors."

"Candy!" Sabrina looked sadly at her daughter. "It's over now." Sabrina walked toward Candy, who tensed. Sabrina wrapped her arms around her daughter. "It's over now," Sabrina said again softly, and Candy's shoulders sagged and the tears began to flow.

"Sabrina, I can't thank you enough," Kelly said. Sabrina just nodded and turned to the officers.

"Can you take us home?" she asked.

"Yes, ma'am," the deputy answered.

"Sabrina," Kelly called to her again. "You will always be a part of Sam and Hazel's family. Thank you again."

Sabrina's breath caught in her throat as she came over and hugged little Sam, Kelly, and Hazel. She started to cry with relief. "Thank you," was all she could say before she let go, leaving in the deputy's car with her daughter.

"Hart?" Kelly looked sober and said, "I need to take my children home."

Hart smiled. "I also got to go to my house today. It's perfect. Not a scratch on it. Big Sam, my man, how would you like to try out a tire swing? I have a great one on the tree in my yard."

"Yes, pwease!" little Sam said and smiled. "Mama," Sam said, putting both hands on Kelly's cheeks. "I love you, Mama," he said clearly.

Hart held out a survivor's blanket and wrapped Kelly and her children up, holding the whole family in his arms.

"You don't understand," Kelly interrupted, stepping back from Hart. "We need to go home—home to Utah, my family."

Hart's face fell as his insides lurched. Stepping toward Kelly, he wrapped her and the children in his arms, "I understand," he whispered. "I want you to be happy."

"You could come," she offered.

"I belong here. I belong . . ." His voice trailed off. Kelly's eyes pooled with tears and he knew. "I belong with you," he said, squeezing them just a little tighter, forehead to forehead, arms wrapped around each other and their new little family

Grace stopped breathing as she watched the embrace. Mabel, standing silently by Grace, reached out and gently brushed Grace's hair back from her face, kissed her cheek, and said, "Sorry, honey."

"Grace!" the county deputy called sharply, gesturing from his car for her to come with him. "We need you, there's a victim at the Seaside hospital," he shouted over the noise of the reunion.

"I'm coming!" Grace shouted back, handing everything in her hands to Mabel and walked toward the patrol car.

"I'll take her," Hart offered, interrupting her thoughts. The deputy nodded and drove away.

Surprised, Grace looked up at Hart who was smiling down at her, still here, while Kelly was loading the kids in her own car.

"Grace," Hart asked, "do you like homemade pasta?" Grace didn't answer. Confused, she pushed back her curls, wiping peanut butter and jam across her forehead. Hart reached out and gently took his thumb and wiped the smear off her face. "I happen to be the world's best pasta maker," he said. "Kelly and I will cook, if you bring your family out after work."

"We'd love to!" Mabel said. "Do you have any handsome friends you could bring over?"

"Mother!"

Mabel cackled and walked away. "How strong is your table, Hart?" Grace asked.

"Why? What do you want to do with it?"

"Spoons, Hart, I want to play spoons."

DISCUSSION QUESTIONS

1. Did you insert yourself into a character in the book? If so, which one and why? Did you see yourself as an advocate, or did you relate more to Amber, Kelly, and Emily?

2. What do you think motivates Grace to go out and meet with strangers in potentially the worst moments of their lives? If you could be an advocate like Grace, would you?

3. Did the book remind you of an experience you, a family member, coworker, or someone in your life has had?

4. One of the most asked questions of victims of intimate partner violence is, "Why don't you just leave?" Did you find yourself asking this question as you read? Did the story give you a new or different perspective on how survivors of violence might feel about leaving?

5. If you could talk to Amber, a petrified teen who reached out and called for help, what would you tell her?

6. If you could talk to the author, what would you ask her? (Set up FaceTime, Skype, or voice calls with book groups.)

7. Oftentimes, society engages in victim blaming. Society suggests that only the poor, drug addicted, or those who deserve

it are victims of violence. There is a theory that we blame the victim, then say to ourselves, "It can't happen to me, because I don't: use drugs, live in poverty, I am safe from being a victim of abuse." Did the book change your perspective of domestic violence victims? Are they always poor, addicted, women, white, heterosexual?

8. If you could give advice to one character in the book, who would it be and what would you say?

9. If you were Officer Joe Hart, whom would you arrest first?

10. Share the following statistics from the National Coalition Against Domestic Violence (ncadv.org/learn-more/statistics) with the group:

   a. 1 in 3 women and 1 in 4 men have been victims of (some form of) physical violence by an intimate partner within their lifetime.
   b. On a typical day, there are more than 20,000 phone calls placed to domestic violence hotlines nationwide.
   c. The presence of a gun in a domestic violence situation increases the risk of homicide by 500 percent.
   d. Only 34 percent of people who are injured by intimate partners receive medical care for their injuries.

Are you surprised by these numbers? Did the book impact your opinions, knowledge, or feelings about domestic violence, its victims, and how our society takes care of victims?

ABOUT THE AUTHOR

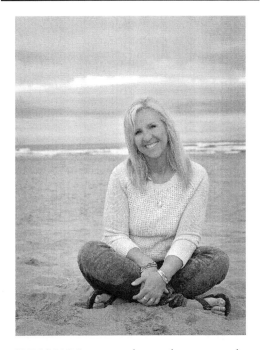

SHANNON SYMONDS currently works as an advocate serving domestic and sexual assault survivors. She has responded with law enforcement and hospitals for over fourteen years, going anywhere she is called to give support to survivors. Shannon lives in an old house on the Oregon coast where she writes, runs, and loves her family. She has a lifetime lofty but worthy goal of ending family and sexual violence.

SCAN TO VISIT

WWW.SHANNONSYMONDS.COM